UNEXPECTED BLESSINGS

Anne Marie St. Clair

Anne Marie St. Clair
Visit my website at www.authorannemariestclair.blogspot.com

Printed in the United States of America

First Printing: July 2018
KDP

ISBN-9781983364549

Dedication
To Kelley Kathleen McCaffrey
March 3, 1987 – September 6, 2004
Your light was so bright
We miss you so much
Another angel taken too soon

CONTENTS

CHAPTER 1

The thing about Rosadel Marshall was she had the courage of her convictions. So, when she delivered her triplet girls thirty-three weeks into her pregnancy on December 24, she decided to give them sufficiently Christian names. And so, Mercy, Grace and Charity Marshall were born into this world.

Now, in spite of the best intentions and the best parenting she knew how to provide, Rosadel often referred to the triplets as the Holy Terror Trio. Only Grace went by her given name. Mercy Louise was known as Lou, and Charity Rose was Rosie. Lou, Grace and Rosie had been creating havoc everywhere they went from the time they could crawl. Rosadel's husband, Clancy, thought the sun and moon set in the girls, and he could never see past the easy way they wrapped him around their little fingers to get out of trouble.

Why Rosadel could remember when they were four, and Mercy decided to go by Lou. "Mommy," Mercy said, "I think Mercy is a silly name. You call Daddy Clancy, and his name is really Jacob Clancy and you call him Clancy. So, you can call me Louise. No, No, Lou! My name is Lou!" Well, Clancy thought that was too cute, so Rosadel was stuck with a daughter named Lou instead of Mercy.

Then at five, Charity announced, "My name is Rose, like the flower, because I never saw a Charity." Rosadel tried to explain that Charity is a virtue, like Mercy and Grace, but it all went over her head. Clancy was no help again, with his "Awe, Sugar, it is good they are strong-willed, no man will ever take advantage of my girls". And Rosadel said, "You just watch that 'Awe, Sugar' stuff because that is how we got these triplets in the first place."

And Clancy pulled Rosadel into his lap and said, "Want to try for boys this time?" And Rosadel said, "You hush, from your lips to God's ears and then Heaven help us!" And Clancy gave Rosadel a big smacking kiss and the girls started laughing, and so did Rosadel and Clancy because that is just how it happened in the Marshall household.

Because truth be told, Rosadel had never been able to resist Clancy when he called her Sugar. And when he put that long drawn out "Awe" in front of it, he always got her to do whatever he wanted. So, in Clancy's senior year of his engineering degree, when Rosadel was finishing up her two-year RN, and he said "Awe, Sugar, we're married and what is the chance this one time without a condom will hurt", and knowing everything Rosadel knew about birth control, she was just as hot for Clancy as he was for her, and decided what the heck, and there you have it, triplets.

She was just glad that Grace liked her name, and Clancy was still the man of her dreams.

So, while Clancy worked as a mechanical engineer at the plant in town, Rosadel took odd shifts at Our Lady of Lourdes nursing home for coverage on nights and weekends when Clancy was home, because there was no way Rosadel was asking any one person to watch the triplets. Clancy's mom would offer, but even Harriet Marshall knew it took more than one grownup to stay in control of the girls. Unless the grownup was Rosadel or Clancy. They had a good life, albeit, an eventful one.

Rosadel loved her girls, and knew they had good hearts, but she also was about out of patience with their antics. She knew something was going to have to change soon, or those girls were going to get into the kind of trouble you can't undo. She'd tried time and time again to get Clancy to see something needed to be done, but he'd just say something useless like, "Awe, Sugar, they're just high-spirited", or "You know they don't mean any harm", so Rosadel knew she was on her own.

She been lighting candles, and saying prayers for guidance, but so far, nothing had come to her. Today, she was going BACK to the Holy Redeemer school office, to answer for another one of the girls' transgressions. It seemed that today, the girls thought it would be a fine thing to do to place a litter of kittens in the crib where the statue of the Baby Jesus had been that morning. With a sign, "Peace on Earth, kittens Free to good homes. Ask yourself, What Would Jesus Do?"

Besides the Momma cat being in a panic and hissing and snarling at everyone that came near the kittens, and nearly running herself ragged chasing the kittens down and dragging them back to the crib, and the sheer irresponsibility of allowing people to just come pick up a living creature, Rosadel knew this was the end of the road for the triplets, and for Clancy. And who even knew where they found the kittens and Momma Cat.

Belinda Collins looked up and smiled when Rosadel came through the door. "What in the world are you smiling at Bee? I was in the middle of making Christmas Cookies when you called, and now I won't have the trays ready to take to the nursing home in time for the pageant tonight."

Bee just smiled harder. "Rosadel, I never used to see you at all, and now the Holy Terror Trio makes sure I see you at least once a week."

Rosadel wasn't smiling. "Bee, you know I love you, but it is not funny. Where did that Momma cat and those kittens come from? One of them could have been hurt or killed. I've got to find a way to get the girls to curb their impulses. I thought it would get better when they started school, but nothing, you know why? No nuns. If they had nuns like we had when we were here at Holy Redeemer, you better believe they would be called Mercy, Grace and Charity and this behavior would be long gone."

Bee held up her hand, "Stop, Rosie, before I hurt myself laughing. Even nuns couldn't defeat your Holy Terror Trio."

Rosadel sank down in a chair. "I should have stuck with my fourth-grade ambition to BE a nun. But no. First day at the regional high school, and what does clumsy me do but trip and drop my lunch tray. I was so embarrassed I got tears in my eyes, and there is Jacob Clancy Marshall, all geeky cute with his glasses and pocket protector saying, 'Awe, Sugar, don't cry, I'll help you clean this up and buy you another lunch' and the rest is history. So here I am twenty-eight years old, and the mother of soon to be eight-year-old delinquents."

Bee wiped her eyes as she tried to stop laughing. "Rosie, you and Clancy were meant to be, and the girls are going to be OK. They really were trying to do a good thing, but that impulse control problem got the better of them. If you've calmed down a little you can go into Principal West's office and talk to her before the girls come down from their classroom."

"And stop calling me Rosie," Rosadel exclaimed. "Rosie is one of the delinquents I'm here about. My name is Rosadel."

"Rosie McPherson Marshall, I have called you Rosie and you've called me Bee since we were in Mrs. Young's kindergarten class here at Holy Redeemer. I'm not going to stop calling you Rosie. And stop calling your girls delinquents! There is such a thing as a self-fulfilling prophesy, and you are starting to create one."

Rosadel sighed and took a deep breath. "OK, Bee, I'm ready to go face the music." Bee buzzed Mrs. West on the intercom and said, "Rosadel Marshall is here to see you Mrs. West." Mrs. West replied, "Give me a minute to finish this letter I'm writing and send her in."

Frances West wasn't writing any letter, but she needed to say a quick prayer for guidance before talking to Rosadel. Frances could still remember when Rosadel and Bee were students in her third-grade class here at Holy Redeemer. She would have been about the same age Rosadel was now.

Frances sighed. Rosadel was such a pitiful little thing at that age. Alicia McPherson had been diagnosed with cancer when Rosadel was six. She hung on until Rosadel was twelve but was always sickly and in and out of the hospital with chemotherapy treatments and radiation. Rosadel tried so hard to be good as a child, she had no idea what an ordinary childhood was like.

The Marshall triplets were high-spirited, to be sure, but they were not mean at all. They did have a less developed impulse control than most second graders, but they had spent the first eight weeks of their lives in neonatal intensive care and had been in and out of the hospital with respiratory infections and pneumonia. If Rosadel were not a nurse and able to provide such a high level of care at home, they probably would have spent even more time in the hospital.

Add to the slight developmental disadvantage the ability of the three of them to reinforce a not so good idea, and the triplets were always into something. Frances knew Rosadel was embarrassed by the way everyone in town talked about the girls and felt like a failure as a mother. Having had essentially no mother she could remember being a mother, Rosadel felt like it was all her fault.

Frances wished she had time for a quick call to her mentor, Sister Dorothy Murphy. Sister Dorothy lived at Our Lady of Lourdes, where Rosadel worked part time. Sister Dorothy had been principal here at Holy Redeemer until her arthritis had progressed to the point that she was often incapacitated by the pain. Her mind was sharp as ever, though, and she and Frances regularly shared a cup of tea and advice.

And that brought Frances right back to Rosadel. Every time Rosadel reported for work at Our Lady of Lourdes, she brought something for Sister Dorothy. Flowers from her garden, a sweet Rosadel had baked, cards or drawings from the girls. Dottie would tell Rosadel in her still soft Irish brogue, "Child, you don't have to be bringing me gifts." And Rosadel would answer, "You lived away from your nieces and nephews to take care of us as children, it is the least I can do to bring you small treats."

And as was the way with Rosadel, without saying a word to anyone about what she did, word got out, and soon many former students were visiting Sister Dorothy, and she never spent a holiday without lots of company.

Rosadel peeked her head in the door of Mrs. West's office before Frances had worked out exactly what to say. Frances hoped the Holy Spirit wasn't too busy to help her get this right.

Rosadel sat with her hands folded in her lap, waiting. Mrs. West had been one of her favorite teachers, but now that she was Principal West, she was a little scary.

Mrs. West asked Rosadel, "You know why you're here, don't you Rosadel?"

"Yes, Ma'am. The girls put a momma cat and kittens in Baby Jesus' crib," replied Rosadel.

Mrs. West thought for a minute, and then replied. "Rosadel, I want you to listen to me with your heart. I know you are embarrassed every time you have to come to school because of your girls, but they really are good girls. They found the box with the kittens and part of the sign on the playground. They thought more people would see the kittens in the Nativity Scene, and the 'What Would Jesus Do?' was their idea. But they were trying to do a good thing this time."

"Mrs. West, to listen to Clancy, they are always trying to do a good thing. But I keep telling them, go get an adult. Don't try to solve things yourself. They were trying to do a good thing when they saw Mr. Wilson's rose bushes looking wilted and turned on his garden hose. Then they forgot, and the hose flooded his crawl space. They were trying to do a good thing when they saw Mrs. Anderson's front door open and closed it for her. Problem was, she had just run out the door to grab her dog, Peanut, and then they were both locked out of the house. She had her daughter's birthday cake in the oven, and by the time the locksmith could come, the cake burned up. Luckily, I was able to bake a replacement cake in time for the party. They were trying to do a good thing when they overheard Clancy saying how tired he was, so they went in our bedroom and turned off his alarm and he was late for work. Do you need more examples? I just don't know what to do anymore."

Frances got up from behind her desk and sat next to Rosadel. She put her hands on Rosadel's clasped hands. "You remember Mrs. White, don't you Rosadel?"

"Yes, Ma'am, she was the other third grade teacher that I didn't have, and I work with her now on the liturgy planning committee. She knows my girls pretty well from planning meetings, and Mass on Sundays."

"I had forgotten that you and Grace work together on the liturgy committee, Rosadel. Well, Miss Dunn, your girls second grade teacher was talking to Grace White about helping your girls learn impulse control. Mrs. White suggested that we all, the school, you and Clancy and Clancy's family and your dad and Jessie all work together on this. This is what she suggested. When Lou has an idea, Grace is supposed to try to talk her out of it, and if she can't Rosie is supposed to go get a grown-up.

If Grace has the idea, Rosie is supposed to try to talk her out of it, and if she can't Lou is supposed to go get a grown-up. If Rosie has the idea, Lou is supposed to try to talk her out of it, and if she can't Grace will go get a grown-up. The girls do well when they have a rule to follow, so Mrs. White thought if we gave them a rule that would work for any situation, we might break this pattern."

Rosadel looked at Mrs. West's hands holding hers and missed her Mama. Again. But Mrs. West sure was trying to give good advice, and so was Mrs. White. So maybe God was answering her prayers and candles with the faculty at Holy Redeemer.

"We sure can try, Mrs. West. But I feel like I need to do something more than that. These kittens and the Momma cat could have been hurt or killed. I need to do something to make an emotional impact on the girls."

At that point, Rosadel noticed the box in the corner of Mrs. West's office, and the noises coming from it. "You have Momma Cat and the kittens in here?" she asked.

"Well, they had to go somewhere until I could take them to the Animal Shelter after work. They are pretty little things. I wish we knew who left them like that on the playground in the first place. The kittens only look about 6 weeks old, a little young to be leaving their Momma. Momma Cat looks like she is used to humans, but the kittens act like they have never been touched or played with. I worry that the shelter won't find homes for them, but my husband and children are all allergic to cats, so I have no choice but to bring them to the shelter."

Rosadel, with the courage of her convictions, thought she had found the right answer both for the girls, and for Clancy.

"Mrs. West, I'm going to take Momma Cat and the kittens home. The girls will have to help Clancy clean the litter box, and handle the kittens, and then find homes for all of them. It will help them learn that actions have consequences. You can't just jump in without thinking. I know they, and Clancy, will get attached to the kittens and I will see lots of tears when they go to good homes, but they need to learn that helping involves not just moments but sacrifice too."

"Rosadel, do you think they are old enough to learn that lesson?" Mrs. West asked gently.

"Yes, Ma'am, I do. My Mama had been sick for almost two years by the time I was as old as the girls. I had already learned a lot about sacrifice, and sorrow. I know lots of people in this town felt sorry for me and thought I was pitiful, but having a sick Mama makes you grow up fast and puts a seriousness in you that never goes away. My Clancy doesn't have hardly a lick of serious in him, even though he has a good job. And he is very kind. But sometimes I feel like the only grown-up in my house. He'll cry as hard as the girls when those kittens leave. But I have to get all of them to develop some caution."

"I'm going to take money out of the Disney jar to pay for taking Momma Cat and the kittens to the vet. We all want to go to Disney World, but that will help impress them. I think God has answered my prayers for how to change things so that my girls grow up responsible."

Frances West truly believed if anyone had a good communication path to God, it was Rosadel, so she added a quick prayer of her own that this plan would work.

"I'm going to call for the girls to come down to the office now, Rosadel. Are you ready?" asked Mrs. West.

"As ready as I can be," replied Rosadel.

The girls walked into Mrs. West's office in a subdued manner, until they saw their Mommy, then they rushed over to Rosadel, all talking at once. "Mommy, we didn't know the kittens couldn't climb out of the box but could climb out of the crib." "Mommy, Mommy, we thought it would help to talk about Jesus." "Mommy, the Momma Cat let me hold her and she purred." "We didn't mean to do a bad thing." "We just wanted the kittens to find a home for Christmas."

Rosadel put her hand up in the "Stop" signal, then opened her arms so the girls could crowd in, Rosie facing Rosadel on the left, Lou standing between Rosadel's knees, and Grace on the right.

"Girls, what does Mommy always tell you?"

Grace was the first to answer, "Don't just do something, get a grown-up." and all three rolled their eyes.

Mrs. West covered her mouth quickly. It really was hard to not laugh at their antics.

Rosadel nodded. "That is right, Grace. And the eye rolling is not necessary for any of you. We are going to have a new rule. And Principal West, and Miss Dunn, and Mommy and Daddy and everybody is going to know this rule and expect you all to follow it. So, listen closely now.

"If Lou has an idea, Grace, you try to talk her out of it, and if Lou won't listen to Grace, Rosie, you go get a grown-up. If Grace has the idea, Rosie you try to talk her out of it, and if Grace won't listen to Rosie, Lou, go get a grown-up. If Rosie has the idea, Lou, you try to talk her out of it, and if Lou can't talk Rosie out of it, Grace, you will go get a grown-up. Now I want you each to tell Mommy what the new rule is for you, and we'll start with Lou."

"Ok, Mommy. If Grace won't listen to Rosie, I get a grown-up, and if Rosie has an idea, I try to talk her out of it." Rosadel high-fived Lou, "Perfect, Baby! Now Grace."

"If Lou has an Idea, I try to talk her out of it, and if Rosie won't listen to Lou, I go get a grown-up." Rosadel kissed Grace on the forehead. "Perfect, Sweetheart! Now Rosie."

"I don't understand why I'm last," said Rosie.

"We all take turns going first," replied Rosadel. "Now tell me the rule."

"If Lou won't listen to Grace, I go get a grown-up. And if Grace has an idea, I try to talk her out of it." Rosadel wrapped her arm around Rosie and gave her a squeeze. "Perfect, Honey. It sounds like you all understand."

Frances West thought again what a great mother Rosadel was and wished Rosadel could see it.

"Now for the next big news. Momma Cat and the kittens are going to come stay at our house, until we find them homes."

The jumping and laughing and shrieking immediately followed. "We're keeping the kittens, we're keeping the kittens." chanted all three girls.

The hand came up again. "No, we are not keeping the kittens. We are taking them home to get them big and strong enough to leave their

Momma. You and Daddy will have to take care of them. I am taking money from the Disney jar so that you and Daddy can take them to the Veterinarian to make sure they are all healthy. And then you will help Mommy and Daddy find good homes for them and say good-bye."

"But what if we want to keep them?" asked Grace. "Will they still have to leave?"

"Yes," replied Rosadel. "Roscoe doesn't get anywhere near the time and attention from you girls that he deserves, so you need to do better by the pet you have before we talk about more pets."

"But Roscoe is old and only sleeps," replied Lou.

Roscoe was a twelve-year-old mutt that had been Rosadel's dog since high school. Clancy gave Rosadel Roscoe as a puppy when he went away to college, to make sure that Rosadel wouldn't miss him too much. Rosadel teased that Clancy just wanted to make sure Rosadel was too busy to find a replacement boyfriend. Roscoe had stayed with Rosadel's dad, Angus, while Rosadel was away at college, but had come to live with Rosadel and Clancy as soon as they moved back home.

Rosadel called Roscoe her "Saint Francis of Assisi dog" because he never met an animal he didn't love. Roscoe had been her biggest supporter when the triplets were babies. He could push a baby swing with his nose, or rock a cradle with his paw to comfort one of the girls while she tended another. No one really knew just how much Roscoe had helped Rosadel in the early years of the girls lives. She had cried buckets of tears into his fur every time the girls were hospitalized. He just let her, and licked her tears, and kept being her staunchest supporter. She just hoped Momma Cat was used to dogs.

"Lou, you know Roscoe loves to go for walks, and play fetch. He does sleep a lot, but I see him bring his toys to all three of you and you shoo him away if you are busy with your dolls or a game, or even a book. Pets aren't like toys to be played with when we feel like it. They are living creatures with feelings that should be treasured and respected. You all have to do better to earn another pet."

The girls all looked at each other, as they had heard this speech before. They knew that no arguing would get Mommy off of this position, so instead, ran over to the box with the Momma Cat and kittens.

"We can call the Momma Cat Holly." said Grace. "And the little black one with the white on it can be Cuddles, and the little grey stripey one is Snuggles," added Lou. "I think the orange one should be Pooh, and the orange and white stripe one should be Peanut." said Rosie. "The one that looks like Momma Cat and is lots of colors with white can be Pokey, and the one with all the colors and no white can be Boo" said Grace.

Rosadel looked to Heaven for guidance. "Girls, you shouldn't be naming the kittens, their new owners will do that."

"But, Mommy," said Grace, "We have to call them something." Rosadel puzzled that for a minute, and agreed, "But you have to be OK if their new people give them new names."

More eyerolls. "Now, girls, we will have to keep the Momma Cat".

"Holly" interrupted Lou.

"OK, we will have to keep Holly and the kittens away from Roscoe until we make sure they are healthy, and then we have to see if Holly likes dogs."

"We'll put Roscoe's travel crate in the dining room, and put Holly and the kittens in it, and keep the door closed so Roscoe can't go in until we have time to work everything out."

"Mrs. West, can I leave the cats here until I can go home and clean up the travel crate and bring it back?" asked Rosadel.

"You certainly can. Now girls, go back to class. Here are your passes. Remember the new rule. I don't want to see you in my office again this year."

"Do you mean until January or this school year?" asked Rosie.

"This school year," replied Mrs. West, glancing up at Rosadel in understanding. "Now back to class with you."

After the girls left, Mrs. West told Rosadel to just come back at dismissal with the crate in the back of her SUV, and she would bring the kittens out to the car pickup line.

"That's awfully nice of you, Mrs. West," said Rosadel. "Thank you for being so good to me and the girls."

"Nonsense, Rosadel. You are the one doing a good thing for these animals, and for your family. I'll pray it all works out for you, and for the cats."

As Rosadel walked out of Mrs. West's office, she was glad to see that Bee was away from her desk, because she just didn't have time to replay the decisions made and get everything done before dismissal.

She knew she needed to call Clancy, and fill him in on the day, and the decisions she had made, but she also knew catching him near a phone at work was a serious long shot.

When Rosadel opened the front door at home, Roscoe, lifted himself from the patch of sunlight where he was sleeping and came over to head butt her hand. Rosadel sank down on the floor and gave Roscoe a hug. Goodness how she loved this dog.

"Roscoe, we're going to have some house guests. There is a Momma Cat and six kittens that will be coming to stay with us until Christmas. I have to go get your travel crate cleaned up, they will be staying in that until we get them checked out at the vet and make sure they are OK, and then until they are big enough to not get hurt. I know you will love them, but we don't know if they will love you, so we'll have to keep you out of the dining room until we figure it all out."

Roscoe tilted his head as if he understood every word, and who knows, maybe he did.

Rosadel called Clancy, and as expected, got his voicemail. She decided the less said the better, and simply said, "Boy will we have a lot to talk about when I meet you at the high school tonight after work. Love you." That should prepare him to not get a word in edgewise.

When Rosadel met Clancy that first day in high school, he had already been on the cross-country track team for two years. Rosadel had never run except in Physical Education class at school, but she would try anything to spend more time with Clancy. It turned out, Rosadel loved to run.

Running became a big part of what Rosadel and Clancy did together. They had the best conversations while they were clicking through the miles. Neither one of them would ever win any awards, but they were consistent, and loved the activity.

It had been easy when they were young, and Roscoe loved to run too. But as Roscoe got older, and the girls got too big to put in the special triplet baby jogger, Rosadel and Clancy had changed their running habits. Rosadel would get the girls on their bikes and take Roscoe for a mile near their house. Then she would pack the girls up in the car, and they would meet Clancy at the high school track on his way home from work. The girls would play in the infield while Rosadel and Clancy ran laps on the track. The nights that the track or field were in use for organized activities, they had to figure out something else. But tonight, was a regular workout at the high school, so it would be a good opportunity to talk.

CHAPTER 2

Clancy Marshall walked into his office and saw the light flashing on his phone. Probably Rosadel. Lately at work, everyone used email or Instant Messaging (IM) to communicate. As Clancy listened to the message, he had a feeling this was another one of those days when the girls had gotten into mischief.

Jacob Clancy Marshall believed that he was one of the luckiest men on earth. Beautiful, loving wife, amazing healthy children, great parents, wonderful brothers, great job. Clancy was the oldest of four boys. He and Pete were a year apart, and five years later, Mike and Donnie were born a year apart as well. They had grown up in a boisterous, happy home. He was a happy person by nature and knew that his lifelong good fortune was part of what shaped his optimistic outlook. His Rosadel was more serious, but that also was a product of her life experience.

Clancy had known of Rosadel for most of his life, even though he never really met her until his junior year in high school. Holy Redeemer parish was the only Catholic parish in Bayou Beni, Louisiana, and with Rosadel's mother being sick for so long and prayed for so often at mass, everyone in the parish kind of knew the McPherson's.

As Allie McPherson got sicker and sicker, the ladies of the parish helped with food and housework, and so Clancy's mom got to know Allie, and Angus and Rosadel from helping out.

Clancy remembered seeing Rosadel come to church with her daddy most weeks, but sometimes Allie McPherson would be well enough to come with them. He was always impressed by how careful Angus and

Rosadel were with Allie. Clancy and his brothers were always being reprimanded in church, but Rosadel sat so still and behaved beautifully.

When Allie died, Clancy was at the same mass as Angus and Rosadel. When the Offertory Prayers were said, and the prayer was for the repose of the soul of Alicia McPherson, Clancy could still see in his mind's eye how Rosadel started shaking, and how Angus wrapped his arms around her and held her as tight as possible.

Clancy had gone home from mass that day and asked his mother if she would write him an excuse for school, so he could be an altar server for Allie's funeral. Harriet Marshall looked carefully at her oldest son as she asked him why. Clancy wasn't sure how to put it in words, but he tried. "They're so alone, Mom. No cousins, or nephews, like we would have in our family. I hate the thought that they would have no altar servers at the funeral mass, when me and Pete could do it."

"Did you even ask Pete if he wanted to?" asked Harriet.

"No, Mom, but you know Pete is usually the one to think about doing nice stuff, so you know he'll be good to go."

Harriet did indeed know that Peter was her "good" son. He never wanted to cause trouble and was always doing nice things for others. She loved all her boys, but Pete was an especially loving and generous boy, so she knew Clancy was right.

"I'll be happy to write notes for you and Pete, and I appreciate that you thought about the McPherson family in this hard time for them. I'm proud of you son." And then Harriet had hugged him and they both noticed that Clancy was a full head taller than his mother, and Harriet realized her oldest boy wasn't going to be a child much longer.

Rosadel didn't notice Clancy at the funeral, and never noticed him at all until the lunchroom incident at high school. Clancy had noticed Rosadel though. He noticed the way her light brown hair would get blond streaks in the summer. And he noticed that while she was slight, she looked strong, not fragile like her mother had been.

When she dropped her lunch tray and he had gone to help her clean up the mess, one look from those big mossy green eyes wet with tears, and Clancy was a goner. He knew Rosadel was the one for him, and the more time they spent together, the more sure he was that they were indeed a match made in heaven.

Clancy also knew that he had been taking the easy way out too often at home. He was not cut out to be a disciplinarian, but he needed to do a better job of backing Rosadel up. It was just that he had so little time with the girls after work that he hated to have any unpleasantness. As Clancy finished his workday, he gave himself a pep talk to really listen to Rosadel, and take a turn being the bad guy with the girls if someone had to do it.

♦ ♦ ♦

Rosadel pulled into the car pick-up line just in time. The crate was clean and in the back of the mini-van. Thank goodness the third row of seats was split so that one side could be folded down. The girls still needed to be in booster seats in the rear, so now the fight would be about who got to sit next to the crate full of cats. Rosadel tried to remember whose turn it was, because usually, that seat was the least favorite. She knew it was written on the chart in her wallet but couldn't pull that out while driving. If necessary, she could look while doing the cat exchange with Mrs. West.

When Rosadel's turn came at the front of the line, Mrs. West was there with the box of cats, and the girls were jumping with excitement. Rosie fist punched the air, "I'm in the back row!". Since the other girls just pouted and didn't say anything, Rosadel knew that battle was over.

Mrs. West held the box while Rosadel placed the Momma Cat and kittens into the crate. The girls strapped themselves into their booster seats. Frances West gave Rosadel a big hug as she closed the door of the van. "Rosadel, you are doing a wonderful thing for these kittens. Thank you so much."

"Really Mrs. West, I think the Lord is providing me a way to teach my girls and Clancy about responsibility, so thank the Lord when you talk to Him."

With that, Rosadel and the girls headed home. The girls would have a half hour to an hour to work on homework while Rosadel got the cats settled, and then they would all head over to the high school to meet Clancy.

The girls had a quick snack of apples dipped in peanut butter and glasses of milk and got started on their homework. There had been a bit of moaning and groaning about not being allowed to play with the kittens, but Rosadel pointed out that Holly and the kittens were very stressed and frightened from all the changes and needed some time out to settle into their new home.

The crate was large, with room for some blankets and towels, and a litter box. Rosadel planned to get a climbing tree with roosts for the crate as well, but for now, with a litter box and water dishes, they would be fine until Clancy got home. Clancy could call Pete, who was a Veterinarian, from the high school, and then could pick up whatever food Pete recommended on the way home. The crate was in the dining room, which wasn't used as a dining room anyway, but was the room where the two treadmills Clancy and Rosadel used when they had to. So, while everyone still called it the dining room, it really served as the exercise room, and Roscoe didn't mind at all being restricted from the room. Rosadel made a mental note to have Clancy ask Pete about how best to introduce Roscoe to their new house guests, because she knew permanent separation was never going to work.

♦ ♦ ♦

When Clancy arrived at the track, he saw the girls playing some sort of hopping, skipping game, and Rosadel was stretching and talking to them. When the girls saw Clancy they ran over, and he had a hard time figuring out what they were trying to tell him, as they were all talking over each other.

"Daddy, Daddy, we didn't do a bad thing!" "We were trying to help." "Someone else put the box on the playground." "Holly and Cuddles and Snuggles and Pooh and Peanut and Pokey and Boo are living in Roscoe's other cage." "Mommy says they all have to go live somewhere else, but can we keep them, Daddy? Can we? Can we?"

Clancy kissed Rosadel over the girl's heads, and then got down in a crouch. "How about you go one at a time, Lou, you can start."

Lou took a deep breath and said, "We found a box of kittens and we put them in where the Baby Jesus was to help, but it wasn't a good idea and we should have got a grown-up so now we have a new rule."

"And we have to take money from the Disney jar to pay Uncle Pete," added Grace.

"And they live in the dining room," said Rosie.

"Wow, it sounds like you girls had an exciting day. Now let me talk to your mom while we run some laps. Give Daddy kisses and then play nice while we run." Clancy had a feeling this story was going to be a good one.

"Sounds like you have had quite a day." Clancy figured he'd open the door for Rosadel to get started.

As Rosadel recounted the events of the day, Clancy got more and more uncomfortable with the decision Rosadel had made to bring the Momma Cat and kittens home. While Rosadel talked, he tried to work out in his mind what exactly was bothering him about her decision. He knew that he had to ask carefully, because he didn't want to sound like he wasn't supportive, but he was having difficulty making the connection between what the girls had done and what this was supposed to teach them. As the story wound down, Clancy asked, "Rosadel, what do you want the girls to learn from caring for and giving away the Momma Cat and kittens?"

"There are a couple of things I want them to learn, Clancy. I want them to learn to curb their impulses, because rushing into things without thinking them through can have unintended consequences."

"But, Rosadel," countered Clancy, "Don't you want them to get involved to try to make things better when they can?"

"Of course I do, Clancy, but taking those kittens out of the box and putting them in the manger actually put them in danger. I know the girls didn't realize that, and at their age, it is unreasonable to think they should, which is why it is so important that they start thinking and involving a grown-up before acting. And when they do decide, with adult help to get involved, I don't want to raise 'write a check' 'make a donation' people. When my Momma was sick, your Momma didn't just drop off a casserole with instructions for how to heat it. She visited with my Momma. She taught me how to make a salad, and how to dust, and sort and do laundry. She and the other ladies from Holy Redeemer didn't take the easy way out. They really helped. And that is what I try to do, and it is what I want our girls to be like. So, they will learn that getting involved is good, but it has a price, and if you are not willing to go all in, you shouldn't go at all."

Clancy knew he was out of his depth here, because he had never needed charity the way Rosadel had, and everything she was saying made sense. He also knew he would be a "write a check" "make a donation" guy if Rosadel wasn't part of his life. His parents weren't those kind of people, but Clancy knew he would use his busy schedule as an excuse for not getting involved if Rosadel would let him. He wondered for a minute why it was so natural for him to take the easy way out, and then let that thought go. Clancy believed God gave him Rosadel because she made him a better person, and this was just one more example of how she made him a better person.

"I know you and the girls are going to get attached to the cats, and you all will cry when they leave, but they will survive, and they will have the satisfaction of knowing they did a very good thing. You know Pete is always looking for foster homes for animals, and we have a chance to do that. Maybe this will inspire one of the girls to be an animal rescuer when she grows up, or a veterinarian. At the very least, they will learn that not thinking things through, not asking a grown up, can have lasting consequences. Think about how they would have felt if one of those kittens would have gotten into the street and been killed. It is time for a significant emotional event to get their attention."

Clancy knew in his heart that Rosadel was right, but he hated the thought of watching the girls' hearts break every time one of the kittens left for a new home. "I trust you on this, Sugar, but the tears are about going to kill me."

"I know, Clancy, and I'm sorry for that, but lots of life's lessons are going to have the girls in tears, so you had better get used to it. Just think what you will feel like when some boy breaks their hearts."

"Don't even open that door! I'll have nightmares," replied Clancy. "They aren't allowed to date until they are at least thirty."

Rosadel punched Clancy lightly on the arm. "That's older than I am now, you goose."

"Wishful thinking, Sugar. I want to protect them forever."

Rosadel and Clancy finished up their run and packed the girls into the minivan. Clancy decided to call Pete before leaving the high school, so that he could stop on the way home and get the right food for the momma cat and kittens.

Pete Marshall had finished up his day at his veterinary clinic and was home deciding what to have for dinner. Bachelor life was not his favorite, but he just hadn't met the right person to share his life with yet. He knew he could go eat at his mom and dad's every night and they would welcome him, but at twenty-nine, he kind of felt like a loser not eating on his own sometimes. The phone ringing was a welcome distraction.

"Hey Bro! What's up?" Clancy immediately launched into the story of the triplets and the kittens. Pete put his vet hat back on quickly as he asked Clancy some general questions about the cat and kittens, which, of course, Clancy couldn't answer.

"Hey, Pete, why not just come over? Rosadel will have enough to feed you, and then you can take a look at the cats and we can go to the store together after dinner?"

Pete quickly agreed to come over. He fed his two rescue mutts, Laverne and Shirley, and promised to be quick. They hung around with him at the clinic all day, so he didn't feel too badly about leaving them home for a couple of hours.

Clancy called Rosadel and told her to expect Pete for dinner, then drove home. Roscoe was waiting at the front door, as usual, and Clancy spent a couple of minutes petting him, and then had a short game of fetch. When he got into the kitchen, Rosadel was busy with the final preparations to put the meatloaf dinner on the table. The girls were setting the table, and Clancy felt his heart fill with love and gratitude.

"Clancy, would you pour the milk for the girls and water for us and Pete? Unless you guys want a beer, and then get that. And I forgot to tell you about a new rule for the girls, so they will tell you about it when we are eating dinner."

Clancy got the drinks, holding off on the beer for him and Pete until later.

At the sound of the front door opening, the girls went running. "Uncle Pete! Uncle Pete! We have kittens and a momma cat, and we are going to take care of them!"

Pete hugged all three girls at once. "Well, if it isn't Moe, Larry and Curly," he said. Pete loved to tease the girls and called them by the names of a different famous threesome every time he saw them.

"That's not our names," said Grace. "You're a big teaser."

Pete ruffled Grace's hair, "I sure am, darlin'. That's part of my charm."

"That's part of why you are still single," added Clancy.

"No brother fighting in this house," warned Rosadel.

"Yes, Ma'am," replied the brothers in unison as they exchanged a man hug chest bump.

"Where are the cats?" asked Pete.

"They're in the dining room, you can wait until after we eat to look at them."

As the family sat down at the table, they all joined hands and said grace. As was the family custom, each girl asked a special blessing as part of the process. "Please help Holly be a good mommy" asked Grace. "And thanks for Uncle Pete" added Lou. "And please help us remember our new rule" said Rosie.

"So, who wants to tell me about this new rule?" asked Clancy. Three hands shot up.

"Well, since Rosie prayed about it, I think she should go first," said Rosadel. "But each girl should tell you how the rule applies to her."

Clancy had to admit he was intrigued by this new rule, so he waited for Rosie to start.

"If we have an idea, we are supposed to get a grown-up. But if one of us forgets to get a grown-up, the others are supposed to help remember. So, for me, if Lou won't listen to Grace, I go get a grown-up. And if Grace has an idea, I try to talk her out of it."

"And if Grace won't listen to Rosie, I get a grown-up, and if Rosie has an idea, I try to talk her out of it." Lou added.

"If Lou has an Idea, I try to talk her out of it, and if Rosie won't listen to Lou, I go get a grown-up." Grace finished.

Clancy and Pete both looked confused, so Rosadel explained that the teachers at Holy Redeemer had come up with this plan. And she explained it more clearly. Clancy actually thought this might work.

After dinner, Rosadel had everyone bring their dishes to the dishwasher, and then sent the girls to the dining room with Clancy and Pete to meet the kittens. Rosadel and Roscoe stayed in the kitchen.

Pete looked over the cat and kittens and confirmed Mrs. West's estimate of about 6 weeks old. He then changed all of Rosadel's plans by informing the triplets and Clancy that the kittens should stay with their momma until at least 12 weeks old, maybe even sixteen weeks. So much for Christmas present kittens. To Pete, the kittens looked to be in pretty good health, and he told the girls that they would have to bring the kittens to see him in the office in two weeks.

"Hey Pete - you want to break the news to Rosadel about how long the kittens will stay here?" asked Clancy.

"Nope, bro - man up and tell her yourself - before the girls do."

"Tell me what?" asked Rosadel, entering the dining room.

"The kitties have to stay for a long time," supplied Grace. Rosadel looked at Clancy, raising an eyebrow.

"Sugar, you are so cute when you do that eyebrow thing," said Clancy.

"Jacob Clancy Marshall do not try to distract me. The kitties have to stay for a long time?" Rosadel crossed her arms and waited.

"They need to be six to ten weeks older to leave the momma cat, according to Pete. So, we will have these babies until mid-January, maybe even mid-February. Maybe we should be looking at them as Valentine kittens."

Rosadel wished she had done more homework before taking this on, but what was done was done. Maybe the triplets got some of their impulse control issues from her.

"Well, I guess that means even more money will come out of the Disney jar, but that is OK. We are going to give these little kittens a good start in life."

Two weeks later, Rosadel was really questioning her sanity, and her interpretation of God's hand in her life. Clancy and the girls were at Pete's veterinary clinic with the cats, and she and Roscoe were giving the dining room a deep clean while they were gone. The Disney jar had been up to almost a thousand dollars and would probably be empty by the time this ordeal was over. Feeding and littering seven cats was expensive, and there would be at least two vet visits for each of the kittens, more if they stayed longer than twelve weeks. Pete would give them as much discount as he could, but he needed to pay his bills too.

Clancy and the girls had been doing a good job with their responsibilities. Rosadel had little interaction with the cat and kittens, she just did the mountains of laundry from the kennel. The girls were good about playing with the kittens, and even good about scooping the litter box. The hard part was knowing how attached the girls were getting to Holly and her babies.

Clancy was supposed to be talking to Pete about how to introduce Roscoe. Rosadel wanted to make sure that her sweet dog wouldn't have to sit at the dining room door looking sad because he couldn't go in for the rest of the time the kittens stayed at the Marshall house.

Holly was getting to the point where she wanted some time away from the kittens, so Rosadel was hoping Pete would approve the plan to let Holly out of the dining room while the girls and Clancy were playing with the kittens.

Rosadel had finished her cleaning and was in the kitchen putting a tray of cookies in the oven when Clancy and the girls got home. She heard them settling Holly and the kittens back into their crate from the travel crates (more money) that had transported them to the vet and back.

Clancy came into the kitchen, and put his arms around Rosadel from the back, leaning in and kissing the side of her neck. "I don't know what smells better, Sugar, you or the cookies."

Rosadel closed her eyes and leaned her head to give Clancy better access to her neck, while cuddling back to be closer to him. "You'll make me get distracted and burn the cookies if you aren't careful," she warned.

"I love burnt cookies," was Clancy's reply.

With that, Rosadel turned in his arms and they were kissing like they couldn't get enough of each other. Which they couldn't, even after all these years together.

Meanwhile, in the dining room, the kittens and Holly were getting reacquainted with their temporary home. Peanut was climbing the wall of the crate, poking his paw through trying to get the girls to play. "I think we should take Peanut out to play," said Lou, reaching for the clasp on the opening.

"Uh-Uh," said Grace, "No opening the crate unless an adult is in the room."

"But Mommy and Daddy are just in the kitchen," said Lou.

At that, Rosie ran into the kitchen. "Mommy, Daddy, Lou won't listen to Grace and is going to open the crate."

Clancy took a deep breath. Dang, he hated to be interrupted when he and Rosadel were kissing like that. "Good job, Rosie. Good job, Grace. Lou, don't you dare open that crate."

Rosadel pulled the tray of cookies out of the oven. "Girls come on in here so we can talk."

The girls scampered into the kitchen, Rosie and Grace very smiley and Lou looking upset. "Come on and tell Mommy all about what Uncle Pete said about the kittens and Holly. Lou, you can go first."

Clancy smiled at Rosadel over the girls' heads. She always knew just what to do to keep things from getting blown out of proportion.

"I'm sorry I didn't listen to Grace, Mommy." said Lou in a subdued voice.

"I know that baby, and that is why you three are looking out for each other and helping each other to not make mistakes. Now tell me what Uncle Pete said."

"Well," said Lou, "Holly does need some time away from the kittens. And they have worms. Or maybe some of them, so Uncle Pete gave them all medicine. But they are doing good."

"And you can let Holly in the kitchen to see how she does with Roscoe." said Grace.

"And Uncle Pete is going to put up signs and pictures at his office to help find homes," said Rosie.

"And he is going to give us certificates to go with the kittens so they won't make more kittens," added Lou.

"Spay/Neuter," Clancy interjected. "That is Pete's Christmas gift to us, he'll provide free Spay / Neuter coupons to go with the cats."

"Isn't that a lot of money?" asked Rosadel.

"Well, you know he provides so many $10 certificates to the animal shelter. He talked to them and told them he was reducing that number by 7 this year, as these cats would be there if you hadn't brought them home. So, it is just a $70 difference to the pro bono work he was going to do next year anyway. And that is his Christmas present to us and the girls."

"Girls, do you understand that your Christmas present from Uncle Pete is going to the kittens?"

"Yes, Mommy, and we think it is a good thing. Uncle Pete explained how too many kittens with no homes is a bad thing and we are stopping that."

"I'm very proud of you girls for sharing your Christmas with the kittens. Now, who wants to help decorate cookies?"

Once Rosadel had the girls all set up with icing, and candies, and cookies to be decorated, she washed her hands and went into the dining room. She had been deliberately limiting her exposure to the kittens, because she really wanted Clancy and the girls to take responsibility. She carefully sat next to the crate and talked to Holly.

"Holly, I'll bet you could use a break from those babies. I know I only had three and sometimes I just needed Clancy to stay with them so I could nap or take a bath or anything. Would you come out with me?"

Holly had been sitting watching as Rosadel talked, but now she walked over to the side of the crate and butted Rosadel's hand where it rested on the side of the crate. As Rosadel scratched Holly, she began to purr.

"Let's get you out of there for a little bit and see how it goes," said Rosadel.

Rosadel carefully opened the crate and fished Holly out, keeping the kittens back with her other hand. Once Holly was out, the kittens started to mewl. Holly didn't seem disturbed by their cries and stretched luxuriously. Rosadel didn't want to leave the girls alone with Clancy and the cookies for too long but didn't want to put Holly back in the crate too soon either. She picked Holly up and opened the door to the kitchen.

Clancy and the girls were doing great with the cookies, but Roscoe came right over to see what was up. Holly didn't seem to react at all to Roscoe, so that was a good first sign. Roscoe just sat by Rosadel's feet and leaned on her leg.

"Will you all be OK without me while I play with Holly for a few minutes?" asked Rosadel.

"Yes, Mommy. We're making beautiful cookies with Daddy."
Rosadel looked at the cookies and was glad they were for family. Beauty was in the eyes of the beholder. She squatted down and kissed Roscoe. "I've got to go back in the dining room, buddy, but I promise I'll save plenty of snuggles for you later."

Roscoe sighed and went back to his bed in the corner, and Rosadel took Holly back into the dining room. After supper when all the food was put away and the girls and Clancy were playing with the kittens, she was going to let Holly loose in the kitchen while she sat with Roscoe. Hopefully, the two animals would form a friendship.

CHAPTER 3

Cassidy Bourgeois had just finished checking all the residents at St. Elizabeth parish animal shelter and was getting ready to check for messages and close for the night. Thank God there were very few animals at the shelter right now.

Cassidy was proud of her work and her choices, but she felt like her heart was getting more and more broken as time went on. This year had been particularly difficult, as they had received a number of senior animals at the shelter, due to the death or disability of their owners. These cases were the hardest on Cassidy. She wanted to take every last one of the seniors home with her. As it was, she had two seniors she had rescued, and she had talked veterinarian Pete Marshall into taking a bonded pair of seniors whose owner had died.

Cassidy had taken a long and winding road to becoming the shelter manager. She had majored in public relations in college and had worked at a veterinarian's office while going to school. Cassidy loved animals and had volunteered here at St. Elizabeth animal shelter in high school. When she went to University of Louisiana at Lafayette, she needed a part-time job, and her history of volunteering with St. Elizabeth Parish Animal Shelter went a long way to helping her get the job.

After a couple of years in public relations jobs in business, Cassidy felt unfulfilled. She missed working with animals, and she missed Bayou Beni. When the job as shelter manager was advertised, she really didn't think she had a shot at it, but decided to try, as it seemed like the right career choice.

To her surprise, she got the Job. One of the first and most important contacts for an animal shelter manager is the local veterinarian who supports the shelter. Cassidy expected that to be Dr. Russell and was surprised to find out he had sold the practice to Pete Marshall.

She had met Pete when they both volunteered at the shelter in high school, even though he was a few years older. Even though they were close in age, they were very different in personality. Pete was very outgoing, and a big tease. Cassidy had a good sense of humor, but was quiet and really very shy, feeling more comfortable with animals than with people.

People often wondered why she went into public relations since she was so shy. What most people don't realize is public relations work is like acting. You put on the costume and read the script, and the people you interact with never really know you or see you. They see whatever you are selling. So, for Cassidy, public relations work was hiding in plain sight.

Cassidy had a few close friends, but mostly spent her time working on plans to improve the plight of the animals that came through the shelter, and her friends were almost all involved in animal rescue. She sometimes worried that the more time she spent with the animals, the less she knew how to interact appropriately with people. As long as she was speaking on behalf of the animals that needed love and care, she could talk forever. Small talk? Cassidy had a hard time wondering why people bothered.

Pete Marshall, on the other hand, could talk about anything with anybody. Cassidy loved being around Pete, because he was always so upbeat and positive. And really cute with his dark brown hair, blue eyes and square jaw. Cassidy thought he was just about the perfect man.

Too bad Cassidy hadn't been able to talk Pete into seeing her as a woman instead of just as a colleague in animal care. She truly didn't even know how to flirt. Cassidy hadn't really had a boyfriend. There had been dates, but with her shyness, they never went anywhere. A twenty-seven-year-old virgin was like a unicorn.

Cassidy finished up her paperwork and headed for home. When she opened the door at her house, she listened for sounds from the dogs.

Maggie, a poodle mix, was sixteen; and Sophie, a terrier mix was fifteen. It sometimes took a loud noise to wake them and let them know Cassidy was home, and every day she was afraid it would be the day she came home to find one of them had died in their sleep.

As she turned on the lights, the two old girls were curled up in their crate, with the door open. They were too old to get into mischief, and too old to wait hours for a bathroom break, so Cassidy had set up a plastic pan with pee-pee pads for the old girls to use if they needed to before she got home.

When Cassidy set her purse and computer on the table, Maggie woke up. She started wagging her tail, and slowly worked her way to her feet and out to greet Cassidy. Maggie's movements woke Sophie, and she began barking excitedly, as she too slowly worked her way onto her feet.

"How are Mommy's good girls?" asked Cassidy.

The dogs now fully awake ran over to where Cassidy sat on the floor to be pet and to climb into Cassidy's lap.

"I sure am glad you girls came to live with me. I love you so much." Maggie and Sophie took turns giving Cassidy doggie kisses, then stood up so that Cassidy could make her way to the kitchen to prepare dinner for all of them.

It was amazing that the dogs, as old as they were when they had come to live with Cassidy earlier that year, were totally at home and in sync with Cassidy's schedule. She often thought about Maggie's owner, who had died, and regularly took both Maggie and Sophie to Our Lady of Lourdes home to visit Sophie's owner, who was still unable to speak or walk after a stroke.

Ms. Bessie Chauvin might not be able to speak or walk, but she knew Sophie, and tears would roll down her cheeks every time Cassidy took the dogs to visit. After the tears would come the crooked smile, since one side of Ms. Chauvin's face didn't work, but Cassidy knew she was brightening Ms. Chauvin's life with her visits.

That was one time Cassidy could small talk. Telling Ms. Chauvin the details of what Sophie had eaten, and the cute things that she had done since the last visit filled the silences. And watching the light come back on in Ms. Chauvin's eyes made it easy to embellish the stories into little comedies that made Ms. Chauvin laugh. Cassidy sometimes thought she should write children's stories based on the stories she told Ms. Chauvin to encourage people to adopt senior dogs.

Cassidy checked her phone and saw that she had a text message from Pete Marshall.

> *Saw the kittens and momma cat that Rosadel is fostering today. They all look good. Deworming the kittens. Will post pictures in my office. Can you post pictures on the Shelter site and petfinder?*

Cassidy thought about how lucky she was that Rosadel Marshall had stepped up to foster that momma cat and her kittens. Kittens really struggled in the shelter, and Cassidy had a short list of people willing to foster entire litters. And she had no idea how Maggie and Sophie would have reacted to a cat and kittens. Just thinking about it made her want to cry. But this time it didn't come to Cassidy saving the day or seeing animals suffer. She had to remind herself to be grateful for the breaks she got when she got them.

> *Sure thing Pete. Email the pictures to the shelter email account and I will get them posted to the appropriate sites.*

> *Thanks, Cassidy. See you Friday.*

Pete Marshall was again experiencing his nightly dinner dilemma. There were a couple of basketball games on TV tonight that he wanted to watch, so he decided to order a pizza.

Laverne and Shirley loved basketball. Since he had gotten them as seniors when their owner died, and they landed in the St. Elizabeth Animal Shelter, he really didn't know a whole bunch of their history. The had lived in Bayou Beni only a short time in the assisted living section of Our Lady of Lourdes. Their owner had moved there because of the pet friendly policy, but had died within six months of moving in. Both dogs were healthy, although overweight when Pete brought them home. They were now a healthy weight.

Most of the time, they didn't care too much about television, but when basketball was on they ran back and forth and barked at the set occasionally. Pete wasn't sure if it was the motion or the noises, but it made watching basketball more fun than ever. Even if the game was a bomb, Laverne and Shirley were great entertainment.

Pete thought about his upcoming visit to the parish animal shelter. Cassidy Bourgeois was a puzzle to him. He had never met anyone so devoted to the care of unloved or unwanted animals. He had seen her work tirelessly to get forever and foster homes for the animals in her care. He had seen her desperately holding back tears when an animal had to be euthanized, either because of severe illness, or because they had behavioral issues that could not be rehabilitated. Pete wished that it would never come to an animal being euthanized for any other reason than to end its suffering, but he knew that there was a long way to go until that day.

Mostly, Pete was grateful for the happy, healthy animals that came into his practice for their annual and semi-annual checks and necessary vaccinations. He was a glass half full guy, so spent most of his time focusing on how many good pet owners lived in Bayou Beni.

Two years ago, Pete had started going to the homes of his patients when they had to euthanize their dogs due to old age or disease. It was much easier on the owners and the pets that way. It was also easier on Laverne and Shirley. They would always get depressed when a dog died at the clinic. It was like they grieved for the animal, even if they never knew it. And they were obviously picking up on the grief of the owners.

But when it came to people, Cassidy was all business. He never could get her to engage in conversation, except about the animals. He thought maybe she just didn't like him, but that was hard to swallow, as Pete was used to people liking him. He was easy-going, nice, and went out of his way to be helpful. He was also pretty ordinary looking. He had darker hair than Clancy, kind of a medium brown, and blue eyes. He wore glasses, as wearing contacts didn't give him the correction he wanted at work. He realized that In spite of the fact he was in really good physical condition, he wasn't the sort of guy who was so good-looking women got tongue tied and uncomfortable around him. So, he just couldn't figure out why Cassidy was so cold with him.

And he was kind of confused as to why it mattered so much.

Cassidy finished feeding the dogs and herself, and decided to give her dad, Prescott, a call. Prescott was forging a relationship with a new post-traumatic stress disorder (PTSD) alert dog. Prescott's first dog, Ulysses, had died over a year ago, and at first Prescott had refused to get a new dog, saying it was too painful to lose another dog. That broke Cassidy's heart, because her dad's PTSD had stolen his quality of life for much of the time since he had returned from Vietnam in 1969. The best years Cassidy could remember for her dad were the years he had Ulysses.

Prescott Bourgeois answered the phone on the second ring, a smile lighting his face when he saw Cassidy's name on the caller ID.

"Hey Baby Girl! How's everything?" he asked.

"Good, Daddy, Good. I was wondering how you are doing with Thor?" Thor was Prescott's new dog. Ulysses had been a Belgian Malinois, and Prescott couldn't bear to have another dog that looked like Ulysses. Thor was a Black Labrador Retriever.

"Thor and I are starting to like each other," Prescott replied. "He is very different from Ulysses. Ulysses was a serious dog. Thor looks like he just heard a joke a minute ago. I swear he does goofy stuff to make me laugh, and then bounces on his paws like he is proud of himself. You know your dad has never been a laughing kind of guy, but Thor seems determined to change me."

Cassidy was delighted by the report. She had picked Thor for her dad for that very reason. Prescott needed light in his life, and Thor was just the one to bring it.

Ulysses had not started as a trained PTSD dog. He had been an abandoned pup at the shelter when Cassidy was in the ninth grade. He was about eight months old when animal control picked him up. No collar, no chip, full of fleas and scared to death, with a broken rib, as if he had been kicked. Cassidy was volunteering when he was brought in, and he was so frightened, it broke her heart.

Prescott had called that night, and Cassidy had been crying and crying talking about this poor scared pup. Prescott hated when Cassidy cried, and he hated the idea that a broken creature had nowhere to go. Prescott thought of himself as a broken creature, and so felt immediate empathy with the pup. The next day, Ulysses had found a home with Prescott.

It took a couple of weeks for Ulysses to lose his fear of feet, making Prescott believe the broken rib had come from a person's foot. He thought if he ever found the person who kicked Ulysses, he might just have found a good reason to go to jail for the first time in his life. After Ulysses got comfortable with Prescott, he started sleeping on Prescott's bed, instead of on his bed beside the bed.

The first time Ulysses woke Prescott up as he was entering one of his nightmares, he thought it was a coincidence. But it happened every time. Prescott never had a full-blown screaming in terror nightmare the entire time Ulysses was alive. Ulysses always woke Prescott up.

And when the daytime anxiety would strike, like at New Year's and Fourth of July with all the fireworks, Ulysses would press himself against Prescott's side, and demand to be comforted, which in turn, comforted Prescott.

It was years before Prescott told Cassidy about Ulysses behavior. When he did, Cassidy told him that dogs were now being trained as PTSD therapy dogs. She had never heard of a dog training himself, but obviously the bond between Prescott and Ulysses had manifested in Ulysses doing instinctively what Prescott needed.

Cassidy could see her dad's quality of life returning now that he and Thor were bonding, and Thor was interrupting Prescott's nightmares. Cassidy was hopeful that Thor would also help her dad learn to laugh a little more often.

"I know you told me things are good, Baby, but I can hear sadness in your voice. Do you want to tell Daddy what's wrong, or do you want me to drag it out of you?"

Cassidy was exceptionally close to her dad. Prescott had been married three times, and Cassidy was his only child. All of his marriages had ended in divorce. He had married Cassidy's mom when she was eighteen and Prescott was thirty-eight. The marriage hardly lasted until Cassidy's first birthday, but Prescott had made sure to stay a fixture in Cassidy's life.

Cassidy's mom, Sandra, had been a wild child looking for a way out of a bad home situation, and Prescott had been generous with alimony and child support, so Sandra always cooperated with him on sharing Cassidy's time. Prescott knew he wasn't good husband material, because of his many issues with PTSD, but somehow, he managed to be a good father in spite of them.

Sandra had remarried when she was thirty and Cassidy was twelve. They had lived in the Baton Rouge area near where Prescott lived and worked but moved to Bayou Beni when Sandra had married Cassidy's step-dad, Mark. Fortunately, Prescott had the opportunity to move to Bayou Beni in 2001, when the plant in Bayou Beni was purchased by the company Prescott worked for.

That had been a really good thing for both Cassidy and Prescott, because when Sandra and Mark had two children of their own, Cassidy had her dad close by to help her feel like she was still important.

Cassidy loved her Mom, and Mark and Candy and Chip, her half sister and brother, but she always felt a little bit outside the tight circle of their family. With Prescott, she was always sure of her place, and his unwavering love.

"The job is hard, Daddy. The dogs and cats whose owners surrender them break my heart. We have some good rescue organizations to help out, but with the oil industry on the downturn again, lots of people are losing their jobs, so we have a harder time placing animals. No creature should be fed and housed and loved for eight or ten years and then end up dying in an animal shelter. I wish I could save them all. And then I'm worried about Maggie and Sophie. I know they are old, and I'm afraid everyday one or both of them will be dead when I get home. And I'm still no good at making friends. I can talk to animals, but people, not so much."

"Oh, sweetheart. I wish I could fix it for you. Isn't there some bright spot you could focus on to help yourself feel better?" asked Prescott.

"I guess there is one thing, Daddy. Rosadel Marshall took a cat and six kittens to foster to keep them out of the shelter, so that is a big deal. Kittens do so poorly without proper socialization, and we just can't give them what they need in the shelter."

"Rosadel's husband Clancy still works for me at the plant. I'll never forget the way Rosadel took care of Ulysses after his stroke. They are good people. And those triplets of theirs are a hoot. I love going to work some days just to hear the stories about their latest antics."

"The triplets are really to thank for Rosadel fostering the momma cat and kittens. They found the box with all of them on the playground and put them in the manger in place of the Baby Jesus with a "Free to Good Home" and "What Would Jesus Do?" sign."

Prescott couldn't help the laugh that burst out of him. "That is priceless, Cass. So how did Rosadel come to bring them all home?"

"She wants the girls to learn that actions have consequences, and that if you are going to get involved in a problem, you need to take responsibility and stay in for the long haul. She is even making the girls pay Pete Marshall for their veterinary care out of the girls Disney fund."

"Well, I sure hope Rosadel and Clancy find good homes for all of them, so you don't have to worry about at least those animals."

"Me, too, Daddy. Thanks for listening to me, I'm going to go do some more paperwork and then watch some TV. I feel better, you always have a way of doing that for me." Cassidy didn't add that part of making her feel better was hearing her dad laugh about the Marshall triplets. It really seemed that having Thor was giving her father back the ability to enjoy life.

CHAPTER 4

Rosadel Marshall was making her start of shift rounds at Our Lady of Lourdes when she heard barking coming from Bessie Chauvin's room. Since Rosadel only worked part time, she didn't know that Cassidy Bourgeois often brought Maggie and Sophie to visit Ms. Chauvin, because their paths hadn't crossed before.

The first thing Rosadel noticed when she entered Ms. Chauvin's room was Sophie lying on the bed, and Ms. Chauvin, smiling as best she could while she stroked Sophie with her good hand.

"Hey Cassidy! Hey Ms. Chauvin! Looks like you have some special company today," said Rosadel as she entered the room.

"Hey Rosadel! Sophie misses her momma, so I bring her up to visit every chance I get," said Cassidy. "And Maggie feels left out if she can't come too, so the three of us all visit. Ms. Chauvin really enjoys seeing Sophie and hearing about her antics, don't you, Ms. Chauvin?"

Bessie Chauvin nodded, and moved her mouth as if trying to speak. Both Cassidy and Rosadel knew that she hadn't spoken since her last stroke, and probably never would again, but they waited patiently to see if words would come out. Finally, Ms. Chauvin just looked at Sophie, then at Cassidy, and her eyes filled with such joy it was easy to see what she wanted to say.

"You just love Cassidy for bringing your Sophie to visit, don't you? And you wish Sophie could stay with you all the time." Rosadel supplied.

Ms. Chauvin nodded, and hugged Sophie to her. Cassidy decided this was as good a time as any to talk to Rosadel about the momma cat and kittens.

"Rosadel, I can't tell you how grateful I am that you are fostering that cat and kittens. I was sick thinking about what I would do with them after Frances West called the shelter. I couldn't bring them to my house with these two old girls, and we just don't have enough foster families to meet all the need. You are a lifesaver for those kittens."

Rosadel blushed a little at the praise and replied, "Really, Cassidy, the Lord sent those animals to help me teach my girls about responsibility, and about getting involved. They are too impulsive, and I'm hoping that they learn to get an adult involved before they take matters into their own hands. They are loving these kittens, and I know I'll have three broken-hearted little girls when they have to say goodbye to the kittens, but hopefully they will learn that you have to be very careful when you take on responsibility for a living creature."

"And maybe one of them will see more foster care in their future." Cassidy warmed to her favorite subject. "We always need foster homes for animals in transition. It is the hardest, most rewarding thing in the world to do, and most people say it is just too hard. If even one of your girls learns how to love and let go, that will be a great gift for many animals in the future."

"You know, Cassidy, I never even thought about fostering animals before this. I think maybe you and I should get together and put together some sort of booth for the next Holy Redeemer church fair, and maybe we can talk to Mrs. West about you coming to a PTA meeting to talk to the parents. There are a lot of good people at Holy Redeemer that might be inclined to help if they knew more about it. How about I give you a call in a few days to talk more about it?"

Cassidy was amazed at how Rosadel just jumped in and tried to help. Her dad was right, Rosadel was just good people. "That would be great, Rosadel. Is daytime or evening better for you? You can call the shelter if daytime is good, or I can give you my number for evening."

"Definitely daytime," said Rosadel with a laugh. "When the girls are home I try not to turn my back for a minute. Now, I need to go make the rest of my rounds."

Rosadel turned to Ms. Chauvin. She placed her hand on Ms. Chauvin's cheek, and looked her in the eye. "It does my heart good to see you so happy. I'll be back later to check on you and give you your nighttime meds. You have a good visit now and I'll see you in a little bit."

Cassidy didn't know when she had ever seen a nurse treat a patient so lovingly. You would think that Ms. Chauvin was Rosadel's mom, the amount of tenderness in her treatment.

Ms. Chauvin nodded her head at Cassidy as if she could read her mind. "She sure is something special, isn't she, Ms. C? Are you related to Rosadel?"

Ms. Chauvin shook her head no, and then yes, then no again.

"So, not family, but feels like family?" guessed Cassidy.

Ms. Chauvin nodded with emphasis.

"You know, Ms. C., I'm not good with people. I'm way more comfortable with animals. I can come here and talk to you, but most of the time when I try to talk to people I don't know what to say. But I think maybe Rosadel and I could be friends. What do you think?"

Bessie Chauvin reached out her good hand to Cassidy, and Cassidy took her hand. Ms. Chauvin squeezed Cassidy's hand and nodded. She then let go of Cassidy's hand and touched her cheek. Cassidy replied.

"Thanks, Ms. C. It helps to know you think I'm a good girl and a good friend. I hope I can learn how to make friends with more people."

Cassidy, Maggie and Sophie visited a little while longer, and as Ms. Chauvin started looking really tired Rosadel stuck her head back in the room. "I'll be back in five minutes to get you ready for bed" she said.

That was Cassidy's clue to go on home. As she kissed Ms. Chauvin's cheek and said goodbye, Cassidy saw the tears glistening in her eyes. "Don't you worry, Ms. C. Sophie is doing fine at my house, and we'll be back tomorrow or the next day so that you two can visit some more."

As Cassidy was leaving the room, Rosadel was about to go back in. "You know, Cassidy, I'd been wondering why sometimes when I come into work Ms. Chauvin seemed so much more at peace than at other times. Now I realize the good days are the days she gets to see Sophie. It is a really wonderful thing you are doing for her bringing Sophie to visit."

"It's really not a big deal," replied Cassidy. "They love and miss each other, and I have the ability to make them both happy. It is such a little thing to do."

"But most people don't bother." Said Rosadel. "I see so much neglect here. So many patients have no one to come visit them. Ms. Chauvin would be one of those if it weren't for you. She has no children, and her only nieces and nephews live in Texas. They come a couple of times a year, when they are on the way to New Orleans for something. They are good people but have busy lives somewhere else. You could take the busy life exemption, but you don't, and I appreciate that. Now you are supposed to say, 'Thank you'."

Cassidy had to smile. Rosadel was a piece of work. "Thank you, Rosadel. I'll give you a call tomorrow to talk about the PTA and booth at the church fair."

"I have a better idea. Why don't you come over for dinner tomorrow night? You can see the momma cat and kittens, and we can talk while the girls and Clancy play with them after dinner. Feel free to bring Maggie and Sophie. My Roscoe loves company."

After agreeing on a time, Cassidy headed home. It looked like she might be finally making a friend after all. Even if they did meet because they had animals in common. Cassidy had a feeling that her lack of small talk ability wouldn't be an issue with Rosadel. That woman could fill any silence.

As Cassidy approached Clancy and Rosadel's door the following evening, she heard barking and children's voices from inside. She rang the bell and was surprised when Pete Marshall opened the door.

"C'mon in Cassidy. Laverne and Shirley are here too, so Maggie and Sophie will have a ball." said Pete as he ushered Cassidy through the door. Roscoe, Laverne and Shirley were all sitting behind Pete, waiting for instruction. "Y'all just sit until Maggie and Sophie are off their leashes," Pete said to the dogs.

Cassidy was amazed that they all obeyed. She knelt down and took off Sophie and Maggie's leashes, Sophie ran to Pete for some love, but Maggie stayed behind Cassidy.

"She's a little scared of everything these days," explained Cassidy.
"I think it is because she doesn't see, hear or scent very well anymore."

Pete released the other dogs, who began playing with Sophie. He
knelt down and put his hand out to Maggie, and said, "How are you
doing, old girl?" Maggie wagged her tail, sniffed Pete's hand and then
head butted his hand to be pet. As Pete sat down on the floor and
gathered Maggie onto his lap, Cassidy felt her heart melt. What a great
guy Pete Marshall was.

Just then, Rosadel called from the kitchen, "Cassidy, in here. We
can talk while I finish up supper."

Cassidy walked through to the kitchen, handing Rosadel the bottle of
wine she had brought as her contribution to dinner. "Thanks Cassidy! I
love an unoaked Chardonnay! That will go perfect with the chicken stew
I made for supper."

Cassidy asked if there was anything she could do to help, and
Rosadel wasted no time putting Cassidy to work on the salad.

"The girls are upstairs getting washed up for supper, and Clancy is
finishing up his shower. We'll eat, and then you can go meet the
momma cat and kittens, and then while Clancy and the girls feed them,
play with them and clean the litter boxes we can talk. Can you believe
that it is December 20th already? We're having Christmas cookies for
dessert. I always let the family eat the broken and really ugly ones before
Christmas. What are you doing for Christmas Cassidy? And how's your
Daddy?"

Cassidy still couldn't believe how fast Rosadel could talk, and how
much she could say without pausing for breath. Rosadel knew Cassidy's
dad from a few years before. Rosadel had pet sat for Ulysses after his
stroke and before he passed away. Rosadel had become very fond of both
Prescott and Ulysses.

"I'm spending Christmas eve with my Mom, Mark and their kids,
and spending Christmas Day with my Dad. And then Dad and I will go to
Our Lady of Lourdes. Daddy will make the rounds. He'll bring Thor and
wear a Santa hat and Thor will wear a hat and they'll bring something
small to each resident. I'll visit with Ms. Chauvin, and we'll meet back at
her room. This is the first year Daddy is doing this, and I'm really

excited. I think now that he is thinking about retirement he is trying to figure out what he'll do with his time, and volunteering at the home is an idea he has."

Clancy had come into the kitchen while Cassidy was talking. "I had heard that Prescott was going to retire soon, but nothing official has been communicated."

Cassidy wondered if she had messed up. "Well, Daddy turned sixty-five this year, so he is talking about it, but I don't think he has settled on a date yet, or even really made a decision to retire. You know how he loves to work and loves his job, Clancy. But he is starting to think it is time for him to get out of the way and let the next generation have at it."

"Well, I'll miss him for sure," said Clancy. "He really understands the plant, and the equipment, and no one is more thorough than Prescott. I'll be happy for him but sad for us when he decides to go."

Cassidy nodded. "I think his biggest fear is that he won't have enough to do if he retires. He really doesn't have hobbies, and that is why he has this plan to go play Santa at Our Lady. He is thinking maybe volunteering there will be a good thing to do. I think my visiting Ms. Chauvin gave him the idea."

Pete walked into the kitchen carrying Maggie cradled against his chest. She had put her paws on either side of his neck and was totally still except for the sweep of her wagging tail.

"Maggie here said she loves going to Our Lady. She says she gets plenty of lap time while she is there," said Pete.

"Maggie spends all her time on my lap or someone else's. While Sophie visits with Ms. Chauvin, Maggie goes from lap to lap. And it is not just the ladies, some of the men really love her too. A couple of times I had to go from room to room to find Maggie when it is time to leave. It tires her out, but she is beside herself with excitement when we pull into the parking lot. And she is such a cuddle bug, it does all the residents good to sit with her." said Cassidy. "I worry constantly because she is so old. She's in good shape for a sixteen-year-old dog, but still, she is sixteen."

At that point, the triplets burst into the kitchen. "Uncle Pete, Uncle Pete! Mommy said you were coming over! Why didn't you come up and get us?"

"Well. lookee here, it's Marcia, Jan and Cindy," said Pete, "And Mommy said to let you finish washing up for supper."

Lou put her hands on her hips, "You are never going to find a girlfriend if you don't learn how to stop teasing girls. You know what our names are."

Cassidy couldn't help herself, she burst out laughing. That put her right in the triplet's headlights.

"Oh, no!" said Grace. "Are you Uncle Pete's girlfriend? Lou didn't mean anything."

Before Cassidy could respond, Rosie piped up. "Even if he is a big tease, we still love him. You don't have to be embarrassed to be his girlfriend."

"Girls," Rosadel admonished. "Cassidy is my friend. She works at the St. Elizabeth Animal Shelter, and she came over to meet the momma cat and kittens. She and Uncle Pete know each other because they both work with animals. Remember when Mr. Prescott brought his dog Ulysses to play with Roscoe? Mr. Prescott is Cassidy's Daddy."

But the girls were more tenacious than that.

"Then who's dog is that with Uncle Pete?" demanded Lou.

"And why is that other dog playing with Laverne and Shirley and Roscoe like she knows them already?" asked Grace.

Pete stepped in. "Well, you girls know that Laverne and Shirley like to hang out with me at the clinic. They know Maggie and Sophie from when they come to see me. And Roscoe loves everybody."

"But you do need a girlfriend, Uncle Pete," said Rosie.

Clancy knew if he didn't open his mouth, he'd be in trouble with Rosadel and Pete.

"Mercy Louise, Grace Ann and Charity Rose; enough. Uncle Pete will find a girlfriend when he is ready, and you are embarrassing Cassidy, who is our guest. Stop with the matchmaking." All three girls were quiet, as whenever Clancy used both their given names, they knew they were in trouble. Gracie's lower lip was trembling. "Come over here and give Daddy some sugar, and then help Mommy set the table," he added.

All three descended on Clancy and the sad faces and quivering chins gave way to giggles as Clancy blew raspberries against their necks.

Cassidy watched in awe, her embarrassment fading as she took in the sight of handsome Clancy Marshall with his little girls. They sure were a handful!

Rosadel took advantage of Clancy distracting the girls to lean over and whisper to Cassidy. "Ever since my Dad and Jessie got married, the triplets think it is their job to find a match for everybody. I'm sorry if they embarrassed you."

"No problem, Rosadel. You and Clancy handle them very well. Stern but loving, the perfect combination. The same combination works wonders with dogs and cats. Not to imply the girls are animals." Cassidy could feel the blush working up her face as she feared her words were offensive.

"I often joke with Clancy that I learned how to parent with Roscoe, and he is in the slow group because his first chance was the girls," Rosadel joked. "Consistency and love is always the key."

The girls set the table and soon everyone was seated and ready for dinner. As was the family custom, after Grace, each girl added a special blessing. "And bless Mommy's friend Cassidy, because she loves animals that no one else does," said Lou. "Bless Roscoe, because he loves everybody," added Rosie. "Bless Daddy because he loves us even when we make him use both names." contributed Grace.

Cassidy found herself blinking away tears from Lou's special blessing, and then fighting laughter with Grace's. She wondered how Lou had worked out that Cassidy's mission in life was to love the animals that no one else did. Cassidy guessed it had to do with fostering the momma cat and kittens.

Dinner was a happy, noisy and delicious affair. The chicken stew was just right, spicy and filling without being too rich, and the salad made a nice compliment. Each of the adults had a glass of wine, which emptied the bottle, and added an air of festivity to the dinner proceedings. After dinner, Rosadel asked Pete to introduce Cassidy to the momma cat and kittens while she, Clancy and the girls cleared the table and loaded the dishwasher.

"Anything to get out of doing dishes," joked Pete.

Clancy clapped Pete on the back of the head. "Way to make Cassidy feel good, oh great brain dead one."

Pete flushed. "Sorry Cassidy. That was a dumb thing to say. Maybe Lou is right about why I don't ever have a girlfriend."

Cassidy didn't know whether she was more embarrassed or amused. "Let's go see the animals, Pete. I have a feeling we both do better with four legged creatures than with two legged creatures."

Holly and the kittens were excited to see company, and immediately began poking their paws through the kennel walls. Cassidy sat down on the floor and opened the kennel door.

The kittens tumbled out, ready to play, and Holly climbed right into Cassidy's lap and began purring.

"Pete, she was somebody's cat. That breaks my heart. She is obviously a house cat and not feral at all. Why would someone dump a pet?"

"Cass, there are so many reasons. Maybe her owner died, and there was no one to take her. Maybe the family lost their job and moved. Maybe there is a sick child or domestic violence situation. I try to not think about it too much, because I don't want to become cynical about people and their motives. I just try really hard to make sure my clients know that I have expectations for how they care for their pets and make them understand that if for some reason they have to give up a pet, they can always bring the animal to me and I will rehome it."

"I didn't know you did that Pete. Have many people brought you their pets?"

Pete shook his head. "So far, no one has taken me up on my offer, thank goodness, because I'm not sure what I would do. Laverne and Shirley are very good about other dogs at the clinic, and here at Clancy and Rosadel's house, but they are a little possessive of my apartment."

"Maggie and Sophie are pretty laid back about new animals, because I have had so many one-night fosters. If you ever do need a place, let me know and I may be able to help you out."

The girls and Clancy came into the room, and the noise level immediately went up more than a few decibels.

"Do you like them Cassidy? Did Uncle Pete tell you their names?" It seemed like the girls were talking in unison.

"No, Uncle Pete didn't tell me you had named the kittens. You know that when they go to their new homes they will get new names, right?"

Lou sighed. "Yes, we know. Everyone tells us that. But we have to call them something."

Pete caught Cassidy's eye, "Can't argue with second grade logic," he said with a wink.

Cassidy felt the blush rising on her cheeks. If she didn't know better, she would think that Pete was flirting with her.

Grace was holding the black and white kitten like a baby, rocking her. "See Ms. Cassidy, this is Cuddles. And I hold her like this, so she learns to trust people."

Rosie was dangling a piece of string that the orange and orange and white kittens were trying to catch. "The orange one is Pooh, and the other one with orange and white is Peanut. We play with them so that they will play nice when the go to their forever homes."

Lou was helping Clancy scoop the litter box. "The mommy is Holly. Does your dogs like cats? Because Holly likes to go in the kitchen and get a break when we play with the kittens."

Cassidy was impressed that Lou was scooping litter. That was not a job most second graders would do. "Yep, Maggie and Sophie are good with cats. So, they won't have a problem with Holly."

"That's good," said Lou. "OK, Daddy, I'm done with poop scooping. I'm gonna take Holly to the kitchen and then come back to play with the kittens."

"How about you let Cassidy take Holly to the kitchen," said Clancy, "Because Cassidy and Mommy have a lot to talk about. You can just stay in here and play with the kittens."

"OK," said Lou, handing Holly to Cassidy. "Now hold her close to you so she doesn't get scared," cautioned Lou.

"Thank you, Lou. I'll be real careful with her." Once again Pete caught Cassidy's eye and winked. Cassidy was glad to escape to the

kitchen, she didn't know quite what to make of the attention she was
getting from Pete.

Rosadel had two cups ready on the counter, and a selection of tea
and coffee K-cups for Cassidy to choose from.

After brewing two cups of decaf coffee, Rosadel and Cassidy sat
down at the kitchen table.

"Really, Cass, I don't think very many people even know that foster
care for animals is a thing you can do. And I know that very few people
think about seniors needing homes. I think we might find some real help
in the community if you talk to the PTA and have a booth at the Holy
Redeemer fair. I know we can get Clancy's mom and dad to work the
booth, and I'll bet your dad would too. Then if we could get some of the
high school kids that volunteer at the shelter for their community service
points, we will have good coverage. We could have Maggie, Sophie,
Laverne and Shirley come out to be the faces of senior rescue." Once
Rosadel got an idea, she tended to run with it.

"I think it could work," said Cassidy, still holding Holly on her lap.
"This sure is a sweet cat. Why do you think someone abandoned her?"

"Well, she could have gotten loose when someone was moving. You
know with all the layoffs in the oil field this year, a lot of the workers
that follow the boom and bust cycle have moved on. She could be feral
but used to contact with humans. But the way she was left at Holy
Redeemer in the schoolyard, I think whoever was taking care of her had
no way to take care of her and the kittens and did what they thought was
the best thing. When you are having a hard time feeding your children, it
is hard to have space in your mind and heart to worry about pets. I know
you and I think of our pets just like family, but not everyone is raised
that way."

"And actually, in this case, leaving them at Holy Redeemer brought
about a better solution than the shelter. But I wouldn't want anyone to
think that is a good choice." Cassidy looked across the kitchen, where
Roscoe, Maggie, Sophie, Laverne and Shirley were all sharing Roscoe's
big bed. "Look at them, you would think they had all been friends for
life."

Rosadel looked over and smiled. "My Roscoe loves everyone of God's creatures, and something about him calms them down. I remember when we had Ulysses after his stroke. He was fine the first day when your dad was here but was nervous as a cat on a hot tin roof when your dad left him here the next day. Roscoe brought one toy after another, and then pestered me for treats, which he took to Ulysses. He was not going to rest until Ulysses was comfortable. They ended up best of friends, and Roscoe really missed Ulysses when he was cleared to stay home by himself. We had him come over one day a week until he died so he and Roscoe could enjoy each other's company."

"I've been worried about Prescott since Ulysses died," continued Rosadel, "I'm glad to hear he has another dog, and that he is giving Thor a chance to explore his own personality."

"I worried about him too, Rosadel, and made sure to get him a trained service dog this time, and one with a very different personality. Thor is a bit of a clown when he is not working, and he makes my dad laugh. I think Daddy has laughed more since he got Thor than he ever did in his life."

"Back to the topic at hand, the church fair is at the end of February. If we have any of the kittens left, they will be ready to go to new homes, so we can do a foster/adoption booth. The next PTA meeting where we will be planning for the fair is the second Tuesday in January. Do you think that you can be ready to come to the PTA meeting and pitch the idea for a booth? I can help. We can tag team it."

Cassidy thought ahead, and conditionally agreed with the plan. "That date sounds fine to me, Rosadel. When is the church fair?"

"We're having a fish fry on February 26th, as it is Lent, and then the fair is on the 27th and 28th. I think we could do the booth both days, but have different animals, especially seniors because that would be too much for them to do both days, don't you think?"

"I think an hour or two in a crowd is as much as a senior can stand. But if we have other volunteers to run the booth, Pete and I can ferry the animals back and forth," replied Cassidy.

"Am I being volunteered, again?" asked Pete as he came into the kitchen. "Rosadel, Clancy told me to tell you to get the milk and cookies fired up because the girls are about done for the night."

"Yes, Pete, you are being volunteered again, but this time it was Cassidy, not me or Clancy. And I can't believe Clancy sent you in here with that message," Rosadel playfully smacked Pete on the arm as she spoke.

"Ouch! Cassidy! You saw that! Protect me before she hits me again!" The dogs got out of Roscoe's bed to see what the commotion was all about, and Cassidy couldn't help it, she laughed out loud.

"Pete Marshall, you big faker! Rosadel barely touched you," Cassidy said.

"But I'm delicate," replied Pete, "And my feelings were hurt more than my arm."

"Do I hear my brother being ridiculous again?" asked Clancy as he came into the room with the triplets.

"Uncle Pete is usually ridiculous," said Gracie.

"And he is a big teaser," added Lou.

"But we love him," said Rosie.

"Thanks Peter, Paul, and Mary, I appreciate your support," said Pete with a wink at Cassidy.

"You need to learn our right names, Uncle Pete," said Lou.

"Or we'll get hurt feelings," added Gracie.

Pete crouched down and opened his arms and the girls crowded in for hugs. "You know I know your names and just tease and would never want to hurt your feelings, don't you?"

"Yes," said Rosie, "But sometimes we need to make you act like a grownup."

All the adults all started laughing at that, and Cassidy returned Holly to her babies as Rosadel set out a plate of cookies and glasses of milk for the girls. Pete and Clancy got themselves cups of coffee, and once again everyone was gathered around the kitchen table.

"Miss Cassidy, did you know our birthday is in four days?" asked Grace.

"We're going to be eight years old," added Lou.

"Can you come to our party?" asked Rosie.

Cassidy looked helplessly at Rosadel.

"I know you said you are going to your Mom's on Christmas Eve, Cassidy, so no hurt feelings if you say no. But we do the girls birthday party from noon to three, then get ready to go to evening mass, then go to George and Harriet Marshall's and have Christmas Eve, so if you are free early, we would love to have you come."

"I can pick you up and drop you off, and you can bring Maggie and Sophie," added Pete.

Cassidy hesitated for just a minute, thinking about how she would change her schedule to have everything finished for Christmas by noon on Thursday, and decided it could be done.

"I'd love to come for your birthday," Cassidy replied, "And thanks for the offer of a ride, Pete. I think I'll take you up on that."

"This year our presents are all for Holly and the kittens." said Gracie.

"We need litter and food," added Rosie.

"And laundry detergent," said Lou.

"Except for Uncle Pete, all our Christmas presents can be for us," said Gracie.

"Wow, that is very generous of you girls," Cassidy was impressed with how matter of fact the girls were about their gifts being for the foster pets.

"Mommy says that if you make a big deal when you make a sacrifice, that you lose all the good in it. And we want to be good girls," explained Lou.

"Well, I still think it is pretty special. I hope that at least one of you learns to love caring for animals enough that I can look forward to you volunteering at St. Elizabeth's Animal Shelter when you are in high school like me and Uncle Pete did." Cassidy smiled at each of the girls as she spoke.

"You knew Uncle Pete that long?" asked Rosie. "That is as long as Mommy knew Daddy."

Pete could see that Cassidy was at a loss, so he tried to help.

"Cassidy and I have known each other for a long time, but we are just really getting to be friends now that Cassidy has moved back to Bayou Beni."

"And the best kind of girlfriend is one who is a friend friend first." Gracie pronounced with all the wisdom of an almost eight-year-old.

Rosadel put up her hand. "Enough! Don't even start on the girlfriend thing. Do you want Cassidy to be so uncomfortable she doesn't come to your birthday party?"

"No, Ma'am," the triplets coursed in unison.

Dessert passed uneventfully, but enjoyably after that, and Cassidy was sincere as she thanked Rosadel and told her she couldn't remember the last time she had so much fun.

"Well, the whole crowd will be here on Thursday. My Dad and Jessie will be back from her business trip to Texas and Michigan, and all the Marshalls will be here too, and the Tate's, along with Belinda Collins and her +1 if she has one right now. It should be a good time." Rosadel hugged Cassidy, and then touched her cheek. "I think we're going to be good friends, Cassidy. I'm just sad it took so long for us to find each other."

Cassidy felt her eyes welling up with tears and didn't know what to say. "There I go again, jumping in saying things normal people don't say. I'm sorry if I made you uncomfortable, Cassidy, but I just say how I feel without thinking sometimes."

Cassidy reached out and grabbed Rosadel's hand. "You are just perfect the way you are Rosadel. And I am really happy that I think we are going to be good friends too."

CHAPTER 5

Angus rolled over on his side to better watch Jessie sleep. The last two weeks on the road had been exhausting for her. Angus hated to wake Jessie up, but it was time to get ready to go to the triplet's birthday party, and they would be disappointed if "Gee-Jay" and "Pop-Pop" were late.

Angus still couldn't believe the beautiful woman sleeping so peacefully beside him had been his wife for almost two years. He thought back to the day he met Jessie at mass at Holy Redeemer, and how he thought that might be the only time he ever saw her. He thought about their meeting again at work, their courtship, and their marriage.

Angus had just about given up on ever getting married again when he met Jessie. At fifty-four, and widowed for fourteen years and a grandfather, he was reluctant to even think that young and beautiful Jessie could be interested in him. But, the triplets opened the door for the conversation, and the rest was history.

Jessie stirred and opened her eyes. "Good morning, beautiful," said Angus. "I was just about to wake you up."

Jessie turned toward Angus and snuggled close. "I sure am glad to be home, and am excited to see everyone, but I could sleep all day," she said. "How much longer did you say this would last?"

Angus pulled Jessie close and kissed the top of her head. "The doctor said you are just entering your second trimester, and that in a few weeks you wouldn't be so tired and will start feeling great. That will last for about three months, and in your third trimester you'll get tired and uncomfortable again."

"I'm just praying that this baby makes it," said Jessie. She and Angus had gotten pregnant practically on their honeymoon, but Jessie had miscarried at eleven weeks. The doctor had assured them that there was no reason a future pregnancy wouldn't be successful and had told them to wait six months before trying again to give Jessie's body plenty of time to heal. They had waited the six months, and then it had taken a while before Jessie got pregnant again. Now that they were at almost fourteen weeks, Jessie was getting less frightened and more confident that this baby would be safely born. Jessie and Angus had already decided if this pregnancy was not successful, they wouldn't risk another one.

Only Jessie's Mom, Dad and Angus knew about the first miscarriage. They hadn't told anyone else at the time the baby was lost. This time, they planned to tell everyone for Valentine's Day, as the baby would be almost twenty-two weeks by then, and Jessie would be starting to show.

"Have I told you lately how much I love you?" Angus asked.

"Mmm, not since last night when I was falling asleep," replied Jessie as she snuggled even closer.

"Well then, Jessie girl, I love you. Every morning when I wake up and see you in my bed, I feel like the luckiest man alive. I hope that I make you at least half as happy as you make me." Angus kissed the top of her head.

"Oh, Angus! I love you too. I never imagined life could be this good. You know how happy you make me." Jessie often thought about how Angus had really been a gift from God. And she really believed that.

"How about I make you a cup of herbal tea to drink in bed, and you can wake up slowly while I shower? Would you like some toast with your tea, or wait and have breakfast together?" Angus loved taking care of Jessie.

"Just tea will be fine. Then I'll get my shower and get ready for the party. I really have missed the girls while we've been gone." Jessie's job had kept her on the road for most of the years between college and meeting Angus. The company had agreed to allow her to stay permanently based in Louisiana, but she still had to travel quite a bit. She usually traveled alone while Angus worked, but he had plenty of vacation time accumulated, and had gone with her on the most recent trip. Angus knew Jessie would have wanted to come home for the weekend between the week in Michigan and the week in Texas and knew that would just put more stress on her body then she needed. By going with her, they had reduced Jessie's travel and stolen a romantic weekend together.

◆ ◆ ◆

Rachel Tate checked the time again calculating what time they should be on the road for the party at the Marshall's. She was loving having great-grandchildren to spoil, even if they felt more like grandchildren. She had made matching shirts for the girls with their names embroidered, plus the words "Ask me about the kittens". She and Daniel had also gotten a big bag of kitten chow, but Rachel thought the shirts would get a good chuckle, and the girls might find homes for the kittens by wearing them.

She was eager to see Jessie, too. When Jessie's first pregnancy ended in a miscarriage, Rachel was as heartbroken as her daughter. She had prayed endlessly to St. Gerard since then and was confident that Jessie would have a healthy baby this time. But, for a first baby, forty-two was definitely high risk, and Rachel knew she would worry until she held that new grandbaby in her arms.

Inserting the triplets' annual birthday party into the Christmas routine had been a challenge, but Rachel and Daniel, along with their children had worked out a plan that was working for everyone. After the party at Rosadel and Clancy's, the Tate clan, including Jessie and Angus went to evening Mass at St John the Evangelist, and then the Tate's celebrated their Christmas Eve. Christmas Day was quiet for Rachel and Daniel, as the children all spent the day with their spouse's families. That made it nice, though, as Rachel and Daniel spent the day going to their siblings' houses for Christmas visits.

With three married children, Rachel knew how lucky she was that she was able to have all of her children and their spouses at her house on Christmas Eve. She knew many of her friends saw their children one at a time or not at all at the holidays. Rachel finished wrapping the gifts and went in search of Daniel. He was making a jambalaya for the birthday party and would want to leave at just the right moment to arrive at the party with the food still hot.

◆ ◆ ◆

Pete Marshall was taking extra care getting ready for the triplets' birthday party, as he wanted to make a good impression on Cassidy. Pete had started to believe that Cassidy might be interested in pursuing a relationship with him the other night at Rosadel and Clancy's house. He was going to do his best to convince Cassidy that they should at least explore the possibility that they could be a great couple.

Cassidy had changed her clothes three times, and her bedroom looked like a tornado had hit. She was currently wearing a pair of brown tweed trousers and a beige sweater, and thought she looked invisible. The problem was that all of Cassidy's clothes had been purchased with the goal of not showing dog hair. She knew there was no time to run out and buy something new but hated that she didn't feel like she looked special or pretty.

What Cassidy didn't see when she looked in the mirror was how the muted colors of her clothes allowed her blond hair to really stand out, and her complexion was a beautiful peachy color. Add in her hazel eyes that looked more green than brown today, and Cassidy was simply beautiful. Cassidy started picking up the mess in her bedroom as she kept an eye on the clock. She had things almost in order when she heard the doorbell ring.

Pete couldn't believe how nervous he was as he waited for Cassidy to open the door. Laverne and Shirley were sitting at his feet, calm in the way that only old dogs can be. When Cassidy opened the door, both dogs stood up and tails started wagging as they saw their friends Maggie and Sophie inside. Pete was glad for the distraction of the dogs, as it helped dispel some of his nervousness. This was Cassidy. They had known each other for years. They would continue as they were in the worst-case scenario.

"Hey Pete! Just let me put Maggie and Sophie in their travel harnesses. Can you carry one of the tubs of litter out? I'll take the other one. And I'll have to transfer their car seats to your car, will there be room?" Cassidy knew her nerves were making her babble a bit.

"I'm the only twenty-nine-year-old bachelor in the world with a minivan, Cassidy, so we'll be fine. Between transporting the triplets on occasion and transporting multiple dogs, I always seem to need multiple booster or car seats. And I feel like I would be setting a bad example as the town veterinarian if I let the dogs ride loose in the car. I'm glad to see you try to set a good example too."

"It's partly setting a good example, and partly I'd be devastated if something happened to the girls in a car accident. Maybe we should have information on car restraints for dogs and cats at the booth at the Holy Redeemer fair."

Pete nodded his agreement. "I have plenty of stuff that I keep at the office to advise people. I can bring materials."

As Pete and Cassidy talked they transferred the car seats and got the dogs all buckled up. Soon, they were on their way to the party.

♦ ♦ ♦

Belinda Collins looked at her reflection in the mirror, and wondered why once again, she was going to a party alone. She wasn't the kind of pretty that stopped traffic, but with her brown hair and blue eyes, she was pretty in "a girl next door" kind of way. And even though she was lazy when it came to exercise, she was naturally very slim and shapely. And she knew she was fun. But when it came to men, it seemed that the guys she met either wanted to be friends with benefits from the first date or were way too demanding. She knew that there were plenty of good guys out there, she just hadn't figured out where to go to meet them. Maybe Bee should take a page out of Jessie McPherson's book and look for an older man. Or maybe not. Whatever, it would be another fun afternoon at the Marshall's.

Angus and Jessie were the first to arrive for the party. The triplets came running to greet them. "Gee-Jay! Gee-Jay! We missed you and

Pop-Pop. You better never leave for this long again!" Jessie squatted down so she could hug all three girls. The girls had decided that Jessie was too young to be called Grandma when she married Angus, so had decided Gee-Jay, short for Grandma Jessie was just the perfect name.

"I think I missed you as much as you missed me. And I heard that you have a momma cat and kittens that you are taking care of until they can find homes of their own." Jessie was amazed at how much you could miss in two weeks where the triplets were involved.

"We are taking care of them until they are big enough to leave their momma. Do you and Pop-Pop want a kitten?" Grace wasted no time in making the offer.

"I think Pop-Pop and I travel too much for a kitten right now," replied Jessie. "But I'll put the word out at work to see if I can help you find homes for them."

Pete and Cassidy were the next to arrive for the party, with four dogs and two tubs of cat litter, they made quite an entrance.

"Uncle Pete! Miss Cassidy! We're so glad you came to our birthday party!" All three girls were talking at once, and Cassidy wasn't sure which was which.

"Happy Birthday, Lou, Grace and Rose!" replied Pete.

"Hey," said Lou, "You used our right names!"

"Yep," said Pete, "That's one of your birthday presents, don't get used to it."

"Oh," replied Rose, "I was hoping it was because you knew to get a girlfriend you were going to have to learn how to behave better."

Jessie couldn't help herself, she burst out laughing. She really had missed the girls.

Pete looked up at Jessie, with an embarrassed grin. "Hey, you, don't laugh, it encourages them. Cassidy, do you know Jessie?"

Jessie reached out to shake Cassidy's hand. "I know who you are, Cassidy, and I've seen you at different events in Bayou Beni, but I don't think we've ever been formally introduced, I'm Jessie McPherson."

Cassidy shook Jessie's hand. "My dad speaks very highly of you, I'm glad to finally meet you officially."

"Well, I think Prescott is the best, so I'm glad to finally meet you too." Jessie took note that Cassidy had arrived with Pete. She had noticed them noticing each other when she and Angus were courting and was hopeful that they were finally moving forward with their relationship.

Pretty soon, all the guests had arrived, and the party was in full swing. George Marshall was telling jokes, Donnie Marshall and Daniel Tate were playing music, and the girls were playing with the Tate grandchildren, Melissa, Mason, Morgan and Madison. The house was more crowded than usual, as the dining room was closed off with the Momma Cat and kittens sequestered from the guests and dogs.

Belinda Collins was helping Rosadel keep the food and drinks stocked up and catching Rosadel up on her life at the same time.

"I just don't get it, Rosie. I'm a nice person. I'm fairly attractive. Why can't I find a man?"

"I'm sure I don't know, Bee. I guess the right one hasn't come along yet. I mean, look at my Dad and Jessie. Jessie was forty when she and Dad got married." Rosadel was trying to be helpful.

"But I don't want twelve more years of bad dates, Rosie. I thought I had found my happily ever after with Gus in college, but that wasn't meant to be. I want to have babies, and sooner rather than later."

Rosadel sighed. She wasn't up for giving dating advice, having never really dated anyone but Clancy. "What about one of Clancy's brothers? Except not Pete."

"Aren't they kind of young, Rosie? I mean, Mike is twenty-four and Donnie is twenty-three. I'm twenty-eight. I know that doesn't seem like a lot, but it feels like a lot."

"They are kind of young, I guess. I just don't know Bee. You could try one of those online dating things." Rosadel was skeptical of that but it was worth putting out there.

"I signed up with one. CatholicMatch.com. I haven't seen anything that looks interesting yet, unless I want to go to New Orleans or Baton Rouge. I was hoping for closer to home." Bee was very laid back about what Rosadel thought was a big deal.

"You signed up for a dating site?" Rosadel couldn't hide the surprise in her voice.

"Yep," replied Bee, "A Catholic one. No big deal. I'm getting desperate, Rosie."

"Twenty-eight is a little young to be desperate," said Pete as he came into the kitchen. "I'm twenty-nine, and not worried a bit."

As Belinda was about to reply, the party was interrupted by screeching cats and barking dogs. Rosadel sprang into action.

"Sounds like someone opened the dining room," said Rosadel as she headed towards the noise.

Inside the dining room, the Momma Cat and kittens were meowing and hissing and generally behaving as if they were frightened to death. Roscoe was pacing in front of their crate, with Sophie and Laverne barking like crazy. Maggie was cowering in the corner, and Shirley was growling.

"Oh, my goodness! Who let the dogs in here?" Rosadel asked, even though she had narrowed the choice of culprit down to one of three.

"We were just going to show Mason and Melissa the Momma cat and kittens," said Grace. "But somehow the door wasn't shut tight and the dogs got in."

Pete and Cassidy had recruited Mike and Donnie Marshall, and each of them had taken one of the four dogs out of the room. Roscoe had left as soon as he didn't feel the need to protect the Momma Cat and kittens anymore, but the cats were still frantic.

"Whose idea was it to come in here without an adult?" asked Rosadel, while Bee and Clancy tried to calm the Momma Cat and kittens.

Lou, Grace and Rosie all looked at each other, but no one answered. They knew they had broken their new rule.

Lou was the first to speak. "It doesn't matter, Mommy, because we all broke the rule. We just got too excited." Grace had tears in her eyes, and Rosie's lower lip was quivering.

"Girls, I know it is your birthday party, and I don't want to fuss you, but do you see how upset Holly is? She was scared to pieces. And the dogs weren't bad, they were just scared too and reacted to that fear. That is why we have to be so careful. We know Holly is fine with the dogs when her kittens aren't around, but this was too scary for her." Rosadel wanted to cry herself.

Clancy knew it was up to him to fix this. "Rosadel, why don't you go back to our guests and I'll have a little talk with the girls." He kissed Rosadel's forehead and gently urged her out of the dining room. "You go too, Bee. I'll handle this."

Rosadel was embarrassed as she went back to her guests. She didn't know what to say to smooth things over.

Pete and Cassidy were the first to start apologizing. "Rosadel, I would never have brought Maggie and Sophie if I thought they would behave like that," said Cassidy.

"And I'm surprised at Laverne and Shirley, too," said Pete.

"It's not their fault and you both know it. When Holly started hissing and screeching, they just reacted. It would have never happened if the girls didn't open the dining room." Rosadel looked at her guests. "I'm sorry for the commotion."

"Never mind about it," said Harriet. "No harm done. And another good story to embarrass your girls with when they get older and start bringing boys home."

"Momma Harriet, if that was supposed to make me feel better it didn't work," said Rosadel, which got everyone laughing.

Donnie started playing Kenny Chesney's "Don't Blink", and Daniel joined in, and the party was back to being a party.

Clancy had gotten Holly calmed down and had three solemn faced little girls to take care of. "Come on over and sit by Daddy," Clancy instructed.

The three girls sat down in front of Clancy. Lou looked heartbroken, Grace kept blinking hard to keep from crying, and Rosie was biting her lip. Clancy felt as broken hearted as they looked.

"You know Daddy loves you more than anything, don't you?" Three little heads nodded. "And Mommy and I wanted you to have the very best birthday ever." Again, three nodding heads. "You know you made a mistake and broke your new rule." Again, with the nods. "What do you think Mommy and I should do?"

This time three heads hung down. Finally, Grace spoke. "I think we should have to give one of our Christmas presents to the Angel tree at church." Lou and Rosie looked surprised, but then nodded.

Clancy had to swallow the lump in his throat. "I think that is a very good and generous idea, Grace, and I think Mommy will think so too. We'll talk to her after the party. Now give Daddy hugs and kisses and let's go have some fun and birthday cake."

Cassidy was still embarrassed that Sophie had behaved so uncharacteristically. Pete was trying to help her feel better. "You do understand that they are dogs, Cass. They respond instinctively. The cat screeched and hissed, so Sophie barked. And we don't know if Shirley started growling or Laverne started barking first. Sophie may have just been back up for Laverne. I think you need to accept that things like this always happen at the triplet's birthday party and let it go."

"That's easy for you, Pete. You're family. I'm just starting to get to be friends with Rosadel and know I'm worried that this will ruin everything."

"Cass, do you really think Rosadel holds you responsible? You know she is feeling as embarrassed as you are that there is always a commotion with the triplets. I think you need to go over to Rosadel and just start talking about anything other than what happened. She needs to be distracted, and that is what friends do." Pete put his arm around Cassidy and squeezed her shoulder. "C'mon, I know you can think of something. How about Prescott and Thor? Didn't you mention Prescott had taught Thor a new trick to do at Our Lady of Lourdes tomorrow?"

Cassidy was surprised at how much she wanted to tuck into Pete's side and never move away. She felt a chill when he dropped his arm from around her shoulders. "That's a great idea, Pete. Daddy taught Thor how to help him take his jacket off, and then set the jacket down on a chair and take a treat out of the jacket pocket. It makes for a great icebreaker, as Thor makes it all look like he is sneaking a treat. I'll go tell Rosadel."

While Cassidy was talking to Rosadel, Pete was thinking about how good it had felt to put his arm around Cassidy, and how pretty she looked when her smile lit up her face as she talked about Prescott and Thor.

Harriet Marshall was observing Cassidy and Pete with an extraordinary amount of interest. It looked like her second son was finally showing interest in a girl that Harriet would have picked for him herself. Harriet caught George giving her the eye. After all these years George was too good at reading Harriet's mind. He gave her that little head shake that said, "Mind your business" so she gave George the raised eyebrow that said, "What are you talking about?" George moved close to Harriet's ear and said, "You know Pete is skittish enough, don't do anything to jinx him. He's not like your other three." Harriet turned and kissed George on the cheek. "Once again, you're right. I'll behave."

Clancy saw his Mom kissing his Dad's cheek as he and the triplets returned to the party, and he said a quick "Thank You!" to the Man upstairs for the loving example his parents had set for him and his brothers. He hoped that he and Rosadel could live up to his parents in the example they set for the girls.

Birthday cake was brought out, and singing commenced, and now it was time to open presents. Even though all the gifts were supposed to be for the Momma Cat and kittens, Angus and Jessie, Daniel and Rachel and George and Harriet couldn't follow the rules. In addition to the "Ask me about the kittens" shirts from Rachel and Daniel, there were new bike helmets from Angus and Jessie, and new booster seats for the car from George and Harriet. The girls were still a little small for their age, and none weighed sixty pounds yet, but were embarrassed about the large booster seats they were using. The small backless boosters would be safe, yet more grownup, and Harriet knew the girls would love them.

Lou, Grace and Rosie loved all their gifts, and especially the gifts that broke the rules. The party ended on a very happy note, with everyone heading out for the rest of their Christmas Eve celebrations. Clancy and Rosadel told the girls they should try to take a little nap, as it would be a late night. The girls knew if they couldn't sleep they were still expected to lie in their beds and read or play quietly, and they were happy to do exactly what Mommy and Daddy had asked.

While Clancy and Rosadel cleaned up the house, Clancy shared with Rosadel Grace's idea for what their consequence should be for not following their new rule. Rosadel got a little choked up, just like Clancy did at the sweetness of Grace's suggestion.

"Sugar, I know you get aggravated with me for saying it, but they really are good girls," Clancy said as he put away birthday decorations and brought out Christmas decorations.

"They are, I know, Clancy. It is just so embarrassing that we can never have anything here without some sort of mishap. But it is very sweet of Grace to want to give a present to the Angel tree. I think we should tell them which one to take tonight to Mass. And I think it should be one of the new pairs of pajamas. I can call Jessie and ask her to pick up replacement pajamas, and then the girls will get to make a sacrifice, and still get what they need for Christmas."

"And I think you need to talk to my mother about the mishap thing. If you think about it, until Donnie was in college there was never an event at the Marshall house without a mishap. I think if you have multiple children, it is inevitable." Clancy was sure that Rosadel had to remember some of the more outrageous mishaps, like the time Mike had thought it would be funny to put a couple of Snickers bars in the punch bowl so it would look like turds. Or the time that Donnie had offered to bake a cake and had put black food coloring in the batter so that everyone's teeth turned black. Harriet hadn't known until they cut the cake.

"I guess I just thought it was because y'all are boys. I expected girls to be different. Less rambunctious." Rosadel knew she would never have done most of the things her girls did.

"Sorry, Sugar. The Marshall gene pool is full of rambunctious. And I'm not sure who we got more from, George or Harriet." Clancy put his arms around Rosadel. "Speaking of rambunctious, how about we get rambunctious while the girls are napping?"

Rosadel shook her head as she threw her arms around Clancy's neck. Life would never be dull in the Marshall household, so she had better get used to it.

CHAPTER 6

Cassidy couldn't help glancing at her watch as Pete drove her home. She had exactly one hour to change clothes, load the car, and feed the dogs if she wanted to get to Sandra and Mark's house on time. And Sandra was a stickler for punctuality. Actually, Sandra was a stickler for everything. Cassidy believed that it was in response to Sandra's wild teenage years that she was so rigid. Cassidy loved her Mom, but often felt sorry for Mark. He had to be all the softness in that household. It wasn't that Sandra didn't love her children. It was just that she was so worried they would make the same kind of mistakes that she had made that she kept them all on a tight leash.

Pete noticed Cassidy's growing agitation and wondered what was up. Was she just anxious to be out of his company? Before Pete let his own insecurities get out of hand, he decided to ask.

"Hey Cass, did I do something to upset you, or has something else working on you? Your anxiety level is going up so fast I can feel it."

"Oh, Pete, it has nothing to do with you. I'm just looking at the time and figuring out how in the world I'm going to get to my Mom and Mark's house on time. If I'm late, there will be hell to pay."

Pete was really surprised by Cassidy's words. Harriet didn't care how late you were, as long as you arrived she was thrilled. Pete couldn't imagine what Cassidy was feeling.

"I'm sorry, Cass. We could have left sooner if I had known."

"It's not your fault, Pete. I was having way more fun at Rosadel and Clancy's house than I will have at Mom and Mark's house. If it wasn't for Candy and Chip, I probably wouldn't go, but I love my little sister and brother, and they need some relief from my Mom and her neurosis. Mark is a great guy, very laid back and that helps, but Mom is a piece of work."

"I wish we had more time to talk, Cassidy. I want to hear all about you, and your Mom and Mark and Prescott. I want to really get to know you. This might be the worst time to tell you this, but I think we have something between us that we need to explore. More than friendship. I would love to go on a date, and then date exclusively for a while and see what develops between us."

Pete's face had gotten red as he spoke, and Cassidy was both stunned and charmed.

"I think I'd like that very much, Pete. I had no idea that you even liked me. I thought we just had our work in common."

"Believe it or not, Cassidy, I'm kind of shy. I mean, I'm good at pretending to be all cool all the time, and I'm great at superficial relationships. But besides my family and my staff, I don't have a lot of close friends. I'm great at making other people comfortable, but I have a hard time being comfortable myself."

Cassidy couldn't believe her ears. She always thought Pete was so confident and in control, and he was hiding in plain sight just like she was. As Pete pulled up in front of Cassidy's and helped her unload the dogs and transfer their car seats, they worked together in a comfortable silence. Pete told Laverne and Shirley he would be right back and walked Cassidy to her door.

"Since Christmas is on a Friday this year, how about I pick you up for dinner on Saturday night? We can go into New Orleans or go local, but I want to start on this dating thing right away."

Cassidy quickly thought about her schedule and realized that Saturday night would work. "I'd love that Pete. What time is good?"

"Let's say six. I'll pick you up." With that, Pete reached his hand up and cupped Cassidy's cheek. He leaned in and kissed her lightly on the lips, then kissed her forehead.

"Have a good time tonight and a great Christmas, Cassidy. I'll be counting the minutes until Saturday night."

With that, Pete hurried back to his car and headed for home to get ready for evening Mass at Holy Redeemer and a night of revelry at George and Harriet's house. He couldn't help smiling as he thought about the kiss with Cassidy. Things were definitely looking good.

Cassidy could hardly believe that Pete had kissed her. And it was a perfect first kiss. Warm and tender, filled with respect. Cassidy wouldn't be sharing any news with Sandra, but she couldn't wait to talk to Prescott tomorrow and tell him about her upcoming date with Pete.

♦ ♦ ♦

Jessie slept all the way to Prairieville after she and Angus had gone home and changed clothes and stopped at Target to buy the girls' pajamas. They would get up early tomorrow to head over to Rosadel and Clancy's to be there when the girls opened their presents. Angus had always been with the girls on Christmas morning, and Jessie hadn't seen any reason to change that. Hopefully, next Christmas there would be toys for four under the Christmas tree.

Angus woke Jessie up about a half hour after they arrived at St. John the Evangelist for Mass. "Sweetheart, we're here," Angus said gently as he kissed Jessie's cheek.

Jessie pulled herself slowly from a truly wonderful nap. "I thought we were going to Mom and Dad's first," said Jessie.

"We were, but when I saw how well you were sleeping, and realized you could sleep for another half hour here in the parking lot if we came straight here, I decided to do that. Don't worry, I called your Mom as soon as we hit the parking lot and told her about the change in plans. She was glad to hear you were napping and endorsed the plan 100%."

"Angus, I'm afraid Heather is going to guess about me being pregnant. She's always been very intuitive with me, and this tiredness is hard to cover up."

"Well, Sweetheart, I'm fine if you want to tell your family. We won't be having any joint family get togethers for a while, so you can tell them and then we'll tell Rosadel later."

65

"I just wouldn't feel right about that Angus. I think Rosadel should be the first to know besides my parents. Next to us, I think Rosadel has the biggest emotional stake in our baby. It's not every day that you get your first sibling at twenty-eight."

"It surely isn't. But Rosadel will be fine. I don't want you putting any stress on yourself about who knows and doesn't know what. A year from now everyone will know you were pregnant this Christmas, and no one will care about anything other than whose turn it is to hold the baby. So, as much as you can, try to relax about it."

Jessie knew Angus was right, and also knew that she could avoid Heather for the evening. Jessie was starting to think that it might be the best thing to tell Rosadel and Clancy tomorrow, and just wait to tell the girls until Valentine's Day. Jessie decided to pray on that decision during Mass.

◆ ◆ ◆

Cassidy arrived at Mark and Sandra's house with time to spare. As usual, Candy and Chip ran to greet Cassidy and the first few minutes were full of their questions and important news that they couldn't wait to share.

Cassidy went into the kitchen to find her Mom and Mark with the two children in tow. "Hi Mama! You sure look pretty today." Sandra was a beautiful woman, with the same blonde hair and creamy complexion as Cassidy, but with bright blue eyes. They could easily pass for sisters.

"Hi Cassidy, I was afraid you were going to be late." For some reason, Sandra never could find a way to not imply criticism where Cassidy was concerned. Cassidy ignored the comment and turned to Mark. He already had his arms open for a hug. As Cassidy hugged her stepfather, Mark whispered in her ear, "She is on a tear today, we don't know why. You look pretty today too, honey."

Cassidy blinked away tears as she hugged Mark hard. It seemed like Mark had been trying to make up for Sandra's words and actions for as long as he had been part of Cassidy's life. Thank God Sandra had married

Mark. Cassidy couldn't imagine what her teenage years would have been like without his mellowing influence on Sandra.

Sandra, in the meantime, was feeling terrible for the way she had greeted Cassidy. Sandra knew her daughter was a wonderful person who she should be very proud of. But unfortunately, Sandra always felt the weight of her own failures when she looked at Cassidy. She had been a wild child, totally not ready for parenthood. She had not been a good mother at first, Prescott had done all the parenting when Cassidy was a baby.

Then when she and Prescott had broken up, Sandra had tried. But she was so tired after working all day. She fell into the role of providing food and shelter, but had a hard time showing love and affection. Mark showed affection as easily as a puppy, and he had drawn Sandra out of her shell somewhat, but she knew her children would all seek their father or each other when they needed love. Mark was the only person Sandra ever felt comfortable being affectionate with.

Candy was very different from both Mark and Cassidy, and at thirteen, felt it her obligation to call out Sandra on her behavior. "Mommy, it is any wonder Cassidy comes here at all the way you talk to her! Chip and I love Cass and if your meanness keeps her away we'll never forgive you."

Cassidy heart was warmed by her little sister's defense but felt bad for her Mom and Mark. "Hey Candy, it's OK. Nothing will ever keep me away from you and Chip."

Sandra bit her lip and cursed her own irritation. Sandra hated nicknames. She called her children Cassidy, Candace and Mark, Jr. That Cassidy and Candace had been shortened to Cass and Candy was bad enough, but calling Mark, Jr. Chip was just terrible. And it was Mark's fault, sort of. He referred to Mark, Jr. as a chip off the old block when he was a baby. Candace started calling him Chip, and Cassidy picked it up. So, to everyone but Sandra, Mark, Jr. was known as Chip.

Sandra had been Sandy when she was wild. Imagining herself Sandy from the musical Grease, or from Bruce Springsteen's iconic songs. Sandra equated having a nickname with making bad choices. She knew it was not logical, but she couldn't help it. Sandra also knew that the two children she shared with Mark would not be as tolerant or understanding as Cassidy was. It was one of the things Sandra knew she had to tackle in the upcoming year. She had to learn to be less rigid, and more loving or risk losing her children's company.

Mark was eager to get the evening back on track, so asked the kids to come finish decorating the tree. The Guidry's had started a tradition the year that Mark and Sandra had gotten married. That first year the tree had been somewhat bare, as Mark and Sandra wanted to create a Christmas tree and holiday that was uniquely their family.

The tree was always put up on the Sunday before Christmas, and the Angel tree topper and lights were put on the tree. The ornaments were always added on Christmas Eve, and the stories that went with the ornaments were told. Mark and Sandra always put the first ornament on the tree, an ornament commemorating their marriage. Then Cassidy put her Christmas 2000 ornament on the tree, then Mark and Sandra and Cassidy put the ornaments they had gotten in Gatlinburg at a Christmas store the summer of 2000, on their first vacation as a family. Next Candy joined in, with the Christmas ornament Sandra had given Mark telling him she was pregnant the Christmas of 2001. With each ornament, and each story, Mark relaxed more as the magic of good memories brought Sandra into a better place.

Mark truly loved his wife, and he knew how often what she felt and what she did were not in alignment. He had finally convinced Sandra that counseling was a good thing to try so that she could overcome the stern and loveless upbringing that she had endured. Mark saw the sad and frightened child who never felt loved or worthy in his sometimes-demanding wife and knew that she thought as long as she acted unlovable, she would know the reason when her children rejected her the way her parents had.

Mark, on the other hand, had grown up in a family full of love and laughter, and so had the emotional reserves to love Sandra unconditionally, and to see past the prickly defenses she tried to hide behind. Mark was eternally grateful to Prescott Bourgeois for helping Cassidy to see her mother in a kind and charitable way. Mark knew he couldn't have loved Cassidy enough to keep her close without Prescott helping Cass understand Sandra instead of rejecting her.

♦ ♦ ♦

Rosadel brought three wrapped packages downstairs to give to the girls to bring to the Angel Tree at Holy Redeemer. "You need to write a Christmas tag that says, 'eight-year-old girl' and replace the tag with your name on it' instructed Rosadel. All three girls were subdued as they took the original tags off of the packages and replaced them. Then the family climbed into the minivan, complete with the new booster seats and headed to Mass.

"Well, at least it was clothes we lost," said Lou to her sisters.

"Lou, that is not the right way to feel, we are supposed to be making a sacrifice," said Grace.

"And I like clothes," said Rosie.

"I'm just trying to make the best of it and not be sad on Christmas Eve," Lou defended herself.

Clancy looked over at Rosadel and rolled his eyes. "Do you girls want to look for Grandpa George and Grandma Harriet and sit with them?"

A chorus of yeses came from the back of the van, and the rest of conversation on the drive to church centered around who would sit next to who during Mass.

As was their Christmas Eve tradition, Rosadel and Clancy took the girls to Our Lady of Lourdes after Christmas Eve afternoon Mass with trays of Christmas Cookies and Roscoe. The girls were all dressed in matching red velvet dresses, and Roscoe was sporting his red and green plaid bow tie. The visit was always the same. Drop off a tray of cookies in the common room of the nursing home side, and then make a circuit of the hallways singing Christmas Carols.

Then, proceed to the assisted living side, and put a tray of cookies in the common room there, and make a circuit of the hallways singing Christmas Carols. The visit always ended with a stop in Sister Dorothy

Murphy's room, and this year, the girls had a special surprise for Sister Dorothy.

Rosadel peeked in the door first, to make sure Sister Dorothy was awake. As soon as the door opened, Sister Dorothy exclaimed, "Rosadel, I've been waiting all day to see your lovely wee bairns. I have a special gift for them now that they are about to receive their First Holy Communion in May."

"Sister Dorothy, you aren't supposed to buy my girls presents. We like to buy things for you."

"Ach, child, and how would I be getting any pleasure if I couldn't buy gifts for wee children? Bring the girls in so I can give them their gifts."

Lou, Grace and Rosie loved to visit Sister Dorothy. Lou thought Sister Dorothy kind of shined, and Grace thought Sister Dorothy was already an angel. Rosie just knew that when Sister Dorothy hugged you or kissed you, it felt like nothing bad could ever happen to you again.

Rosie was carrying a tray of cookies for Sister Dorothy, and Grace held a package. Lou had Roscoe's leash.

"Children, come and give me hugs and kisses," Sister Dorothy opened her arms wide.

Lou handed Rosadel Roscoe's leash, and Rosie and Grace sat their gifts on the table, as they ran up to Sister Dorothy's wheelchair to hug her and give kisses.

"How are my best girls doing?" she asked.

"We have a new rule, Sister Dorothy," said Lou.

"But we broke it today," added Rosie.

"And so, we gave a present to the Angel Tree to show we're sorry," Grace finished.

"I'm sure that Baby Jesus is pleased with your sacrifice," Sister Dorothy soothed as she looked to Rosadel for my information.

"How about I stop in Saturday night before my shift and we can have tea and I can fill you in?" said Rosadel.

"That would be lovely, child. Another thing to look forward to. Now, Clancy, go to the top of my dresser, and you'll see three wrapped boxes for these angel girls of yours."

Clancy retrieved the boxes and gave them to Sister Dorothy.

"Now, girls, these are a very special birthday and Christmas gift. I've waited until you were old enough to appreciate them. And I think you are ready, so here they are."

"Can we open them, Mommy?" asked Grace.

Rosadel knew that most of the pleasure for Sister Dorothy would come from watching the girls open their gifts, so she gave them permission. As the girls opened their gifts, Sister Dorothy watched closely for their reactions, and she was not disappointed.

"Rosary Beads! They are so beautiful! Not plastic like for babies. Thank you, Sister Dorothy!" The girls spoke over each other in their excitement, and more kisses and hugs followed.

"They are Connemara Marble Rosary Beads," explained Sister Dorothy. "From Ireland. I ordered them especially for you girls, and know I think you are grown up enough to have them."

"I promise to take good care of them," said Grace, "And I'll make sure Lou and Rosie do too."

"You won't have to make me," said Lou, "I'll take good care of them on my own."

"I take care of all my things" said Rosie.

"Girls, Grace was just trying to be helpful. I know you will all treasure your grown-up rosary beads and take good care of them. Sister Dorothy, thank you so much. What a perfect gift. Now the girls have one more gift for you before we go to their grandparent's house."

The girls had been practicing their new Christmas song for weeks and were excited to finally sing it. As they sang "Christmas in Killarney" Sister Dorothy smiled so hard her cheeks ached.

"That was beautiful," she told the girls when they finished. "Sure, and I don't miss the old country anywhere near as much as I did before you sang to me."

As the Marshall prepared to leave, Clancy wheeled Sister Dorothy down to the common rooms to take part in the planned Christmas Eve celebrations. The festivities were already in full swing, and many of the residents immediately called for Sister Dorothy to join their group.

Knowing that Sister Dorothy would have a fun evening of her own made it easy to leave with smiles to head to George and Harriet's house.

◆ ◆ ◆

Pete had headed straight back to George and Harriet's house after Mass and was helping Harriet get food and drinks set up. Mike and Donnie would be home later, as usual they both had last minute things to buy between Mass and the gathering at the Marshall house.

"It still feels a little strange with no Angus on Christmas Eve," Harriet said as she took a tray of mini muffulettas out of the oven. "He was a fixture here for a lot of years."

"But this is way better, isn't it, Ma? I mean, I think Angus is the happiest I've ever seen him." Pete was busy setting up a vegetable tray as they talked. There was a pot of gumbo on the stove, the rice was in the rice cooker, and the trays of fruit and cookies were ready for dessert.

"It is better, Pete, but I was expecting our Christmas Eve to grow, not shrink as Dad and I got older." It seemed like a perfect opportunity for Pete to share some of his news with Harriet.

"Ma, promise me you won't get too excited and go crazy, but Cassidy and I are going out on a date on Saturday night." Harriet wanted to do a little dance for joy but restrained herself.

"She seems like a real nice girl, Pete. And you know Dad and I just love Prescott. I hope you have a good time."

Pete was relieved that Harriet was going easy on him, so he figured he might as well keep going. "I really like her, Ma. And I have for a long time. But it seemed like she was only interested in being work colleagues. Then we started to spend more time together because of the kittens that Rosadel and Clancy are fostering, and I started to think maybe Cassidy is just shy, not uninterested. Well, I worked up the nerve to ask her out, and she said yes. So, wish me luck."

Harriet looked at her second son and wondered again why he lacked confidence when it came to the opposite sex. She thought Pete was very attractive, and she knew he was the nicest and most considerate of her sons, even if he was a bit of a tease. Harriet knew the teasing was Pete's way of making sure people were comfortable and at ease.

"I'll wish you luck if that is what you want, Petey, but I don't think you need luck. I think you and Cassidy are a good match, and I think she will appreciate what a good man you have turned out to be."

Pete washed his hands as he finished his work on the vegetable tray and went over and gave Harriet a hug. "Thanks for always being my biggest supporter, Ma. You're the best."

Harriet hugged Pete back, and thanked the Lord for this sweet boy of hers. While the others were more likely to go to George for advice, Pete had always been her special one. The little boy who brought her flowers, the one who would notice that she wasn't feeling well and offer to help with laundry or supper. She knew that whoever ended up with Pete was going to be one lucky woman, and Harriet was delighted with the thought it might be Cassidy.

◆ ◆ ◆

Prescott Bourgeois was deep in thought as he drove home from the Southeast Louisiana Veterans Home in Reserve on Christmas Eve. He and Thor had visited and entertained as many of the residents as they could. Prescott worried less about the long-term residents than the people in rehab. So many of them didn't have adequate support systems to manage outpatient care. So many veterans with mental health issues that ended up homeless. Prescott was sure that he could make a positive difference, he just had to figure out how to do it.

Thor was resting quietly in the backseat of the extended cab of the truck. As Prescott started feeling hopeless, a big black paw landed on his shoulder. "I'm OK, Thor. Just worried about the guys. I know life was hard for me before I had you and Ulysses, but I could always work and function. I'm afraid some of the guys we met today won't make it on their own."

People might find it crazy the way that Prescott talked to his dogs, but they just didn't know how much it helped to vocalize worries to a non-judgmental ear.

"I think I'm getting an idea about retirement, Thor. I think you and I are going to talk to Cassidy about it soon. There are a bunch of ideas running over each other and coming together, but I think I'm onto something." Thor rested his head on Prescott's shoulder for a minute before sitting back down. The harness and tether system allowed the big dog to change positions but kept him restrained so that both he and Prescott would be safe if they were in an accident.

Most people did not know it, but Prescott Bourgeois was a very wealthy man. He had worked hard at his job for nearly forty years, and lived simply, and saved money. From the initiation of a 401k plan at work, Prescott had saved the maximum allowable amount. He wasn't one to constantly trade his investments, but twice when the company's stock crashed, he had liquidated all his holdings and bought stock, selling when the value returned to a reasonable place. The first time Prescott went all in on company stock, he turned $100,000 into $500,000. The last time, he turned 2 million dollars into 8 million dollars. Prescott had seen that 8 million dollars grow to 18 million dollars over the past 8 years. He hardly ever thought about the money, but lately, he was thinking that his extraordinary good fortune might give him the opportunity to do something great in retirement.

As Prescott arrived at home and got his and Thor's dinner, he thought about Cassidy, and hoped she was having a good time at Sandra and Mark's house. He was grateful that Sandra had married such a great guy, as he knew Sandra tended to be too hard on Cassidy, and Mark tempered that. He sure was looking forward to Christmas, as any day he spent with his wonderful daughter was a good one.

CHAPTER 7

Jessie had found a few minutes to talk privately to Rachel on Christmas Eve, and Rachel gave Jessie a shirt that Rachel had made for Rosadel, embroidered with "I'm the Big Sister".

"Mama, when did you do this?" Jessie asked.

"I had made it as soon as you found out you were pregnant the first time. I thought it would be a cute way for you and Angus to tell Rosadel. I put it away for a while, praying you would need it. I had a feeling you would want to tell Rosadel soon, so I got this out when we got home from the triplets' party." Rachel knew her oldest so well, it was almost like they communicated telepathically.

"Thank you, Mama. This will be perfect. I just have to find a time without the girls in the room." Jessie felt her eyes filling. Pregnancy certainly brought emotions close to the surface.

Rachel hugged Jessie one more time. "With the weather as warm as it is this year, I'm sure the girls will go outside to play at some point and give you adults a chance to talk privately."

Angus popped his head into the kitchen, "Jess baby, are you about ready to leave? We have an early start tomorrow."

"I'm ready, sweetheart. Just let me say goodbye to everyone." Angus suppressed a grin. That meant they would get on the road in about forty-five minutes to an hour. Goodbyes at the Tate house were a long affair for Jessie. As Jessie went into the family room to start her goodbyes, Angus gave Rachel a hug. "Thanks for trusting me with your girl, Rachel. She has changed my world."

Rachel hugged Angus back. "We knew God had made someone special for our Jessie, we just didn't know it would take so long for His plan to come together. I'm glad you two found each other."

Angus estimate was correct, and it was close to an hour later that they got on the road. Jessie stayed awake long enough to show Angus Rosadel's shirt, and then slept the rest of the way home.

Morning came too fast, and Jessie felt like she was still half-asleep when she and Angus headed over to Rosadel and Clancy's house at seven the following morning. Even with the triplets being up late at George and Harriet's house the night before, it was hard to keep them in bed any later than that on Christmas morning. Rosadel had called at six-thirty, she and Clancy were keeping the girls upstairs with breakfast in Clancy and Rosadel's bed until Angus and Jessie rang the doorbell. Then Angus and Jessie could let themselves in, and the girls could run down the stairs to greet them and see if Santa had arrived.

The girls came running down the stairs as Angus was opening the door, and to their credit, all three girls took the time to hug and kiss Jessie and Angus before looking in the family room at the tree.

"Pop-Pop, we've been waiting for you" "And we had hot chocolate and cinnamon toast in Mommy's bed" "And Roscoe got in the bed too!"

"Gee-Jay! We made you a present!" "Mommy helped, but we worked real hard on it!" "You have to open it first!"

And Jessie and Angus were dragged into the family room by three very excited little girls. An hour later, the wrapping paper had been put in garbage bags, the girls were dressed in play clothes, and the adults were gathered in the kitchen, drinking coffee.

"Mommy, can we go outside and play with our Hippity Hops?" asked Lou.

"Go ahead, baby. Take Roscoe with you," replied Rosadel.

"Okay, Mommy! Let's go girls!" Lou tended to be the ringleader. Rosadel knew that Roscoe would watch over the girls and bark if they got too rambunctious and needed intervention to not get hurt.

Angus had slipped out to the car as Rosadel was getting the girls outside. He walked into the kitchen and handed Rosadel a small wrapped package. "We wanted to give you this present without the girls in the room, June Bug. You'll see why when you open it."

Rosadel looked at Clancy, he shrugged his shoulders to let Rosadel know that he didn't know any more about what was in the package than she did. Rosadel's face was priceless as she opened the package and read her shirt.

"Squee! Jessie, Daddy! This is great! When?" Rosadel ran over and hugged Jessie, then hugged Angus and held on tight.

Jessie was crying, of course. "Pregnancy hormones, I was afraid you would be upset."

"Jessie, how many times did I tell you not to worry about me. I'm ecstatic. When are you due?" Rosadel was just about dancing she was so excited.

"We're due right around the twenty-fifth of June," said Angus. "Looks like June is a lucky month for me."

"So, it will be a little longer before you'll know if I am having a brother or a sister. Are you going to find out?" Rosadel went back over to Jessie and put her arm around Jessie's waist.

"I think if it is easy to see, we'll know, but it isn't that important to us," replied Jessie. "We are just praying for healthy."

"I'll start praying for that too. I'm thinking because you waited until the girls were outside, you don't want to tell them yet," Rosadel was pretty sure she was right on that one.

"That's right, June Bug. We want Jessie to get past twenty weeks or so before we tell a bunch of folks." Angus hoped Rosadel wouldn't question that decision, as he didn't want to bring up Jessie's previous miscarriage.

"That's smart, Daddy. People get all up in your business once they know and putting off those comments as long as possible is a good idea. You really only have to say something when you start to show, and that could be as far out as twenty-four weeks, as long as it is only one baby." Rosadel smiled really big again. "Are you sure it is only one baby?"

"As sure as we can be at this point," Jessie was smiling now too. Rosadel's joy was infectious. "Have you picked out names, yet?"

"Daniel Fergus If a boy, and Allela Angelle If a girl," Angus replied. Now it was Rosadel's turn to start crying. She hugged Jessie again. "Jessie that is the sweetest thing for you to do."

Jessie was crying again too. "I know it may be silly, Rosadel, but I feel like your Mom is smiling down on me and Angus and wishing the best for us. I would love to be able to honor her memory this way."

Clancy knew he had to interrupt the cry fest, before the girls came inside and starting to pick up on the emotions in the room.

"Coffee and cookies, and I'll hide that shirt. The girls will know something is up if you two don't get a grip. Find something else to talk about." Angus smiled at Clancy, appreciating as always how well he and Rosadel fit together.

"Let me tell you about the plan Cassidy and I have for the next PTA meeting," Rosadel said, and the conversation switched to pets, and fostering and finding the kittens homes. Mostly. As they were going over the plans that Rosadel and Cassidy had made, Jessie couldn't help herself.

"Rosie, do you think something is developing between Cassidy and Pete? I swear those two have been circling each other since before your Dad and I got married. I sensed they are moving forward yesterday at the party."

"Well, Jessie, I think so, but have been careful not to say anything in front of the Holy Terror Trio. If they get wind of something, they will torture Cassidy and Pete just like they did you and Dad. I think the foster cat and kittens put them in a position to spend more time together, and that was all it took to get Pete to make a move. In spite of how easily he relates to people professionally, Pete is really shy around girls. I always forget that, because in the family he is such a cut up. I hope they do get together, I think they are perfect for each other."

The girls chose that exact moment to burst into the kitchen. "Who is perfect for each other?" Lou demanded. "Are we going to fix another couple up like Pop-Pop and Gee-Jay?" asked Rosie. Grace knew she better keep her mouth shut, because Mommy didn't want them matchmaking.

"Mr. Prescott and his new dog, Thor." Rosadel said a quick prayer of Thanksgiving to God for helping her think that one up. "Thor is very different from Ulysses, and that makes it easier for Mr. Prescott to love him without missing Ulysses so much."

Jessie was astonished at how fast Rosadel could think on her feet. Being Mommy to the triplets probably gave her a lot of practice.

"Mommy, how old was Ulysses when he died?" Grace looked worried as she asked. Rosadel knew where this was going and hated that it was going there.

"He was twelve, honey." Rosadel waited.

"But Mommy, isn't Roscoe twelve?" asked Rosie.

"Yes, he is, but Uncle Pete says he is a very healthy twelve. I don't think you have to worry about Roscoe dying anytime soon." Rosadel hoped God was listening, because she certainly wasn't ready to lose Roscoe either.

The front door opened, and Harriet Marshall called out, "Where are my favorite granddaughters?" and Rosadel got the reprieve she needed.

♦ ♦ ♦

Prescott and Cassidy were having a wonderful time at Our Lady of Lourdes. Thor, while trained as a PTSD alert dog, was not technically a service dog, because Prescott was not disabled by his PTSD, and Thor did not provide essential alert tasks in public. So, Thor was an Emotional Support Dog, and as such could also be a Therapy Dog.

Thor had completed the required obedience training, and Christmas was his first official visit as a Therapy Dog. Prescott was a little nervous about how Thor would do, but so far, he was amazing. Thor was wearing his Santa hat, and had perfected his signature move; a bow followed by offering his paw to shake. Everyone was charmed by the big Labrador Retriever with the smile on his face. When Thor helped Prescott out of his jacket and then stole the biscuit out of the jacket pocket, he brought down the house.

Cassidy had dropped Sophie off with Bessie Chauvin, and she and Maggie were making their rounds. Maggie didn't have a special move like Thor, she just gently sat on laps, and offered kisses to those who wanted them, but Maggie's visits were as appreciated as Thor's.

Finally, Cassidy collected Maggie and went to Bessie's room. She was only there for a few minutes when Prescott and Thor joined her.

Cassidy had waited until both her dad and Ms. Chauvin were settled to share her news. "I have a date tomorrow night."

Ms. Chauvin smiled, and Prescott asked, "Anyone I know?"

"As a matter of fact, Daddy, yes. Pete Marshall." Cassidy was blushing a little as she shared Pete's name.

"He is a fine man, Cassidy, and comes from a fine family. You two should have a lot in common, given how much you both love animals."

Bessie Chauvin was looking on with a smile and nodding her head,

"That's right," observed Cassidy, "You know Pete too, from taking Sophie to see him."

Ms. Chauvin smiled even more and gestured to her face with her good hand. Cassidy blushed even more as she interpreted what Bessie was saying. "And you think Pete is handsome."

Bessie Chauvin's smile confirmed that Cassidy understood her perfectly. Cassidy had arranged for Bessie to come out with her and Prescott for the day. Prescott's house easily accommodated Bessie's wheelchair, and Cassidy was comfortable helping her while at Prescott's house. They had a simple dinner planned, Prescott had made a salad and gotten a Honey Baked Ham, and Cassidy had made baked macaroni. There were cookies from Rosadel for dessert, and a dessert tray from Rouses.

Prescott decided to rescue Cassidy from her embarrassment. "It's about time to get to the house and get dinner on. I'll push Bessie out to your car and help her transfer, and then you can follow me to the house."

♦ ♦ ♦

Rosadel and Clancy were sitting on the couch with Roscoe, enjoying the quiet at the end of another happy Christmas Day. From the sounds of things, the girls had finally fallen asleep. Clancy was sipping a beer, and

Rosadel a glass of wine, as they looked at the fire in the fireplace, and the lights on the Christmas tree.

"I'm going to be a big sister," Rosadel couldn't keep the smile off of her face as she said it. "If it's anything like being a big brother, don't get too excited," joked Clancy.

Rosadel looked at Roscoe. "Can you believe he said that Roscoe? You love Uncle Pete and Uncle Mike and Uncle Donnie, don't you?"

Roscoe wagged his big tail and smiled. "See, Clancy, you should be ashamed of yourself."

Clancy put his arm around Rosadel and pulled her close to his side. "The only thing I have to be ashamed of is that I haven't kissed you since the girls went to bed, Sugar. I can't believe I'm wasting an opportunity like this."

As Clancy turned Rosadel so that she was reclining across his lap, he leaned in and kissed her. And like always, kisses got heated quickly.

"Unless you want the girls to get an impromptu biology lesson, I think we need to take this to our room," Clancy murmured against Rosadel's mouth. "I'll take care of the fire and the tree if you let Roscoe out one more time."

As Rosadel took care of Roscoe, she thought about her and Clancy and their life. She also thought about Angus and Jessie. Maybe it was time for her and Clancy to think about another baby. She'd pray on it, and then bring it up to Clancy.

As Rosadel and Clancy took their time showing each other with their bodies how very much they cherished each other, their minds were very much in tune as well. Neither one of them thought that life could get any better than it already was.

CHAPTER 8

Cassidy got up early on December 26, determined to go shopping for something that made her feel beautiful for her date with Pete tonight. She really wanted company for shopping but didn't know who to call. At thirteen, maybe Candy was old enough to make a good shopping companion.

Before she could over think it, Cassidy called Sandra and Mark's house. She was relieved when Mark answered instead of Sandra.

"Hey Mark, Is Candy home? I'm going shopping and wondered if she would like to come with me?"

"Hey Cassidy, I bet she would love that! She thinks she is too old for the same activities as Chip, so Sandra and I have been trying to figure out what we could do with both of them today without one of them being bored. If you take Candy shopping, we can take Chip to New Orleans to City Park and Mini Golf and maybe even the Amusement Park. Let me get Candy and you can ask her." Mark was glad he had answered the phone as well, he'd manage Sandra, and Cassidy and Candy would have a great time together.

"Um, Mark, the thing is I have a date tonight so would have to have Candy home by four, will that still work?"

Mark thought for a minute before answering. "It's only nine now. If you were planning to go to Lakeside, we could meet you there at three. Sandra can shop a little with Candy, I'll take Chip to the arcade, and then we can all have dinner somewhere in Metairie before we come home. What do you think?"

Cassidy didn't have to think before answering. "I think I hit the stepfather jackpot. Thanks Mark. That is a great plan."

Candy was beyond excited to be going shopping first with Cassidy, and then with her mom. Sandra was a little upset that Cassidy hadn't asked for her, but Mark pointed out how important it was for Cassidy and Candy to have a relationship that was independent of Sandra and won her over.

Cassidy discovered that Candy was a great shopping companion and ended up with an outfit far more colorful than she would have ever purchased for herself. The deep crimson color was really great with her hair and skin, and the dress was feminine and sexy without being flashy or trashy. Candy convinced Cassidy to get a new pair of shoes to go with the dress, because all of Cassidy's usual shoes were "Maw-Maw" shoes in Candy's opinion.

The meeting with Mark, Sandra and Chip was accomplished without a hitch, and Cassidy found herself a bundle of nerves as she drove home to get ready for her date with Pete. She was worried she would be too dressed up. She was worried she'd be too nervous and too quiet. She was just plain worried about everything, because this date with Pete was really important to her. She knew she was close to in love with Pete already, and was frightened that she would fall hard and fast, and Pete would lose interest once he got to know her.

As Cassidy got ready for her date with Pete, Maggie and Sophie offered continuous silent support. Cassidy felt bad for how much time they were ending up on their own, but she knew after all the excitement yesterday, they would sleep most of the day anyway.

At precisely six o'clock, Pete rang Cassidy's doorbell. She answered the door almost immediately. Pete was dazzled. "Cassidy, you look great! I love that color on you!" Cassidy blushed as she took in Pete's blazer, tie and dress pants. "You look pretty fabulous yourself, Pete. I don't think I've ever seen you this dressed up." Cassidy noticed how the blue of Pete's shirt made his eyes look even bluer.

"I wasn't sure what the dress code for tonight was, because I forgot to ask. Looks like we match though," Cassidy was really glad she had gone shopping.

"I thought we'd drive into New Orleans for dinner. I made reservations at Antoine's for seven, so we need to get on the road." Pete hoped traffic was light.

Cassidy settled Maggie and Sophie and picked up her coat. "I'm ready, let's go."

Cassidy was surprised to see Pete was driving a car instead of his minivan. "Mom lent me her car for tonight, I wanted to be more special than a dog hair covered minivan for our date." Pete explained.

"Well your Mom sure knows how to ride in style," said Cassidy as she sat in the well-appointed Lincoln MKZ. "This is a super nice car."

"Yeah, Mom and Dad always had practical cars while we were growing up. Mom decided she deserved a special car after all these years, and now that all of us are off the payroll, she indulged herself. Dad was happy to see her finally spending money on herself for a change."

"So, your mom knows about our date?" Cassidy was intrigued, as the last person she would confide in was her mother.

"Yep, that is another geeky fact about me. I'm really close to my Mom. Closest of her boys. She and I just click. I can talk to her about anything. You seem kind of surprised. Didn't you tell your mom about our date?" Pete was wondering if Cassidy was embarrassed to be going out with him or something.

"I think you kind of got the picture on Christmas Eve that my mom and I have some stuff to work on. I told my Dad and Bessie Chauvin, but I don't tell my mom much of anything that I don't have to."

"Wow," said Pete, "I can't imagine that. I talk to both my parents about just about everything. Why don't you tell me more about your Mom?"

"It's complicated, Pete, and kind of a downer. Are you sure you want to talk about such heavy stuff on our first date?" Cassidy could see Pete wanting to run for the hills when he found out what a dysfunctional family she came from.

Pete glanced over at Cassidy and reached one hand over to rest on hers. "Cassidy, I want to know everything about you. That is what dating is for. And I have a feeling until you and I get past the heavy stuff, neither one of us will relax enough to have fun. So, go ahead, help me understand you."

Cassidy squeezed Pete's hand before letting go so that he could keep both hands on the wheel. "So, my mom, Sandra, was eighteen when I was born. I don't know my grandparents. Apparently, it was a bad situation, and the day Sandra graduated high school at seventeen, she moved out. She was working at a grocery store and rented a room at one of her friend's parent's house. They kind of knew she was in a bad situation at home. She was a little on the wild side, and the room she rented had a private entrance and bath, so she came and went as she pleased. My dad shopped at the grocery store where she worked and worked with the dad of the family she lived with. Prescott was a lot older than Sandra, but he was a really handsome man. He started talking to Sandra whenever he was at the store, because he felt sorry for her. Well, one night, Prescott was leaving the grocery store, and saw Sandra in the parking lot struggling with someone. He of course intervened. It was Sandra's boyfriend, and it was not the first time he had gotten rough with her, just the first time someone stopped him. Prescott didn't do anything physical, just told the other guy to go. He yelled some curses at Sandra and left. Prescott put Sandra in his car, took her to his place, and patched her up. Her clothes were torn, and she had a fat lip. From then on, Prescott took care of Sandra, and Sandra developed a case of hero worship of Prescott. They got pregnant and got married on her eighteenth birthday. I don't think Prescott ever loved her the way a husband should love a wife, but he wanted to take care of her. Then, there was me."

Cassidy stopped to take a breath. "I don't ever remember Prescott and Sandra together. I kind of have some snapshots in my head, but in my memory, they always lived apart. They split up when I was two. Prescott paid Sandra plenty enough child support that she could have stayed home with me, but she wanted to work. It was like she had no idea how to be a mother. Prescott was the one to take time off work if I was sick or something. Sandra was never abusive, but she was never loving either. And she is great at finding fault. Prescott was always telling me that Sandra really loved me but didn't know how to show love because of her parents. I think the only reason I never stopped loving Sandra is that Prescott would have been disappointed in me if I did.

"Mom and Mark met when I was nine and got married when I was ten. They moved to Bayou Beni in 2000, when I was twelve. I missed Prescott something awful, because I could only see him on weekends, but Mark has been great from the beginning. In 2001, Prescott got transferred to Bayou Beni, and between him and Mark I had a great childhood. Sandra mellowed a little being married to Mark but is still tough. I love Mark, and Candy, and Chip; and Mark has been working on Sandra. As I understand it, she has agreed to go for counseling. Mark and Prescott both believe the scars from her childhood make it hard for her to be an affectionate and supportive mother. Sometimes I think that the reason me, Candy and Chip are so close is that we all cover for each other when it comes to Sandra."

Pete was stunned. Cassidy was such a thoughtful, compassionate person it was hard to believe that she had a mother who was so emotionally remote. Prescott and Mark had done a really good job.

"Gosh, Cassidy, I can't imagine how hard that was for you growing up. I sure am glad you had Prescott and Mark."

Cassidy turned in her seat to face Pete. "Sandra is not a bad person, Pete. In fact, she has lots of friends at work, and is thoughtful and kind most of the time. It is like she is afraid to be kind or loving with us kids, as if something bad will happen if she shows us affection or support. I hope the counseling helps her. I do love my mother, and I hate seeing her trapped in patterns that keep her unhappy."

"Well, I think you are remarkable for being so tolerant and understanding of your mother." Pete couldn't help but think about the contrast with his childhood. "I had such a storybook life. Great easy-going Dad, super bossy but super loving Mom, the best brothers any guy could ever hope for, and Rosadel has been a sister since Clancy brought her home when I was fifteen. Add in the triplets and Angus, and now Jessie, I live a dream life. I never wanted to be anything other than a veterinarian, and here I am owning a practice in the town I grew up in. The only thing missing has been someone to share my life with, and the more I know you, the more I think I may not have anything missing anymore."

Pete pulled into the parking lot near Jax Brewery as he finished speaking. After paying for parking, Pete and Cassidy walked the few blocks to Antoine's. Cassidy was glad that the new shoes were comfortable as well as pretty.

Dinner was wonderful, and Pete and Cassidy found that they could talk about anything and find common ground. Their conversation veered towards more light-hearted subjects, and they both laughed at the same things. Cassidy didn't think she had ever found it so easy to talk to anyone. As they walked back to the car, Pete tucked Cassidy's hand into the crook of his elbow. "This is quite possibly the best date of my life," he said, "And I don't want it to end. I was going to suggest we go to Celebration in the Oaks at City Park, but I think we're overdressed. If I asked you to come back to my house to watch a movie or something, would that be OK?" Pete didn't want Cassidy to think he was putting a move on her or trying to move the relationship forward too fast. "We could stop at Mom and Dad's, return the car, pick up Laverne and Shirley and hang out at your place if that would be better. I'm just not ready for the night to end."

Cassidy was sure she wanted to spend more time with Pete, she was also sure she didn't want the relationship to move forward physically too fast. And she had no experience with how to manage this.

Pete could see Cassidy's tension, and decided to try and help. "Cassidy, I'm not going to tell you that I'm not attracted to you, but I will tell you that Harriet raised four gentlemen. You do not have to be worried about being alone with me, either at my house or yours. I want to spend time with you and get to know you, not jump your bones. Well, I do, but I'll wait until you're ready."

Cassidy couldn't resist Pete when he blushed. And couldn't help laughing. "I think I'm flattered," Cassidy said with a chuckle. "How about we pick up Laverne and Shirley and go to my house. That way when you leave my house and get home, you can stay home for the night."

Pete squeezed Cassidy in close and dropped a kiss on her forehead. "I think that sounds perfect."

Harriet Marshall was surprised to hear the knock on the front door, and Pete call out at just after 9:30. She had expected his date to last longer than that. When Pete came into the family room with Cassidy, she breathed a sigh of relief.

"Hey Pete, Hey Cassidy. You're home early." Harriet was fishing for information, but delicately for her.

"Hi Mrs. Marshall. Thanks for lending Pete your car. It is one sweet ride." Cassidy was smiling ear to ear.

"I'm going to pick up Laverne and Shirley and go over to Cassidy's for a while, and I didn't want to get dog hair in your fancy car," added Pete.

"Thanks for that Pete. I appreciate that the car still smells new, and I don't want to lose that any sooner than I have to." Harriet had enjoyed the dogs and cats that had been family pets over the years, but she was kind of glad to have been pet free for a while. George was getting a yen for a pet, so Harriet knew this pet free stage wouldn't last much longer.

"How was dinner?" Harriet wanted to get as much time observing Pete and Cassidy as she could and wasn't above stalling. "Would you all like something to drink? I can make tea or coffee."

"No thanks on the drinks Mom, and dinner was great," Pete knew Harriet was on a fact-finding mission and wanted to get out of there as quickly as possible.

"I'd never been to Antoine's before," said Cassidy, "And it was on my New Orleans bucket list. The food was delicious, but the dessert! I had the Meringue glacee sauce chocolat - it was the most delicious dessert I ever had."

Harriet smiled at Cassidy's enthusiasm. "George and I went there to eat when we were engaged, and I had the Meringue glacee back then. I still talk about it - so I'm with you - that is one exceptional dessert."

"Mom, Dad says you remember food better than you remember anything else, and I'm starting to agree with him." George chose that moment to walk into the room.

"Yep, every vacation we ever took, I can tell you what we saw and did, and Harriet can tell you what we ate." George was smiling as he commented.

"Y'all stop. If I didn't remember food I wouldn't know what your favorites were, and you would never get them. If you don't hush and not embarrass me in front of Cassidy I am fully willing to go on strike." Harriet was laughing as she delivered her speech, so Cassidy knew it was all in fun.

"Ma, that threat just doesn't work as well since I got my own place," said Pete, "But I'll stop tempting Dad to get in the doghouse."

Cassidy loved watching the Marshall's interact. It was so obvious that they all loved each other so much, and Harriet was obviously the center and most important part of the household. Cassidy wondered if her mother, Sandra, ever felt as comfortable and loved as Harriet did. It was certainly something to think about.

Pete shook his Dad's hand and kissed his Mom and got Cassidy out the door as quickly as he could. Pete dearly loved and appreciated his parents, but he didn't want to end up spending an hour with them and losing his private time with Cassidy.

Cassidy made some decaf for her and Pete, and then sat down on the couch with him. "Want to watch a movie, or talk, or what?"

Pete had decided earlier, he wanted Cassidy to know him and all his strangeness early on. "You wouldn't happen to have a Scrabble game, would you?"

Cassidy grinned, the smile lighting up her face. "Are you kidding me? Me and Prescott play Scrabble all the time. Prepare for an epic battle." Cassidy got out the Scrabble board, and she and Pete played two very close games, with Pete getting two "Bingos" or seven letter words in the first game, and Cassidy getting three in the second. There was a lot of talking and laughing to accompany the game.

It was well after midnight when Pete decided it was time to collect Laverne and Shirley and head home. Cassidy walked him to the door.

"Pete, thanks so much for tonight. I had a great time." Cassidy felt like her cheeks would hurt tomorrow from smiling so much.

"Me, too, Cass. This was the best date of my life. What do you say we get together tomorrow afternoon and take the dogs over to Our Lady of Lourdes? I want to see you as much as I can. But only if you are comfortable."

"That would be great Pete. We both know it will be tough to see each other during the week, so tomorrow will be great."

"I'll pick you up around two, that way we will visit between the resident's lunch and dinner." Pete turned to face Cassidy. "I'm going to kiss you goodnight now."

Cassidy looked up at Pete catching the intensity of his gaze as he lowered his mouth to hers. This was no polite touch of the lips like their previous kisses. Pete's lips lingered on Cassidy's with just enough pressure and movement to make Cassidy want more. When Cassidy was sure Pete was going to tease her mouth open with his tongue, he backed away, leaning his forehead on Cassidy's.

"We're going to take the physical side of this relationship slow, Cassidy, because already I know I've never felt this way about anyone before. I think you could break my heart without too much effort." Pete kissed Cassidy's forehead, patted his leg for Laverne and Shirley to follow him, and pulled the door shut behind him.

Cassidy locked the door and stood for a few moments with her fingers on her lips. Pete wasn't the only one who had never felt this way before. And Cassidy was pretty sure Pete already had the power to break her heart.

CHAPTER 9

When Pete and Cassidy walked into Bessie Chauvin's room at Our Lady of Lourdes on the Sunday after Christmas, with Maggie, Sophie, Laverne, and Shirley, Bessie's eyes lit up even more than they usually did when Sophie came to visit. Her crooked smile was out in full as Cassidy put Sophie up on the bed.

As Sophie and Bessie were settling in together, Bessie kept looking at Cassidy, and then at Pete. Pete knew Bessie wanted the full story from Cassidy, so he took the other three dogs to make the rounds.

Bessie looked at Cassidy with a question on her face as soon as Pete left the room. "Ms. Chauvin, for someone who can't speak you sure know how to get information out of a girl," Cassidy joked as she sat on the edge of the bed. "Do you want me to get you up and into your chair for a while, or did you just get in bed to take a nap before dinner?" Bessie nodded, letting Cassidy know that she was planning to take a little nap before dinner. Bessie raised an eyebrow at Cassidy.

"I'm not trying to avoid answering, honest I'm not. Pete and I had a wonderful date, we went to New Orleans and ate at Antoine's and went to Pete's Mom's house and then Pete came over with Laverne and Shirley and we played Scrabble. I really like him, Ms. Chauvin, and it scares me."

Bessie Chauvin nodded, her wise eyes seeing how very important Pete was to Cassidy. Bessie pointed at her dresser. On top, there was a picture of a soldier, the picture looked to be World War II vintage. Cassidy realized that while she saw the picture every time she visited Ms. Chauvin, she didn't know who the picture was. And with Bessie unable to speak, she had never asked. It seemed like Bessie wanted to tell her something about the man in the picture, so Cassidy went over to the dresser, and brought the picture back over to the bed.

"Is this a picture of your husband?" asked Cassidy. Bessie shook her head no. "Your brother?" Again, Bessie shook her head no. "Your boyfriend?" Bessie shook her head yes, but also touched her heart and her ring finger. "You were engaged to him?" Bessie nodded vigorously this time.

Cassidy was pretty sure how this love story had ended. "Was he killed in World War II, Ms. Chauvin?" Bessie again nodded her head yes. "I sure wish you could talk, Ms. Chauvin," Cassidy said, "I would love to hear your story, and how it relates to me and Pete."

Bessie Chauvin made a gesture like the opening of a drawer, and then pointed to the dresser the picture sat on. "You want me to get something from the dresser?" Bessie nodded again.

Cassidy opened the top drawer of the dresser and found a scrapbook. She lifted it out and brought it over to the bed, sitting down next to Bessie again.

Cassidy opened the scrapbook so that both she and Ms. Chauvin could see the contents. On the first page was a picture of a young couple, dressed for a special occasion.

"Is this you?" Cassidy asked. "Ms. Chauvin, you sure were pretty!" As Cassidy paged through the scrapbook, the story of Bessie Chauvin and Edward Scott started to come together. They had met at Southern University in New Orleans, both of them students. They had started dating in 1941, and rapidly fell in love. Then came December 7, 1941, and Edward enlisted in the Army. He wanted Bessie to marry him before he went to war, but she wanted to wait until he came home.

The scrapbook was full of letters from Edward to Bessie, each one full of details of the life they would build when he came home from the war. Edward often praised Bessie for making him wait to marry her, as he said it made him that much more careful to have her to come home to and take as his bride. The last page of the scrapbook had the letter that Edward's mother had written to Bessie after Edward's mother had been notified of his death in battle.

Bessie took Cassidy's hand in hers and looked deeply into Cassidy's face. She slowly shook her head back and forth, as she pointed to the picture of her and Edward in the front of the scrapbook.

"What is it Ms. Chauvin? What do you want me to know?" Bessie touched her heart, she touched her head, and she touched her watch. Then she touched her heart again and placed her hand on the picture of her and Edward.

"You never stopped loving him, did you?" Cassidy asked. Bessie shook her head, as she had never stopped loving her Edward. Bessie then held her good arm like she was holding a baby, and then held up her hand in an empty gesture.

"You never got to have babies, because you lost your love, I understand. But what are you trying to tell me?" Cassidy hated that she wasn't figuring this out.

Bessie touched her head, her heart and her watch again. Cassidy tried to figure out what Bessie was trying to tell her. "Ms. Chauvin, I'm trying to understand. Is there something about time?" Bessie used her good hand to turn the pages in the scrapbook to one particular letter. She pointed to it, and so Cassidy read it carefully.

> *Dearest Bessie –*
>
> *I hope this letter finds you well and happy, but selfishly, I hope you miss me near as much as I miss you.*
>
> *I'm sorry that we argued before I left. I know that you are right, and that we should wait to marry until I get home. I know it is important for you to finish your education, and that taking the chance of making a baby could have made finishing school impossible for you, especially if something prevents me from coming home. I'm doing everything I can to be the smartest soldier I can be, but war is dangerous. I've seen and heard things I never wanted to know could happen. I try to chase those thoughts away with thoughts of us living in a nice little house, you teaching school, me working at a garage or factory where I can put my mechanical skills to good use. I picture lots of pretty babies, growing up in our happy home. I truly love you, Bessie. I feel like I met the other half of my*

soul when I met you. I comfort myself with memories of all the fun times we have had together, and dream of all the wonderful times our future will hold.

Keep working hard on your studies, and write when you can. I keep your letters with me all the time. If you could send a picture, that would be great. I would love to make all the guys jealous seeing what a pretty girl I have waiting for me at home.

If you can, please write my Mama as well. She sure does love you already, and I know it makes me feel better to think of you and Mama spending time together while I'm gone. I know it is a long trip from New Orleans back to Belle Terre, but when you are home visiting your family I know Mama is not too far away in Houma for you to get to visit.

I need to get back to my duties, dearest Bessie. Know that I am holding you in my heart and in my dreams, counting the days until I can come home to you.

Love Always,
Edward

As Cassidy finished reading the letter, she felt her eyes tearing up, and looked at Bessie Chauvin who had tears rolling down her cheeks. Bessie was shaking her head again, and Cassidy thought that now she understood.

"You wish you would have married Edward before he left. And you wish you would have had his baby. You did the smart thing, the careful thing, and you lost the chance to have a piece of Edward forever." Cassidy's heart broke as she said the words.

Bessie Chauvin nodded her head, to show that Cassidy finally understood. "And you want me to make sure I don't waste time, and don't wait too long with Pete. But Ms. Chauvin, there is no World War II, and Pete is not in the military."

Bessie pointed to her watch again and raised her empty hand.

"But nobody knows how much time we have." Cassidy leaned over and kissed Bessie Chauvin's cheek. "I think I get it now. And I think I have to stop calling you Ms. Chauvin, because you are too important to me for such a formal title. I never knew either of my grandmothers, but I feel like you are the grandmother I never had. Would it be okay if I start calling you Grandma Bessie?"

Bessie hugged Cassidy with her good arm and kissed her cheek. "I'll take that as a yes, Grandma Bessie."

Pete came back into the room with the three dogs. He saw the two women sitting on the bed together with Sophie, the scrapbook, and the traces of tears.

"Is everybody okay? Did something bad happen?" Pete was distressed to see two of his favorite people looking so emotional.

Cassidy smile was like the sun coming out after the rain. "Ms. Chauvin showed me her scrapbook of her fiancé who was killed in World War II, and we got kind of weepy. Then we decided that since I don't have a grandmother, that Ms. Chauvin will be my honorary grandma, and I'm going to call her Grandma Bessie from now on."

"Well, Ms. Chauvin, you sure did pick a good girl for your adopted granddaughter. Cassidy is just about the nicest person I know." Pete knew he blushed as he spoke, but he couldn't help it. This relationship was great for both Cassidy and Bessie.

Bessie smiled her crooked smile and handed the scrapbook to Cassidy to put it away. Cassidy realized that it was probably time to take the dogs home and allow Bessie her nap before dinner.

"I'll be back Tuesday to visit, you have a nice nap now and enjoy your dinner and evening." Cassidy picked Sophie up off the bed and sat her on the floor. Cassidy then leaned over and hugged and kissed Bessie one more time. "I love you, Grandma Bessie," she whispered. Bessie patted her heart with her good hand to let Cassidy know she loved her too.

As Pete and Cassidy walked the four dogs to Pete's minivan, he bumped Cassidy with his shoulder. "That was a really good thing you did, Cass. You gave Ms. Chauvin the greatest gift anyone ever gets, the gift of family."

"Pete, you just don't know how good Ms. Chauvin has been for me. It started with me realizing Sophie didn't belong at the shelter, and when I found out the whole story and started coming to visit Grandma Bessie, I also started realizing that I could make friends, I just needed some confidence. Visiting with her and seeing her smile as I told her stories about Maggie and Sophie, gave me the courage to try to have conversations with others. I don't think I would have ended up friends with Rosadel without Ms. Chauvin, and then maybe we wouldn't be dating either. My Dad has been telling me my whole life the best way to have a friend is to be a friend, but I always got trapped inside my own head. Grandma Bessie made me feel like I had something to offer, and she really changed my life."

By now, Pete and Cassidy had loaded the dogs into their car seats and were in the front seat. Pete leaned over and kissed Cassidy gently on the lips.

"If Bessie Chauvin had anything to do with you sitting here with me right now, I need to buy her the biggest bouquet of roses I can find. But don't sell yourself short, Cass. You have been the sunshine for Ms. Chauvin ever since the first time you brought her Sophie to visit her."

"It goes back to what my Dad says, if you live your life for others, you get more than you can ever imagine." Cassidy was really starting to realize how wise Prescott really was.

"I hear you Cassidy, but there is one thing that I am determined to do for me, and that is to take this relationship as far as it can go. Just two dates and I think I want forever. And don't let that scare you, we can take all the time you need, and if you don't feel the same, we'll still work together successfully. But I've been knowing you and watching you for years, and now that I'm really getting to know you it is even better than I imagined."

Cassidy was surprised by Pete's words. She knew she really liked and admired Pete but was afraid to go too fast into talk of love or happily ever after. She was struggling to think of what to say when Pete solved the problem by changing the subject.

"So how are the plans for the PTA meeting coming along? Have you had a chance to work on anything yet?"

Cassidy was grateful for the change in subject, but uncomfortable that she hadn't really done any concrete planning yet.

"With Christmas and everything, I haven't done more than think about it. I was planning to bring Maggie and Sophie, as they are good in public and are great faces for the problems that senior dogs can face. If I could just find homes for all the seniors, that would be great progress. In the almost three years that I have been the St. Elizabeth Animal Shelter director, we have cut the euthanizations down to almost zero, besides the dogs that are too sick or too broken to rehome. But we still have a high mortality rate for kittens and puppies that we can't find foster homes for, especially when we don't get the pregnant moms, but the delivered litters. I want to concentrate my presentation on senior foster and litter foster."

Pete was well aware of Cassidy's experience as shelter director, as he was the veterinarian that provided the services to the shelter. "I think that is a great focus for your pitch at Holy Redeemer. Do you have any pictures of Laverne and Shirley at the shelter before you convinced me to take them home? I think if we could do before and after posters of Laverne and Shirley and Maggie and Sophie we can clearly show how important a foster or forever home is to the seniors. I think we can get Rosadel to take some pictures of the kittens that she is fostering, maybe even some video clips to give people a realistic idea of what kind of commitment they are making without losing that 'Awww' factor."

"Exactly, Pete. I don't want people to underestimate how big a commitment foster care is, but I don't want them to think it is without reward either. And fostering an animal can be temporary for someone who is ill, or for deployed military. There are so many variations on foster care that most animal lovers can help in some way. And those that can't foster for some reason can always volunteer at the shelter like you and I did." Cassidy was very hopeful that the session at Holy Redeemer would lead to even more community participation in St. Elizabeth's Animal Shelter.

As they pulled up in front of Cassidy's house and unloaded the dogs, Pete thought about what his next steps should be. He wanted to see Cassidy every day but didn't want to scare her by being too intense. They had a nice relaxing evening, watching TV and talking, and it seemed like only minutes had gone by and it was time for Pete to leave.

"So, Cass, if I call you every day, will that make you feel crowded? I know the weeknights can get crazy, but I hate to wait until next weekend to see you. Do you think we could get together on Thursday for New Year's Eve? Mom and Dad have a party every year, and I'd like for you to come. There is usually a mixed crowd, Rosadel and Clancy will be there, and Mike and Donnie and then some of Dad and Mom's friends and some of my aunts, uncles and cousins. It is a crowded noisy event, and everyone seems to have a great time. We can stay as little or as much as you like." Pete knew he was babbling a little, he tended to do that when he was nervous.

"I usually spend New Year's Eve with my dad, Pete. It is kind of our thing." Cassidy was disappointed turning Pete down, but hated to miss out on her and Prescott's tradition.

"How about Wednesday night, then? We could go eat somewhere local, or I could cook for you." Pete knew he was pressing a little but didn't want to say goodbye without a plan for the next time he and Cassidy would see each other.

"Wednesday will work. I'll take the girls and go see Grandma Bessie on Tuesday. I think I'd like for you to cook for me, can I bring the girls or anything to contribute to the meal?" Cassidy was excited to see what Pete's house was like.

"Just bring you and the girls, and their food if you don't want them eating what Laverne and Shirley eat. I'll take care of the rest." Pete leaned in and kissed Cassidy softly on the lips.

"I'll give you a call tomorrow night just to say 'hi', hope you have a good day at work." And with that, Pete headed for home.

Cassidy thought about how much fun she had with Pete, and how easy it was to be with him, and wondered what she was so afraid of. Maybe on New Year's Eve she could talk to Prescott about it. He may not have been able to make any of his marriages work, but he was the smartest person when it came to people that Cassidy had ever known. She hoped that Prescott could help her figure out what was holding her back, because she really did want a future with Pete.

CHAPTER 10

Cassidy was really looking forward to her New Year's Eve with her Daddy. Pete had called both Monday and Tuesday nights, and Pete and Cassidy had talked for nearly an hour each night, just sharing their day's activities. Wednesday night dinner at Pete's had been lots of fun. Cassidy had been wondering what Pete would make for dinner and was pleasantly surprised by a really nice dinner of chicken and sausage gumbo and salad. They had played a couple of games of Scrabble before Cassidy had packed up Maggie and Sophie and headed home.

Pete had given Cassidy lots to think about, as the good night kiss the night before had been the most passionate kiss of Cassidy's life. She wondered if she was the only girl in the world who would be talking to her Dad about her love life, but she really didn't feel comfortable talking to anyone else.

Cassidy had just put a tray of mini muffulettas in the oven, and the pot of jambalaya was finishing on the stove. She had plenty of Zapp's Potato Chips, Elmer's CheeWees and beer, wine and soda.

Cassidy and Prescott's New Year's Eve tradition had started when Prescott and Sandra first broke up. Sandra like to go out and party on New Year's Eve, and Prescott had no interest in that at all. Cassidy had seen Sandra getting all dressed up and wanted to get dressed up too. So, Sandra had called Prescott and explained that Cassidy wanted to get dressed up and go to a party too.

Prescott told Sandra not to worry, Cassidy would have a party with him. And they did. Party food, noisemakers, silly hats and Dick Clark's

Rockin' New Year's Eve on the television. Cassidy had a blast, and a tradition was born.

As Cassidy hit her teens, Prescott expected her to want to do things with her friends, but Cassidy loved the New Year's Eve tradition with her Dad too much to have it end. They didn't dress up anymore, and wine and beer had joined the soda and juice but Dick Clark's Rockin' New Year's Eve, party food, noisemakers and silly hats were still part of the evening.

Prescott and Thor arrived just as Cassidy was taking the tray of mini muffulettas out of oven. Thor was already wearing a party hat and looked like he was enjoying it. Prescott had a bag with him that Cassidy knew had noisemakers and party hats. Sometime in the past five years, Prescott had begun searching all year for the silliest hats he could find. If the Shark head hat that Thor was wearing was any indication, he had outdone himself this year. Cassidy wondered how in the world she was going to have a serious conversation with Prescott with an animal on her head.

"Smells good in here, baby girl. I've been looking forward to this all week. Seems like we've both been too busy to visit for the past couple of weeks." Prescott hugged Cassidy and kissed her on the cheek.

Cassidy leaned into her dad and held on tight. "I've been looking forward to it too, Daddy. I love Christmas, but it was an awfully busy December. And when I tell you all the plans I have for the new year, you'll see January and February won't be much better. But it is all good stuff."

"Let's put on our hats before we eat. I bought a couple more shark heads for the girls, and you get your pick from the selection in the bag." As he spoke, Prescott pulled a monkey hat, a bear hat, a tiger hat and a lion hat out of the bag.

"I'll take the monkey," Cassidy was laughing as she put on her hat, and then tried to get Maggie and Sophie into theirs. Thor seemed to like wearing a hat far more than they did, but they kept them on. "I don't think Maggie and Sophie's hats will last very long, because they look kind of miserable. Put one on, Daddy, and I'll get a picture for the collection and let Maggie and Sophie go back to being happy dogs."

Prescott put on the bear hat, and Cassidy took a picture of them all to add to her New Year's Eve album. Neither Prescott or Cassidy were big drinkers, but Prescott had a beer with his supper, and Cassidy had a glass of wine. They would pop a bottle of champagne at midnight. Prescott always spent the night in Cassidy's spare bedroom, as neither one of them liked the idea of anyone being on the road after midnight on New Year's Eve.

As they settled down in front of Dick Clark's Rockin' Eve, Prescott took off his bear hat and looked at Cassidy. "So, Monkey Girl, what is on your mind. I can tell there is something bothering you that you need to talk about."

Cassidy removed her monkey hat and tried to figure out where to begin. "You know that I went on a date with Pete Marshall the day after Christmas."

"Yes, I did. How did it go?" Prescott had been hoping that things would work out for Cassidy and Pete.

"It was great, Daddy. We talked and talked, and then played Scrabble. Pete went to Our Lady of Lourdes with me on Sunday, and we talked on the phone both Monday and Tuesday, and he made dinner for me last night at his house."

"Well, Cass, that sounds like things are going pretty well." Prescott knew that more had to be coming.

"I'm scared, Daddy. I'm scared of how Pete makes me feel. Comfortable and excited at the same time. It has only been less than a week since our first date, and I think about him all the time. I'm afraid that I'm falling in love with him."

"Cassidy, you've known Pete since high school, and always admired him. What scares you about falling in love with him?"

"I'm afraid once he knows me he won't love me back. I'm afraid I don't have what it takes to be in a relationship. I'm not saying this to make you feel bad, but you don't have relationships, and if Mark wasn't a saint, Mom would never have lasted in a relationship. How can I trust myself to get it right?"

"OK, baby, let's take this one step at a time. Me and Sandra's mistakes belong to me and Sandra, not to you. I'll start by talking about me. This might be a little uncomfortable for both of us, but we need to talk about some things that you probably never knew and are old enough to know now. You know that your mom was my third wife. The first two were good women, just like Sandra. I was messed up in my head when I got back from Vietnam. You know my Dad was killed in the Korean War, and my mom died when I was in Vietnam, so I was looking for connection to someone. Well, Vivian was the first someone. And she truly loved me, But I didn't love her back, not the way a husband should love a wife. And she couldn't help but know it. She got tired of the nightmares, and the silences and the lack of intimacy, and we got divorced. I still wanted to belong. So, I married Stephanie. And it was like Vivian all over again. I just didn't love her the way a husband should love a wife. She too got tired of the nightmares, and the silences, and the lack of intimacy, and we got divorced. I decided that I wasn't going to ever get married again, because I just wasn't good at it.

"Then I met Sandra. She was so lost, and needy. Her father was a mean and violent man, and her mother was so beaten and hopeless that she couldn't do anything for Sandra. I never meant to marry your Mom, Cassidy, I just wanted to help her get to a better place. Then she got pregnant, and we got married. I found out what real love feels like when you were born. And I never felt that way about any other living creature. Sandra never resented how much I loved you, but she knew that I didn't love her as much as she loved me. That eats at a person. So, we divorced.

"You never talk about the years between when Sandra and I split up, and when she married Mark, but I know you remember the parade of men. Sandra just wanted to be loved. And she tried all the wrong things. And there you were, loving her like crazy, and she just didn't know how to love you back.

"I decided that I had to be the stable parent. There would be no women paraded through your life the way the men came and went. That is not to say that I have lived like a monk. I enjoy women, and the company of women. But I have been very discreet, and very honest. The women that I have had relationships with know that there is no future, just mutual companionship and affection. When I was younger, the women were usually divorcees, who when they decided they wanted a committed relationship, moved on. Lately, they are widows, who move on for a variety of reasons.

"By the time that Sandra and Mark were married, and it was clear they would be together forever, I knew that I liked living by myself. I have no desire for the compromise of a committed relationship. I like my own company, and I like to be alone. I loved Ulysses, and I love Thor, but a dog is the right creature for me to share my life with. I'm too set in my ways to share every day with another person.

"But I have become a great studier of humans and human nature. I watch the people that I know at work and at the Veterans Administration, and see the qualities that make marriages work, and the qualities that cause marriages to fail. The two biggest things are communication and compatibility. And a serious dose of attraction. The happiest marriages I see are where the two people like each other enough to work through things when they don't love each other anymore, and where they love each other enough to work through things when they don't like each other anymore.

"Because if you spend fifty years with a person, feelings are going to cycle. Now, Cassidy, you are my baby girl, and I love you, and you probably believe that I am prejudiced. But you are a wonderful person who knows how to compromise, and how to show love. I watch you with Candy and Chip, with Sandra and Mark, and with all the residents at Our Lady of Lourdes. You have all the right qualities to be a good partner."

"How can you know that, Daddy? How can you be sure? I see Mark and Mom, and I wonder how he puts up with her. I wonder if I'm going to be just like her. And then I think Pete would never put up with that, and he'll end up disappointed and unhappy and leave."

"Cass, do you think you are borrowing trouble? You are endlessly patient with your dogs. You always have something kind to say to everyone. You can be a little bossy, but I don't think that will be a problem with Pete. I mean, you've met his mother, Harriet."

Cassidy had to laugh a little. "Mrs. Marshall is kind of bossy, isn't she? But in a very loving way."

Prescott nodded and smiled. "I call her the general. George obviously loves her to pieces and so Pete has seen a good marriage and what it takes. I think he is a good risk, Cass, and that you should give the two of you a chance."

"I know you are trying to make me feel better, Daddy, but I'm still scared. And I never had a good marriage to watch and learn from, except maybe Mom and Mark, and I think he must be a saint to put up with Mom. How will I know how to be a good wife?" It hurt Prescott's heart to see Cassidy so upset.

"You and Pete will learn together how to be a good couple. There is no one right answer. I know you two have a lot in common, and there is a lot of mutual respect. It sounds like you agree on many subjects and like to do the same things for fun. That is a great start. It sounds like you are attracted to Pete, and that is important. My advice is to just relax, and let your relationship develop. Anyone who isn't a little scared going into a relationship that could last a lifetime is the crazy one."

Cassidy could hear the wisdom in Prescott's words, but still felt insecure about allowing her feelings for Pete to deepen. "I'm scared too of the changes that will have to happen. Pete invited me to go to a party at his parent's house, but I wanted to spend New Year's Eve with you like always. I like routine, Daddy, and change is hard for me."

"Cassidy, I appreciate you wanting to preserve our tradition, but you know that I am getting older, and I won't live forever. It will be good to add other people to our circle and keep expanding it so that when I'm gone you will still be wearing funny hats and watching Dick Clark's New Year's Rockin' Eve. Dick Clark died, and this tradition continues without him, I want it to be the same when I die, but we have to expand our circle for that to happen."

Cassidy could see the wisdom in Prescott's words, and she wanted to take a chance on what she and Pete could have, but this was a big step, and she was truly frightened of opening up her heart.

Prescott put his bear hat back on and handed Cassidy her monkey hat. "Enough seriousness for what is supposed to be a party. Want to play Scrabble or Trivial Pursuit?"

"I'll get the Scrabble board, I've been playing with Pete, so prepare to be defeated." Prescott breathed a sigh of relief as Cassidy retrieved the Scrabble board and they started playing. It was time for Cassidy to get past her relationship fears and move on with her life. Prescott believed she and Pete were an excellent match and hoped his little girl had found a man that she could share a rich and wonderful life with.

CHAPTER 11

Marie Theriot looked at the agenda for the PTA meeting in January. As one of the cafeteria staff at Holy Redeemer, she and the other staff were always invited to attend. Usually, she stayed home, but this time, she really wanted to attend.

Marie was a lonely person. She had made a great many mistakes in her life that she wished she could correct, and life had dealt her some harsh blows.

Marie was born Marie Lafont, daughter of Michael Lafont, and Elyse Dugas Lafont, the only child of only children. Michael and Elyse had grown up in White Castle, LA, and had moved to Galliano, LA after Michael returned from World War II. Michael had served in the Navy with a commercial fisherman from Galliano, who had offered Michael a job after the war. Michael loved being on the water and fishing, so he married Elyse and moved to Galliano.

The small Lafont family in Galliano was a happy family. They enjoyed their friends in the small community and lived a nice, if somewhat simple and secluded life until Marie was fifteen. When Hurricane Hilda struck the coast of Louisiana, and an F4 tornado struck Galliano. Twenty-two people were killed, two of those were Michael and Elyse Lafont.

Marie moved to live with her only remaining grandparent, Maw-Maw Aimee after the storm. Aimee Dugas was only sixty-three, but a hard life and many sorrows had taken their toll on her. While she was alive, she was very good to Marie, but when Marie was a senior in high school, Aimee passed away.

With the little bit of life insurance Aimee had, Marie was able to support herself until graduation, along with her wages as a part time waitress at a small restaurant in White Castle. After graduation, she started waiting tables full time, and the owner of the restaurant started allowing her to take extra shifts as a prep chef. Marie had made some friends in her two years in high school in White Castle and had a decent life.

Marie was a pretty girl, and a good waitress. And in her job as a waitress she met Burl Theriot. Burl was a Vietnam Veteran, handsome as the day is long. Jet black hair and dark brown eyes, and a blinding smile. And charming. And a flirt.

Burl set his mind on winning Marie, and after a couple of weeks of persistent invitations, Marie went out on a date with Burl. He swept her off her feet. Flowers, gifts, Burl treated Marie like a princess for the first couple of months they dated. The only problem was whenever Marie made a plan with her friends, Burl would have something come up so that she had to cancel.

When Marie looked back at her life, she couldn't believe how easily Burl had reeled her in and trapped her. She had spent a lot of time with counselors in the past two years and was learning a lot about how abusers create their victims. She was hoping to go work in a women's shelter as a volunteer soon, to tell her story and help other woman.

As Marie made more and more excuses to her friends and cancelled activities, Burl got more amorous. Finally, he proposed to Marie and she said yes. It was a small wedding at Our Lady of Prompt Succor in White Castle, Marie had to ask Father Lorio to provide witnesses for her and Burl, as she was embarrassed to ask any of her friends after disregarding them for so long.

At first, married life was good. Burl was still loving and attentive, even if he was controlling. Marie continued to work at the restaurant but was now working as a prep chef and sous chef, as it bothered Burl for her to interact with the customers. Burl worked at the car dealership, where he was usually the lead salesman.

Marie was excited when she found out she was pregnant, and at first, so was Burl. But as Marie's pregnancy advanced, Burl got more and more frightening. He would rant about how this baby was not going to rule his house, and how he expected to always come first. Marie put his behavior off to nervousness about the responsibilities of fatherhood, and let it go.

Marie was lonely, but she accepted her lot. Soon, she would have a baby, and she would never be without family again.

The first time Burl hit Marie was when Sandra was about a month old. Burl wanted to make love, and the baby was crying. Marie tried to tell him to wait until she soothed the baby, and he slapped her across the face, telling her to always remember he was the first priority in the family.

The abuse didn't stop there and became routine. Burl was not the abuser that would abuse than apologize, he was the type to tell Marie she deserved it. And he had so isolated her by that time, Marie believed she did deserve it. She also made sure there would be no more babies.

Marie learned that she could lavish love and affection on Sandra while Burl was at work, but if she showed Sandra any affection when Burl was home, they both got a beating. Burl repeatedly told Marie that if she left him, he would have her declared unfit, and would take full custody of Sandra. Then he would make sure Marie knew that Sandra would be the object of his anger.

Marie hated herself that she had stayed. Her counselors had worked with her to understand how Burl's abuse had stolen her ability to do anything other than what she did, but she was having a hard time forgiving herself.

When Sandra was three, Burl decided it was time for Marie to go back to work. That took away any alone time for Marie and Sandra. It also ended Marie showing Sandra any affection.

Burl left Sandra alone as long as Marie devoted herself to him when he was in the house. It was the least she could do, and she believed the most she could do to protect Sandra.

Sandra saw the way her father treated her mother and tried to be as invisible as possible so as to not provoke him to beat her. She wasn't allowed to have friends over, so tried to create a story to tell at school that would make her home life seem more normal.

Marie and Sandra lived trapped in Burl's prison until Sandra graduated from high school. Sandra had a good friend whose parents offered Sandra the use of their garage apartment until she got on her feet. Marie watched her go with a breaking heart, and a fervent wish that Sandra would find a better life than Marie had found.

Marie was frightened when she learned that Sandra had married Prescott Bourgeois. She was afraid that Sandra would get trapped in the same cycle of abuse that Marie was in. Marie did her best to keep tabs on Sandra, but it was very difficult, because Burl had forbidden Sandra's name to be spoken in their home.

Sandra and Prescott moved to Brulee, and Marie lost track of Sandra for a while, but prayed for her every day.

Marie's life continued in the pattern of working and serving Burl until 1998, when Burl was killed in an automobile accident. Marie wore her widow's black and walked behind the casket at his funeral at Our Lady of Prompt Succor but felt nothing but joy that she was finally free.

Burl had a lot of life insurance, and Marie immediately hired a private detective to find Sandra. By the time he found her, Sandra was married to Mark, and had moved to Bayou Beni. Marie moved to St. Elizabeth Parish in 2001, in the hopes of reconciling with Sandra. But she never had. Until 2013, she had worked at Holy Redeemer as a cafeteria worker, attended Mass, and gotten more and more bitter and lonely.

When the school secretary, Belinda Collins, had approached Marie after lunch one day, Marie didn't know what to expect. Belinda apologized to Marie, saying she had noticed that Marie didn't seem to have any friends, and wanted to get to know her better. It was the breaking point for Marie in her now self-imposed prison of loneliness.

Marie had started to cry, and the next thing she knew, she and Belinda were in the teacher's lounge with the door locked, and Marie had poured out her story, leaving Sandra's name out. Belinda encouraged Marie to go talk to Father LeBlanc about her life, and Marie did. Father had set Marie up with counseling through Catholic Charities, and she had made tremendous progress overcoming her shame and her regret. She had yet to forgive herself.

And so, when Marie Theriot saw that Cassidy Bourgeois, Director, St. Elizabeth Parish Animal Shelter was speaking at the PTA meeting, she could hardly believe it. Her precious granddaughter. Marie was sure Sandra had never told Cassidy about her or Burl and thought she would be safe going to the PTA meeting to get to see Cassidy.

CHAPTER 12

The time between New Year's Eve and the PTA meeting had flown by for Cassidy. She and Pete continued to progress their relationship, seeing each other a couple of times a week and talking nearly every day. They had started going to Our Lady of Lourdes together on Sundays, and Laverne and Shirley were as popular with the residents as Maggie and Sophie.

Cassidy and Grandma Bessie were progressing in their relationship too. Bessie was spending far more time up and, in her wheelchair, than in the bed. She was still going for physical therapy to strengthen her arm and leg, and still doing speech therapy to try to restore her ability to speak. Occupational therapy was still focused on good transfers, bed to chair, chair to bed, chair to toilet and on hair brushing, tooth brushing and personal care.

Even though it had been months since Bessie's stroke, her care team was still hopeful that Bessie could graduate to assisted living from full nursing care, and Bessie was motivated to work towards that.

As Bessie's physical capabilities were improving with therapy, her frustration with being unable to speak was increasing. She could now hold a pencil and draw, but words were lost, both in speech and in writing. Cassidy hated to see Bessie so upset, and wanted better information about her condition and prognosis, but because of medical privacy rules, didn't have access to better information.

Cassidy was certain that there were electronic tools that could help Bessie communicate better and wanted to find a way to get Bessie access to them. Pete and Cassidy had talked themselves in circles trying to figure out how to help but had come up with nothing so far.

The Monday before the PTA meeting, Cassidy called Prescott after she got home from our Lady of Lourdes. Prescott immediately noticed that Cassidy sounded subdued.

"Hey Baby Girl, isn't tomorrow night your big night at the PTA Meeting talking about foster care opportunities in the community? What has you sounding so discouraged? Are you nervous about tomorrow night?"

"Oh, Daddy, everything is fine for the PTA meeting tomorrow night. Between Rosadel and Pete, I think we are going to have a very successful presentation and sales pitch. It is Grandma Bessie that I'm upset about."

"She didn't have another stroke, did she?" Prescott knew Cassidy would be heartbroken if something serious happened to Bessie.

"Oh, no, Daddy. It is just that I know there are alternate tools that could help Bessie communicate in addition to her therapy, but because of medical privacy rules, I can't talk to anyone about her disability or prognosis. I feel like if I had more information, we could do some things to alleviate Bessie's frustration with the pace of her rehabilitation."

Prescott thought for a minute before answering. "I wish you would have mentioned this sooner, Cass. I know Bessie's great-nephew, Gil Chauvin. He works in maintenance for the company at our Texas site. Clancy and I met him at a maintenance meeting last year, and when Clancy mentioned that Rosadel worked at Our Lady of Lourdes, Gil shared that his "Tante" or Aunt Bessie was staying there. I can call Gil, fill him in on what is going on, and maybe get you in touch with the right family member to help Bessie. I know that they all love her very much, but it is hard to manage your own life and a family member who is far away. As I understood from Gil, his Dad wanted to move Bessie over to a facility in Texas, but she was determined to stay in Louisiana. I'm sure he will be thrilled to hear that Bessie now has a 'granddaughter' here in Louisiana taking care of her."

Cassidy couldn't believe it. Her dad always seemed to have a way to fix things. "Daddy, how do you do it? How do you know so much about so many people?"

"Baby Girl, I've told you your whole life that people love to talk about themselves, and they love for you to be interested in them. I just listen a while, then ask a few questions, and before you know it I have people's life stories. It helps that I don't judge, because I know we're all carrying burdens that no one can see. Just listening has helped me see how I can help people over and over again." Prescott wanted Cassidy to understand it was nothing special about him, that listening to people was something that anyone could do and that it would open up brand new worlds for them. "I'm glad this time it is helping you. I'll give Gil a call tomorrow, and when you call me after the PTA meeting to let me know how it goes I'll let you know what he said."

Cassidy and Prescott talked for a few more minutes, and then hung up. Cassidy thought about calling Pete to let him know that Prescott had a contact for helping Bessie but decided to wait to tell him tomorrow. She was still a little uncomfortable about moving too fast into a relationship with Pete.

Cassidy called Rosadel early Tuesday morning from the St. Elizabeth Animal Shelter.

"Hey Rosadel, are we all set for tonight?" Cassidy had prepared a slideshow with pictures of animals that had passed through the shelter, including the cat and kittens that Rosadel was fostering, and Maggie and Sophie and Laverne and Shirley. She also had a picture of Ulysses and had Prescott's permission to share how that special dog had changed Prescott's life. All she needed was a computer with projection so that she could run her presentation from a memory stick or from a file server.

"We'll have a computer with projection, but we are on a private network, so you can either mail me the file and I will have Bee put it in the folder with the other presentations, or you can bring your memory stick."

"You know how I am, Rosadel. I'll mail you the file and bring a memory stick. I've got some really cute pictures that I think will help sell the PTA on giving us space for a booth at the fair. Some of the pictures Pete took of the kittens are ridiculous they are so cute. And someone had taken a picture of the kittens, momma cat and What Would Jesus Do sign. Are you OK that I put that one in there?"

Rosadel sighed. "Everyone already knows the story, so it can't hurt. I'll just be embarrassed again."

Cassidy was conflicted. "Rosadel, I don't want to embarrass you, but it is so important that if any message gets across to the audience tonight it is to bring your animals to the animal shelter, don't just abandon them in a public place. I thought if I could get people laughing a little, it would open them up to the rest of the message. But if that will be uncomfortable for you, I still have time to rework my presentation."

Rosadel sighed again. "No, Cassidy. I think you need to use it. The girls would never have had the opportunity to put the kittens in the manger if they hadn't been left in the church parking lot. And that is what started this whole thing and made me think Holy Redeemer can help. So, I'm good."

"And you should be proud of what you are doing to help, Rosadel. Not embarrassed. And proud of how well the triplets are doing with caring for the kittens, and with following their new rule." Cassidy was shocked that she had been that outspoken with Rosadel and immediately started to apologize. "I'm sorry, I shouldn't be telling you how to feel. That was very impertinent of me."

Rosadel had to start laughing. "Oh, Cassidy, as bossy as I've been with you, that was nothing. It just means we are really friends and you are comfortable with speaking your piece. You should hear how Bee talks to me."

Cassidy chuckled a little too, having had the opportunity to hear Bee in action. "I just don't want to overstep." Cassidy was still learning about how normal friendships worked.

"Don't overthink with me," replied Rosadel. "If I have something to say, you can count on me saying it. I won't let silly misunderstandings come between me and my friends. Life is too short and unpredictable for that."

Cassidy knew she had a long way to go before she was as comfortable managing the nuances of relationships the way Rosadel did. But she was very glad that she had such a great role model in Rosadel.

Pete pulled into the parking lot at Holy Redeemer close to a half hour before the PTA meeting was due to start. He and Cassidy had decided to meet in the parking lot so that she could do a dry run of her presentation with him. Pete spotted Cassidy's car and pulled into the spot next to her. He got out of the van and into the passenger seat of Cassidy's car.

Pete wanted to kiss Cassidy but was afraid that kind of public display of affection might make her uncomfortable, so he settled on squeezing her hand. "How are you doing Cass? Are you ready for your big performance?"

Cassidy squeezed Pete's hand back, answering, "Yes, I think so. I have some good news to share before I run through my presentation with you. Daddy knows Grandma Bessie's great nephew, and he is going to talk to him about getting better communication tools for Grandma Bessie."

"That's great, Cassidy. How in the world does your dad know Bessie's great nephew? I thought all the family she has left is in Texas."

"Turns out Clancy knows him too," Cassidy replied. "His name is Gil Chauvin, and he works for the same company as Dad and Clancy at their Texas location. He was at a maintenance meeting with Dad and Clancy, and when Clancy mentioned that Rosadel worked at Our Lady of Lourdes, Gil shared that his great aunt Bessie was a patient there. Daddy was going to call Gil today and talk to him about Bessie to see if we could get something working on different treatment options."

"I would have never guessed at that connection. I guess what they say about Louisiana is true, where everywhere else there are no more than six degrees of separation, here in Louisiana, it is really only two."

"Honest, Pete, I think that is true. That's why Daddy always told me to never say anything ugly about anybody, besides it being bad manners. He always told me that whoever you are talking about, somebody in the room knows them or is related to them, so always be careful when you speak."

Cassidy opened her laptop and brought up her presentation. "I need to run through this with you to make sure it flows, and we're running out of time. Are you ready?"

Pete was entranced watching Cassidy practice her presentation. She was so animated and passionate as she talked about the challenges of animal rescue and foster care, and the many reasons animals had to be surrendered or fostered. When Cassidy shared the picture of herself, Sophie and Bessie Chauvin, and referred to herself as Sophie's long-term foster mom, Pete got a little choked up. Cassidy had no idea how good she was at this. Pete was sure that the good people of Holy Redeemer would not only be approving a booth at the parish fair, but also, they would be getting much more involved in supporting St. Elizabeth's Animal Shelter.

As Cassidy wrapped up her presentation, Pete clapped lightly. "It's good, Cass, it is really good. I'm sure we will get to have a booth, and I wouldn't be surprised if a few parents didn't ask about volunteering at the shelter for service hours for their older children. I'm really glad Rosadel thought of this."

When Cassidy had shut down her laptop, she placed it in her large purse, just in case she needed it while inside. Cassidy and Pete went into the Holy Redeemer Parish center, where a good-sized crowd had already assembled. Cassidy spotted Rosadel and Clancy and touched Pete's arm to point him in their direction.

Rosadel gave Cassidy a quick hug while Pete and Clancy shook hands. Rosadel explained the order of the evening.

"At seven, Fr. LeBlanc will say a quick prayer to start us off. Then Frances West, the principal, will say a few words about how things are going at the school. Then Michelle Guidry, the PTA president this year will go through all the committee leads and get an update. The last committee is the fair committee, and Belinda Collins is the chairperson. She will talk about the booths, vendors and sponsors we have so far, and then will introduce you to pitch the booth for the animal shelter. I have seats saved up front for the four of us, so let's get settled in before this thing gets going."

The program progressed quickly, and soon it was Cassidy's turn to speak. As Belinda was introducing Cassidy, she opened Cassidy's presentation, which started with the pictures of Holly and her kittens in the manger in front of Holy Redeemer school.

As good-natured chuckles spread through the room, Cassidy began her talk.

"Hi, and thanks for allowing me some time to speak tonight. As Belinda said, my name is Cassidy Bourgeois, and I am the shelter director at St. Elizabeth Animal Shelter. I'd like your support to have a booth at the Holy Redeemer Parish fair to promote fostering and adoption of the animals at the shelter. I know that the fair is the biggest fundraiser of the year, and that my booth won't raise any money, so you will be making a sacrifice to lose that income producing space. But Holy Redeemer was thrust into the unwanted animal problem we have in this parish, and I wanted to give you all a chance to help be part of the solution."

As Cassidy continued to speak, Pete glanced around the room and noticed that most everyone was paying attention and listening intently. He took that as a very good sign.

Cassidy continued speaking.

"We will always have a need for people willing to foster animals, as well as to adopt. There are two groups of animals that struggle the most in the shelter environment, and those are babies and elders. There are many misconceptions about how and why animals end up at the shelter. I'd like to share a few of examples that have happened just since I have been shelter director."

Cassidy's next slide showed a picture of a young man with his arm around a dog, and another picture of the same dog with a family group.

"Within the first month, a young man living in Bayou Beni was killed in a motor vehicle accident on Interstate 10. His five-year-old German Shepherd dog was brought to the shelter by the police, because when the police notified the young man's family, they immediately advised the police about the dog. The dog was terrified. The young man's family wanted the dog but had to deal with all of the other details surrounding an unexpected death. Lindy Russell was able to take the dog to Dr. Russell's house for a month until the family was able to come and get him."

Cassidy switched to a slide showing Laverne and Shirley.

"These two beauties are familiar to everyone that goes to Dr. Pete Marshall's veterinary clinic. Laverne and Shirley had just moved into Our Lady of Lourdes assisted living with their owner when she passed away unexpectedly. They were brought to the shelter as a bonded pair of seniors who had lost their home and their owner. Fortunately, Pete needed some companions in his new home, and we were able to place Laverne and Shirley with him."

Cassidy's then showed a slide with multiple dogs and cats.

"With so many active military here in St. Elizabeth Parish, we often have animal surrenders with deployments to combat. Working with my dad, Prescott Bourgeois, we try very hard to find long-term foster homes to keep the animals until their owners return. So far, we have been able to foster and reunite all our veterans with their beloved pets when they return from deployment, but the need for more foster families never goes away."

Bessie Chauvin, Cassidy, Maggie and Sophie were featured on the new slide.

"I brought Maggie home when she was found wandering the streets. We have no idea where she came from. But Sophie came into the shelter when Bessie Chauvin had a stroke. I brought her to my house, in the hopes that Ms. Chauvin would have a speedy recovery. Well, Bessie is still at Our Lady of Lourdes in rehabilitation, and Sophie is still with me. All of us except for Maggie hope that Sophie and Bessie end up living together again."

"And we will finish where we started, with the Momma cat and kittens left at Holy Redeemer. Rosadel and Clancy Marshall have been fostering these pets, and they will be ready for adoption in early February, so their time commitment was about eight weeks."

"As you can see, there are many ways to get involved, some longer term and some short term. Not all animals that end up in the shelter are there because they have some sort of problem. Many of them are wonderful animals whose owners have become unable to care for them. Many are wonderful animals who didn't get the chance to be with a family who would love them. We work very hard at the shelter to make certain that we don't adopt out or put in foster care any animals who are dangerous, or too damaged for ordinary families, so the risk to your family of having an unsuitable pet is low if you work with us on what type of pet best fits your family's needs."

"With the high volume of attendance at the fair, I think we could really educate the people of St. Elizabeth Parish on who we are, what we do, and what they can do to help. I ask your consideration to allow us to have a booth. Thank you."

Belinda Collins took over at the podium as the audience applauded Cassidy's presentation. "Cassidy, I will let you know by Friday if we are going to have a booth at the fair."

The meeting wrapped up, and Cassidy found herself surrounded by people. Many thanked her for the presentation, sharing that they never even knew that dogs could go into foster care. Others apologized for thinking that only problem animals ended up in the animal shelter. Still others asked how they or their children could sign up as volunteers. A few asked about adopting the kittens, and many promised to come by the shelter to see the available animals.

Cassidy was overwhelmed with the support. Rosadel had said the people at Holy Redeemer were a special group, but Cassidy had never expected this. Cassidy took the names and email addresses of the people interested in the kittens and promised to send them applications for adoption. She reminded them that the kittens needed to stay with their mother until at least the second week of February, but that she would work with Rosadel to facilitate a meeting before then to pick a kitten.

Marie Theriot stayed in the background, but she watched Cassidy closely. Marie could see Sandra in Cassidy, and she had to work hard to keep her emotions in check that she had missed out on so much of Sandra and Cassidy's lives. Now that Marie had seen Cassidy and heard her speak, she was more determined than ever to find a way to reconnect with Sandra. Marie decided to talk to her counselor at their next session about the best way to try to reconnect with Sandra. It was time for Marie to risk losing the hope of a reunion with her daughter for the chance of restoring their relationship.

As Cassidy and Pete walked to their cars, Cassidy was still bubbling over with excitement. "Pete, even if we don't get a booth at the fair, just talking to these people has done a great job of getting the word out. Maybe I should try to go to all the public-school PTA meetings too."

"That's a great Idea, Cassldy, but don't expect the same level of enthusiasm you found here at Holy Redeemer. I'm sure you will get a positive response, but there is something really special about this parish and how they take their responsibilities to all God's creatures. Growing up going to church here, I thought the whole world was full of people like the ones I went to church with. In high school I learned that the level of kindness and inclusion at Holy Redeemer is way more unique and special than I had realized. It's not that there won't be good people at those other PTA meetings, it is just that you will see a more normal distribution then you find here."

Cassidy realized Pete was making a good point but didn't let that temper her enthusiasm. "I know that Pete, but every person we can influence to get involved, or to just take better care of the animals they own is a victory. I think that I can deal with the disappointment of a less than perfect reception in exchange for the opportunity to make things better."

Pete leaned over and gave Cassidy a kiss. "I know you want to take it slow, and I'm trying. But if you keep acting this way, I'm going to keep falling more in love with you." And with that, Pete walked over to his car and got in.

Cassidy stood there for a minute in shock, and then walked over to Pete's car and knocked on the window. "Are we still on for dinner and Scrabble at my house tomorrow night?"

Pete nodded, "I wouldn't miss it for the world. Since we missed visiting Bessie tonight, should we meet there first and then go back to your house?"

Cassidy thought about that for a minute. "How about you come over, we eat dinner, and then we take the dogs and go see Bessie? That way we won't have to worry about showing up while she is at dinner."

"I'll see you tomorrow, Cass, and congratulations again. I think you have started something big tonight."

◆ ◆ ◆

Marie was still deep in thought as she let herself into her house after the PTA meeting. It wasn't often that Marie was out this late at night, and she realized it was lonely and kind of scary going into an empty house so late at night so far out in the country.

Marie lived outside of Bayou Beni, in a section of St. Elizabeth Parish known by the locals as Audela (oodella). Audela was a rural area so people in Audela had septic systems and wells and pumps. Audela is the French word for 'beyond', and that is how the area got its name. Audela is the area beyond city services.

Marie thought about Cassidy, and about how passionate she was about the care of unwanted animals. Marie thought back to her childhood in Galliano, and to her beloved dog, Bijou. Bijou was a mixed breed, long haired and short legged, and she loved Marie. Sadly, Bijou was killed by the same tornado that had killed Marie's parents. When Marie had arrived to live with her grandmother, she was too sad to even think about asking for a dog, and then when her grandmother died, Marie knew it would be impossible for her to own a pet, as she was barely able to care for herself.

Marie had asked Burl about a dog shortly after they were married, and he had promised they would get a dog in a few years. By the time Sandra was six months old, Burl told Marie that she would never have a dog, as she was miserably unable to care for him and a baby.

Marie gave up her hope of a dog of her own, knowing that Burl would abuse the poor animal to punish her if she had one.

But there was no more Burl. And it got lonely out here in the country. And Marie could see Cassidy again if she went to the shelter just to see. The more Marie thought about the possibility of having a warm, loving, living creature to share her life, the more excited she got about the idea. She would go to the shelter tomorrow before she lost her nerve.

CHAPTER 13

When Cassidy arrived at work the following morning, she was surprised to find a number of voicemail messages inquiring about available animals. She wrote down the phone numbers and decided to prioritize the callbacks to immediately after she completed her morning rounds to check on the staff and the resident animals.

There were only four animals currently at the shelter, the rest were in foster homes. Of the four at the shelter, three were black dogs. Cassidy knew that the research showed that there really isn't statistical data to support that black pets are harder to place in homes, but it seemed like she always had a couple of black dogs in the shelter.

Lester was about 2 years old, and some kind of retriever mix, with long black hair and a white blaze on his chest. He wore a perpetual doggie smile, and his tail could start a wind storm. Cassidy stopped by his cage and gave him a good scratch behind the ears. "You'll get your walk in a few minutes buddy, right after the staff meeting." Cassidy knew her two full-time employees had walked the dogs at the start of their shift at 7:00 that morning, so didn't feel badly that Lester had to wait a few minutes.

Pippen was next. Pippen was less than a year old and looked like a greyhound/German shepherd mix. He had the features of a shepherd and the build of a greyhound. He was more timid than Lester and had a beautiful brindle black and brown coat. He had chocolate brown eyes that would melt your heart. "Hey Pippen!" Cassidy rubbed under his chin. "How's my good boy this morning?" Pippen wagged his tail and leaned into Cassidy's hand. "I'll be back in a few minutes, boy."

Inca was a probably a beagle/Labrador retriever mix. She was solid black, and looked like a small retriever, but could howl like a beagle. She also had a beagle's mournful expression, rather than the happy grin of a retriever. Cassidy thought there might be some basset hound in the mix as well, contributing to the look. In spite of her sad appearance, Inca was a happy little dog that would make someone a great pet. She was around six years old and had been found wandering the streets. It was obvious that she had been a pet at one point, as she knew basic commands and walked beautifully on a leash. Her tail had started wagging and banging the side of her enclosure the second Cassidy had entered the kennel area. "Hey Inca girl! That tail of yours is doing overtime." Cassidy rubbed Inca's ears as the little dog's whole body wagged with excitement.

The last dog in residence was the one Cassidy worried the most about. Max was a black pit bull mix. He was large, at around sixty pounds. It was obvious that he had a lot of different breeds in his lineage but had a big square head and powerful body. He was the oldest dog in residence, at about eight years old. He had been turned in by his owners when they lost their jobs and their home and had to move in with her parents in another state. Dogs like Max broke Cassidy's heart. His previous owners had said they loved him, but they just couldn't keep him. Max was not doing as well in the shelter environment as the others, and Cassidy was still trying to find him a foster home. She hoped one of the phone calls she returned would work out for Max. He had never lived around children though, so she thought it would be best if Max went to an adult home. Max had his face pressed up against the front of his enclosure as if trying to get to Cassidy. She knelt down and pressed her forehead to his cheek. "We're going to find a home for you, Max, I just know it."

Cassidy left the kennels and went into the conference room, where her two full time employees, Dustin Tassin and Katelyn Aucoin were already waiting.

"Good Morning! I have a bunch of phone calls to return from people wanting animals. We may empty the shelter today!" Cassidy couldn't help being excited about the prospect.

"Can't happen too soon, boss," replied Dustin. "You know in another two weeks we are going to start getting the Christmas mistakes back from the 'never should have had a pet' people."

"I know, Dustin. I still love Christmas, but it gets harder and harder with knowing that January and early February are going to be heartbreaking for a bunch of animals that never did anything but get picked by the wrong people." Cassidy wished that there were no pet stores. Reputable breeders did background checks and required veterinarian recommendations. Shelters and animal rescues did the same. But many pet stores would give anyone with money or credit a living creature. It hurt Cassidy's heart.

Katelyn shook her head. "Dustin, could you just once not be Mr. Gloom and Doom? Is there anything that you can't answer with a negative statement?" Katelyn tended to be an optimist and was always trying to keep things as light as she could. Working in the animal shelter could be hard, heartbreaking work and Katelyn was committed to finding the good in the work they did, instead of focusing on the negatives.

"I'd find something positive to say if Max found a forever home, I swear I would," replied Dustin, and Katelyn immediately forgave him. Dustin's biggest fault was probably that he loved all the animals too much.

Cassidy sensed the shift in Katelyn's mood, and so Cassidy got the morning meeting started. Katelyn would do the daily checks with the foster homes to see if everything was working well with those. In addition to the momma cat and kittens that Rosadel was fostering, the shelter had another eight cats in foster homes. It was looking like at least three of those foster situations were going to become long term adoptions.

Dustin would be caring for the resident animals and preparing for an adoption event the upcoming weekend. Dustin was also going to call the local rescue groups and check to see if any of them would like to bring animals to the adoption event.

Cassidy would be returning the calls and focusing on fundraising, and the financial reports for the calendar year that just ended. The meeting adjourned with the plan to meet again at three that afternoon, before Dustin and Katelyn's shift ended at three-thirty. Cassidy had two volunteers that came in from three to five, and then Cassidy put the dog's last meal out, walked them one last time, and closed up the shelter for the night.

As Cassidy returned to her office, she thought about how lucky she was to have Dustin and Katelyn as full-time employees. She knew that both of them would move on to other jobs at some point, but for as long as she could she wouldn't forget to appreciate their great fit for the job they were doing.

Dustin was twenty-three, and an army veteran. He hadn't decided what to do next, and since he loved animals, and had volunteered at the shelter in high school, he had applied when he got discharged from the military. Cassidy knew that Dustin would be moving on soon, and also knew she would miss him. It seemed likely that he would be using his veterans' education benefits to become a veterinary technician. Cassidy thought Dustin had the ability to be a veterinarian, but Dustin wasn't sure he wanted to spend eight years in school.

Cassidy knew Prescott was working with Dustin to try to help him figure out what to do next, and Cassidy realized she would probably be looking for a replacement for Dustin in the fall, when she was sure he would be heading off to school.

Katelyn worked at the shelter because the jobs hours worked well to coordinate child care with her husband's work schedule. Kyle Aucoin was a nurse and worked a three to eleven shift at the local hospital. With only the slight overlap in shifts, Katelyn and Kyle's three children stayed in after school care until Katelyn picked them up at four each afternoon. The children were in second, fifth and seventh grade, and so Cassidy anticipated that Katelyn would be working at the shelter for the foreseeable future.

By the time Dustin and Katelyn left the shelter that afternoon, Cassidy had probable homes for Lester, Pippen and Inca, and needed to call Rosadel to set up four visits to meet the kittens. While the successes of the day made Cassidy very happy, she was even more worried about Max. Cassidy hated the idea that he would be alone in the shelter, without at least the sound of other animals to keep him company at night.

Knowing she couldn't solve that problem, or any problem, for that matter by worrying about it, Cassidy decided to call Rosadel to set up the visits for the potential kitten owners.

Rosadel was thrilled to hear that there was so much interest in the kittens and arranged for Cassidy to bring the prospective owners over to meet the kittens on Saturday. The triplets were not as thrilled.

"But Mommy," said Lou, "Uncle Pete said the kittens wouldn't be ready to leave until Valentine's Day. Why are people coming to see them in January? That is just silly."

"And what if those people scare them?" added Rose. "You made everybody stay away from the kittens at our birthday party because you said it would be too much simulation."

"Stimulation," Rosadel corrected automatically. "And all of those people would have been. Miss Cassidy will be bringing the people over two at a time, so it will be just like Grandma Harriet and Grandpa George or Pop-Pop and Gee-Jay coming over to visit. The kittens won't be going anywhere until they are old enough, but if they can meet their new families, and then visit with them regularly until they leave Holly, it is best for the kittens."

"But it's not best for us, Mommy," said Grace as her eyes filled with tears. "It makes us sad and reminds us that as much as we love these kittens they are going away."

Rosadel knelt down and hugged Grace. "I know it makes you sad to think about the kittens leaving, Gracie, but it is what we knew would happen. And by having the kittens' new families come to visit us and them for the next month, we can make friends with them and then we can always know how the kittens are doing. So, we have to do the right thing for the kittens, even if it makes us sad."

"Well, I think it is stupid," said Lou.

"Mercy Louise, we do not talk like that in this house," Rosadel was quick and firm in her response.

Lou rolled her eyes. "I think we should wait until the kittens are bigger before we have people come to get them."

"I appreciate your opinion, Lou, but the visits will start on Saturday, and that is the final word on it."

All three girls were on the verge of a major sulk. Rosadel hardened her heart. "You three can take your long faces up to your room, and play quietly until you find a better mood, or you can find a better mood now and we can get out your bicycles and take Roscoe for a walk. It is up to you."

Hearing his name, Roscoe stood up and started wagging his tail, and nosing Lou. "Well, to be nice to Roscoe and make sure he gets his walk, I think we can find a better mood." Lou looked at the other two girls and they nodded.

"But it still won't be a good mood," said Rosie.

Rosadel had to hide a smile. "I understand you are too sad for a good mood, but maybe some exercise will cheer you up." Rosadel was not looking forward to the next six to eight weeks, as she knew the girls were going to fight her on the kittens' adoptions every step of the way. Thank God for Roscoe and his intervention. It was like he knew Rosadel needed his support to get the girls to behave better. What a gift this wonderful dog was.

◆ ◆ ◆

Cassidy was just getting the dogs settled for the night when she heard the bell indicating that someone had entered the lobby of the shelter. Hoping that it was not an animal surrender, Cassidy hurried up front.

Marie was nervously looking at the posters on the walls of the small reception area, thinking how surprising it was that the animal shelter smelled like pine rather than like animals. It was very clean and bright, not sad and dingy like Marie had expected it to be.

Cassidy saw an older woman in the lobby as she came up to the reception desk. "Can I help you?"

The older woman jumped slightly, as if startled.

"I'm sorry," said Cassidy, "I didn't mean to startle you. Can I help you?"

Marie stuck out her hand to Cassidy. "I'm Marie Theriot, one of the lunch ladies at Holy Redeemer. I heard you talk at the PTA meeting last night. I had a dog when I was a girl. My husband wouldn't let me have a dog when he was alive, but I'm alone now and think I could give a dog a good home. I wondered if you have any dogs here that need someplace to go." Marie knew she was babbling a little, but she was really nervous to be having a real conversation with Cassidy.

Cassidy shook Marie's hand. "Well, I'm glad to meet you Mrs. Theriot. Why don't you come in the back and meet our residents? If you think you would like to adopt, you can fill out the application, and we can see how everything works out. You might find that none of the dogs in residence are a good match for you, but once you fill out the application and get approved, we can keep you advised as to other available dogs through local rescue organizations, and let you know when we bring more dogs in."

Marie was beginning to see that this was more complicated than she had thought. But the more she thought about having a dog last night, the more it seemed that it would be one more step in healing all the scars on her heart. "I would love to meet the dogs. How long will it take to go through the application process if I meet one I want?"

Cassidy liked the enthusiasm she was getting from Marie. "The application process usually takes three to five days but can go faster. Let's go see what you think of our residents."

All the dogs were standing at the front of their kennels when Cassidy and Marie entered the kennel area. Marie noticed all but one of them were wagging their tails, even though the one tail-wagging dog had a mournful expression. "Hey kids, this is Marie, and she is looking for a forever friend."

The three tailwaggers wagged harder, but it was the dog in the last kennel, standing silent and still who caught Marie's attention. He looked so lonely. And sad. And he looked like his heart had been as battered as Marie's.

Marie walked over to Max's kennel. She leaned over so that her face was level with his. Max just sat still and watchful. Marie put her hand against the kennel door, and Max leaned into her hand. Marie stuck her fingers through the wires, and scratched Max under the chin. Max closed his eyes and sighed.

Marie turned to Cassidy with tears in her eyes. "Can I have him? What is his name? Why is he here? Why is he so sad?"

Cassidy was blinking back her own tears. She had seen a lot of people find a pet, but she had never seen such an immediate emotional connection between a human and a dog before.

"His name is Max, he is eight years old, and his owners lost their jobs and couldn't keep him. He has been grieving. We, that is Dustin, Katelyn and I try to give him all the love we can, but he is so confused as to why he is here and where his family went."

Marie thought about how she had felt after Hurricane Hilda had taken her home, her parents and Bijou. Marie knew exactly how Max felt. "I meant what I said. I want Max."

Even though she could see the emotional connection, Cassidy had to be rational in the execution of her job. "Let me take you to the play area, and then I will bring Max in so that you two can spend some time in a more comfortable environment. After you spend a few minutes together, I'll bring Max back to his kennel, and you can fill out the adoption application if you still want him. Then we'll both go home, and I'll call you and let you know if the application is approved, and when you will be able to pick up Max and take him home. If you'd like, you can come visit Max and walk him between now and when the application process is complete. I find that taking the time to bond with your new pet prior to taking them home can make a big difference."

Cassidy took Marie to a room that looked like a family room. There were a couple of leather look couches, and toy boxed filled with dog toys. There was a television in the corner, tuned to the Animal Planet channel. "Make yourself at home, and I'll be right back with Max."

Marie sat on the edge of one of the sofas and wondered what in the world she was doing. Would Sandra be angry that Marie had approached Cassidy this way before reaching out to Sandra? All of the anxiety of the past came flooding back to Marie. What if she had ruined her chances of reconciliation with Sandra with this impulsive move? As Marie started to move into a full-on panic, Cassidy and Max came into the room. Cassidy removed the slip leash from around Max's neck, and he walked over and put his big head in Marie's lap.

As quickly as the panic had threatened to overwhelm Marie, it faded away. Marie bent down and kissed the top of Max's head. She all but forgot Cassidy was in the room. "I lost my whole family at once too, Max. So, I know how you feel. I still miss my family. But I have plenty of love to give you. Can you be brave enough to love me back?" Max lifted his head, stood up on his hind legs and put his paws on Marie's shoulders, and then leaned his big head against hers.

"I think that is a yes," Marie rubbed Max's sides, careful not to hug him. She remembered her Daddy telling her to never hug Bijou, as it could scare a dog to be restrained like that.

Cassidy watched in approval. Marie Theriot may not have owned a dog for many years, but it was obvious she knew how to interact properly with an animal. Marie was letting Max set the pace for what he was comfortable with.

"We're going to be good for each other, Max. I have a house and a big yard, so you will have plenty of space to play. I'll walk you every day. You may never stop missing your old family, but I'll never leave you."

Max sat down and leaned against Marie's leg. "I'm positive Max is supposed to be my dog, Ms. Bourgeois. Can I fill out the application now?"

"You can call me Cassidy, and I can get you a paper application, or you can fill one out online. Which would you prefer?"

Marie was a little old-fashioned. "I'll fill out a paper application if you don't mind. I have a computer, but I still do most of my business with paper. The people at work tell me it is time to come into the 21st century, but I'm taking my time with it. And I don't want to mess up the application and have it take longer for me to get Max."

Cassidy couldn't believe that Max had found a home so easily. "Let me settle Max for the night, and I'll come back with an application."

Marie rubbed Max behind the ears, "I'll come to see you every day until you come home, boy. Be good until tomorrow."

As Cassidy settled Max back in his kennel and collected a blank application for Marie, she thought about calling Pete and Prescott after work to let them know she had found a home for Max. Her phone buzzed as she was walking out of her office. It was a text from Pete. Answering would wait until Marie was working on the application.

Cassidy found Marie staring into space when she came back into the playroom. Cassidy couldn't help thinking Marie looked as sad and lost as Max did. "Here is the application form. Do you mind if I answer a text while you fill out the form?"

"No problem at all. I just realized I am probably holding you over. I'm sorry, that was thoughtless of me." Marie hadn't been thinking at all about how late it was getting.

"It's fine, Mrs. Theriot. One of the first things I learned when I took this job is that you have to be flexible. Just take care of filling out the application, it won't take long at all."

Cassidy unlocked her phone and saw her text from Pete.

Dinner still on?

Cassidy knew it would be too late to visit Grandma Bessie if she and Pete had dinner first.

Still at the shelter. Processing an application for Max. Can we have dinner after we visit Grandma Bessie?

Pete was quick to reply.

Max? Sure thing we can wait on dinner. Just text when you are leaving the shelter and I will pack up the girls and meet you at your place.

Cassidy smiled as she read Pete's answer. He was as excited as she was that Max was finding a home.

Perfect. See you soon.

Marie took only a few minutes to complete the application. As she handed it to Cassidy, she said, "I meant what I told Max. I'll come every day until I can take Max home. I get off work at between 2:30 and 3:00 most days, so I can be here by 3:30 if I don't go home and change like I did today. So, I won't make you late again."

"Really, Mrs. Theriot, it is fine. And Max will be glad to see you tomorrow. I hope by Friday we can send him home with you."

Cassidy was still bubbling over with excitement when Pete picked her up. "Pete, I've never seen anything quite like it. Max and Mrs. Theriot just bonded right before my eyes. I sure hope everything checks out with her references so that Max can go home with her on Friday."

Pete loved seeing Cassidy this way. He wondered if she knew how beautiful she was when she was lit up like this from finding the perfect home for one of her shelter residents. Pete squeezed Cassidy's hand. "Cass, I'm so happy for you. I know how worried you were about Max. Tell you what, I'll be happy to give Mrs. Theriot a coupon for a free initial visit. That way, hopefully, I'll be Max's vet, and we'll be able to keep track of how they are doing together."

"Really, Pete? That would be great. She lives out in Audela, so could just as easily go to a vet out that way. I think if she meets you and your staff, she'll come back into Bayou Beni."

"Why, Cassidy, did you just compliment me and my staff? Thank you. I'm proud of the work we do at the clinic, but I'm prouder still of how we try to make our clients feel like family."

"Did I never tell you before what a great job I think you do? And how much I appreciate your staff? Gee, Pete, sorry about that. I guess I thought you knew." Cassidy felt badly that she didn't do a better job of talking about her feelings, even on such benign topics. "I'm going to work on doing a better job of telling people I appreciate them. I never thought about it until lately, but part of why I have a hard time with relationships is that I spend too much time inside my head."

Pete reached over and squeezed Cassidy's hand again. "It is good to think about how to be a better person. But don't change too much, I kind of like you just the way you are."

Cassidy leaned over and kissed Pete on the cheek. "Thanks, Pete. Between you and Grandma Bessie, I'm going to have to be careful that I don't get conceited."

The next few minutes were busy with Pete parking the van, and Pete and Cassidy getting the dogs organized to go into Our Lady of Lourdes for visits. Pete was taking Laverne and Shirley over to the activity room on the assisted living wing, and Cassidy was taking Maggie and Sophie to visit Bessie in the rehabilitation and full care wing.

Bessie was still dressed and sitting in her chair when Cassidy got to her room. "Grandma Bessie! You are looking great. And sitting in a regular chair so late in the day. Are you strong enough now to use your walker right up until bedtime?"

Bessie smiled, and Cassidy was pleased to see that Bessie's mouth was less droopy, and that when Bessie held up her hands, her right arm looked much stronger.

Cassidy placed Sophie in Bessie's lap, and Bessie began petting Sophie with her right hand. "Grandma Bessie, your right hand is working really well again."

Bessie smiled and nodded. It looked like everything but Bessie's speech was being recovered. Cassidy made a note to herself to call her dad tomorrow and find out if Prescott had talked to Bessie's great-nephew.

Cassidy sat on the edge of Bessie's bed and caught Bessie up on the events of the last two days. Bessie nodded and smiled as Cassidy talked about the PTA meeting the night before and gave Cassidy a thumbs-up as she related the numerous calls that she had gotten at the shelter that day.

When Cassidy told Bessie about the end of day visit with Marie Theriot, and that Marie was working on adopting Max, it was obvious that Bessie had something to communicate.

"Do you know Mrs. Theriot?" Cassidy asked. Bessie nodded her head yes, and then made a sign of the cross.

"You know her from church at Holy Redeemer?" Cassidy was amazed at how good she and Bessie were getting at non-verbal communication.

Bessie nodded again, and then shook her head back and forth, and touched her heart. "She is a very sad person, isn't she Grandma?" Bessie nodded again. "Do you know anything about why she is so sad?"

Bessie shook her head no, and then drew a box with her hand. "Okay, Grandma, that one is going to take me a minute to figure out." Cassidy thought about what it could mean.

Bessie thought for a moment, and then crossed her arms across her chest, grabbing her shoulders.

"She keeps to herself and doesn't let anyone get close," Cassidy guessed. Bessie nodded her head yes again. And then Bessie put up one finger. "Except for one person?" Bessie nodded again.

"Now I'm curious as to who that could be," Cassidy said, "And I have a feeling we can't sign language that one. But I'll ask Rosadel when I see her this weekend. Rosadel knows everyone at Holy Redeemer." Bessie smiled and nodded again.

It wasn't long before Pete stuck his head in the door of Bessie's room. "Hey, Ms. Bessie! Don't you look beautiful tonight." Pete walked over to her chair and kissed her cheek. "It looks like I'll be taking you dancing soon if your recovery keeps going so well." Bessie smiled and blushed as she patted Pete's cheek.

Cassidy pretended to be outraged. "Grandma are you trying to steal my boyfriend?" And then Cassidy blushed as she realized what she said.

Bessie laughed and shook her head no, as Pete pumped his fist in the air and said "Yes! She finally called me her boyfriend!"

Cassidy couldn't help joining in the laughter, and the visit ended on a happy note. As Pete and Cassidy walked to the van with the dogs, Cassidy was marveling to Pete at how much Bessie had improved in the last few weeks.

"I'm amazed, Pete. Grandma Bessie had the stroke around Halloween, and I brought Sophie to my house. At Thanksgiving, she had made very little progress. Then as December went on, it seemed like little bits of progress were being made in therapy, but since Christmas, Grandma Bessie's recovery has been remarkable."

"Did you ever think that you might have something to do with it? You've given Bessie a reason to get well. She wants to have more time with you. Just like I do." Pete was certain that Bessie having family close by, albeit family that Cassidy created, was critical in her desire to get well and back engaged in life.

"Love makes life worth living, Cass. Bessie had Sophie to love, and at first, you taking care of Sophie made dying less scary. But as you and Bessie formed your relationship, I think the love you give Bessie, and the fact that you have shown her you need her, are powerful motivators. None of us like to feel dispensable, you have given Bessie purpose again."

Cassidy blinked back tears. "I do need her, Pete. Grandma Bessie has helped me come out of my shell and interact more naturally with people. I can never repay the debt I owe her."

Pete reached over to squeeze Cassidy's hand. "There is no debt to repay, Cass. Love doesn't work like that. Love just helps us lift each other up, no score keeping. You and Bessie have enriched each other's lives, easily and naturally, because you were both thinking about the other. My mom has always taught us that the best life is one lived looking out for others, and the older I get the more I know how right she is."

"My dad lives by the same rule, Pete. I guess living with my mom has made it harder for me to accept the wisdom my dad has always had. My mom lives more of an inward facing life, except for Mark. I know she loves me and Candy and Chip, but she always seems so concerned with appearances, and what other people think. Mark told me at Christmas that Mom is going for counseling to try to work through some of her issues, I sure hope it helps. I want to have a close relationship with my mom, but until she can meet me halfway, I always feel like I'm trying and coming away disappointed."

Pete had a hard time imagining Cassidy's relationship with her mother. Harriet might be a little too interfering and opinionated, but Pete always knew Harriet loved him and his dad and his brothers unconditionally.

As Pete and Cassidy prepared and ate dinner, conversation switched to easier topics, with Pete sharing funny stories about his childhood, and Cassidy talking about her plans for the Holy Redeemer church fair. As Pete was leaving for the night, he kissed Cassidy good-bye.

"I've been nervous about asking you this, Cassidy, but I feel like I need to before we go too much further. You know I'm Catholic, and that my faith is important to me. Would you come to church with me this Sunday? I'm not asking you to become Catholic, I just want to share that part of my life with you." Pete couldn't believe how nervous he was asking.

"Sure, I'll come to church with you, Pete. Neither my mom or my dad were church goers, so I didn't grow up going to church, or talking about God much for that matter. I've had such positive experiences with the people at Holy Redeemer, I don't mind finding out more about it."

Pete hugged Cassidy tightly. "I'll see you before Sunday, but plan for 11 AM Mass and brunch afterwards. Do you want me to check and see if we can bring Bessie to church and out to brunch with us?"

"That would be great Pete, thanks for thinking of it. I can't wait to call my dad tomorrow and catch him up on all that has been happening."

Pete was smiling as he drove home. It looked like everything he ever wanted in life was about to become real.

CHAPTER 14

The message waiting light was lit on Prescott Bourgeois' phone when he returned to his office after the morning meeting on Thursday. Prescott checked his watch to see how much time he had before his next meeting as he listened to the message. With over an hour before his next meeting, Prescott decided to return Cassidy's call. She sure sounded happy this morning.

"Hi Daddy! How are you?" Cassidy's voice was a sure indicator that her mood had not taken a downturn since she left her earlier message.

"I'm good Baby Girl, what's up? You said you had good news for me." Prescott wondered if the good news involved Pete Marshall.

"Max has found a home, Daddy. A lunch lady from Holy Redeemer heard my talk at the PTA meeting and came and filled out an application last night. She and Max fell in love at first sight! I've never seen anything like it. I've been checking out her references this morning, and everything is checking out. I think Max may be able to go to his forever home today."

"Oh Cassidy, that is great news, I know how worried you have been about Max." Prescott knew that Cassidy had been seriously worried that Max wouldn't find a home.

"And Daddy, I have three families coming today to see the other dogs, and four families lined up to meet Rosadel's kittens, and two calls this morning about two of the cats we have in foster care that are up on Petfinder. We may have an empty shelter by this time next week!"

Prescott was glad to hear it, but like Dustin, knew the inevitable post-holiday pet drop off would begin soon at the shelter. "That is great,

Baby Girl! I know how hard you work to find all of your animals' homes."

"And I think that I'm getting a booth at the Holy Redeemer fair to talk about adoption and rescue. All the local rescue groups that I have talked to are interested in helping and rotating animals through the day. I think we may have an opportunity to turn the corner in St. Elizabeth Parish so that we don't have to euthanize animals anymore."

"That would be great, Cassidy." Prescott wondered if it was time to talk to Cassidy about his retirement plan but decided it would be better if the plan was more developed before he talked to her about it. "I had faith that once the people of Bayou Beni understood the challenges more, they would step up and help. This is a special community we live in."

"I know, Daddy, and I'm realizing that even more since I moved back. Let me tell you more good news. Grandma Bessie is using her right hand more, her face hardly droops, and she is spending most of the day in a chair and using her walker and managing her own transfers. She really is getting better, Daddy, I'm so happy for her."

"Wow, Cassidy, no wonder why you are so excited. Any one of those things would be great, but all in a couple of days, this is wonderful. Congratulations, Baby Girl." Prescott was proud of the positive difference Cassidy was making in so many ways. She had always been his pride and joy, but she was really living up to her potential since she took the shelter director job and moved back to Bayou Beni.

"Have you talked to Grandma Bessie's nephew yet? As much as she is progressing with her therapy, her speech is just not coming back."

"Yes, I did talk to Gil, he is going to be calling Our Lady of Lourdes to talk to them about alternate therapy for Bessie. He is also going to ask them if he can add you into the information chain, but he is pretty sure the medical privacy rules won't allow that. He told me that I could give you his phone number so that if you have questions or concerns, you can call him directly."

"Thanks, Daddy, that will be great. That brings me to the next thing, and I need to ask your advice." Some of the excitement had left Cassidy's voice, and Prescott wondered why. "Pete asked me to go to church and to brunch with him on Sunday. He's going to check and see if

Grandma Bessie can come with us. The thing is, I'm afraid Mama is going to be upset if she hears I went to a Catholic Church. I don't know what the story is, but I know Mama is against organized religion, and especially against the Catholic Church. I don't want to upset her, but I want to go. And if me and Pete end up staying together, I may want to become a Catholic, or at least go to church with him all the time. What should I do?"

Prescott sighed, and thought carefully before answering. "No need to say anything right away, Cassidy. See how you like church on Sunday. See how things develop with Pete. When the time is right to introduce Pete to your mom and Mark, let Mark know first that Pete is Catholic, and follow his lead. He handles your mom better than anyone else. He'll give you good advice when the time comes."

"OK, Daddy. It feels a little like kicking the can down the road, but I see your point. Do you have any idea why Mama has such an issue with Catholics?" Prescott thought hard about how much to disclose to Cassidy, because it was really Sandra's story to tell.

"Well, Cass, the most I can tell you is that Sandra's parents were practicing Catholics, and she doesn't remember them as good people, and I think she feels the church didn't do right by her. That's all I can say. At some point, you may have to ask your mother about it, but I'd wait until I had to, and I'd get Mark involved first. You know your mother acts tough but is really fragile, and you don't want to make life harder for her."

Cassidy wondered how many children of divorce got counseled to be kind and gentle with the other parent by the parent that was left in the first place. She knew Prescott held himself responsible for not being a good enough husband to Sandra, but she was amazed at how even after all these years, Prescott was still so protective of Sandra.

"I'll just wait then, Daddy. But if things keep going well with Pete, I'll have to talk to Mark about how to tell Mama Pete is a Catholic."

"Don't borrow trouble, Cassidy. By the time you tell Mark, maybe the therapy your mother is getting will have helped the situation."

"I sure hope so, Daddy. I want Mama to be happy, and I want to be closer to her. Well, I guess I should let you go back to work and get back to work myself. If I call the next references and get good news, maybe Max can go home with Mrs. Theriot tonight."

Prescott was glad that all the years of counseling military veterans with PTSD had given him the ability to respond calmly even when he was shocked.

"Mrs. Theriot?" he questioned. "That is who is adopting Max?"

"Yes, Daddy, Marie Theriot. Do you know her?" Prescott thought a minute before answering. "I knew a Marie Theriot a long time ago. It is a common enough name in Louisiana. Probably not the same person. The Marie Theriot I knew lived up near Baton Rouge." But Prescott knew he needed to check. Could it be possible that Sandra's mom was in Bayou Beni?

After Cassidy and Prescott hung up the phone, Cassidy called the rest of Marie Theriot's references, and was thrilled that everything checked out and Max would be able to go home with Marie today. Cassidy called the office at Holy Redeemer and left a message for Marie with Belinda Collins that Max was ready whenever Marie was. Then Cassidy called Pete to let him know the certificate for a free exam was needed today. Pete was busy with a patient, but Hannah Falgoust, Pete's office manager had been prepared for Cassidy's call.

"He is with a patient, Cassidy, but I can email a certificate to you if you can print it there," Hannah was glad to help. And she was glad that it looked like a romance was developing between Pete and Cassidy.

"Thanks, Mrs. Falgoust. I can print it here no problem. How is JT doing?" Hannah's son JT had a rough time after returning from Afghanistan, and Prescott had worked with him to get him the help he needed.

"JT is doing great, Cassidy. Thanks for asking. I know that working at Home Depot isn't a permanent solution, but it is paying his bills and allowing him to save up some money. I'm just as happy to have him home for a little longer. Your Dad convinced him to enroll in night classes at University of New Orleans to see if maybe he wants to study to become a mental health counselor with the VA or a volunteer organization. Your dad has convinced JT that his experiences, and the way he has coped with them would make him a great resource for other struggling individuals. I hope JT goes that route. He was always a sensitive person, and that is why combat was so hard for him. He would be a wonderful counselor."

"That sounds like a good fit for him, Mrs. Falgoust. I remember JT being one of the good guys in school. Always looking out for the kids that got picked on, always sitting with the kid that was eating lunch alone. I think he would be a great counselor."

"Thanks for sharing that with me, Cassidy. A mother sees the best in her children, it is good to hear that other people see the same things."

"Well Mrs. Falgoust, I've got to get back to work. Tell JT I was asking for him next time you talk to him, would you?"

"I surely will, Cassidy. And just to let you know, I'm available to help at the booth at the Holy Redeemer fair if you need me."

"That's great! I'll add you to the list, thanks again."

As Cassidy hung up the phone she thought again how lucky she was to have gotten this job in a town like Bayou Beni, with the support of the people at Holy Redeemer.

Prescott had not been able to shake the nagging sense of worry since talking to Cassidy. Yes, Marie Theriot was a common name in Louisiana, but he just couldn't discard the idea that this Marie Theriot was his ex-wife Sandra's mother, and Cassidy's grandmother. Since Cassidy had said that Marie was a lunch lady at Holy Redeemer, Prescott decided to go talk to Angus McPherson.

At the end of the work day, Prescott made his way to Angus' office, knowing Angus always stayed a few minutes late to make sure everything was running smoothly before he left for the day. Sure enough, Angus' door was open, and his office light was on.

"Hey Angus, do you have a minute?" Prescott waited at the door of the office.

"Sure thing, Prescott. Do we have an equipment problem?" Prescott was quick to answer. "Nope, this isn't about the plant, Angus. I need to talk to you about something. Is it OK if I shut the door?"

"Go ahead, just let me know if I should give Jessie a call to let her know I'll be late. We carpooled today."

"Gee, Angus, I don't want to disrupt your evening, maybe another time would be better." Prescott hated to put anyone to any trouble.

"To tell the truth, Prescott, Jessie is elbows deep in some data analysis about a problem at the plant in Texas, and I'll have to pry her out of here. Just give me a second to call her and tell her she has another hour to play with her data. That will give us plenty of time." Angus' wife Jessie was a data analyst and manufacturing problem troubleshooter, who was based in Bayou Beni, but who solved problems globally for the company.

Prescott paced around the office, looking at Angus' pictures while Angus called Jessie and told her about the delay. Prescott sat down in the chair in the office as Angus finished the call and turned to him.

"Prescott, you are like a cat on a hot tin roof. What is going on, man?" Angus was worried, because Prescott was normally the calmest, steadiest guy in any room.

"To be honest, Angus, I'm not sure where to start, so stay with me as I try to make sense of this for both of us. I'll start with the easy question, do you know Marie Theriot, the lunch lady at Holy Redeemer?"

Now Angus was really curious. "I know who she is. I've seen her at Mass, and at the Grandparent's Day lunches since the triplets were in preschool. Why?"

"Well, she just adopted a dog from Cassidy at the shelter." Prescott knew that didn't account for this visit.

"And?" asked Angus. "We both know that is not why you are here. What about Marie has you so stirred up?"

"Cassidy's mother Sandra's mother's name is Marie Theriot. Do you think it is possible it is the same one? Cassidy knows nothing about her mother's family, because that is how Sandra wanted it. Sandra moved out the day she graduated high school, and her parents disowned her. I knew her father a little bit from the VFW. He was a womanizer, and a mean man. I didn't know Marie, but always got the feeling Burl kept her on a very short leash. I kept track of where they were until Burl died to try to protect Sandra from them as much as I could. Once he died, I stopped, as I never thought of Marie as a bad person, just a victim."

Angus had been listening intently to Prescott and knew what he was about to say was not going to make things any better.

"As I said, I don't really know Marie, but she was kind of a burr under Rosadel's saddle from the time the girls started school. Always had something negative to say. Rosadel was complaining about Marie one day, and I suggested that most negative people were unhappy people, and that she should try to befriend Marie. Well, Rosadel told Bee Collins, and Bee approached Marie. Turned out Marie is a domestic violence survivor. She has been in counseling and has set up a ministry at church where the parish ladies coordinate donations for a safe house here in St. Elizabeth Parish operated by a United Way Agency. So, it really could be the same Marie Theriot." Angus felt for Prescott, what an awkward position.

"I don't want to frighten her, Angus. But I need to know her intentions. Sandra is still a fragile person, and Cassidy is my life. I can't see Marie hurt them, but if she just wants to reconnect, I want for her to have that chance. I don't feel like sitting and waiting to see what happens is the right answer, but I have no idea what to do." Prescott didn't really think Angus had any answers either, but it sure helped to talk about it.

"Prescott, do you mind if I talk to Jessie about this? She is a problem solver all the way down to her DNA. If anyone can think of a way to get to the bottom of this, it is Jessie. I'll talk to her tonight and give you a call later if that works." Angus honestly didn't know what else to offer by way of advice.

"Thanks, Angus. That will be fine. But please, other than Jessie, can we keep this quiet? If it is a different Marie Theriot, there is nothing to talk about. If, on the other hand, it is Cassidy's grandmother, there could be a lot of people hurt if things aren't handled carefully. I can hardly believe that Marie has been working at Holy Redeemer for fifteen years, and Sandra has never bumped into her somewhere in town." Prescott could hardly believe he had never run into Marie either.

"Well, as I understand it, Marie's life was work, Mass, and home. No friends to speak of. And she could have shopped somewhere else so as to stay under the radar. From what I know, she is a sad and broken woman, who is now determined to help other women escape abusive situations. I'm glad to hear she got a dog. That unconditional love will probably help her heal even more. And if it is the same Marie Theriot, maybe she can heal her relationship with Sandra. It must be a pain that never goes away to be estranged from your parents." Angus thought about how his parents had both died before he was twenty-one.

Prescott shared Angus' sentiments. "I never knew my father, he was killed in Korea when I was a baby. My mother died while I was deployed in Vietnam. I can't imagine having parents and not being close to them, seeing as I have wished for parents my entire adult life."

Angus and Prescott sat in silence for a few minutes, before Prescott got up to leave. "Thanks for helping, Angus. I hope Jessie can come up with something to do. I hate the thought of just waiting for the other shoe to fall."

"I hear you, Prescott, but that might be the only choice we have. I'll give you a call later." Angus was thoughtful after Prescott left his office. He thought about how the entire Holy Redeemer parish had been there for him and Rosadel when Rosadel's mother Allie died. He thought about how Prescott had been there for him as well. It was hard to imagine being as isolated as Marie was. Angus said a quick prayer for healing for Marie as he finished his day's work. He was looking forward to talking to Jessie on the way home. Jessie may not have an answer, but Angus was a big believer in a trouble shared being a trouble halved.

When Angus stopped at the door of Jessie's office, Jessie was packed up and ready to go. "Did you find your answer, sweetheart?" Angus asked.

"Yes, and it was right under my nose. I don't know how I missed the information the first time. The plant changed suppliers for a key raw material. The Certificates of Analysis show a higher carbon content on the new material. That carbon is what is causing the quality problem. Now it is out of my hands and in purchasing's hands to either get the quality we need from the new supplier or switch back to the old one."

"So, no need for travel to solve this one?" Angus was pleased if that were the case.

"No travel!" confirmed Jessie. "I love it when I can solve a problem from home. What's up with you, Angus? You seem troubled."

"We'll talk about it in the car, Jessie. It is why I'm late, and what Prescott and I were discussing."

Jessie's curiosity was piqued, but she realized that Angus needed to wait until they were in the car out of respect for Prescott's confidentiality. As soon as they were settled in the car and on the road, Jessie turned to Angus.

"Ok, Honey, I can't stand it – what is up with Prescott?"

Angus sighed. "Be patient as I tell the story, Jessie, because it is complicated. You know how close Prescott is to his daughter, Cassidy?"

"Yes, Honey, I've seen them together and they remind me of you and Rosadel."

"I can see where they would, but Cassidy's mom is still alive. She and Prescott divorced when Cassidy was little, and even though Sandra remarried, Prescott is still very protective of Sandra. Well, Cassidy called Prescott yesterday to tell him that one of the dogs at the shelter had been adopted by Marie Theriot."

"Our Marie Theriot? The lunch lady?" Jessie asked.

"Yes, our Marie Theriot. Well, it turns out that Sandra's mother's name is Marie Theriot. Sandra moved out of her parent's house when she graduated high school, and her parents disowned her. Cassidy knows nothing about her grandparents, not even their names."

"And Prescott is worried that Marie is Sandra's mom?"

"Yes, and worried that if she is, it could be a problem for Sandra and for Cassidy. It turns out that Prescott always suspected that Sandra's father, Burl, abused Marie, but had no proof. When I shared that Marie is a domestic violence survivor, it seemed more likely that it is the same Marie."

"You can put all doubt to rest, Angus. Marie has mentioned her husband Burl at our meetings while packing up donations for the safe house. She also has mentioned a daughter named Sandra." Jessie wasn't sure it that information made it better or worse.

"I need to call Prescott his evening and let him know. He doesn't know what to do, do you have any ideas?"

Jessie knew what she was about to say wasn't going to be the answer anyone wanted. "Angus, Prescott can't 'do' anything. If he approaches Marie, she will be terrified. We have a meeting on Saturday to sort and box up more donations for the safe house and for women's shelters around the parish. I'll stay after and tell Marie that she has been recognized and encourage her to talk to her counselor about it. This is Marie's to handle, not anyone else's".

"I know, Jessie, and I said as much to Prescott. I'll reinforce that tonight when I talk to him. And I'll keep praying for Marie and for Sandra. I can't imagine the pain of being estranged from your child."

Jessie reached over and squeezed Angus' hand. "I know, love. But there are many broken and hurting souls out there who can't find their way back to their loved ones. I'm hoping that with the support of her Holy Redeemer family, Marie can reach out and heal the breach with Sandra. I know she has wanted to but has been too ashamed for failing to be a better mother, for failing to leave Burl, for failing to stand up for herself to make the contact. This may be just the incentive she needs to take that final step."

Angus thought for a moment before he spoke. "Marie had to know she was taking a risk both by going to the PTA meeting and by going to the shelter and adopting a pet. Maybe she is more ready than she knows."

"I hope so, Angus. Since Bee started pulling Marie out of her shell, I have come to know her as a sad and broken woman, but not mean at all. She has a heart full of love but feels like her love is a curse. She has been getting steadily better since she has been in counseling, and she is comfortable with many of us women now, but only truly close to Bee. We'll just have to pray extra hard that the Holy Spirit works in the hearts of everyone to reach a happy outcome."

As Angus pulled into the driveway, he had one more question for Jessie. "This won't be too stressful for you, will it? I don't want to you to take on anything that could hurt you or the baby."

Jessie leaned over and kissed her beloved husband. "No, darling. Not too stressful for me. I love solving problems and talking to people about difficult things has become easier for me because I have had to do it for so many years as part of my job. Yes, it is different when it is personal stuff rather than work, but difficult conversations are just that, difficult. I'll be fine, and so will the baby."

Angus call Prescott as soon as he went into the house, while Jessie was starting dinner preparations.

"Prescott, we're just about sure that Marie Theriot is Sandra's mother. Jessie said she has mentioned a husband, Burl, and a daughter, Sandra, before at the meetings where they sort donations for the victims of domestic violence." Angus waited while Prescott digested that news.

"Did Jessie have any ideas on what I should do?" asked Prescott.

"Yes, she did. And, Prescott, I know this is hard for you. But you can't do anything but be supportive of Cassidy and Sandra when the time comes. This belongs to Marie and Sandra. Jessie is going to talk to Marie on Saturday and let her know she has been recognized and encourage Marie to talk to her counselor about it. Jessie and I are going to be praying for everyone. I know you like to fix things, but this one has to be fixed by the principals, not by you."

"I know that in my head, Angus. But my heart wants to protect Cassidy. I wish I was more of a praying man, because I could use the comfort right now."

CHAPTER 15

Rosadel knew by the time that breakfast was on the table that Saturday was going to be a tough day. The girls had been moody since learning that prospective owners were coming to meet the kittens. And the full out revolt started this morning.

"I don't like this cereal, Mommy," Lou was first, as usual, to start complaining.

"Well, just eat your toast then," Rosadel was determined to not engage.

"I don't like the toast either," said Lou.

"Then drink your milk and go take care of the litter box. If you're hungry, something will taste good."

"You don't care if I starve," said Lou, and started crying.

This was not the time for tough love. Rosadel picked Lou up and put her in her lap. "Go ahead and cry it out, baby. I know you don't want the kittens to leave, and that your stomach is all upset because you are upset. But they have to go to their forever homes. If you feel like eating something later, you just let me know. I don't want you to starve, but I know what it is like to be too upset to eat."

"Mommy why are you making us give the kittens away if you know it makes us sad?" Gracie looked close to tears too as she asked.

Rosadel held out her arm for Gracie to come over for a hug. "This is how it has to be, Gracie, and I told you all that when we brought the kittens home. We don't have time or money for seven cats. And they wouldn't get the love and attention they need. We have to look at this like how our family is. Everyone you love doesn't live here, do they?"

"No, Pop-Pop and Gee-Jay and Grandma and Grandpa and Uncle Pete, and Uncle Mike and Uncle Donnie and Nanny Bee all live at their own houses," replied Gracie.

"And it will be just like that with the kittens."

"But Mommy," Rosie this time, "The people can come visit us, and we go visit them. The kittens can't come visit."

"That is why Miss Cassidy is bringing people to our house to meet us and the kittens. That way we can make friends and then maybe we will be able to go visit the kittens in their new homes." Rosadel was wishing Clancy hadn't had to go out to the plant this morning, as she surely could use some backup.

"But maybe isn't very good, Mommy," Lou again. "You and Daddy say 'Maybe' to wait to say 'No'."

Rosadel sent up a quick prayer for guidance, and the phone rang. Rosie ran and picked up the phone.

"Hi, Gee-Jay! We're having a bad day. Can you come over with Pop-Pop?" Rosie got right to the point.

"Why are you having a bad day, Rosie?" Jessie wondered what in the world had happened.

"Miss Cassidy is bringing people over to meet the kittens. And Lou is so upset her stomach hurts, and Gracie wants to cry and I'm just mad. And Mommy says that 'maybe' we will get to see the kittens after they leave, but we know what 'maybe' usually means."

Jessie did know what 'maybe' usually meant. "Can I talk to your Mommy for a minute, sweetheart?"

Rosie ran the phone over to Rosadel. "It's Gee-Jay, Mommy, and she wants to talk to you."

"Hi Jessie! What's up?" Rosadel was glad for the distraction.

"Hey, Rosadel, I was calling to see if you were going to the meeting at Holy Redeemer this morning to package up the donations for the woman's shelter and safe house, but I'm guessing not because of Cassidy coming over."

"That's right, Jessie. I wasn't going to be able to go anyway, as Clancy had to go out to the plant this morning."

"Tell you what, I'm going to ask your dad if he wants to hang out with you while I go to Holy Redeemer, it sounds like you could use some backup today."

Rosadel couldn't turn down an offer that good. "Praise the Lord! I would love for Daddy to be here to help with all this emotion. I feel like I'm hanging on by a thread here."

"I'm ready to walk out the door, and your dad can be ready in less than five minutes. We should be there shortly. Just hang on, baby, we're coming to help." Jessie wasted no time in filling Angus in on the situation, and in no time at all they were at Rosadel's house.

By the time they arrived, the girls were playing with the kittens, tears at bay for the time being. "Pop-Pop, Gee-Jay, we're glad you came. Mommy is being mean to us." Lou was in full revolt mode again.

Angus knelt down and gently placed his hands on Lou's shoulders. "Mercy Louise, you may be my granddaughter, but your mommy is my baby. She is never mean. I will not tolerate you talking about her that way."

Lou immediately burst into tears, but Angus was not moved. "You can be as mad or as sad as you want to but saying hateful things about your mother is not acceptable."

Gracie and Rosie just watched, they had never seen their Pop-Pop like this before. Angus continued to gently hold Lou. "Now, I need you to apologize to your mommy, or I need you to go to your room."

Lou was still crying as she obviously debated what she was going to do. "But Pop-Pop, you don't even know why I said it."

"Doesn't matter, kid, Not acceptable. Now what is it going to be? Time out, apology, or both?" Angus had no difficulty being firm when he needed to be.

Lou finally said, "I'll apologize."

Angus turned Lou towards Rosadel and said, "Well, go ahead and apologize then."

Lou was still hiccupping as she said, "I'm sorry, Mommy." Angus turned Lou back around and hugged her. "I love you Lou, but you have to learn that it is not OK to be mean or hurtful just because you are hurting.

Do you think it is easy on Mommy to give these kittens away? It is just as hard for her as it is for you."

Lou turned and looked at Rosadel, "Is it Mommy?"

Rosadel nodded, "Yes, it is, baby. But doing the right thing is hard sometimes, but we still have to do the right thing."

Rosie and Grace moved over to Rosadel and hugged her. "I'm sorry, Mommy," said Grace. "I didn't mean to make everything harder for you."

"Me, either," said Rose.

Jessie knew it was up to her to interrupt the moment and move the girls to a better place. "C'mon and show me the kittens while Pop-Pop and Mommy have a minute together. I have to leave for a meeting at Holy Redeemer, but I don't want to miss seeing them."

The girls and Jessie went into the dining room, and Angus gave Rosadel a long hug. "I hate to be stern with those girls, but they have to learn to not take their pain out on other people. When I think of what you had been through by the time you were their age, and never a problem, I get kind of protective."

Rosadel hugged her dad back tightly. "I felt bad for Lou, but you're right, it is never okay to hurt someone just because you are hurting. I want to protect them too much sometimes, and I feel like I did a terrible thing with fostering these kittens, they are getting their hearts broken."

"Sometimes our hearts have to break, baby. And it is better that they learn how to love and let go as children than to have to learn that as adults." Angus knew better than most that love and pain often went together. "Do you think I could have married Jessie and be as happy as I am now if I had stayed afraid of the pain that might come if I lost her like I lost your mother? When we choose love, we open ourselves up to pain, but we also open ourselves up to immense joy. We have to trust in God and appreciate the joy to live a full life."

"I know, Daddy. And I know in my head that I am doing the right thing for the girls, but my heart hurts when they hurt, and I wish I could protect them from that." Rosadel was getting a little teary-eyed again.

Angus gently kissed her forehead. "June Bug, every parent wants to protect their children from pain, and none of us can do it. What we do instead is teach them that pain is part of life, and we have to learn from it, and allow our pain to give us more compassion for others when they are hurting. Your job is not to protect your girls from pain, but to teach them that pain isn't a reason, or an excuse or a validation. Pain is part of life. When we hurt, we may want to strike out, but that is not the solution. Admit to the pain, ask for help, and accept that sometimes, there is no relief in sight, so you seek comfort, because it is all you can get."

Rosadel rested her head on Angus's chest. "I wish sometimes I was a little girl again. You always made the world safe and not scary for me, even when Mama was dying. I don't know how you did it, but you still make me feel safe and not scared. Thank you, Daddy."

"You'll have me crying in a minute, June Bug, we need to stop this. How about a cup of coffee for me? I hadn't finished mine when Jessie rushed me out of the house."

As Rosadel and Angus went into the kitchen for coffee, Jessie was working her magic with the triplets while visiting with the kittens.

As Jessie sat on the floor with the kitten, Snuggles, on her lap while the kitten, Pokey, was trying to fight with her shoelace, she decided to share a story with the girls.

"Did you guys know that Paw-Paw Daniel and Maw-Maw Rachel used to live on a farm?"

She got their interest right away with that one.

"Really?" asked Lou. "With cows, and pigs and horses?"

"Really," replied Jessie. "Cows, pigs, horses, chickens, and a few goats. Plus, some crops, like tomatoes and cucumbers and squash and cauliflower and broccoli. It wasn't a really big farm, and Paw-Paw had another job, but he and Maw-Maw and Paw-Paw's brothers and nephews all shared in the work."

"How old were you?" asked Grace. "Did you like it?"

"We lived on the farm until I was about 11 or 12," replied Jessie. "I liked it a lot, most of the time, but when I was about seven, I didn't like it at all."

"Why not?" asked Rosie.

"Well, it started when my dad, that would be Paw-Paw Daniel, and his brothers decided it was getting to be too much trouble to have all those animals, and they started to sell them. I didn't spend a lot of time with the cows or pigs, and they were keeping the horses, so at first, I didn't think it would change much for me."

"But what happened?" asked Lou.

"Well, when you have a farm, you always have barn cats. And the number of cats you have is always changing, but you never have more cats than you need. And the cats live in the barn, and that is their home."

"Well, I loved all the cats. And when the brothers started selling the animals, they had a buyer who wanted to buy the animals, and the barn they lived in, and some of the land. And so, they sold that barn, and all the cats, that lived in that barn, who I loved, got sold with the barn."

"All of them?" asked Rosie. "How many?"

"There were eight," replied Jessie. "And I was heartbroken. I cried, and I fussed, and I told my Mama that I was going to go over to that barn and get those cats and bring them back to the horse barn that we still had."

"Did you do that?" asked Grace.

"No, I didn't, because my Mama, Maw-Maw Rachel, sat down and taught me a very important lesson."

"What did she teach you?" asked Grace.

"Mama told me that those cats were right where they belonged, and they were happy. And I told her that I wasn't happy, and I loved those cats and I wanted them to be with me. And Maw-Maw Rachel told me this. She said, 'The love in your heart wasn't put there to stay, love isn't love till you give it away'. And then she told me what that meant. Maw-Maw Rachel told me that love is only real when you want what is best for who you love, not what is best for you. So, what was best for those cats was to stay living in the barn they lived in and have new humans to take care of them."

Lou was the most insightful, and the most argumentative of the triplets, and she got right to the point. "But our kittens have lived here their whole lives, so our story is different."

"Yes, they have, Lou. But here is the thing. Does your Mommy still live with Pop-Pop? Does your Daddy still live with Grandma Harriet and Grandpa George?"

"No," Lou answered hesitantly, because she knew something she wouldn't like was coming.

"That's right," said Jessie, "Because children are supposed to grow up and leave their parents and make families of their own. Kittens are the same. These kittens are supposed to leave Holly and have families of their own."

"And if we love them, we want what is best for them," said Rosie.

"Even if it makes us sad," added Grace.

"That's right," said Jessie. "And I'm very proud of you for understanding that."

"But I still feel all tangled up and mad inside," said Lou.

"I know, Lou, and it will take time for that sad, tangled up feeling to go away. And you will cry. And miss the kittens. But if you remind yourself that the best way to love them is to want what is best for them, some day in the future you will feel better. And your mom is right. If you meet and make friends with the people the kittens go to live with, you can keep in touch with them and always know how your kittens are doing."

"I'll never like it," said Lou.

"And didn't I start this story by telling you how I didn't like it at all when I lost my barn cats? Life isn't always the way we like it to be. But if we put love first, it always works out in the end." Jessie believed that with all her heart, so it was easy to encourage the girls to trust her.

"Gee-Jay, I'm going to try really hard to love the kittens enough to let them go to forever homes," said Gracie. "But I think I'm going to cry a lot too."

Jessie held out her arms for the girls to come in for a hug. "Come on and hug me, all of you. I know that you will cry, but you will be okay. And me and Pop-Pop will be here as much as you need us with hugs and kisses. And Mommy and Daddy always love you too."

Rosadel and Angus came into the dining room in time to witness the group hug.

"How's my girls?" asked Angus.

"We're good, Pop-Pop." said Rosie. "Did you know Gee-Jay used to live on a farm?"

Angus looked at Jessie and saw the love shining in her eyes, along with a shine of accomplishment. "Well, as a matter of fact, Rosie, I did know that."

"But did you know her cats got sold with a barn and she was sad?" asked Gracie.

"You got me there kid," replied Angus. "I didn't know that."

"And Maw-Maw Rachel says, 'The love in your heart wasn't put there to stay, love isn't love till you give it away'." Added Lou.

"And here I thought it was Oscar Hammerstein," said Angus. Rosadel and Jessie laughed, and the girls looked puzzled.

"Never mind Pop-Pop being silly," said Rosadel. "That is a very good thing for you girls to remember. "Rosadel turned to Jessie. "Thank you for sharing with the girls. They seem much calmer now."

"Glad I could help, Rosadel, but this is just a temporary lull. The next weeks will be emotional. Please don't hesitate to call on me and your Dad anytime you need us to help manage the emotion. We love you all and know how hard this is. Now, I need to get out of here and over to Holy Redeemer. I need some good-bye kisses and hugs."

As the girls hugged and kissed Jessie goodbye, Rosadel reached over and whispered in Angus' ear. "It sure was a great day for our family when you married Jessie."

Angus smiled as he put his hand on Jessie's back to walk her to her car. "And an even greater day for me, June Bug."

It was no time at all until Cassidy arrived at the house with the first family wanting to meet the kittens.

As soon as the doorbell rang, all three girls rushed to open it. Cassidy was waiting outside with a tall African-American woman and a little girl.

"Hi Miss Cassidy!" said Lou. "We've been waiting for you."

Gracie looked at the little girl. "Don't you go to Holy Redeemer?"

Rosadel arrived just as she heard Gracie's question.

"Please come in. Gracie, let our guests get inside before we start asking questions." Rosadel stuck out her hand, "Hi, I'm Rosadel Marshall. Thanks for being interested in adopting one of the kittens."

The woman with Cassidy shook Rosadel's hand saying, "Nice to meet you Rosadel. My name is Bethany Williams, and this is my daughter, Michelle."

Rosadel turned to Michelle, "Nice to meet you, Michelle. Do you go to Holy Redeemer?"

"Yes, Ma'am," Michelle responded shyly. "We just moved here, and I am in second grade in Mrs. Russo's class."

Rosadel gestured to the triplets, "This is Lou, Grace and Rosie, my daughters. They are also in second grade, in Miss Dunn's class."

"Hi, Michelle," Lou said, "Do you want to come and meet the kittens?"

And with that the three girls went into the dining room. Angus came out of the kitchen and did a quick double take. "Bethany! What are you doing here? Wait, never mind, you are here about the kittens."

"Daddy, do you know Bethany?" Rosadel knew she shouldn't be surprised, because Angus knew so many people.

"Sure do, June Bug. Bethany just transferred to the plant. She is a quality control expert, in addition to being a control systems engineer. We finally convinced the company we couldn't share one control systems engineer between the plant here and the one up near Baton Rouge, and Bethany took the new position. She and Jessie spend a lot of time together, and she knows Clancy too."

"I wondered if you were related to Clancy when I heard your name is Marshall, but I wasn't sure." Bethany smiled at Rosadel.

"Well, I'm married to him, so I think that counts as related. Why don't we go into the dining room and see how the girls are getting along, and if everything is okay in there, we can go into the kitchen and have some coffee."

Cassidy just watched in wonderment as all of this transpired. She really had never seen anything like the way Rosadel and Angus just made people comfortable.

The girls were busy introducing Michelle to the kittens, one at a time, and filling her in on their different personalities. All four girls appeared to be having a good time and getting along, so the adults retired to the kitchen, but left the door open to the dining room.

Roscoe got up from his bed to greet Cassidy. "Hey, big boy. Good to see you. I had to leave the girls home today, I promise I'll bring them over to see you soon."

Angus smiled. "Not trying to embarrass you Cassidy, but you and Pete sure are a good match. He always greets Roscoe before talking to me too."

Cassidy blushed as she apologized. "I'm sorry Mr. McPherson. I didn't mean to offend you."

"No offense taken, Cassidy, and please, call me Angus. I think it is great the real love you have for animals." Angus turned to Bethany. "How are you settling in to Bayou Beni, Bethany?"

"We're working on it, Angus. I bought a house in Audela and are almost completely unpacked. Michelle is having some difficulty with the transition, and making new friends, so I thought a kitten might help with the loneliness."

"Bethany, I know we just met, but I'd love to arrange a playdate for my girls and Michelle. I have to confess with triplets, I have never had to worry about my girls having friends to play with, but since I was an only child I know how important friends are. Before you leave today, let's set up a playdate either here or at your house for the girls." Rosadel felt bad that she never thought about starting a ministry at Holy Redeemer for new parishioners, and she made a mental note to talk to Bee and Jessie about it.

Bethany looked slightly overwhelmed at the suggestion. Angus reached over and covered her hand. "She just charges in, Bethany. With everything. I've been trying since she was a little girl to convince her to look before she leaps, but my Rosadel always leaps in to help and to make others feel more comfortable and welcome. I know it can be a little intense, but I can vouch for her, she means well."

"Daddy!" Rosadel flushed. "I'm sorry, Bethany, if I made you uncomfortable. Daddy is right, I do jump in with both feet to try to help before I even understand if help is needed. Take your time and let me know if you decide the girls should have a play date."

Bethany struggled to put into words what she was feeling. "Rosadel, I'd love to set up a playdate for the girls. It is just that for the past couple of months, I've been feeling so isolated, and now all of a sudden, one phone call to the St. Elizabeth Animal Shelter, and I'm finding the community I need. It's just a little overwhelming."

Cassidy reached over and placed her hand on Bethany's. "It is what my dad has always told me. If you want to make your life better do something good for the world. The good will come back to you."

At that point, Michelle came in from the dining room. "Mommy, can I come over and play with my new friends someday? They want me to come over any time."

Bethany started to laugh as she reached out to Michelle. "Of course, you can, Baby. Mrs. Rosadel and I were just talking about getting a play date set up."

Lou, Rosie and Grace came spilling into the kitchen. "Mommy, Michelle has to go to after school care every day until her Mommy gets off work. Don't you think she could come to our house some days? We would still do our homework and everything." Lou was very excited to have a new friend.

"And Mommy," added Grace, "Then we could play all kinds of games that work better with four people and you could have some private time."

Angus looked at Rosadel. "Private time?" he asked. "Where in the world did Grace pick up that one."

Grace answered Angus directly. "We learned about it at school Pop-Pop. Miss Dunn said that everyone needs some private time to think about things and sometimes to pray and sometimes to do things they like to do. Miss Dunn said our parents are always making sure we get what we need, so we should try to find things to do so that our parents can have some private time."

"Well," Angus replied, "Sounds like Miss Dunn is a very smart lady. And it sounds like you girls are having fun together."

"Pop-Pop, did you know Michelle used to live in Texas? And that her Daddy lives in heaven?" Rosie wanted to have a part of the conversation too.

Rosadel and Cassidy both glanced at Bethany and Michelle, while Angus answered. "Yes, I did know that Rosie, because Mrs. Williams works with me at the plant. Mrs. Williams works with and knows your Daddy too."

Lou turned to Bethany. "Mrs. Williams, do you really know our Daddy?"

"I sure do," said Bethany. "But not as well as I know your grandfather. I've only been at the plant for a little while, and I've had more work in common with your grandfather and Jessie. But your Daddy has always been very pleasant to me."

"Daddy is more quiet than Mommy and Pop-Pop. They never met a stranger." supplied Grace.

As all the adults laughed at that little bit of wisdom, Rosadel couldn't help but ask where that came from.

"Grandma Harriet," said Lou. "She said that you and Pop-Pop and Grandpa George just talk to everybody like you knew them forever. She said Daddy is more like her, and she hasn't really figured Uncle Pete out yet."

Cassidy thought that was funny coming from Harriet. From Cassidy's perspective, Pete was outgoing and friendly to everyone, but mostly, she saw him in his role as veterinarian. Maybe he and Cassidy were more alike than she knew.

Michelle leaned against Bethany, "Mommy, I really like two of the kittens, Pokey and Boo. Do you think we could have two? Then they could be company for each other and we could each have one to pet when we watch TV at night."

Bethany rolled her eyes. "I don't know, Michelle. Let Mommy think about it."

"Tell you what, Bethany. I'll tell the next couple of people that both of them are promised, just in case. We can always change our minds later and put one of them back on the available list." Rosadel didn't want to encourage Michelle, but she also didn't want to see the little girls heart broken.

Cassidy looked at her watch. "I hate to rush this, but I've got to get back to the clinic to meet the next family and bring them over."

"Bethany, if you came in your own car, you and Michelle are welcome to stay awhile and visit. The girls are really enjoying having a new friend to play with." Rosadel was looking forward to getting to know Bethany better as well.

"We did come in a separate car, but I have to get to the store and do my grocery shopping and get home and get going on housework. When you work all week, the weekends stay full of more work, but thanks for the offer." Bethany really was excited that maybe she and Michelle would finally start making connections in the community.

Rosadel knew she was being a little pushy but went for it anyway. "Why don't we set up a playdate for Wednesday for the girls after school? I'll pick up Michelle when I pick them up, and then you both can have dinner with us after work. Will that work?"

Bethany thought about her schedule, and they made a date.

"Don't forget to send a note to school with Michelle that I can pick her up," Rosadel advised. "Even for me they won't let me pick up a child without a permission slip."

"I won't forget," promised Bethany. "Let's go, Michelle. Say good-bye to the kittens and the people and let's get on the road."

As good-byes were said and Bethany, Michelle and Cassidy left the house, Angus put his arm around Rosadel. "Now I'll bet that went far better than you imagined."

"It sure did, Daddy," Rosadel couldn't actually believe how good it had gone.

"Mommy, we already made a new friend!" said Lou. "And if she takes two kittens, they will always be our friends too."

"Jessie said if you try to do everything out of love good things happen, and she sure was right." Grace said

Angus knelt down and faced the girls. "Jessie was 100% right. When we act in love, good things follow."

"I felt sad for Michelle that her Daddy is in heaven," said Rosie. "She said she doesn't remember him, because she was only a baby when he died. She misses her family back in Texas and is kind of mad at her mom for moving here."

Rosadel looked at Angus for more information, but he shook his head gently, indicating this was not the right time for a conversation.

Angus instead talked to the girls. "Thanks for telling us that about Michelle, Rosie. It is hard being a single parent. You know it was just me and your Mommy for a lot of years, and I was lucky that Mommy never was angry with me. Bethany had good reasons for moving here with Michelle, and it would be good for you girls to help Michelle be happier with the move by being good friends to her."

"We'll be great friends, Pop-Pop. We are like you and never met a stranger." said Lou.

The kittens were put away for some quiet time, and the girls went upstairs to play quietly until Cassidy got back with the next family.

Rosadel and Angus cleaned up the kitchen in a harmony perfected over years of doing chores together.

"If I drink coffee with all four families, I'm never going to sleep tonight. I guess I could switch to decaf." Rosadel wanted to make sure everyone that came to meet the kittens was welcomed properly.

"I think that is a good idea, June Bug. You're a little intense without a caffeine load. Don't want to go scaring people away."

"Daddy, I've never scared anyone away in my life. But you are right. I'm like a chipmunk on speed with too much coffee. I feel so sad for Bethany. Can you tell me more about her?"

"Well, I can tell you her husband, Derek, was killed in Iraq. But I think in the interest of you two developing a friendship on your own terms, the rest of Bethany's story should come from Bethany." Angus didn't want to misrepresent anything that he knew, and he also knew that Bethany would probably share more details with Rosadel than he had.

"That is probably a good idea, Daddy. We probably won't get too much time to talk on Wednesday, but maybe I can have Clancy watch the girls next weekend, and Bethany and I can go out to lunch or something to really get to know each other." Rosadel was excited at the prospect of making a new friend, especially a friend with a daughter the same age as the triplets.

The next family interested in a kitten was the mother of an eighth-grade student at Holy Redeemer, who was looking for a kitten for her mother, whose elderly cat had recently died. The girls were quiet while the two women played with the kittens, and it looked like Cuddles found a forever home. As the women were about to leave, Lou spoke up.

"Mrs. Devereaux, we would like to stay in touch with Cuddles after he comes to live with you, would that be alright with you?"

Miriam Devereaux smiled in delight. "Of course, it would. My grandchildren are all boys, and I've missed having little girls to visit with. You just tell your Mommy whenever you want to come over, and I'll make sure to have plenty of cookies to spoil you with."

"We don't need cookies or anything, Mrs. Devereaux, we just want to see Cuddles." Grace thought it was important to tell Mrs. Devereaux that.

"No worries, it will give me an excuse to eat cookies too. I think I am going to change Cuddles name to Marshall. That way I'll think of your family every time I talk to him."

Cassidy couldn't believe how well this day was going and promised to be back soon with the next prospective owner.

Unfortunately, the next prospective owner called and cancelled, so that left just one more visit on the day.

The final visitor was Grace White, the third-grade teacher. "Mrs. White, Mrs. White!" Lou ran up and gave her a hug. "We are so glad you want a kitten. We can ask you at school every day!"

Grace and Rosie ran up to give and receive hugs as well. Grace White gave each girl a hug before standing up to greet Rosadel. "Even though they haven't reached third grade yet, I have gotten to know your girls and I think they are delightful. You are doing a great job with them."

Rosadel blushed a little as she thanked Grace White. "I appreciate the plan you helped Miss Dunn with. So far, it is really helping with impulse control."

Grace White smiled at the girls. "So, which kitten do you think should come live at my house?"

And with that, Mrs. White and the triplets went into the dining room to meet the kittens.

Cassidy smiled at Rosadel. "I had no idea you were friends with Grace White."

"Actually, Cassidy, seeing that the calls you got all came from the Holy Redeemer PTA meeting, Bethany might be the only person I didn't know. Holy Redeemer has been my family for my whole life." Rosadel was glad of that too.

Cassidy nodded. "I've never been part of a church family, but you sure make it look attractive. Pete invited me to come to Mass with him on Sunday and then go out to brunch. I'm more excited than ever now to get to know more about Holy Redeemer, and the Catholic Church."

Angus was proud of Rosadel for not pouncing on that piece of information and running with it. "Clancy and I always go to brunch with Daddy, Jessie and the girls after Mass. We promise we won't invite you to join us and mess up your date."

Cassidy blushed as she answered. "We're bringing Grandma Bessie with us, so it wouldn't mess up our date. But it might be overwhelming for Grandma Bessie on her first outing to have so many people. If she does well tomorrow, maybe another Sunday we could join you."

Rosadel liked the sound of that. "We'd love that Cassidy. And you're right. It will be exhausting for Ms. Chauvin to go to Mass and to brunch without adding the chaos that seems to follow the Marshall triplets. I'll make sure to say 'Hello' to Ms. Chauvin at church. It will be great to see her at Holy Redeemer again. We have missed her."

Grace White looked up from the kittens. "Did I hear you talking about Bessie Chauvin? How is she?"

Cassidy answered. "She is doing great, Mrs. White. She is using her hand well again and is using a walker most of the time. She can self-transfer from the bed to the walker to a chair and everything. We still like to have someone nearby when she transfers, but her recovery has been amazing. The only thing is that her speech has not come back. I've gotten contact information for her nephew in Texas and will be calling him to plot a new strategy for her therapy."

"That sounds wonderful, Cassidy. If you don't mind my asking, how did you come to be so involved with Bessie?"

"Well, it was because of her little dog, Sophie. When Bessie had her stroke, the EMTs who answered the 911 call called the shelter to let us know that there was a dog at the property. I went over with the police to pick up the dog and met Sophie. Well, it was obvious Sophie was well loved, and didn't belong in the shelter, even temporarily. So, I brought her to my house as a foster. The next day, I went to the hospital to tell Ms. Chauvin that I would take care of Sophie until she could come home from the hospital. As soon as Ms. Chauvin was transferred to Our Lady of Lourdes, and I could bring Sophie to visit her, I started visiting every couple of days with Sophie, and my other senior rescue dog, Maggie. We just clicked with each other, and now I call Ms. Chauvin Grandma Bessie, because she is just like a grandmother to me.""

Grace White reached out and hugged Cassidy. "Thank you, Cassidy. You may not have been raised as part of a church family, but you are surely doing God's work on earth."

"I've decided the little striped cat the girls call Snuggles will be my cat. And her name will be Elyse. I'm excited for the next few weeks to pass quickly so that I can bring her home."

"You can come visit her any time, Mrs. White," said Rosie. "We will always be glad to see you."

"Thank you, Rosie, and I may take you up on that, but I'll check with your Mommy first."

Rosadel was always happy to spend time with Grace White, so she echoed Rosie's invitation.

"Just call to make sure we're home, Mrs. White, we'll be glad to see you."

Clancy got home from the plant just as Cassidy and Grace White were leaving. The girls ran up to Clancy as he opened the door.

"Daddy! Daddy!"

"We made us a new friend today," said Lou. "Her name is Michelle and she may get two kittens."

"And Cuddles is going to be named Marshall, and live with Mrs. Devereaux, and we are going to go visit." added Grace

"And Mrs. White is going to take Snuggles and name her Elyse." Rosie wasn't going to be left out of the information exchange.

"Well, it sounds like quite a morning here," said Clancy as he leaned in to kiss Rosadel hello.

"You have no idea," Rosadel said as she kissed him back.

Just then Clancy noticed Angus. "Hey Angus, didn't realize you were here. Where's Jessie?"

"She's at a meeting at Holy Redeemer, but she should be back soon. You're stuck with me until then."

Clancy laughed. "Nope, just means we're not outnumbered for a little while."

All the adults laughed while the girls pretended to be mad. Cassidy and Grace White took their leave, and the girls busied themselves putting the kittens away.

"We had quite a morning, Clancy. That is why Daddy is here. But it is all okay now. I'll tell you all about it over lunch."

CHAPTER 16

The morning had passed quickly for the volunteers at Holy Redeemer, and over 60 boxes of supplies were ready to be shipped to various women's shelters and the St. Elizabeth safe house. Marie Theriot was doing a last-minute check of the boxes to make sure that all were properly labeled so that they would get to the correct destinations.

Jessie noticed that Marie was separated from the other women, and decided it was a good time to try to talk to her privately.

Marie startled slightly when Jessie spoke her name. "I'm sorry, Marie, I didn't mean to startle you."

Marie smiled as she replied. "Not your fault, Jessie. One of the lingering after effects of years of systemic abuse is an enhanced startle reflex. I've learned so much about myself these last two years. It is a tremendous relief to no longer be angry. If I could just get past the guilt for the mistakes I made, and the shame for letting myself be a victim for so long, it would be a wonderful thing."

"Well," Jessie replied, "I think you are amazing. The way you have pulled this group together to raise awareness of domestic violence, and the way you have committed yourself to helping others find a way out of abuse is impressive. I know the journey has been long and hard for you, but you are an inspiration to the women we are helping. You never gave up, Marie. And you never stopped believing in God, even though it had to feel like He abandoned you. We are lucky to have you as part of the Holy Redeemer family."

Marie was obviously touched by Jessie's words. "Thank you, Jessie. I'm trying my best to find peace through this volunteer work. I'm so grateful that Bee reached out to me and helped me find a way out of the darkness I had lived in for so long. Father LeBlanc and my counselors at Catholic Charities have helped so much, but I still have a long way to go. I'm hoping having Max will help even more. I think it is good for me to have a living creature depending on me again. It means I can't ever go back to the darkness, because Max is depending on me"

Jessie knew she had to get to the point quickly, before they were interrupted. "Marie, I have something to tell you, that you may need to talk to your counselor or Father LeBlanc about. In a roundabout way, Max is the reason you may have a problem."

"What is it, Jessie? Is there something about Max I don't know?" Marie looked truly worried.

"It is not Max, Marie. It is Cassidy. Cassidy mentioned you adopting Max to her dad, Prescott, and he immediately wondered if you were the same Marie Theriot whose daughter he married. Prescott went to Angus to see what he knew about you through Holy Redeemer, and when he talked to me, I knew you were the same Marie Theriot."

Marie paled, but she was not shocked. She knew this might be an outcome or approaching Cassidy. "What does Prescott want?" Marie asked.

"He just wants to make sure neither Cassidy or Sandra gets hurt. I don't know how well you ever knew Prescott, as he and Sandra got together after you were estranged from her, but Prescott is one of the world's good guys. Even though he and Sandra have been divorced for more than twenty years, he still is very protective of her. And he is a fierce papa bear when it comes to Cassidy." Jessie felt bad for Marie, that anyone would think she meant harm to her daughter or granddaughter, she knew she had to be honest with Marie.

Marie asked what seemed to be the next logical question. "What is Prescott planning to do?"

"Angus talked to him earlier this week and told Prescott that it is not his place to do anything. This belongs to you, and Sandra and Cassidy. I know Prescott well enough to know he will respect that, but once one person knows, Marie, it is just a matter of time."

Marie looked over at the rest of the women. "Jessie, can we go out for lunch after this to talk more? I don't want to be overheard, but I feel like I need some time to process this with a friend."

Jessie reached out and squeezed Marie's hand. "Thank you for trusting me as your friend, Marie. I'll call Angus and let him know we are going to lunch. He is at Rosadel and Clancy's house. I may need to drop off my car there so that Angus can go home, would that be okay?"

"I don't want to put you out, Jessie. Maybe I should work though this on my own." Marie still felt the weight of always being viewed as an encumbrance.

"Nonsense, Marie. Just let me call Angus, and then we'll know what to do next." Jessie softened her words with a quick hug.

Angus was happy to hang out at Rosadel and Clancy's house for a few more hours, as he and Clancy had decided to tackle trimming some of the trees in the backyard.

"I don't know how long I'll be, sweetheart, but I'll be home as soon as I can." Jessie was happy to tell Marie they could take as long as they needed for lunch.

Jessie and Marie decided to meet at the Hungry Pelican. It was a local seafood restaurant, with high backed booths lining the walls, so it was a perfect place for a private conversation. The food was very good too.

As Marie and Jessie sat down in a booth in the corner of the restaurant, Marie folded her hands on the table and took a deep breath.

"How much of my story to you know, Jessie?" Marie asked.

"Well, I know that you were abused by your husband, Burl, and that to protect Sandra, you allowed the two of you to become estranged. I know you moved here to try to reconcile with your daughter but have never been able to take that last step." Jessie outlined the bare bones.

"That is the spare truth, Jessie, but I think the part of the story that has kept me from reaching out to Sandra is what I need to talk about with a friend instead of a counselor." Marie felt in her heart that Jessie was the right person to talk to.

"I was orphaned by Hurricane Hilda in 1964. The tornado that struck Galliano killed my mother and father, and my little dog, Bijou. I went to live with my grandmother in White Castle, but she died when I was a senior in high school. Burl Theriot charmed a poor orphan girl with no one into becoming his wife. He didn't show his true colors until I was pregnant with Sandra. He had been very controlling, and had separated me from my friends, but was never abusive. While I was pregnant with Sandra the ranting and raging started, and when Sandra was a baby, the physical abuse started. I was able to be a normal loving mother when Burl was at work and I was home, but when Sandra was three, Burl made me go back to work. Any time I showed affection to Sandra, it meant a beating for me and for her. I felt like it was my fault, and that there was no one to turn to. So, I stopped showing affection to Sandra, and only I got beaten. Burl was so careful and controlled. There were never bruises on my face, and rarely on my arms. I tried to protect Sandra and be invisible. I know she knew her Daddy beat me. I know she became a ghost in our house. I know she moved out as soon as she could, and I was afraid to contact her and bring her back into the circle of Burl's wrath. What she doesn't know is how often Burl threatened me with Sandra if I tried to leave him. He told me he would get custody, and then she would be his punching bag. I was too afraid to do anything but believe him." Marie had been carefully folding and unfolding a napkin while she spoke.

Jessie placed her hands on Marie's before she spoke. "You know that you were a psychological prisoner, don't you, Marie? You know that Burl used the classic tactics to separate you from support groups, and then to trap you with him and his abuse. You did the best you could in a terrifying situation. And you did save Sandra. She has a wonderful husband, Mark, and three wonderful children. So, you may feel like you failed. But you succeeded in the most important way of all. Your child survived and is living a good life. And you greatly minimized the damage Burl could do to her."

Marie wiped her eyes before continuing. "But I know Sandra felt unloved. I know she thought I didn't love her as much as I loved Burl, and that I chose him over her. I don't know how to explain it all to her."

Jessie thought carefully before she answered. "I would talk to my counselor about that Marie. I don't know if a letter would be better, or if a facilitated meeting would be better. But I think God is forcing your hand to do something now."

Marie nodded. "I've been praying and praying for God to lead me to an answer. To either show me I should give up or show me it is time to come out of the shadows. I think this is God's answer, now I have to be brave enough to follow through."

Jessie smiled. "I prayed for either peace with my single status, or to meet my future husband, and then when I met Angus I was terrified. My Mama had to set me straight, or I would have let my chance at happiness pass me by. I think we are all the same. When what we pray for doesn't look like what we expected, we are afraid to trust it."

"I'm embarrassed to admit that I've always had the fantasy that I would be in the grocery, or the mall, and Sandra would walk up to me and say 'Mother?' and I would open my arms and we would hug and cry and act like we were in a Hallmark Channel movie." Marie was able to smile ruefully as she shared her fantasy.

"Oh, Marie. If life could only be a Hallmark Channel movie, there would be no need for the Hallmark Channel." Both Jessie and Marie laughed at that.

"Not to push, Marie, but do you plan to do anything about Prescott?" Jessie knew she needed to report back.

"I think I need to talk to him myself, Jessie. I'll write my number down so that you can give it to him. I'm not proud to say that when Burl died I used some of the money to hire a private investigator to find Sandra, and I also paid him to research Prescott. If he was a threat to my granddaughter, I was planning to come out fighting. What I found instead is that he is a real asset to the community and everyone that knows him. My counselor says that I have to start to learn to talk to men as well as women about my past, because men are important in the battle against domestic violence. I have only ever talked to women and Father LeBlanc. I think talking to Prescott would be good for both of us."

"I think so too, Marie. I'll be sure to give him your number. I think you two will both feel better after you talk."

At the point, Marie and Jessie's food arrived, and they concentrated on food over conversation.

◆ ◆ ◆

The Hungry Pelican was busy that afternoon, and unbeknownst to each other, both Pete and Cassidy were in separate booths. Cassidy had picked up Candy for a sister's lunch, and Pete's vet tech, Lindy, had asked him to have lunch with her after the clinic closed at noon, as she had something to talk to him about. Pete wasn't surprised that Lindy wanted to talk. They had been friends for practically their entire lives, and Lindy had been obviously preoccupied lately.

As Pete and Lindy sat down at their booth, Cassidy and Candy arrived at the restaurant, and were sat at a booth on the other side of the restaurant, near where Jessie and Marie Theriot were seated. As the hostess walked Cassidy and Candy to their booth, they passed right by Jessie and Marie. Cassidy was a little surprised to see them together, as she hadn't known that Jessie was friends with Marie Theriot, but then again, Jessie seemed to be like Prescott, and friends with everyone.

"Hi Mrs. Theriot! Hi Jessie! I didn't know you two were friends. How is Max settling in?" Marie was startled to see Cassidy on the heels of the conversation she had been having with Jessie, and had difficulty responding. Jessie jumped in.

"I'll let Marie swallow that mouthful of food before she answers you about Max. Marie and I work together on a committee at Holy Redeemer, and since Angus decided to help Clancy with some tree trimming at Rosadel's, Marie and I decided to have lunch together. How did the kitten introductions go? Did the girls do alright? Were there any problems?"

Cassidy looked puzzled. "No problems. Were you expecting some?'

Jessie hated to tell tales, but she had backed herself into a corner, so she decided to offer the most sanitary version of the morning's activities that she could. "The girls were pretty emotional this morning about the kittens finding new homes, that is why Angus was there for moral support for Rosadel. Sounds like they did fine though."

Cassidy knew how hard it was going to be on the girls to say goodbye to the kittens, so was immediately sympathetic. "They were great. We had a no show, but three out of four people visited, and one of them might take two kittens. So, fingers crossed there are only two more kittens and Momma Cat to find placements for."

Candy was looking at the floor and fidgeting, and Cassidy realized she had never introduced her sister. She put an arm around Candy and said. "This is my sister, Candy. Candy, this is Jessie McPherson and Marie Theriot. I'll explain how I know them over lunch."

Marie had found her voice. "It is nice to see you again, Cassidy, and nice to meet you, Candy. Max is adjusting well to living with me. I crated him while at work yesterday, and he is crated today. He seems very happy in his crate. But in the evening, he is my shadow, and slept on the floor next to my bed on Thursday night, and on the foot of the bed last night. We walk the perimeter of my property a couple of times in the evening, and his leash manners are beautiful. I think we are going to be very happy together."

Cassidy was thrilled. "That's great Mrs. Theriot. Please take advantage of the certificate for a free exam at Pete Marshall's veterinary clinic. I think you will be very pleased with Pete and his staff. I don't want to take up too much of your time, and the hostess needs to seat us and get on to other customers. A pleasure to see you both." With that Cassidy and Candy made their way to their table.

After Cassidy and Candy were out of earshot, Marie looked at Jessie and said. "I need to move fast, now that I have met two of my three grandchildren. Candy looks like my mother. It was all I could do to keep my composure."

Jessie hastened to reassure Marie. "You gave nothing away. But you're right. It is time to find out if Sandra is open to you being part of her children's lives. I'll be praying for all of you Marie, that God's will is for you all to be reconciled."

"Thank you, Jessie. I'll be praying the same thing."

As Cassidy and Candy placed their orders, Candy's curiosity got the better of her. "Who were those ladies? And aren't they kind of old to be your friends?"

Cassidy smiled as she answered. "Friends come in all ages, Candy, but I guess when I was your age I didn't know that as well as I do now. I just met Mrs. Theriot this week when she came to the shelter and adopted Max. She picked him up on Thursday after work. Jessie McPherson is Angus McPherson's wife. Angus McPherson is Rosadel Marshall's dad, and Rosadel is Pete's sister-in-law."

"And the kitten lady," supplied Candy.

"And the kitten lady," agreed Cassidy.

"So, how is it going with Pete?" Candy asked. "And I promise I will not go back to Mom with a full report."

Cassidy laughed, and she and Candy caught up on how things were going with Pete, and with Bessie Chauvin; and Cassidy heard all about the new boy at school that Candy thought was too cute.

Meanwhile at Pete and Lindy's table, the conversation had yet to get started, even though Lindy had invited Pete to lunch because they had to talk. Pete and Lindy had placed their food orders, and now Lindy was drumming her fingers on the table and biting her lip.

Pete placed his hand over Lindy's drumming fingers. "Well, kid, you said you wanted to talk, and here I am."

"I didn't realize how hard this was going to be," replied Lindy, blinking as her eyes filled with tears.

Pete was truly concerned when he saw Lindy's tears. In all the years of their friendship, Pete had only seen Lindy cry when they lost an animal.

"Hey, Lindy, whatever is it, I'm here for you. We've been friends forever. You are as much of a little sister to me as Rosadel. Whatever it is, I'll do whatever I can to help. Just tell me what you need."

Lindy turned her hand over and gripped Pete's. "Pete, I've decided to go to veterinary school, and I've been accepted at LSU for the fall semester. I'm going to move to Baton Rouge to live while I'm at school."

"Lindy! That is awesome. If you want to buy the practice when you graduate, I'll understand. Is that what you were so upset about? Were you afraid I'd be angry?" Pete was a little nervous about what he would do if he had to sell the practice to Lindy, but that was years away, and he wasn't going to borrow trouble. "Did you finish your undergraduate degree? I thought you just had an associate degree from Delgado."

"I have been going to LSU at night and on my flex days to finish my bachelor's degree in biology. With my degree from Delgado, the biology degree from LSU, Dad being an alumnus, and my work at the clinic, I got accepted to start in the fall. The fact my GRE scores were near perfect didn't hurt either."

"That is awesome, Lindy. Are you upset about leaving the clinic? I'll give you hours whenever you want them, and you can do your clinicals with us. Heck, the way Bayou Beni is growing, maybe we can be partners when you graduate." Pete was getting enthused now, thinking about a growing practice.

"No, Pete. That is not what I'm upset about. I guess I'll start with why I decided to go to Delgado and not LSU in the first place. I didn't want to go away to college because I was afraid that having too much freedom would encourage me to make a terrible mistake."

Pete felt like he was walking in an emotional minefield. "Lindy, you've always been level headed, and not impulsive or reckless, what made you think you would make a terrible mistake?"

Lindy decided that the only way to do this was to just come right out and say what was on her mind. "I'm gay, Pete. And I thought if I went away to college I might not be able to resist acting on my temptation to have a relationship. My parents are so Catholic, and they raised me very Catholic, so since I realized I was gay in high school, I thought my only choice was to be celibate and alone to stay a good Catholic. But I don't feel that way anymore. Pope Francis being open to not judging people by their sexual orientation, the Supreme Court making gay marriage the law of the land, I no longer feel like pursuing a relationship would be a terrible mistake. I haven't told my parents yet, as a matter of fact, you are the first person I've told. But I want to learn to date. And have crushes. And hopefully, fall in love and get married. I used to think that I had to forgo all of that, but now I don't. I'm tired of being alone. I'm tired of being lonely. And most of all, I'm tired of pretending to be someone else. Someone that wants to date men. I want to date women, and to find someone to share my life with."

Pete hoped that he was doing a good job of hiding his shock. Of all the things he had imagined, this simply wasn't on the list. Pete knew he had to use his words carefully.

"First of all, Lindy, thank you for trusting me with your honesty. I love you, and I am so grateful that you knew you could share your true self with me without fear of rejection. I'm going to be a little embarrassed as I say what I have to say, but it is important that I tell you this. I know it was a huge step for you to tell me that you are gay, and I am humbled by your faith in our friendship. But it doesn't make any difference to me. "

Pete knew he was turning red as he continued. "I never thought about your sex life before, and I still won't. You are my friend, my sister from another mister, Lindy. You are the best vet tech I know. You are one of the smartest people I know. You have an enormous capacity for compassion and love. Your smile lights up a room. I trust you more than anyone when I need a surgical assist. I would rather consult with you on a difficult patient than other vets I know from school. I know that telling me you are gay is a big deal, but it is a big deal that makes no difference to me. Except I will never try to fix you up with Mike again."

Lindy smiled a little bit, even though she was still very emotional. "I decided to tell my mom and dad tomorrow after church. They know that I got accepted into LSU Veterinary school, and they are very excited. They think that what I have been so nervous about is telling you that I'm leaving. I'm so scared of what is going to happen when I tell them tomorrow."

"Lindy, I can't possibly predict what your parents will do, but I can promise you this. If they throw you out, you can go to the clinic and stay there for the night. Then, you and I will decide if you want to move into my place for a while or go stay somewhere else. You won't be homeless, and you won't be alone." Pete had a brief moment of panic as he wondered how he would explain it to Cassidy if Lindy moved into his house but decided to not worry about that until he had to.

"Pete, I know this puts you in a tough position, but could you keep this between us until after I tell my parents? I'll let you know on Monday how that goes."

"Not a problem, Lindy. I'll be praying for you that everything goes well with your mom and dad. And that after you tell them, you get comfortable telling everyone. At least at the clinic, I'm confident it won't change how anyone treats you or feels about you. Except Hannah will have to stop trying to fix you up with JT."

"Honestly, Pete. The fixing up has been the worst part. I'll be so glad to not have to make up lame excuses for why I don't want to date this son or nephew or brother or cousin."

"Look at the bright side, Lindy, they may all start to try to fix you up with girls you might be interested in." Pete smiled as he said it.

"One step at a time, big guy. I think I'd like to do my own looking for a little while at least." Lindy felt like a huge weight had been lifted from her shoulders. She couldn't believe how accepting Pete was, but then again, she could. His personality and innate goodness had made it easy for Lindy to pick Pete to be the first person she came out to.

Pete and Lindy dug into their food when it came, and talk migrated to lighter subjects. As luck would have it, Pete and Lindy left the Hungry Pelican just minutes before Cassidy and Candy. Pete and Lindy were hugging each other tightly by Lindy's car as Cassidy and Candy walked into the parking lot.

"Cass, isn't that Pete? Who is that girl? Why is he hugging her? Isn't he supposed to be your boyfriend?" Candy was not liking what she was seeing.

Cassidy felt kind of queasy about it herself. "That is Pete, and the girl is Lindy, one of the vet techs at his clinic."

"That doesn't look like a boss-employee hug to me," Candy was agitated. "We should go over there and see what is going on."

Cassidy knew that was not a good idea. "No, Candy. I trust Pete. I'm sure he'll tell me what this was all about when I talk to him tonight."

Candy wasn't so sure. "I hope you're right Cass. I was starting to like Pete, even though I only know him from your stories. I'd hate for him to turn out to be a screw up."

"Me, too, Candy. Now do you still want to come to Our Lady of Lourdes with me to meet Bessie Chauvin?"

"Yes, even though I'm a little nervous. I never met a really old person before. What should I call her?" Mark's parents were in their seventies, and his grandparents were dead, so Candy had never met someone in their nineties before.

"You can call her Ms. Bessie, Candy. And when you meet her you will never believe that she is ninety-two, she is amazing. I know she is going to be very excited to meet you."

CHAPTER 17

Candy was unusually quiet on the drive home from Our Lady of Lourdes. Cassidy didn't worry too much about it, thinking Candy was probably tired. It also allowed Cassidy to think about Pete and Lindy, and to try to talk herself out of making a big deal over it.

When they were about five minutes from Sandra and Mark's house, Candy finally spoke.

"Cassidy, why didn't you tell me Ms. Bessie is black?"

Cassidy was a little surprised by the question. "Um, I didn't think it mattered?" Cassidy felt bad that it might matter to Candy. "Why, Sweetheart? Is it important to you what race Ms. Bessie is?"

Candy sighed. "Not really, Cass. But it is all so confusing now. When I was little, everybody just played together, and nobody talked about race. But lately, race seems to be part of every conversation. I was just thinking about you and Pete and Ms. Bessie going out to brunch tomorrow and worrying that someone would say or do something hateful when you called Ms. Bessie Grandma."

"Let me find a good place to park so we can talk, Candy." As Cassidy maneuvered the car into a strip mall parking lot, she thought about what she wanted to say to Candy. There was no doubt that this was going to be a difficult conversation. "I know things are different than they were when I was your age, Candy. I never worried about going out in crowds with multiple races and ethnic groups. Is it different now?"

"I guess yes and no. At school, the kids mostly hang out by what they do. You know, the sport kids hang together, and the super smart kids hang together, and the band kids hang together, and the kids that don't belong to something just kind of float around the edges. You have white kids that only hang with white kids, and black kids that only hang with black kids, and Asian kids that only hang with Asian kids, and Hispanic kids that only hang with Hispanic kids, and then you have this big pile of kids that are mixed and hang together. I don't know if it is because I'm in eighth grade now, or what, but everyone seems more aware of who you hang out with, and some of the kids are starting to hassle the kids that hang in the mixed crowd. They say ugly things."

Cassidy had a feeling that Bessie being black had given Candy the opening to have a conversation that she had wanted to have for a while. "When I was in school, it was mostly the same. But no one hassled the kids in the mixed group. Still, it was a big deal if there was a mixed couple. Unless they were an athlete and a cheerleader, and then everyone kept their mouth shut."

"That's the same now," said Candy. "It is just...there's this feeling all the time. Like a bunch of kids are walking around angry all the time. And it makes me uncomfortable. There have been a couple of times that kids have come to school with stuff that has been confiscated by the office, and then they send another letter home about what is and isn't allowed on school property."

"What kind of stuff gets confiscated?" Cassidy asked.

"Well, confederate flags are one. And gang stuff, bandanas and pins and stuff that people put on their uniforms to show they belong to a group that isn't supposed to be on campus. Some of the kids are scary. I was in the lunchroom one day, and a group of kids went over to another group of kids and started calling them names. The cafeteria lady called the disciplinarian, and they name callers all got suspended, but that didn't do anything but make them meaner and madder when they came back to school. They're careful to not get seen by adults, but other kids see them. And we're all scared to report what we see."

"Have you talked to Mom and Mark about this?" Cassidy was worried and had no idea what to do.

"Uh-Uh, Cass. I mean, what are they going to do about it? I have to go to school. And you know how Mom can get crazy. She'd start calling the school and demanding stuff and I think they are doing everything they can at school." Candy looked so dejected, it hurt Cassidy's heart.

"Candy, do you feel like it isn't safe at school? Because if that answer is yes, we have to tell Mom and Mark." Cassidy was sure of that, at least.

"I wouldn't say I feel unsafe, just uncomfortable. I don't like it Cass, and it's made me wonder about things. Mom and Dad always say that people are people, and that skin color and where you were born and who you love doesn't matter, but it sure matters a lot to a lot of the people I go to school with. And it sure seems to matter to a lot of other people, based on what I see on TV. I'm wondering if Mom and Dad are right after all."

"Oh, Candy, Mom and Mark are right, it shouldn't matter. And I have never been able to figure out why it does matter to so many people. We're all people trying to share a planet and have a decent life for us and those we love. We have to keep on believing that especially when we are among people who want to make more noise about our differences than our similarities." Cassidy was quiet for a moment. "I hate that things are so tense at school right now. What about your friends? Are they feeling like you are?"

"I've only talked about it to a couple of them that I'm really close to, and they feel the same way. Without ever really talking about it, we all started trying to travel in a pack and make sure no one is ever alone."

"That is a really good strategy, Candy. I honestly don't know what to tell you, other than I think you should talk to a counselor at school about what you are seeing and how you are feeling. Sometimes it is only one or two ringleaders who make the follower kids feel like they can do bad things. It might be that the counselors are not able to do anything because they aren't getting complaints from the students. Do you think you could go talk to one of the counselors?"

"I guess so, Cass, but if it gets out that I went to the counselor, and then something happens to one of the kids, I'm afraid it will come back on me."

Cassidy hated what she was about to recommend, but it seemed like the best choice. "You have to set it up, Candy. Tell your friends that you are having problems with Mom. It is never a lie, you just need to exaggerate a little bit. One of them is bound to recommend you talk to a counselor. Then you talk to the counselor about the problems you are seeing at school instead. That should protect your privacy."

"Cass, if Mom found out, she'd be upset. And hurt. I don't know if I can do that."

"Could you say that you are having problems with me? That since I have a boyfriend you feel like I don't have time for you anymore? And that you need advice on how to talk to me about it?"

Candy was quiet for so long that Cassidy thought she would reject the idea. "Um... Yeah. I think I can make that work, Cass. Thank you."

"Thank you for confiding in me, Candy. And don't worry about me and Grandma Bessie. If anyone has anything rude to say, I can more than stand up for myself. All these years in public relations have taught me a lot about diffusing situations. I'll be fine." Cassidy was sure of that.

"I would hate for Ms. Bessie to be hurt, too, Cass." Candy had really liked Bessie Chauvin.

"Tell you what, Candy. I think that Ms. Bessie probably has stories that would shock us both if she could talk. I know that she went to college in the 1940's when hardly any women went to college, much less black women. Her fiancé was killed in World War II and she never married. I'm not sure what she did, but she made enough money to own a nice home in Bayou Beni. She lived through Jim Crow laws, and the Civil Rights movement. I'll bet Ms. Bessie doesn't get upset too easily by ignorance. And that is what being rude or unkind to someone because they don't look like you. It is just plain old ignorance.

"Now I better get you home before Mom starts calling the police and the hospital."

Candy laughed. "You know she's not that bad, Cass."

"I know, but I needed to make you laugh." Cassidy leaned over and hugged Candy before starting the car and driving on to Sandra and Mark's house.

Cassidy was glad that Sophie and Maggie had slept quietly in their car seats while she drove Candy home and was even more glad that she could use them as an excuse for why she couldn't stay at Sandra and Mark's for dinner.

"I don't know why you have to travel everywhere with those dogs, Cassidy. Normal people don't do that." Sandra could never seem to see Cassidy without having something to complain about.

"I don't go everywhere with them, Mom. But Candy and I took Sophie to see Ms. Chauvin, and I didn't want to stop at home and drop them off and make Candy even later getting home. I promise to come by for dinner one night this week, how does that sound?" Cassidy felt like she spent most of her conversations with Sandra either apologizing or asking forgiveness.

Mark met Cassidy's eye over Sandra's head and gave her the familiar, sorry she is doing this to you look.

"I'll make meatloaf. That is your favorite right?" Sandra really did try hard to be a good mom, it was just hard for her.

"You bet. And your meatloaf is the best, Mom. I'll give you a call tomorrow evening and we can decide which day." Cassidy kissed Sandra, Mark and Candy and yelled goodbye to Chip before heading for home.

As Cassidy drove home she thought about Pete and wondered how to bring up that she had seen him with Lindy. She didn't want to seem like she was spying on him, but knew if she didn't mention seeing him, she would be uncomfortable. Cassidy was also afraid that she would sound accusatory if she brought up seeing Pete and Lindy, and she didn't know if she could pull off bringing it up without acting weird.

She was still thinking about it as she pulled up in front of her house. It looked like Cassidy was going to have to figure out what to do, because Pete was sitting on her front steps.

Pete walked over to the car as soon as Cassidy parked, and helped her get Maggie and Sophie out of their car seats. "Where are Laverne and Shirley?" asked Cassidy.

"They're at home," Pete replied. "I know we don't have plans for tonight, and I'm not going to stay long, but I really wanted to see you."

Cassidy couldn't help the sense of dread that came over her. Pete and Lindy were a thing, and he was here to break up with her.

"What's up, Pete? Why did you want to see me so badly?" Cassidy was proud of how calm she was acting.

"Can we go inside? I'd like to give you a big hug, and a kiss, and then sit with you on the couch and tell you about my day if that is alright. And you can tell me how things went with the kittens and with Candy and Ms. Bessie." Cassidy was starting to feel better about whatever Pete wanted to talk about, and they went inside.

Cassidy didn't think she was imagining that Pete kissed her with more passion than usual after they were inside the house. As they sat down on the couch, Pete kept Cassidy close by his side.

"Emotional day, Cass. And I hope I said and did the right things. My vet tech, Lindy, got accepted at LSU Veterinary School, and will start her classes in the fall. I offered her the opportunity to buy the practice when she graduates, as it was her dad's. I know that was the right thing to do, but now I'm worried that the practice won't be big enough for two vets, and then what? And Lindy shared some other personal stuff that I have to respect her request for me to keep private, but I know I was way out of my league when it comes to advice. Lindy and I have been friends forever, and I am humbled that she would come to me, but I'm just a guy. I'm not very good at navigating emotional situations. I have brothers. We played football in the yard and didn't discuss feelings."

Cassidy hugged Pete as she snuggled into his chest. "I'm sure you did fine, Pete. You always do with me. I saw you and Lindy in the parking lot at the Hungry Pelican, that is where I took Candy for lunch. You guys were hugging, and I didn't want to interrupt, because it looked pretty emotional."

Pete was quiet for a moment as he let Cassidy's words soak in. "Thanks for telling me that, Cassidy, and thanks for trusting me that Lindy and I were together as friends."

Cassidy chuckled a little. "Candy wanted me to confront you. She got a little ferocious at the idea you could be a two-timer."

Pete pulled Cassidy away from him so that he could look her directly in the eyes. "You know I would never do that to you, don't you Cassidy? I'm not that kind of guy. I wouldn't be pursuing you if I didn't think we have a future. I've dated other girls casually, and they always knew it was casual. There is nothing casual about this for me, I want to invest in us and see if we have what it takes to be like my mom and dad or Rosadel and Clancy."

Cassidy felt the last of her doubts melting away. "I want that too, Pete. I'll be honest. I worry that I don't know how to be half of a good couple. I never saw a marriage that was an even partnership. I have always felt like Mark is too good to be true, and I don't know how he has put up with my mother for all these years. I'm afraid that I'll be like my mother and be impossible to live with."

Pete pulled Cassidy close again. "I'm not sure if my feelings should be hurt because you think Mark is too good to be true and I'm not, or if I should be shaking my head because you think you could be impossible to live with. Cassidy, I swear to God I'm not making this up. My mom has told all of us boys our whole lives that everyone is impossible to live with. But when you love someone enough, you find a way to live with them anyway. That is what dating is for. It is to find out if you love someone enough to live with them even if they are impossible. Obviously, Mark loves your mom like that. Now, tell me about your day with Candy."

Cassidy sat up again so that she could face Pete. "Mostly, it was good. We had a nice lunch, even if Candy did want to call you out for hugging Lindy. We had a good visit with Grandma Bessie, but then things got a little uncomfortable on the drive back to Mom and Mark's."

"What happened?" asked Pete.

"Well. Candy asked me why I had never told her Bessie is black. And that started a whole conversation about race and racial tension, and some problems at Candy's school. I have complete sympathy with you for feeling out of your depth, because I am terrified I gave Candy the wrong advice."

"What did you advise her to do?" Pete asked.

"Long story short, I told her to talk to one of the school counselors. She was afraid that somehow talking to a counselor could get her in trouble with the scary kids if something disciplinary happened to one of them. So, I told her to talk to her friends about having a problem with me ignoring her now that I have a boyfriend. I know one of them will suggest she talk to a counselor, and that can be the cover for the real conversation. I hope I did the right thing."

"I think pointing Candy to a counselor is the only right answer, unless she is willing to talk to her mom or dad. And I hate to hear about racial tension at her school. We really didn't have a lot of issues when I was in high school. And all I remember about middle school was how embarrassing it was when my voice changed." Pete was truly disappointed to hear that things had changed so much.

"I know, Pete. It wasn't like that for me either. I hate the thought that Candy has to deal with that sort of tension in school. It feels like society has gone backwards instead of forwards sometimes. Now I'm really wishing Grandma Bessie could talk. I know she has lived through enough to find the right words to encourage me, because I'm having a hard time finding them for myself."

Pete hugged Cassidy tighter. "My mom always says that giant steps forward are always followed by small steps back, but we keep making progress. I want to believe this is a small step back. Think about all the friends we have, and all the people you know who race doesn't matter to. I'm hoping that it is a small but loud group at Candy's school, and that the problem gets addressed sooner rather than later."

"I hope so too, Pete. I hope so, too."

CHAPTER 18

Cassidy knew that Bessie Chauvin had been a parishioner of Holy Redeemer prior to her stroke, but she didn't realize that bringing Bessie to Mass on Sunday morning would be like appearing with a celebrity.

As Cassidy and Pete helped Bessie out of Pete's van and set her up with her walker, people from all over the church parking lot surrounded them. Cassidy knew she would never forget the smile on Bessie's face as person after person hugged her and welcomed her back. It was a good thing that they had arrived early, because it took almost twenty minutes to get from the car into church.

As Pete and Cassidy got Bessie settled into the pew, and her walker folded out of the way, Rosadel, Clancy and the girls came into church and settled into their usual pew. Angus and Jessie slipped into the pew right behind Pete, Cassidy and Bessie.

Although Bessie attended mass every day in the chapel at our Lady of Lourdes, it was obvious to Cassidy that coming to Holy Redeemer had really given Bessie a spark. She had walked confidently with her walker into church and was sitting and standing as required during mass. Cassidy tried to talk Bessie out of kneeling during the consecration, but Bessie was determined to kneel, and got up with limited assistance from Pete.

But the best moment of all was when Pete leaned over at the greeting of peace, and kissed Bessie cheek, saying, "Peace be with you." Without missing a beat, Bessie replied "And with your spirit." Granted, her speech was slurred and whispery, and if Pete hadn't known what to listen for, he might have missed it. As it was, he just about lifted Bessie up in the air when he heard that whispery sound.

Cassidy was on the other side of Bessie and was doing her best to follow along with the unfamiliar church service. She knew something dramatic had happened when Pete reached behind Bessie to squeeze her hand. "She spoke!" he said in a whisper to Cassidy, "It was whispery and soft, but she spoke."

"Grandma Bessie!" exclaimed Cassidy and hugged her tightly.

Jessie observed all of this interaction from the pew behind and wondered what had happened. Whatever it was, it was obviously good news.

As Pete helped Bessie up to the altar to receive communion, Cassidy said a prayer of thanks, and hoped that this was the breakthrough that Bessie had needed to regain her speech.

From the smile on Pete's face as he brought Bessie back to the pew, the good news wasn't over. Cassidy was excited to talk to Rosadel after mass, since Rosadel would know more about how significant this development could be.

As the mass ended with song, Cassidy was certain she heard Bessie humming along with the music. As the singing ended and Pete went to get Bessie's walker, Cassidy asked, "Grandma Bessie, were you humming?" Bessie nodded with a big smile on her face.

As soon as Pete, Cassidy and Bessie got outside, they were joined by the McPherson's and the Marshall's.

"Uncle Pete! Ms. Cassidy! We didn't know you would be here. Want to come to brunch with us and Pop-Pop and Gee-Jay?" Before Pete or Cassidy could answer, Lou stopped dead in her tracks. "Hey, what are you two doing together? I knew it, Ms. Cassidy is your girlfriend, Uncle Pete."

Cassidy turned bright red, and Jessie had to turn away so as to not be caught laughing. Bessie's smile couldn't get any wider.

"Lou! You know we talked about that and you are not supposed to ask about people's girlfriends or boyfriends." Rosadel was about to apologize for Lou when Lou spoke up again.

"I didn't 'ask', Mommy. I made a declarative sentence." At that, all the adults had to start laughing.

Angus knelt down next to Lou. "Sweetheart, any sentence, or question that could embarrass someone should stay inside your head, not come out your mouth. Does that make sense?"

Lou thought for a minute. "Yes, but Mommy and Daddy are always saying stuff that embarrasses us. So, I still don't understand."

Rosadel looked like she was having a hard me staying out of it, but she let Angus handle it.

"Well, Lou, I'll bet when Mommy or Daddy embarrass you or one of your sisters, it is because you forgot a rule, or made a mistake. Mommies and Daddies have to correct their children, even when it is embarrassing. I had to do it to Mommy, and Grandpa George and Grandma Harriet had to do it to Daddy and Uncle Pete and Uncle Mike and Uncle Donnie. You're smart enough to see the difference."

"OK, Pop-Pop. But I really thought I wasn't breaking a rule."

Angus put his arm around Lou and looked at Rosadel. "Well, June Bug, what do you think?"

"I think we should go to brunch, Daddy. It was good seeing you, Pete and Cassidy. And it was a real treat to see you back at Holy Redeemer Ms. Chauvin."

"Wait, Rosadel," Cassidy was too excited to let Rosadel get away. "Grandma Bessie spoke in church, she said something to Pete at the greeting of peace, and she said "Amen" when she took communion."

"That is great!" Rosadel was as excited as Cassidy. "It isn't unusual for the first words to be prayers or mass responses, because they are stored differently in the brain because of the ritual and repetition. But it is still a breakthrough. Congratulations, Ms. Chauvin. Cassidy, make sure to tell the nurse on duty about this when you get back to Our Lady of Lourdes.

"I'll make a note to talk to Ms. Chauvin's speech therapist the next shift I work. This is very good news. Now we'll be on our way so that you all can enjoy your outing, without the peanut gallery and their commentary."

Pete was grateful for the reprieve. "Huey, Dewey and Louie, I'll see you later in the week."

"Uncle Pete!" Gracie this time. "You really need to learn how to act more like a grown-up. We still love you, but sometimes you are too silly."

Clancy clapped Pete on the back. "Enjoy your brunch, bro. C'mon girls, let's load up and go eat with Pop-Pop and Gee-Jay."

As Cassidy helped Bessie into Pete's van, she couldn't help chuckling. "Grandma Bessie, those girls are really something, aren't they?"

Bessie was laughing herself. As Cassidy was making sure she could get her seatbelt on, she noticed the sparkle in Bessie's eyes, in addition to the smile on her face. "Maybe in a few weeks, we could have the Marshall's and McPherson's join us for brunch. Would you like that?"

As Bessie shook her head emphatically yes, Pete met Cassidy's eyes. "You realize that you have to admit you and I are dating for that to happen, don't you Cass?"

Cassidy smiled brightly at Pete. "Yep, I'm ready to tell the world, Pete. Are you okay with that?"

"More than okay, Cass. I might even steal a kiss in the restaurant. What do you think about that?"

As Cassidy blushed and Bessie laughed, they made their way to brunch.

◆ ◆ ◆

Marie had been pacing around her house since she got home from early Mass. Max was pacing right beside her. When Marie realized her anxiety was transmitting itself to Max, she knew she need to do something different.

"C'mon boy, let's put your leash on and walk around the yard for a while." Max knew the word leash and sprinted to the foyer where he sat patiently waiting for his leash.

Marie dropped her cell phone in her jacket pocket and put Max on his leash. Marie lived on a five-acre piece of land, with a small two-bedroom house set near the front in the center of the land. If she and Max walked the perimeter of the property three times, they would get a little more than a mile walk. Marie figured a mile walk would help settle both her and Max down.

As Marie and Max walked, she thought about how little time she had spent outside on her property in the many years she had owned her home. She had hired a lawn service to tend to the yard, and most days she simply got up, went to work, came home and stayed inside. She had wanted a big piece of property so that she didn't need to see her neighbors often, and it had worked. As it was, Marie didn't know any of her immediate neighbors. The lot wasn't fenced, so Marie had been walking Max on his leash since she brought him home. She wondered if she should put up a fence so that he could run loose but decided the exercise of walking him was good for her for the time being.

As Marie and Max reached the back of her property, Max began sniffing the air. "What is it, Max? Are the neighbors cooking something good?" Marie thought she heard a faint sound of barking. "Do you smell that barking dog, Max?" Marie wondered if the barking dog was loose and decided to head towards the front of the property just in case. Maybe the fence was a good idea, to protect her and Max. Marie decided to make some phone calls in the coming week.

Back inside the house, Marie wondered what she could do with herself to pass the time while waiting for Prescott to call. She knew it was ridiculous to be in such a state of anxiety but couldn't find a way to calm down. It wasn't as if she had any idea when Prescott could call, and it could be days or even weeks.

Marie decided to take Max for a long ride and go to White Castle to visit the graves of her mother, father and other relatives. It always made Marie feel better to go and talk to her mom. Max had been good in the car so far, and she hoped that the longer drive would go as smoothly as the short trips had gone. Marie and Max were on the road in a matter of minutes.

♦ ♦ ♦

Prescott had looked at the paper in his hand at least a dozen times. Now that he had Marie's number and her permission to call, he had no idea what to do. It had seemed so simple in his mind to call Marie and ask her intentions. Now that it was possible, Prescott realized he would have to move forward carefully. Marie had suffered much in her life and did not need him adding more suffering to what she had already borne. But Prescott also realized that now that Marie was anticipating his call, putting it off could actually be adding to her stress. Prescott decided that he needed to carefully plan what he had to say, and call Marie tomorrow, Monday, after work.

Thor, feeling the tension in Prescott, leaned heavily against his side and placed his head on Prescott's lap. "I'm okay, Thor, just worried about how to talk to Marie about Sandra and Cassidy. I tell you what. I'm going to stop worrying about it and start working on my plan for retirement. How does that sound?"

Thor grinned his big doggy grin at Prescott and danced across the room to get his favorite tug toy. After a rousing game of tug-of-war, Prescott sat in front of his computer and pulled up his business plan.

Prescott had decided to retire in June. He planned to make the announcement at work at the end of January. Prescott had been working up a business plan for his post-retirement life, and it was finally taking shape. All he needed to do was find an appropriate piece of property, and it looked like there was one available in Terrebonne Parish. The property was around 100 acres, had a five-bedroom home, a barn, a stable, and multiple one and two-bedroom cottages. As Prescott understood the story, there had once been a 1000-acre sugar plantation on the property. The plantation was subdivided sometime in the 1850's but through marriages, births and deaths, this 110-acre parcel had all been owned by the same people.

The last owners had tried to make a restaurant and wedding destination venue on the property, but never recovered from the impact of Hurricane Katrina. The property had been vacant since 2008, although enough repairs had been affected to prevent further decay before the property was abandoned.

Prescott planned to open a sanctuary on the property. A sanctuary where military veterans could learn to cope with life after the military before fully reentering society. But also, a sanctuary where they could live long term if their scars were too deep to heal properly. A sanctuary where animals could find a home rather than be euthanized. And hopefully, a sanctuary where service animals could be matched with veterans so that both could return to being productive members of society. Prescott almost had his business plan complete and was ready to file for his tax-exempt status.

Prescott planned to secure a million dollars of his 401(k) as Cassidy's inheritance, and to put the rest of the money into a trust to run the sanctuary. He had plans to meet with his attorney and financial advisor the first week of February to start the legal proceedings. He had decided to tell Cassidy about everything right before he shared the news of his retirement with the people at work.

As Prescott documented more of the details of his business plan for the sanctuary, he thought about what to say to Marie when he called. He thought perhaps he should start with an apology. He had suspected that Burl was an abuser but had chosen the easy way out. Prescott knew that he had neither the knowledge nor the ability to have made an intervention at that time, but he still felt badly that Marie had been trapped for so long.

He knew that it was very gracious of Marie to talk to him, as it really wasn't his business. He wanted to make sure that he expressed his appreciation correctly. Preston prepared himself to answer questions about both Sandra and Cassidy. He hoped that Sandra would find it in her heart to give Marie a chance. It seemed unfair that one person should suffer as much in one lifetime as Marie had without the opportunity for reconciliation.

♦ ♦ ♦

When Cassidy and Pete dropped Bessie off at Our Lady of Lourdes, she was exhausted. After brunch, the trio had stopped by Pete's to pick up Laverne and Shirley, and then had gone to Cassidy's for a couple of hours. Bessie held Sophie in her lap while Cassidy showed Pete and Bessie photo albums of her growing up. Pete noticed most of the pictures were of Cassidy and Prescott, with fewer pictures of Sandra, Mark, Candy and Chip. Pete hoped that those photos existed at Sandra's house.

As Cassidy got Bessie settled in her room, Pete stopped by the nurse's station to update the on-duty nurse as to the surprising progress Bessie had made. The nurse was delighted to hear about the breakthrough and promised to make sure the speech therapist knew about it before her next session with Bessie.

Pete knocked on the door before entering Bessie's room. He found Cassidy tucking Bessie in for a nap.

"Grandma Bessie is going to take a little nap before her dinner. This was a big day. Grandma, I'll bring Maggie and Sophie by to see you on Tuesday. I'm going to give Gil a call tomorrow night and tell him about your day, and I'll have a full report for you when I see you next." As Cassidy leaned down to kiss Bessie goodbye, her eyes were already drifting shut. Pete placed a kiss on Bessie's forehead, and he and Cassidy left hand-in-hand.

♦ ♦ ♦

Marie was tired but calm when she and Max returned from their visit to the cemetery in White Castle. Max had behaved beautifully in the car, and in the cemetery. Marie had tidied the graves of her parents and grandparents, and left flowers for everyone. Whenever Prescott called, she was ready. As Marie prepared an evening meal for her and Max, she thanked God for her new companion. Everything just seemed easier with Max by her side.

CHAPTER 19

Pete didn't remember a day at the clinic passing so slowly. Other than a thumbs-up from Lindy when she arrived at work on Monday morning, he had no idea how her conversation with her parents had gone the day before.

Finally, all the staff had gone home except for Lindy, and Pete left Laverne and Shirley in his office while he went back to the boarding area where he knew Lindy would be feeding their guests before taking them out one last time before they locked up for the night.

"So, Kid, how did it go?" Lindy smiled at Pete as she answered.

"Way better than I expected, to be honest." Lindy replied. "My mom cried a little, but my Dad was amazing. He said that while he was surprised, he wasn't shocked. And that he hoped I knew that he loved me no matter what. Mom was in the 'Are you sure? This is going to make your life harder' place until Dad told her that there couldn't be anything harder than being unable to be your whole self all the time. I was so proud to hear him say that. When he did, then I started crying. I don't think they are ready for me to bring a girlfriend home tomorrow, but they made it so much easier than I expected."

Pete gave Lindy a quick hug. "I hoped it would go that way, Lindy. I've known your Dad forever, and I never saw him indicate that he had any prejudices at all. I know it is different when your daughter is concerned, but I just couldn't imagine him not loving you or being proud of you."

"It's the whole Catholic thing that made me nervous, Pete. But even Mom came through there. Mom said she never could accept that God would make a child that He didn't love just the way He made them. I never expected her to say something like that. I have heard and read so many stories of people's families turning their backs on them for being gay. I feel so lucky that my parents are the way they are."

"So, what's next, Lindy? Are you going to tell your older brother and sister? Are you going to keep the circle small for a while?" Pete believed Lindy's siblings would be as accepting as her parents had been, but really it was up to Lindy.

"I'm calling my brother tonight. And the plan is to call my sister tomorrow night. And then I'd like to tell the staff here at the clinic about my going back to school. I think I'll wait until the next time Hannah tries to fix me up with JT to tell her, and then of course, everyone will know within hours. Now that I've started telling people, I just want everyone to know so that this feeling of hiding is over with."

Pete hesitated, but asked the question he needed to ask. "Are you OK if I tell Cassidy?"

Lindy looked questioningly at Pete. "Cassidy Bourgeois? Sure, but why is that important?"

Pete could feel his ears turning red as he answered. "Because we're dating. And she saw us hugging in the parking lot of the Hungry Pelican. And she trusted me even though I couldn't explain why we looked so intense. And I want to make sure that nothing goes wrong between us."

Lindy's smile was big enough to light a room. "Why, Pete! A girlfriend! And one I would have picked for you myself! Will wonders never cease! Of course, you can tell Cassidy. Can I tell people you have a girlfriend?"

"Sure. Until yesterday, I wasn't sure if Cassidy was comfortable with people knowing we have been dating, but now that I know she is ready for people to know, what the heck. I just hope the gossip and speculation isn't too bad."

Lindy really was happy for Pete, and for Cassidy too. It was always nice when two of your favorite people became a couple.

♦ ♦ ♦

Cassidy was surprised when the phone was answered on the first ring. "Gil Chauvin, can I help you?"

"Um, uh, Hi Gil, this is Cassidy Bourgeois."

"Cassidy! So excited to finally talk to you. I am so grateful for all you have done for my Tante. It has been hard to be so far away, and now I find from your father that you have become family."

Cassidy was taken aback, both by Gil Chauvin's beautiful baritone voice, and by the warmth with which he greeted her. His voice had a lilt, as if English was his second language, but there was also some Texas twang as well.

"I love Ms. Chauvin, Gil. She has been so good to me and for me. I consider her my honorary grandmother."

"So, your father told me, Cassidy. I must say again, I greatly appreciate your care and concern for my Tante. My sisters and I have been so worried and feel so guilty that we are far away and cannot do more."

"Gil, you should know that Bessie is getting the very best of care. The only problem is that I can't help more. Without the ability to interact with her care team on her care, I can't make suggestions. I think that she has progressed enough in comprehension to use technology to help her communicate. There are programs that will talk for her, where she can type or touch pictures on a screen to communicate. If you could talk to her care team about providing those tools, that would be great. Her insurance probably won't pay for those; will that be a problem?"

"No, Cher, Tante has plenty of money, and we all would help if needed. I will talk to her care team and get things started. Why don't we plan to talk once a week, so I can fill you in on my talks with her care team?"

"Oh, Gil! That would be great. I almost forgot the best news of all. Pete and I took Grandma Bessie to church yesterday, and she talked twice. I'm not Catholic, so I'm not sure what exactly she said, but Pete said that they were the right responses. Her voice was whispery and slurred, but she talked! And she hummed with the hymns. Pete told her care team, and hopefully, that will give them more to work with."

Gil wondered who Pete was, but decided that question could wait. He was enchanted by the voice on the other end of the phone. He could feel how deeply Cassidy cared for his Aunt Bessie just by listening to her voice. "I'll be sure to talk to them about that when I talk to them tomorrow. Usually, I get an update every Friday, but I'll make a special call tomorrow. Would you like me to call you tomorrow night and give you an update?"

"That would be great, Gil, but it will have to be late. I promised Grandma Bessie that I would bring Sophie to visit tomorrow night after work. I should be home by eight, if that is not too late for you to call.'

"I'll call at eight tomorrow Cassidy. It has been a pleasure meeting you. I'm looking forward to meeting you in person soon."

As Cassidy hung up the phone, she was exhilarated. She had talked to a stranger without a work script and with no problems. Bessie was going to get enhanced communication devices, and she would be getting regular updates on Bessie's progress. She couldn't wait to call Pete and tell him all about it.

◆ ◆ ◆

Prescott held the phone in his hand, knowing that he had put this call off for long enough. Thor rested his head on Prescott's knee.

"I'm OK, boy. You can relax. I just need to make this phone call, and now I don't know why I started this whole thing. I get this savior complex going, and I stick my nose where it doesn't belong. I hope I'm not making a big mistake here."

Thor stood up and placed his paws on Prescott's shoulders and rested his head on Prescott's chest. As Prescott rested his head against Thor's he felt his tension and anxiety ease. "Thanks, Thor. You know better than I do what I need sometimes." Thor laid down by Prescott's feet as he dialed Marie's number.

Marie had just finished washing up the supper dishes when her phone rang. She took a deep calming breath before she answered.

197

After Marie's "hello", Prescott jumped right in. "Hello, Marie, it is Prescott Bourgeois. I want to thank you for taking my call. I realize I have no business interfering, and you are being very gracious to talk to me."

Marie was surprised that Prescott sounded so nervous, apologetic, and sincere. "I appreciate that you care so much about my daughter and granddaughter, Prescott. I never did meet you in person, but I've heard good things about you, so I'm fine with talking to you. Jessie McPherson told me you were worried about what my plans were with regards to Sandra and Cassidy."

"Marie, I've come to realize that I am out of line here. Your life and your decisions are your business. I apologize for inserting myself into your life and understand if you tell me to mind my own business. Your relationship with Sandra or with Cassidy is your business, not mine."

Marie thought for a minute before answering. "Well, to tell the truth, Prescott, I've been trying to get up the nerve to contact Sandra for almost twenty years. As soon as Burl died, I started looking for her. I just felt like I didn't deserve to have her back in my life, seeing as how I'd failed her as a mother. I've been going to counseling for a few years now, and realize that I did my best, even though it wasn't very good."

Prescott felt the weight of guilt at Marie's words. "Marie, I apologize for not speaking up way back then. I didn't know you, but I knew how Burl acted and talked at the VFW hall, and someone should have tried to help you. I know it is too little, too late, but I am truly sorry the community stood silent while you were so badly treated."

"Prescott, what I've learned through my counseling is that it is always possible to look backward and see what you could have done better, or different. But that most of us are doing the best we can when we're doing it. If you need my forgiveness, you have it. But it wasn't your fault. I'm having to accept it wasn't my fault either. It is just what happened. What is important is what is in front of us. And I want to have a relationship with Sandra and her family. But I understand that is up to Sandra. I know I complicated matters by meeting Cassidy. But I couldn't help myself. And I have to tell you, Max has improved my life dramatically, just in the few days he has been with me."

"Marie, I don't know if you know this, but I suffered greatly with Post Traumatic Stress Disorder after coming home from Vietnam. I got a dog, Ulysses, and he saved me from PTSD. Ulysses died, and now I have another dog, Thor. You don't have to tell me how life changing the love of a dog can be. Cassidy was beside herself with worry over Max, afraid he would never find a loving home. Whatever happens with Sandra and Cassidy, you did a great thing by adopting Max."

"Thank you for saying that Prescott. I'm afraid I can't tell what the future holds, but I can promise you I have no intention of doing anything to hurt Sandra or Cassidy."

"Marie, I have to apologize again. I should have known that and left you in peace. It was enough to let you know that I knew who you were, and that your secret was bound to come out. You didn't owe me this conversation, or your reassurance, and I am grateful for both. If the time comes when I can help you with something, please let me know, and I'll be glad to do what I can for you."

"Thank you for that, Prescott. I just ask that you speak kindly of me to Cassidy if she asks you about me."

"I can do that, Marie. Good luck with Max, and with your continued healing. I'm not a praying man, but I will send good thoughts into the universe for you."

As Marie hung up the phone, she realized she was ready. She would talk to her counselor this week about sending Sandra a letter. Marie believed she was finally strong enough to stand it if her letter went unanswered.

♦ ♦ ♦

Pete was happy to hear Cassidy so excited about her conversation with Gil Chauvin, he just wasn't sure he was excited about Cassidy being so excited about talking to another guy. He knew he was being unreasonable, but hearing "Gil" this and "Gil" that made him cut their phone call short. As he was feeding Laverne and Shirley, and preparing his own meal, he started feeling like an idiot. Instead of being at

Cassidy's sharing a meal and time together, he let jealousy steal his chance at a nice evening.

Cassidy had trusted him when she saw him and Lindy embracing. He couldn't even listen to the recounting of a phone call without being a jerk. This relationship stuff was harder than he realized.

Cassidy was puzzled as to why her call with Pete had gone so strangely. She was trying not to make too much of it and decided to call her dad to get her mind off the call.

Cassidy knew as soon as Prescott answered the phone that something was bothering him. "Hey Daddy, are you upset about something?"

"Just a little down, baby girl. Sometimes memories of the past take root and won't let go. I was just about to go outside and play fetch with Thor. That usually gets me out of the past and into the present. Is there something you needed to talk about?"

Cassidy thought about mentioning how strange Pete had acted, and then decided to keep it to herself. "Nothing special, I just wanted to let you know I talked to Gil Chauvin this evening, and he is going to talk to the people at Our Lady of Lourdes about getting better communication devices for her. Thanks again for helping make that connection for me."

"No problem at all, Cass. I'm going to go play with Thor and see if I can shake off this dark mood. I love you."

"I love you, too, Daddy. Talk to you later in the week."

As Cassidy hung up, she looked at Maggie and Sophie. I should just stick to dogs, thought Cassidy, humans don't make any sense at all.

CHAPTER 20

Pete tried his best to act like everything was normal when he picked Cassidy up on Tuesday night to go to Our Lady of Lourdes. Cassidy took her cue from Pete, and they chatted somewhat normally as they loaded Maggie and Sophie into Pete's van.

The ride to Our Lady was quieter than normal, Cassidy feeling uncomfortable, and Pete feeling guilty. Cassidy was relieved to get out of the van when they arrived. As was their custom, Pete took Laverne and Shirley to the activity room on the assisted living side of the facility, and Cassidy took Maggie and Sophie straight to Bessie's room.

Cassidy was really upset at Pete's coldness, and didn't know what to do. But she also didn't want to upset Bessie. As Cassidy walked into Bessie's room, she was so surprised she forgot everything else. Bessie was sitting up in her chair, with a laptop computer on the rolling table in front of her.

"Grandma Bessie! You got a computer. Do you like it?" Bessie nodded, and then slowly typed a message for Cassidy.

Yes. I am slow but I can talk now.

"I think that was pretty fast, myself. Did you use the computer much before your stroke?"

Bessie nodded again and began typing.

Yes. Facebook and Email and Pinterest.

Cassidy smiled. "How about that? You are more hip than me Grandma. I've got a Facebook account, but I hardly ever look at it. I use email mostly for work. I've heard about Pinterest, but I've never used it. Maybe you can teach me some things."

Bessie laughed and nodded. Sophie had been standing on her hind legs with her front paws on Bessie's leg, but she was tired of waiting for lap time, and let out a sharp little bark.

"Okay, Sophie. I'll move the table, so you can get on Grandma's lap." As Cassidy moved the table out of the way, Sophie jumped up onto Bessie's lap and curled up contentedly.

"I guess Gil must have called and gotten the computer arranged for you. That was awfully quick."

Bessie nodded and smiled and gestured for Cassidy to roll the computer back into place.

Cassidy complied, and Bessie typed.

You're sad.

"I was trying to hide it, Grandma, but I am. Or maybe I'm confused. Everything was fine with me and Pete on Sunday night. Then last night we hardly talked at all before he had to hang up, and today he is just distant. I don't know what to think."

Bessie typed again.

Patience. Men?

Cassidy had to laugh. "I guess none of us ladies understand men. Do you want to stay here with Sophie, or do you want me to get your walker and come with me and Maggie to visit?"

Bessie typed.

Go.

And so, they went. Cassidy knew that they didn't get to see as many people with Bessie along, but it was good for everyone. Bessie increased mobility encouraged the other patients in rehab, and Cassidy got to see how much more comfortably the residents interacted with Sophie and Maggie with Bessie there.

By the time Cassidy, Bessie, Maggie and Sophie got back to Bessie's room, Bessie was exhausted. Pete arrived with Laverne and Shirley just as Cassidy had gotten Bessie settled into her chair with Sophie on her lap and her computer table angled so she could reach it.

"How's my best girl?" asked Pete as he kissed Bessie on the cheek. "Look at you with a computer! That should help you get your point across, shouldn't it?"

Bessie nodded, as Cassidy replied. "Gil got Bessie a computer just that fast! I'm so impressed that he was able to make that happen. I never expected one phone call would make such a difference."

Bessie noticed the shadow that passed over Pete's face when Cassidy mentioned Gil. Now Bessie had a good idea what was making Pete act funny, but that was something Cassidy and Pete would have to work through together. She smiled and shook her head.

"NO, what? Why are you shaking your head, Grandma?" Cassidy asked.

Bessie typed.

Shaking cobwebs. I'm tired.

"I'll bet you are, this has been a full day. We'll get going, and I'll stop and tell the nurse you are ready to get in bed."

Bessie smiled and nodded. As Pete and Cassidy took the dogs and headed to the car, Cassidy told Pete that Bessie had made the rounds with the dogs using her walker.

"That is great, Cassidy. Hopefully, Bessie progress will continue, and she'll be able to move over to the assisted living side, or maybe even go home again."

Cassidy sobered, as she thought about how hard it would be for Maggie to lose Sophie as a companion. But, she remembered what

Prescott always said about not borrowing trouble and pushed the thought aside.

The drive back to Cassidy's house wasn't any more comfortable than the drive to Our Lady had been. When Pete parked in front of Cassidy's house, Cassidy invited him in. After a long silence, Pete declined.

"I have a couple of surgeries tomorrow, and I need to read up on the case notes, and do some research on what I might find, so I'll pass. I'm going to my Mom's for dinner tomorrow, so I'll see you on Thursday."

Cassidy was disappointed, and wanted to ask what was wrong, but thought about Bessie's advice to be patient, so saying goodnight, she took Maggie and Sophie inside and hoped that Pete would return to normal soon.

Pete drove home in a funk. If Cassidy wasn't losing interest in him and getting interested in Gil, it wasn't because he deserved it. Pete was embarrassed that he lied to Cassidy. He did have surgeries tomorrow, but he was ready for them. And he wasn't going to have dinner at his Mom's tomorrow until he called and asked her if he could come over. He hoped the answer was yes. Even though it hurt to admit it, Harriet was the only person he could talk to about his tangled feelings related to Cassidy. He really was a Momma's boy. Oh, well, at least he had a good Momma.

◆ ◆ ◆

Marie had arranged for a fence installer to come by that afternoon to give an estimate. When Marie opened the door, and stepped outside so that Max wouldn't get loose or scare the contractor, she realized the young man that had come to do the estimate had been a student at Holy Redeemer, and was a regular at Mass.

"Miss Marie! The lunch lady. Do you remember me? I'm Ricky Thibodaux, I graduated from Holy Redeemer in 2003."

Marie smiled as she shook his hand. "I recognized you, but I'm afraid I didn't remember your name. I love when I see my kids from Holy Redeemer continuing to attend Mass at Holy Redeemer. I see you with a wife and baby at Mass now, don't I?"

"Yes, Ma'am. And I'd like to get home to them soon, before the baby goes to sleep. How about you show me where you want the fence to go, and I'll take some measurements. Then we can talk about different types of options and prices."

"That sounds great. Are you OK if I bring my dog, Max? He'll be leashed."

"No problem at all, Miss Marie. I love dogs."

Marie stepped back inside the house and put Max on his leash. "We're going to get a fence for you so that you can run around." Marie hugged Max as she clipped his leash on.

"Handsome dog you have there," Ricky remarked. "Is it OK if I pet him?"

Marie hesitated. "To be honest, Ricky, I just brought Max home on Friday. You are the first person to come to the house. I'm not sure how he will react, but if you are good with that, I would love for you to pet him."

Marie told Max to sit, and Ricky offered his hand to be sniffed. Max leaned into Marie's leg, and looked up at her. "He's good, Max. Ricky won't hurt you."

Ricky rubbed Max's ear, and Max closed his eyes and leaned into Ricky's hand. "He sure is a sweet dog, Miss Marie, where did you get him?"

"He was at the St. Elizabeth Animal Shelter, Ricky. His owners moved and couldn't take him. I need the fence, so he can have more freedom."

"Well, let's get going then. If you decide to hire me, I'll get Max his fence just as fast as I can."

Marie liked Ricky, and she liked the price and design of the fence he suggested, so she signed the contract right away. Ricky would start installing the fence on Monday of the next week.

As Marie prepared dinner for her and Max, she decided to write the letter to send to Sandra. Marie had an appointment on Wednesday with her counselor, she decided to bring the letter and go over it with her counselor, and then mail it to Sandra as soon as possible. It was time to stop living in the shadows and finally put her life in order.

✦ ✦ ✦

Bethany Williams helped Michelle pick out play clothes to put in her book bag to take to the Marshall's house the following day after school.

"Mom, you called the school, right?" Michelle didn't want anything to mess up her playdate.

"Yes, and I'll drop off the permission slip for Mrs. Marshall to pick you up in the morning when I bring you to school. Then I'll come over after work and meet you at the Marshall's."

"I'm really excited, Mommy. I play with kids at school, but I miss having real friends. Lou came and got me at recess yesterday and today. I like playing with her and Grace and Rosie. And they know everybody."

"I'm really glad, Michelle. I know you didn't want to move, but I want us to be happy here."

Michelle crawled up on Bethany's lap. "I love you Mommy. But I miss my grandma's."

"I know honey, and we will drive over to Texas next weekend to see everybody. Making friends here will help. I promise."

Bethany poured herself a glass of wine after Michelle was in bed and sat in the living room staring into the fireplace. Even after six years, Bethany had trouble believing Derek was really gone forever. She supposed it was because they had spent so much time apart when they were married. They had met in high school, and both joined the military after graduation. Bethany in the Air Force, Derek in the Army. They got married at twenty, and Bethany left the Air Force and started college when her first enlistment was up.

Michelle was born when Bethany was twenty-two, and her and Derek's moms helped tremendously with Michelle so that Bethany could finish her engineering degree. Derek had deployed to Iraq twice and returned safely, so when he deployed right after Bethany's graduation, she was sure he would come home. They had decided that once his current enlistment was over, he would leave the Army and take his turn going to college. He never got that chance. Three months into Derek's third deployment an IED took out his vehicle, and him and two other soldiers.

Bethany was shattered. As the years had gone by, she had gotten used to missing Derek, used to the empty place. But she was tired of it. Tired of being a widow, tired of being alone. Whenever she mentioned thinking about moving on, thinking about dating, the mothers went wild.

"You'll never find a man as good to you as Derek." "No man wants to raise another man's child." "You need to wait until Michelle is grown to even think about that."

Maybe they were right, but Bethany wanted to date. She might never introduce a date to Michelle, but maybe she would. Bethany wanted to live again.

Both mothers were widows but widowed more recently than Bethany. Bethany had been twenty-six when her dad died, and Derek's dad had died about six months after Derek. Bethany thought he died from a broken heart. The mothers had become each other's support group since Bethany's dad had died. Neither one had worked outside the home during their marriage, so they were the queens of the volunteer army in their town. They knew everyone, and kept busy and mostly happy in their widowhood, and didn't understand why Bethany couldn't be a happy widow too.

Complicating everything was the fact that Michelle was the only grandchild on both sides. Derek's sister Devon was happily single, and Bethany's sister Anitra had just gotten engaged. Bethany thought that the distraction of planning Anitra's wedding would help her mother cope with the move. She knew it was hard on all of them for her and Michelle to move to Louisiana, but it was only a six-hour drive, and she planned to visit often.

The other reason she had wanted to move away was the "Poor Michelle" nonsense. The mothers had gotten into the habit of excusing any bad behavior of Michelle's with "the poor child doesn't have a father". Bethany knew that it was hard on Michelle, but she didn't really remember Derek, or his father, and really missed Bethany's father, who she had called "Pops".

Bethany knew that Michelle needed to be held accountable, and they both needed to figure out life as a family unit on their own. Bethany knew they might end up moving back home at a point in time, but for now, Bethany wanted her and Michelle to be independent.

Bethany finished her wine and got ready for bed. As she said her nightly prayers, she prayed that her girls would find friends in the Marshall girls. And she prayed that she would find a friend in Rosadel.

CHAPTER 21

Harriet Marshall put the meatloaf and baked macaroni in the oven and checked the time on the clock. Both would be ready at six-thirty, and Pete and George should both be home by then. Donnie and Mike could float in any time or not at all, so she didn't worry about them. But she was worried about Pete. Her usually unflappable son has sounded so down last night when he called and asked if he could come for dinner that she had gone to the store today to make him his favorite foods.

Harriet kind of hoped that Pete arrived before George got home from work. Pete was more comfortable baring his soul to Harriet than to George. Harriet had never figured out why, because George was as easy going as a person could be, and Clancy, Mike and Donnie all sought George out more than Harriet when they needed advice. But Pete was different.

The door opened at six, and when Harriet heard the scrabble of paws, she knew it was Pete and not George. Pete, Laverne and Shirley made their way into the kitchen. Harriet was relieved to see Pete looking good, although he did look sad.

"Hey Ma! What's for dinner?"

"Meatloaf, baked macaroni and green beans, your favorites. I figured if you were coming for dinner I should make it a happy occasion."

Pete gave Harriet a hug and a kiss. "Thanks for being such a great mom. I don't know if I tell you enough how much I appreciate you."

Harriet hugged Pete hard before pushing away. "Don't go getting all schmaltzy on me or I'll start crying, but thanks, Honey. Help yourself to something to drink. There is beer, wine, cokes and water in the fridge."

Pete grabbed himself a beer and put a water bowl down for Laverne and Shirley before sitting at the table.

"Mom, I think I'm screwing up, and I can't seem to stop." Pete picked at the label on his beer bottle as he spoke.

Harriet checked the clock and sat down at the table with Pete.

"What do you think you are screwing up, Pete? And why?" Harriet reached over and put her hand on Pete's.

"It's Cassidy. We've been spending lots of time together, and things have been progressing really well. We even went to church together on Sunday and brought Bessie Chauvin with us. It was a great day. Then on Monday, Cassidy called Bessie's nephew Gil to talk to him about getting Bessie better accommodations for her rehabilitation. When Cassidy called me on Monday night, she was all excited about the Gil guy. And I got my feelings hurt that she could be so excited about another guy, so I cut the call short. Then I was embarrassed about how I acted, so I promised myself I would just act like nothing happened when we took the dogs to Our Lady of Lourdes last night. But I was uncomfortable and so was Cassidy on the ride over. So, I gave myself a good talking to, and decided to end the night better than I started it. But when I got to Bessie's room, she had a computer, and Cassidy was all excited about how quickly Gil was able to help. I got upset again and dropped her off without going inside or explaining."

"I hate to say it, Pete, but it sounds like you are acting like a spoiled brat." Harriet loved her kids but pulled no punches.

"I know, Mom. And it gets worse. On Saturday, Cassidy saw me hugging Lindy Russell in the parking lot of the Hungry Pelican, and she trusted me without question. So, Cassidy sees something that she could misconstrue and doesn't, and I just get crazy jealous over a phone call. I know I'm being a jerk, but I can't seem to help myself."

Harriet took both of Pete's hands in hers. "Pete, maybe you are not mature enough for a romantic relationship. If you are going to try to build a love relationship with Cassidy, you have to trust her. It is obvious she trusts you. What is going on in your mind that you feel you can't trust her? And if you really believe you can't trust Cassidy when she has given you no reason to mistrust her, then the problem is you, not her. And you shouldn't pretend that you are ready for a relationship when you aren't."

Pete nodded his head. "I want to be ready, Mom, I do. I've never felt like this about anyone before, so I never felt jealous. This stinks."

"Pete, jealousy comes from insecurity. You are old to be falling in love for the first time. I understand that it is scary and uncomfortable to feel that deeply. But you have to be fair to Cassidy. If you can't figure out how to go to her and tell her just what you told me, you need to cool down the relationship. Cassidy deserves better than a person who blows hot and cold and doesn't communicate. Everyone deserves better than that."

"I know that Mom, I just don't know how to start."

"Well don't start if you can't stop acting foolish. But if you are serious about being sorry and doing better, go get some flowers, go over to Cassidy's house and start with 'I'm sorry I've been such a jerk' and then explain. Tell her you need her help to not be such an idiot. And hope she forgives you. Make a plan for how you can tell her when you are feeling jealous or insecure, so that she knows. But, Pete, make sure you are sure you are ready for this before you go any further. Maybe you two need to put the brakes on romance and focus on being friends for a while."

"Mom, we've been friends since we both volunteered at the shelter when I was in high school. I want to move forward. I just have to trust Cassidy. She has never given me any reason not to."

They both heard the front door open as George got home. "Can we not tell Dad?" Pete asked.

"I'll tell him after you leave, you know we don't keep secrets." Harriet stood up to kiss George hello as he came into the kitchen.

"What secret?" George asked. "Hi Pete, good to see you." Pete stood up and he and George shook hands.

"Hey, Dad. Mom will tell you later, but I do have something to tell you that was a big secret until this weekend."

Now Harriet was intrigued. "What is that?"

"Lindy Russell is going back to LSU to veterinary school. She got accepted and starts in the fall."

"Wow, Pete, that is great news for Lindy, but I'll bet you are going to miss her at the clinic."

"I know, Dad. But I have plenty of time to find a replacement, since she is staying until August. I think I can stretch my payroll to have both Lindy and her replacement on staff for a month. I've depended on Lindy for so much, I have to really think about my other vet techs and analyze if one of them is ready to step up and fill Lindy's spot, or if I should try to hire a more experienced tech. But all that is small stuff. I'm really excited for Lindy. She'll make a great vet."

As Harriet got busy putting supper on the table and George went to wash up for dinner, Pete thought about what Harriet had said. Maybe he wasn't ready to fall in love. Maybe he was too much of a jerk to have a love relationship.

Conversation over dinner turned to family matters, conversation about Rosadel and Clancy, and whether or not they would find homes for the rest of the kittens and the momma cat. Harriet worrying that Mike was working too many hours at the restoration garage and would never have a life besides work, and then worrying that Donnie was so busy taking care of making music with his band that he was neglecting his "real" career. Pete let the conversation wash over him, loving the familiar rhythm of Harriet worrying and George teasing her about it. They were so comfortable, so much two halves of the same whole, and Pete could never remember it being any different. He knew that he had always gone to Harriet for advice, but Pete found himself wondering if maybe this time he should talk to his Dad.

As dinner and conversation wound down, Pete decided to try to get some private time with George. "Hey, Mom, since you cooked, how about I clean up the kitchen and put the food away? That way I can have some time with Dad like I had with you before dinner."

Harriet was a little surprised that Pete wanted to talk to George, but also pleased. Maybe George would have the magic words to help Pete figure out what to do.

As Pete put the food in containers for George to put away, Harriet couldn't help but to interfere from the living room. "Pete, make sure to pack some leftovers to take home," she shouted.

George winked at Pete before he shouted back, "I'm sending everything home with Pete. You can cook for me anytime." Harriet harrumphed, but George and Pete both knew she was pleased that Pete was taking the leftovers home.

As George cleared the table and Pete loaded the dishwasher, Pete finally asked his dad the question weighing on his mind. "Dad, have you ever struggled with jealousy over Mom talking to or about some other guy?"

George remembered why he was glad Pete usually talked to Harriet and answered carefully.

"No, Pete, I never did, but there is probably some history on that you would have no reason to know about. You probably never knew that Uncle Vince and Aunt Grace almost got divorced long before you were born. Vince is enough older than me that he went to Vietnam. He and Grace got married right out of high school, knowing there was a good chance Vince would get drafted. He was born in 1950, and it was hard to miss the draft. Sure enough, Grace was pregnant by September, and Vince enlisted, because he thought that he would have a little more control that way.

"While Vince was deployed in Vietnam, a bunch of the guys he served with thought it was funny to mess with the married guys about what their wives were doing at home. Grace never did anything the least little bit suspect. She went back home to live with her mom and dad and took care of your cousin Maryellen. Vince's letters got crazier and crazier, as he accused Grace of all kinds of things. She just wrote back about life and sent pictures of the baby. Vince finally sent a letter telling Grace that when he got back, he was going to divorce her. I still remember her sitting at the table at my parent's house, crying and crying. Your grandfather told Grace not to worry, he'd straighten Vince out when he got home. Your grandmother was beside herself. She loved Grace and of course, Maryellen was the first grandchild, and she was afraid she would lose them both because of Vince's behavior. Well, thank

God, Vince made it home from Vietnam. He was a mess in more ways than one, but with counseling, he got his act together and he and Grace have made a good life.

"I was a teenager, just noticing girls when all that drama went on. I promised myself I'd never do that to someone. Either you trust someone enough to have them in your life, or you don't. Jealousy comes from one of two places. Either it comes from a person's own insecurity, or it comes from a lack of trust in the other person's commitment to the relationship. There is no reason to pursue a relationship with someone you can't or don't trust.

"When your Mom and I started dating, we were older, and she had plenty of male friends. I realized that Harriet is just outgoing, and likeable, and will always have a crowd of people around her. She would say the same about me. We knew pretty early on in our relationship that we were exclusive, and never let those friends of the opposite sex mess with the exclusivity or importance of our relationship. But we talked about it early. We decided to be exclusive and trusted each other to keep that promise.

"Now, would you like to tell me what is going on? Why are you asking?"

Pete was still processing all that George had told him. He had never seen anything but love between Uncle Vince and Aunt Grace. After Maryellen, they had five more children, the youngest the same age as Pete. And since Wayne was five years younger than his next sibling, he had spent more time with Clancy and Pete than with his siblings. The three boys spent many summer nights all sleeping at one house or the other. Aunt Grace and Uncle Vince were like a second set of parents.

"Wow, Dad, I never would have guessed Uncle Vince and Aunt Grace had any problems. They always seemed as solid as you and Mom to me."

"Well, Pete, by the time you were born they were solid, and the hard times were almost twenty years behind them. No ducking the question, why are you asking."

Pete hated having to admit to his dad what was going on, but knew he had to. "I've been a jerk with Cassidy lately."

George simply raised his eyebrow, and Pete knew he had to tell the whole story again.

"I've been acting like a jerk with Cassidy because she has been talking with Bessie Chauvin's nephew Gil about Bessie's care. I got insanely jealous when on the phone the other night it was 'Gil this' and 'Gil that'. I promised myself on Monday night I wouldn't be a jerk again on Tuesday, and then I was. Mom said maybe I'm too immature for a relationship, and maybe she's right."

George looked up at the ceiling for a moment, and then looked at Pete. "Mom doesn't pull any punches, does she? Well, Pete, I think you're scared, not immature, and I guess you got Uncle Vince's jealous gene. Have you and Cassidy talked about being exclusive?"

"Well, I said that I wanted to be early on, and I think Cassidy does too. I'm got so tangled up on Monday night, I can't remember if Cassidy ever agreed to that or not."

"Well, son, my first piece of advice would be to talk to Cassidy. Tell her you got jealous, make sure she knows that you are in an exclusive relationship with her, and make sure she feels the same. Then, apologize for being a jerk, and ask for Cassidy's help with managing your emotions. Unless you want to slow things down. But no matter what you want, you need to apologize to Cassidy. And hope she wants to forgive you and help you through this."

Pete nodded, "Just for the record, you and Mom gave me the same advice."

George laughed. "I'd say your Mom trained me well, but we've been so happy together for so long because we match. We never did fight all that much because we both approach the world the same way. Be honest and say what needs to be said. Don't hold a grudge and remember how much you share that would be awful to lose. It isn't rocket science Pete. The Golden Rule - treat others the way you want to be treated."

"I know Dad. It is just I never felt like this before. It scares me to feel this much about someone who isn't family."

George walked over to Pete and put his arm around Pete's shoulder. "Then work on making Cassidy family, boy. We could use another daughter, and I think you will never get over it if you let her get away."

Harriet couldn't stand it anymore and came into the kitchen. "And usually I am the pushy one telling the boys what to do."

George smiled. "Can't let you have all the fun, Harriet."

♦ ♦ ♦

Bethany Williams took a deep cleansing breath after she parked her car in front of Rosadel and Clancy's house. She knew it was just dinner with friends, but it felt like so much more. This big move for independence had left Bethany lonelier than she had ever been, and she knew Michelle was lonely too. A friendship for Michelle with a bonus friendship for Bethany seemed too good to be true.

As Bethany raised her hand to ring the doorbell, she heard the sound of excited voices from inside. She hoped Michelle was having a good time. Maybe if Michelle made some friends, she would start adjusting to life in Louisiana.

As Bethany rang the doorbell, she heard a cascade of footsteps headed for the door, and heard Rosadel call out, "Make sure you look to see you know who is at the door before you open it."

Bethany saw four faces pressed up to the side lights, as the girls followed instructions.

"It's Michelle's Mommy!" yelled Lou, as Grace opened the door.

"Hi Ms. Bethany! Want to come say 'hi' to your kittens?" Bethany thought the speaker was Rosie.

"Hi Mommy!" Michelle hugged Bethany around the waist. "I really think we need to take Pokey and Boo. They love each other a lot and it would be sad if they couldn't live together."

Bethany thought for a minute and decided two kittens couldn't be that much more trouble than one. "If I say yes, you have to be in charge of cleaning the litter box."

Michelle's smile lit up her face. "I can do that Mommy! I've been helping Lou and Grace and Rosie clean the litter box today. And two kittens won't be as stinky as six. I'll do it."

Rosadel came out of the kitchen wiping her hands on a dish towel. "Girls, you didn't even let Ms. Bethany in the house before! It is normal for Michelle to want to see her Mommy, but you all need to back up a little and give Ms. Bethany some space.

"Bethany, do you want to come into the kitchen, or would you like to see the kittens, or would you like to freshen up?"

"Thanks for asking, Rosadel. I think I'd like to go see the kittens with Michelle and the girls, and then wash my hands and join you in the kitchen."

Rosadel pointed to a door under the stairs. "The powder room is right there. Clancy isn't home yet, so dinner will be a half hour or so. Just come on into the kitchen when you are ready."

When Bethany entered the kitchen ten minutes later, Rosadel was preparing a salad. "Is there anything I can do to help?" she asked.

"Nope, this is the last of it. Easy supper tonight, jambalaya and salad. The jambalaya is finishing itself in that pot, and the salad is almost done. The girls will set the table, and if you don't mind, I'll ask Michelle to help."

"That would be great, Rosadel, thank you. And thank you for having Michelle over to visit this afternoon. How did she do?"

"The girls were great together. They played with the kittens, did their homework, and then played with the kittens some more. I wouldn't have a problem in the world with Michelle coming over any time, Bethany. She is a great little girl."

"Thanks, Rosadel. I think so too, but I wasn't sure how she would do today. She has been a real handful since we moved."

"I can't imagine, Bethany. I've lived in Bayou Beni my whole life, with the exception of college. I don't know how you had the courage to pick up and move here."

"It was more like desperation than courage, but I don't want to talk about that when Michelle can overhear."

"How about the two of us go out for lunch on Saturday, and you can tell me all about it if you want to. Michelle can come over and play with the girls and Clancy can watch them while we have some grownup time.
"

"That would be great, Rosadel. I need to talk through some stuff, and I haven't found anyone that I was comfortable enough with to get it all out. I know we just met, but I feel really comfortable with you."

"Thanks, Bethany. I feel really comfortable with you too. I think we are going to be great friends."

Bethany offered up a silent prayer of thanks and felt a huge sense of relief. Maybe this move to Louisiana was going to work out after all.

CHAPTER 22

Pete was nervous as he pulled up to Cassidy's house to pick her up for their Thursday visit to Our Lady of Lourdes. He grabbed the bouquet of flowers off of the passenger seat and retrieved Laverne and Shirley from their car seats. As he rang Cassidy's doorbell, he mentally rehearsed what he wanted to say to Cassidy.

Cassidy's eyes widened in surprise when she saw the flowers in Pete's hand. Pete handed Cassidy the flowers, saying, "These are for you, to help me say how sorry I am for acting like a jerk the last few days."

Cassidy took the flowers, and gestured for Pete to come in. "Thank you, Pete. The flowers are beautiful. But I need to know why you've been acting strange."

Pete flushed. "It's embarrassing, Cassidy. I got crazy jealous of Gil Chauvin and acted like a jerk."

Cassidy looked at Pete in surprise. "But Pete, I never even met Gil, just talked to him on the phone."

"I know, Cassidy. I can't explain why I reacted the way I did. I've never cared about someone the way I care about you. When you talked about Gil, I felt like I was losing your interest. And so, I decided my feelings were hurt and pouted. It was all me, not you at all, and I'm sorry. I'm going to try really hard to do better."

Cassidy was quiet as she looked for and found a vase to put the flowers in. She was glad that Pete had apologized and cleared the air, but she was also troubled by his confession. She decided to act as normally as possible but knew that the conversation with Pete wasn't over.

"Let me get Maggie and Sophie ready to go, and we'll talk more after we visit Grandma Bessie. Will you be able to come in and stay for a while when we get back?"

"Sure thing, Cassidy. I want to get us back to normal." Pete was even more nervous now that he had apologized. Something was obviously going on in Cassidy's mind and he had a feeling it wasn't good.

Cassidy was quiet on the trip to Our Lady of Lourdes, and Pete got more nervous. They parted at the door to go their separate ways, agreeing to meet up in Bessie's room in an hour.

Bessie was using her computer when Cassidy got to her room. The computer would say a word, and then Bessie would try to repeat it. Bessie's speech was far from normal, but it felt so good to hear her make any kind of sound, Cassidy had to wipe a tear from her eye before going into the room.

"Grandma Bessie! I heard you!" Cassidy hurried over to plant a kiss on Bessie's cheek.

Bessie gestured for Sophie to come up on her lap. "Soapy," Bessie held her little dog tight.

"I'll bet Sophie is too excited to hear you say her name!" Sophie's tail was indeed wagging as she stood on Bessie's lap showering her face with kisses. "I'm so proud of you Grandma! You are making great progress."

Bessie nodded, and said, "Slow".

"I know it will be slow and take a long time. But you are moving forward and that is great. Do you want to come with me and Maggie to do visits today?"

Bessie nodded her head yes and pointed to cane in the corner. "You graduated from the walker to a cane?" Cassidy asked.

Bessie smiled and nodded. "Before too much longer, you will be able to move over to assisted living and have Sophie come stay with you." As Cassidy said that she worried what would happen to Maggie if her roommate moved out. She could hear Prescott's voice in her head saying to not borrow trouble, so she let the thought go.

As Bessie and Cassidy made their visits on the nursing home side of the facility, Pete, Laverne and Shirley made their visits on the assisted living side. Bessie noticed that Cassidy was subdued as they made their visits and wondered if there were still problems with Pete. The child would talk if she wants to talk, thought Bessie, and focused on the joy that Maggie and Sophie were bringing to the residents they visited.

As Bessie and Cassidy returned to Bessie's room, Bessie finally decided to ask. She looked at Cassidy and asked, "Sad?".

Cassidy hugged Bessie and answered. "A little Grandma. I have to do something that I don't want to do, but I know I have to. I'll come by tomorrow and tell you all about it."

Pete overheard Cassidy talking to Bessie, and wondered what Cassidy had to do that she didn't want to do. He realized he hadn't really talked to Cassidy since Sunday and didn't know if there was something going on at the shelter. He mentally shook a fist at himself for being so foolish. As he walked into the room, he saw Cassidy startle, as if she didn't intend for him to have heard what she said to Bessie, and that feeling of unease he had had since the beginning of the evening returned.

Bessie sensed the tension in the atmosphere and knew she had just the thing to diffuse it. "H'lo" she said to Pete.

"Why, Ms. Bessie! That is surely the most beautiful greeting I have ever gotten. It is so good to hear your voice!" Bessie smiled at Pete, thinking again what a nice young man he was, and hoping whatever was happening between him and Cassidy would not take too long to resolve.

As Pete and Cassidy said their goodbyes, and got the dogs packed up in the car, Pete couldn't contain his excitement. "I'm so happy to hear Ms. Bessie speak, Cassidy. Did she talk more to you?"

"Just one word at a time, Pete, but it is very exciting. She was practicing with a program on her computer when I got here. The first thing she said was 'Sophie'. It sounded like 'Soapy', but Sophie knew and got all excited and it was just beautiful."

Cassidy had almost confided in Pete her worry about Maggie and Sophie being separated but decided to hold her peace. If the conversation at her house went the way she suspected it would, Cassidy would need to learn to confide in someone else, the way she used to.

The rest of the trip to Cassidy's house was completed in silence, and Pete grew even more nervous. Cassidy, on the other hand, was more certain with each passing minute of what she had to do.

After they were in the house and settled, Cassidy offered Pete something to drink, and got them both a glass of ice water. Cassidy knew she had to jump in and get this conversation over with.

"Pete, I told you about my mom, Sandra."

"Yes, Cassidy, you did. Has something happened?" Cassidy took a deep breath and prayed for guidance.

"Not with Sandra, Pete, but with you. I have spent my whole life dancing around Sandra's moods. Never knowing what was going to set her off, not knowing what I was going to be criticized for this time. I promised myself that I would not have relationships by choice with people who would hold me responsible for their emotions. I need to have relationships where there is honesty, and where I am not punished for simply being myself. This last few days have been hard on me, as I have second guessed what in the world I did wrong. I didn't do anything wrong. I am not willing to give anyone the power to make me feel bad when I have no reason to. And because of that, I think we need to slow down, and back up in this relationship. We can be friends. Maybe if we are friends for longer, you will trust me enough to not jump to conclusions without talking first. It may not be fair to you to put my baggage with Sandra into our relationship, but that baggage is part of me. And it is not fair to me to ask me to commit to another relationship where I will always feel like I am walking on eggshells."

Pete was gob smacked. "Cassidy, I swear I'm sorry, and it won't happen again. Please, just give me another chance."

"I am giving you a chance, Pete. A chance to be friends. And if we can be friends without any more crazy silences or long pouts that I have no control over, maybe we will try to move to more than friends. But I'm not willing to invest more than friendship until I see that I won't be riding someone else's roller coaster for the rest of my life."

Pete was heartbroken, but he knew that he had been the one to mess up the relationship, and he would have to be the one to fix it.

"I promise I'll win back the right to court you, Cassidy. I can't tell you how sorry I am, but I know you are right. My mom even told me that maybe I'm not mature enough to have a romantic relationship if I acted so foolishly for no reason. I'm going to show you and my mom that I can be the kind of man you deserve."

As Pete collected Laverne and Shirley to head home, he thought about what Cassidy had said, and what Harriet had said. It was time for Pete to grow up and prove himself worthy of Cassidy's trust and her love.

As Cassidy shut the door behind Pete, the tears that she had been holding at bay all evening slipped down her cheeks. She sat down on the floor of the foyer, and Maggie and Sophie climbed into her lap. "It's already too late, girls. I think I already fell in love with him. But I can't spend the rest of my life with a man that doesn't talk to me instead of pouting and acting distant. I can't. I hope Pete does better, because I'm not sure that I'll ever get over it if he doesn't."

♦ ♦ ♦

Marie's appointment with her therapist had gone well, and the therapist approved of Marie's plan to send a letter to Sandra. Marie had brought the letter with her to her appointment, and the therapist had offered some advice for revisions. Marie decided to re-read the letter one more time before putting it in the mail.

> *My dearest Sandra –*
>
> *I don't blame you if you never read this letter. If you do choose to read it, I hope you read it with an open heart.*
>
> *I am so sorry for being such a bad mother to you. I have been in counseling for several years now, and I know I did the best I could in a bad situation, but you were the one to suffer for my inadequacy.*
>
> *I want you to know I love you. I have always loved you. Burl Theriot was a cruel and violent man, and the only way I knew to protect you from him was to push you into the shadows of our lives.*

Burl hated for me to show anyone affection but him. When I realized that showing my love for you resulted in him abusing both of us, I stopped. I should have had the courage to leave, but Burl told me he would get custody of you, and you would be his target.

I should have had the courage to leave when you did, but I was so broken by then.

When Burl died, I hired a private investigator to find you, but then felt unworthy to ask your forgiveness.

I would love to be reconciled with you, and to meet your husband and my grandchildren. I realize that may not be something that you can do, and I respect whatever decision you make.

Please know that you were never the problem. You are a wonderful person, and were a wonderful little girl. I wish I could have given you a better childhood.

Whatever you decide, know that I love you with every breath in my body, and I am so proud of who you are.

Love Always,
Mom

Marie put the letter in an envelope and sealed it before she could change her mind. Max was leaning against her leg with his head resting on her lap. "Let's take this out to the mailbox, Max, and then take a walk around the yard."

Max wagged his tail as Marie clipped his leash on his collar. Marie knelt down and placed her forehead against Max's. "I'm sure glad you are here, boy. You give me the courage to try. I don't know how I lived so long without you." Max pushed his forehead against Marie's as if to say, "Right back at you".

Marie put the letter in her mailbox and raised the flag so that the letter would get picked up in the morning. Now all she had to do was wait. As she and Max walked the perimeter of her yard, she noticed the sounds of dogs barking at the property behind hers. It sure sounded like they had a lot of dogs, but Marie supposed they were hunting dogs, and many people had four or more. Max moved closer to Marie, and seemed uncomfortable, so Marie headed up towards the front of the property.

"Don't worry Max. We'll have a fence soon, and you'll be as safe in the yard as you are in the house."

As Marie got her and Max ready for bed, she prayed that Sandra would find it in her heart to forgive Marie. And then she asked God to please give her the strength to accept it if Sandra did not.

◆ ◆ ◆

Prescott looked at the clock and thought about calling Cassidy. He hadn't talked to her since Monday night, and knew she was probably worried about how abrupt he had been. Prescott had thought quite a bit about his conversation with Marie and had realized that there was nothing he could do to fix the past, so fixating on it was taking him down a bad road. The best cure for the guilt he would always carry for the mistakes of the past was to do everything in his power to make the future as beneficial to as many people as he could.

Prescott realized it was too late to call Cassidy, so he spent the evening finalizing the paperwork to take to his attorney on Monday. He still hadn't figured out what to call the sanctuary and decided to see if Cassidy was available on Saturday so that he could fill her in on his plans and get some help from her on a name. Prescott thought Pete might have Cassidy's Saturday booked, but he decided to call her tomorrow at work and see if she could come over for lunch and to talk. After meeting with his attorney on Monday, Prescott planned to give his notice and start telling the people at the plant that he would be retiring at the end of June. The plan was all coming together, and the dream of spending the rest of his life helping veterans and animals was about to come true.

CHAPTER 23

Cassidy hoped that her visit with Bessie Chauvin this evening was going to cheer her up, because it had been a tough morning so far.

The shelter was almost at capacity for residents again, only a week ago, Cassidy had been looking at an empty shelter. Lester, Pippin and Inca had all gone to forever homes over the past week, but the Christmas present puppies and kittens had started rolling in. Cassidy knew that being mostly young, they would be easier to place, but it was so depressing to see this cycle repeat every year. At least Cassidy had the foster/adoption booth to look forward to at Holy Redeemer at the end of February, hopefully, the good people at Holy Redeemer would come through in a big way to help the shelter.

When the phone rang at around 11:30, Cassidy honestly thought about letting it go to voicemail. She was glad she picked up when she heard Prescott's voice on the other end of the line.

"Hey, Daddy, what's up?" Cassidy couldn't help smiling hearing her daddy's voice.

"I was hoping my best girl could meet me for lunch tomorrow," replied Prescott.

"I'd love to Daddy. Do you want to go out, or would you like me to make lunch for us?" Cassidy was thinking that it would be nice to see Thor too.

"I don't want to make work for you, but it would be nice to bring Thor, so you can see how well he is doing."

"Daddy, you know you can bring Thor anywhere with you. He is an official assistance animal and is allowed." Cassidy didn't know why Prescott was so resistant to taking Thor everywhere.

"I know, Cassidy, and I have started bringing Thor to lots of places. Because he is an official assistance dog, he has to be at work when I take him out in public. If I come to your house, I can release him from work and he can play with Maggie and Sophie and just be a dog for a while."

That made sense to Cassidy and made her feel better. "I'd like you to come over, Daddy. I have a bunch of stuff I need to talk to you about, and it will be much more comfortable if we are at my house."

Prescott wasn't sure he liked the sound of Cassidy's voice when she shared that she had a lot to talk about, but he knew tomorrow would come soon enough.

"How about I pick something up for us to eat, and you can just worry about drinks? I've had a craving for crawfish etouffee. I'll pick us each up an order at the Hungry Pelican and bring it over if that works for you."

"That will be great, Daddy. I can't wait. Today has been a real bummer. Just last week I was all excited that we had homes or prospective homes for all of our animals. We have had such a busy intake week we are almost full again. Lots of young dogs and cats, mostly Christmas presents that didn't work out." Cassidy hadn't meant to unload on her dad, but it had just come spilling out.

"I'm sorry to hear that Cass. Don't let it get you down. I'm sure you'll find homes for all of them. You found a home for Max, and so you should be confident that you will place these animals too."

"I know Daddy, and if we never had animals I wouldn't have a job, but sometimes it just gets me down. I promise I'll be in better spirits tomorrow."

"Baby Girl, you can be in any spirits you want to be, and I'll always be glad to be with you. I'm going to get back to work. I'll see you around noon tomorrow."

As Cassidy went back to work, she felt better. Talking to Prescott always did that for her. Maybe after she talked to her dad tomorrow she would have more peace about her decision with Pete. Cassidy certainly hoped so.

Pete was struggling through his day as well. He was trying to keep a good face on things, but he had noticed Hannah and Lindy watching him closely. He knew there was nothing to talk about, that he had to work on himself and his behavior. Pete was planning to call Cassidy later that afternoon, and just talk. Friendly, not too pushy. He was going to ask if they should try to take Bessie out to Mass and brunch again on Sunday. Just as friends.

Pete checked his appointments for the rest of the day and was pleased to see that Marie Theriot and Max were coming in at 3 PM. That would give Pete the perfect reason to call Cassidy. He couldn't believe that last week at this time everything was looking so good, and that he had made such a mess of things. As soon as that train of thought started, Pete shut it down. There was no going back and fixing the past, he had to concentrate on convincing Cassidy he was worth planning a future with.

Marie was nervous as she and Max headed to his first veterinary appointment. Marie had never taken a dog to the vet before and had no idea what to expect. Plus, she had never taken Max anywhere with other animals, and didn't know how he was going to react. When they got to the veterinarian's office, Marie was surprised at how calm Max was. She remembered her dad talking about how nervous Bijou always got when taken to the vet, and had expected similar behavior from Max.

Marie was relieved to see that there weren't any dogs or cats in the waiting room when she and Max went in. He walked politely on his leash to the reception desk, and Marie was pleased to see him sit without instruction.

Hannah Falgoust greeted Max before she greeted Marie. "Aren't you a handsome fellow? And so well behaved." Looking up at Marie, Hannah asked, "Can I help you?"

"Yes, thank you," replied Marie. "I have a 3 PM appointment for Max with Dr. Marshall. We have a certificate from St. Elizabeth Animal Shelter for a free initial appointment."

"So, this is Max! Cassidy was worried about him finding a good home, but it looks like he hit the lottery. I have some forms for you to fill out, Mrs. Theriot. I know you just got Max a week ago from the shelter, so just tell us whatever you know. We understand that Max was left at the shelter without a lot of history, so we'll do the best we can with what we have. If they didn't have a date of birth for Max, we can ask Dr. Marshall to estimate his age." Hannah wanted Marie to feel comfortable so that Max would keep coming back to see Pete. She knew Cassidy wanted that to happen.

"The shelter told me he was around eight years old but didn't give me a date of birth." Marie wasn't sure what to do.

"We can use his adoption day as his date of birth and just adjust the year, or you can pick a day that means something to you, Max won't mind as long as he gets extra treats that day." Hannah could see how nervous Marie was and wanted to help her relax but could see nothing she was trying was working. Hopefully, Pete would work his magic.

After Marie filled out and turned in the paper work, Lindy took Marie and Max back to an examining room and promised to be back soon with Dr. Marshall.

When Pete came in the room with Lindy a few minutes later, Marie was surprised to see a handsome young man that she recognized from the PTA meeting the previous week.

"Hi, Mrs. Theriot," said Pete, offering his hand to shake. "I'm Pete Marshall. I think you know my sister-in-law, Rosadel, from Holy Redeemer."

"Yes, I do, Dr. Marshall. It is nice to meet you." Marie was embarrassed because Dr. Marshall must have noticed how sweaty her hands were.

Pete gestured to Lindy to help him lift Max onto the table. "Lindy and I are going to put Max on the table to examine him. Lindy will hold his head, and I will pick up his body. Since we don't know him yet, I don't want to take a chance on picking him up without someone keeping him engaged from the front. He may be frightened or react poorly to being out of control."

Marie stepped back and said a quick prayer that Max reacted well, and her prayer was answered as Max was very docile while being handled.

"Did we weigh Max?" Pete asked Lindy.

"We did, and he is sixty-three pounds," replied Lindy.

Pete invited Marie over to the examining table. "Mrs. Theriot, you can pet Max and talk to him while I examine him. It will help keep him calm."

Marie positioned herself in front of Max, and he laid his big head on her shoulder.

"Looks like he loves and trusts you," said Pete, "I'd never guess he had only been with you a week."

Marie swallowed the lump in her throat before answering. "I can't believe it either, Dr. Marshall. I love him so much already, I can't imagine life without him."

"That is just the kind of answer I always hope to get from my patient's caretakers." replied Pete.

As Pete checked Max out, he was impressed with how calm and obedient the big dog was. Max's shots were all up to date from the shelter, and was already on heartworm and flea medication, so this was basically a wellness and getting to know you check.

"Everything looks and sounds good, Mrs. Theriot. I'd recommend you continue with the heartworm and flea medications that were started at the shelter. Hannah will fix you up with a six-month supply of each. Max had his last set of booster shots at his intake at the shelter in December, so we will want to see him in June. Of course, if you have any problems or questions, please call us at any time."

"No questions, thank you Dr. Marshall. It was a pleasure meeting you." Marie was relieved that this first visit had gone so well. Looks like she had been nervous for no reason.

Pete was glad that he could report that Max and Marie Theriot had bonded and were doing great. There was something about Marie that bothered him. She seemed familiar to him somehow. He knew she didn't come to Holy Redeemer until he was in high school, so he had to assume it was just that he had seen her at Mass over the years. Pete honestly believed he had never met a person who seemed lonelier. He was glad she had Max and hoped that would help ease her loneliness.

Pete was nervous as he dialed Cassidy's number at St. Elizabeth Animal Shelter. He was glad that he had the report on Marie and Max as an icebreaker and hoped that he would get a positive response from Cassidy.

Cassidy was surprised to hear Pete's voice when she answered the phone late Friday afternoon.

"Hey Cassidy, I just wanted to let you know that Marie Theriot and Max just came in for their first visit. They are getting along fine and appear to have really bonded with each other. I thought you would want to know."

"Thanks, Pete. That is good news. I hoped they would do well, it seemed like they made an immediate connection."

"If you didn't know Marie had only had Max for a week, you would think they had been together forever." Pete thought about mentioning how lonely Marie seemed, but decided that was a conversation better had in person. "I know things are weird now, Cass, but can we still take Bessie to church and go to brunch on Sunday?"

Cassidy bit her lip and thought for a moment before answering. "I don't think that is a good idea this weekend Pete. Why don't we just go over and visit at Our Lady of Lourdes in the afternoon, like we did the week before last?"

Pete swallowed his disappointment and made sure he kept his voice upbeat. "How about I pick you up around 1:30 Sunday then?"

"That will be fine, Pete. I need to get going, I've got a lot to finish up before the end of the day." And with that Cassidy hung up.

Pete shook his head as he looked at the phone in his hand. Getting back to a romantic relationship with Cassidy was going to take more work than he had initially assumed.

Closing up the shelter for the night took a lot longer this Friday, as there were so many animals in residence. Dustin and Katelyn were both scheduled to work tomorrow, and Cassidy went over the coverage schedule for the weekend. None of the animals were so young that someone needed to sleep at the shelter. Katelyn was going to work the phones on Saturday to see if any of the local rescue groups could setup foster home arrangements to ease the population at the shelter.

By the time Cassidy left work, she decided to just pick up Laverne and Shirley and head over to see Bessie. She'd grab something to eat after she got home, not that she was very hungry these past few days.

Bessie had already finished eating and was in her room, practicing words on her computer when Cassidy arrived.

"Hey Grandma! Do you ever take a break?" Cassidy leaned over and kissed Bessie's cheek while Sophie clamored to get some lap time.

"No break. Must talk." Bessie answered, and then smiled.

"Well, I think you are doing fantastic, Grandma. I never would have believed at Christmas that you would have made this much progress before January is even over."

Bessie smiled proudly. "Walk. Talk. Go Home." Although the words came out slowly, it was obvious Bessie's speech was getting more clear and natural every day.

Cassidy heard Bessie's proclamation with joy and a fair bit of trepidation. Cassidy wanted Bessie to go home, too. But she was worried about the reality of Bessie living alone, especially since Bessie had no relatives close by.

"Do you want to come with me to visit with Maggie, or do you want to stay here with Sophie and keep working on your exercises?" Cassidy was fine either way, and knew that her conversation with Bessie was best left for after their visits were accomplished.

"Visit. Talk. Practice with people." Cassidy knew the other patients would be excited by Bessie's progress, as it gave them all hope for their own rehabilitation when they saw a success story like Bessie.

As Cassidy and Bessie made the rounds with Maggie and Sophie, Cassidy thought about Pete, and how much she wanted to share with Bessie. Cassidy knew that Bessie was excited about Pete and her as a couple and didn't want to disappoint her. But Cassidy also knew that Bessie knew something was not right, and that it would be foolish of her to try to pretend everything was normal.

As soon as they finished their visits and got back into Bessie's room, Bessie looked at Cassidy and asked, "Pete?"

Despite the fact that thinking about the situation with Pete made Cassidy feel sad, she couldn't help by smile at Bessie's perception.

"Oh, Grandma, the Pete thing is kind of in a mess right now. Why don't you sit down with Sophie, and I'll sit down with Maggie and I'll explain the whole mess?"

As Cassidy explained the progression of the past week, Pete's silence and strangeness, his explanation and apology, Bessie just listened as she pet Sophie. Cassidy realized she had never told Bessie about Sandra, and realized that without that part of the story, Cassidy was overreacting as much as Pete had. Cassidy wondered if something in Pete's past had influenced his reaction. Filing that thought away for later, Cassidy told Bessie how much Pete's unexplained silence felt like her entire life with Sandra, never knowing what she would do that would cause silence and hurt feelings. As Cassidy finished pouring out her heart, Bessie reached over and took her hand.

Bessie's mouth worked as she tried to find and say the right words. "Pete scared. Cassidy scared. Love scary."

Cassidy squeezed Bessie's hand. "Yes, love is scary, and Lord knows I'm scared of what I feel for Pete. I never thought about Pete being scared by what he feels for me. Do you think I'm being too harsh, Grandma? Should I just accept his apology, move forward and hope for the best?"

Bessie thought for a moment before trying to answer. "Your time not mine or Pete."

"That is just what I think, Grandma. I'm not ready to just let it go. Maybe I will be soon, maybe not. I promised Gil I would call him tonight and give him an update on how you are doing. I'm going to do that, and I'm going to tell Pete about the call when he picks me up on Sunday with Laverne and Shirley to come visit. That will be Pete's first chance to show me he can act like he trusts me. I hate feeling like I am testing him, but I don't know what else to do. I can't live with a husband who always finds fault with me. It has been hard enough living with a mother who does that."

Bessie squeezed Cassidy's hand again. "No fault you. His fear."

As Cassidy processed what Bessie was telling her, she wondered if some of her interactions with Sandra were actually different when viewed from Sandra's perspective. Cassidy decided to talk to Prescott about it when they had lunch on Saturday.

As Cassidy prepared to leave with Maggie and Sophie, she hugged Bessie and kissed her cheek. "Thanks for listening, and for the advice, Grandma. I feel better now than I have all week." Cassidy knew she had a lot of thinking to do, but maybe, just maybe, everything could work out alright.

◆ ◆ ◆

Gil Chauvin glanced at the clock and wondered when Cassidy Bourgeois was going to call. He was relieved that his Tante Bessie had someone who cared so much about her but couldn't shake the nagging guilt that it was a virtual stranger who was making sure that Tante was taken care of. Although Gil had been born and raised in Texas, he felt the pull of his Louisiana roots far more than his sisters did.

He had looked at the company's internal job posting system, and there was nothing that fit his skill set either at the Bayou Beni plant or the Baton Rouge facility. Gil knew that he had too many years with the company to move to Louisiana without the benefit of relocating with the company, but he also knew there were not many years left to spend with Tante, and he wanted to live in Louisiana while she was still alive. Gil had a strong suspicion that he would stay in Louisiana once he moved there, now all he had to do was find an opportunity to pursue there.

Cassidy unloaded Maggie and Sophie, got them fresh water, and decided to call Gil before trying to eat supper. She felt better after talking to Bessie, but still didn't feel much like eating. Maybe talking to Gil would improve her mood.

Gill picked up the phone on the first ring. "Sounds like you were waiting for a call," said Cassidy, "Is this a bad time?"

"No, Cher, I was waiting for your call," replied Gil. "How are things with my Tante Bessie?"

"Gil, you wouldn't believe the progress Grandma Bessie has made since I talked to you on Monday. If she keeps doing better at the same rate, I think we can do a phone call for you and her soon. She is talking, slowly, and not real sentences, but communicating. She has been practicing with the speech therapy program on the computer you got her whenever she is not doing some other kind of therapy. She is working on getting promoted to assisted living so that she can have Sophie with her again." Cassidy knew she was rambling, but she was so excited to share with Gil.

"Cassidy, that is wonderful news. I have some news myself. My work travel has finally slowed down, and I will be coming to Bayou Beni next weekend to visit Tante Bessie. I hope I will get to meet you as well and thank you in person for taking such loving care of Tante. Perhaps we could take Tante to dinner?" Cassidy didn't want to be ungracious, but she also didn't want to push Pete too far.

"I'd like that Gil, but I usually keep my weekends reserved for time with my boyfriend, Pete. He is also a great friend to Bessie."

"Then please extend my invitation to Pete as well," replied Gil. "I want to get to know everyone who has been so good to Tante Bessie since her stroke. It has weighed on my mind that I have not been back to visit since Tante left the hospital for Our Lady of Lourdes. I knew that Clancy Marshall's wife Rosadel was a nurse there, and so also knew I would know whatever I needed to know, but I feel terrible for neglecting my Tante."

"She has been fine, Gil. She is very well loved by the staff and the other patients. Pete and I took her to Holy Redeemer for Mass on Sunday, and you would have thought we brought a celebrity to church. She has had many visitors, and while I know she misses you, she has not been neglected or lonely since her stroke. In fact, I know she has more friends now than she did before. Grandma Bessie just attracts people to her."

"I'm excited to see her and meet all of her friends in Bayou Beni. My plan is to come into town on Friday, and to leave Monday morning. Can we plan to take Tante Bessie out to dinner on Saturday night?"

"Could I suggest Mass on Sunday morning and brunch instead? Bessie does best earlier in the day. By evening, she is tired, and I know she will enjoy the time out more if she is less tired."

"That sounds perfect. I'll plan to visit Tante on Friday as soon as I get to Bayou Beni. Thank you again, Cassidy for the wonderful care you give to Tante Bessie. I will never be able to repay you."

"Gil, Bessie has given me so much, it is I who will never be able to repay her. She has changed my life. Even though there is a huge age difference, she is my very best friend. She understands me in a way that is magical to me. I love her dearly and am so grateful that she came into my life."

Gil was so touched by Cassidy's words, he choked up a bit. "I look forward to meeting you, Cassidy. Have a wonderful week." As Gil and Cassidy said goodbye, Cassidy thought about Pete, and decided it wasn't too late to call him.

"Hey Pete, I just got off the phone with Gil Chauvin. He is coming into town next week to see Bessie and invited me to dinner. I told him I saved my weekends for you, and he said to invite you too. So, we are invited to go to Mass and brunch with Bessie and Gil next weekend."

Pete sat in somewhat stunned silence. He couldn't believe Cassidy had called him, and he really couldn't believe how she casually referred to him as her boyfriend.

"Um, that sounds great, Cassidy. Thanks. Did you have a good visit with Bessie tonight?"

"I did, Pete. And I'm having lunch with my dad tomorrow. Do you have plans this weekend?"

"I'm going to Rosadel and Clancy's tomorrow. Rosadel is going out to lunch with a new friend, and I'm helping Clancy keep the triplets and Rosadel's new friend's daughter entertained. I'm looking forward to the girls keeping themselves entertained so I can have a good visit with Clancy."

"I think I know Rosadel's new friend. Her name is Bethany Williams, and I brought her over to Rosadel's last weekend to meet the kittens. She has a daughter in second grade at Holy Redeemer." Cassidy fought her own twinge of jealousy when she thought about how beautiful Bethany was, and how she was already connected to Pete through Clancy. This relationship stuff was harder than she realized.

"That sounds like the one. I didn't pay really good attention, because I'm mainly interested in spending time with Clancy."

Both Pete and Cassidy fell silent. Cassidy decided to trust Bessie and her heart. "Pete, I'm still having a hard time with everything that happened this week but talking to Bessie tonight I realized that my reaction to your behavior has more to do with me and Sandra's relationship than it does with our relationship. I still think we need to take things slowly, but I didn't want to go to sleep another night feeling so far away from you."

"Cassidy, I swear, I have no idea why I acted like such an idiot, other than that the way I feel about you scares me. We're going to figure it all out, though. I think what we have is too special to not figure it out. I'll see you around one on Sunday. Have fun with your Dad tomorrow."

As Cassidy hung up the phone, she called Maggie and Sophie over to sit on her lap. As she cuddled her dogs, Cassidy thought about Pete, and about how much she wanted everything to work out for them. She thought about how most women would be calling their mother to talk about relationships, but that would never be Sandra and Cassidy. Thank God she had Prescott.

CHAPTER 24

Bethany looked in the mirror and wondered if she was too dressed up, or not dressed up enough. Usually, she only went out with family, and everyone knows their family's dress code. She hoped the leggings, boots and sweater tunic she was wearing hit the right tone. Michelle popped her head into Bethany's bedroom. "You look really pretty, Mommy. Like someone in a magazine."

Bethany crouched down and opened her arms, and Michelle ran in for a hug. "You are amazing, Michelle! You always know just what to say to make me feel better. I was wondering if I was dressed okay, and now, I'm not worried, because you made me feel like a million bucks."

Michelle hugged Bethany extra hard. "I love you, Mommy. Even if you did move me to Louisiana."

"Do you think you will ever not be upset with me for that?" Bethany was concerned that Michelle would seriously never get over the move.

"It is getting better now that I am friends with Lou and Grace and Rosie. And pretty soon we will have kittens. I like my school and teacher. I just miss Grandma Billie and Nana Beverly. And Neetee (Anitra) and Deedee (Devon)."

"How about we plan to call everyone when we get home from the Marshall's house this afternoon? I know they will all want to hear about your kittens, and I think Neetee will want to talk to you about the wedding and being flower girl."

"I think I'm old enough to be a junior bridesmaid, Mommy." Michelle had her hands on her hips.

Bethany kissed the tip of Michelle's nose and replied, "You have to take that up with Neetee. Are we ready to go have some fun?"

As Bethany and Michelle headed over to the Marshall house, Pete Marshall was also preparing for his day with Clancy. Laverne and Shirley had been fed and were waiting to be loaded into the van. Pete had picked up a couple of bags of kitten food before he left the clinic to bring with him to help Clancy and Rosadel with expenses. He knew that Rosadel was trying to teach the girls a lesson by taking money for the kittens care out of their Disney fund, but at the rate the money was disappearing, the girls would be in high school before they ever got to Disney.

Pete and Bethany ended up pulling up in front of the Marshall house at the same time. Pete smiled to himself as he thought about Cassidy's response to him meeting Bethany. Bethany was absolutely stunning. Maybe he wasn't the only one who was struggling with jealousy.

As Pete was getting Laverne and Shirley out of the car, Bethany and Michelle walked towards the front door. Michelle was watching Pete more than where she was going, but she was holding her mother's hand, so Pete wasn't worried that anything would go wrong. He was actually kind of glad Michelle was watching him, that we he wouldn't startle them when he followed them to the door.

Laverne and Shirley were eager to get inside to see their friend Roscoe, and so getting to the front door was accomplished before anyone had answered the door bell.

"Hi, I'm Pete, Clancy's brother, and these two lovely ladies are Laverne and Shirley." Bethany smiled at both Pete's easy manner and the dog's eager faces. She stuck out her hand.

"I'm Bethany Williams, and this is my daughter, Michelle. Nice to meet you." At just that moment, Lou opened the door.

"Uncle Pete! What are you doing holding hands with Ms. Bethany? You are supposed to be Ms. Cassidy's boyfriend. Boyfriends don't hold hands with other girls." Pete had no idea who was more embarrassed, him or Bethany.

"LOU!" Rosadel might win the contest for most embarrassed. "What in the world are you asking a question like that for? Did it ever occur to you to wait and see what is really going on before jumping to conclusions?"

Lou's lower lip quivered for a second, then jutted out and got firm. "I'm just looking out for Ms. Cassidy because she has been so good to us. Uncle Pete shouldn't be holding hands with Ms. Bethany." Pete realized he had to speak up and fast.

"I just met Ms. Bethany and we were shaking hands in introduction. And your Mommy is right. Uncle Pete has gotten himself in trouble his whole life by jumping to conclusions without keeping my mouth shut until I know the whole story. You really don't want to make all the mistakes I've made."

Rosadel was intrigued by Pete's statement, and knew she would have to get the rest of that story. But for now, she wanted to get everyone in the house, so she and Bethany could go to lunch.

"Let's all get inside so that Daddy and Uncle Pete can get set up for me and Ms. Bethany to go out to lunch." Rosadel smiled at Bethany and Michelle as she herded everyone inside. "Pete, Clancy is in the yard with Roscoe, why don't you go outside with Laverne and Shirley while I take Bethany and Michelle in to see the kittens?"

"I'll do that Rosadel, but don't let me forget, I've got two bags of kitten food in my van for you and the girls."

"Thank you, Pete, but the girls are supposed to be buying the food." Rosadel could be as stubborn as Lou.

"And I'm a grown man and can spend my money on foster pets in St. Elizabeth Parish if I want to," replied Pete, winking at Bethany as he and Rosadel continued to bicker. "And you shouldn't argue with family in front of company and make them uncomfortable."

"Goodness me, I'm sorry Bethany. I need to learn to keep my mouth shut as much as Lou and Pete apparently." Bethany's nerves were completely forgotten with all the interchange just getting into the Marshall house.

"No problem, Rosadel. You and Pete sound like me and my sister Anitra. I would have thought you two were brother and sister if Pete didn't look so much like Clancy."

"That is what happens when you know each other practically your whole lives. Rosadel has been just like my little sister since I was still a kid. We actually bicker more with each other than either of us do with Clancy."

Rosadel smiled. "That is only because Clancy is impossible to argue with. He just thinks about what you said and then either comes back with a reasonable compromise or apologizes for creating a misunderstanding. I really got lucky in the husband department. But he does pick on Pete, Donnie and Mike enough to be normal."

Pete laughed. "As if there is any such thing as a 'normal' Marshall."

The girls' heads had been going back and forth as if they were watching a tennis match.

"Momma Harriet says 'normal' is just a setting on the clothes dryer. Now go on outside with Clancy so that the girls can visit the kittens, and me and Bethany can go out to lunch and be adults for a while." Rosadel was smiling and steering everyone in the direction she wanted them to go as she spoke.

Lou had taken Michelle's hand and was leading her into the dining room. "Pokey and Boo play together all the time, so it is good that they are both coming to live with you. Mommy, can we get the kittens out of the kennel to play?"

"Yes, Lou. But you'll have to put them away when me and Ms. Bethany leave, and then it will be up to Daddy whether or not you can take them out. Got it?"

"Got it, Mommy. C'mon Michelle."

As the girls fussed over the kittens, Rosadel reached over and squeezed Bethany's hand. "Sorry it is always such a zoo here. I try so hard to keep the chaos at a minimum, but it always seems to get away from me."

Bethany squeezed back. "No apology necessary, Rosadel. This house is so welcoming and full of love, I feel bad for Michelle that our house is so quiet. I'm hoping the kittens will add some life to our home."

"And isn't that just life in a nutshell, it seems we all want what we don't have. If you're ready to go, I'll go alert Clancy that he and Pete are in charge and we'll hit the road."

✦ ✦ ✦

Cassidy was glad that she was going to have time with her Dad to talk through her tangled emotions. For most of her life, Cassidy had considered herself a rational person, who thought things through and reacted with logic, not emotion. Since she had started falling in love with Pete, it seemed like her emotions were always too close to the surface, and she really wanted to get back on a more even keel. Prescott was always so level-headed, Cassidy knew she would feel better after she had a chance to talk to him.

Prescott was looking forward to spending the afternoon with Cassidy. He was excited to share his plans with her for his retirement, and also for the animal and human sanctuary. He was hoping Cassidy would help him think of a good name.

Prescott was surprised to see Bethany Williams and Rosadel waiting for a table at the Hungry Pelican when he stopped to pick up his and Cassidy's lunches. "Hey Bethany, Rosadel. I didn't know you two knew each other."

Rosadel laughed as she answered. "So, you wouldn't know that Cassidy introduced us. It is exactly like my Daddy always says. Never say anything bad about anybody in Louisiana to somebody else in Louisiana. Because everybody knows somebody that knows somebody."

"And that is the truth," replied Prescott. "I'm picking up lunch to spend the afternoon with Cassidy."

"Could you do me a favor?" asked Bethany. "Could you tell Cassidy that I have decided to take two of the kittens that Rosadel is fostering?"

"She will be really pleased to hear that, Bethany. When I talked to her yesterday she said the shelter is back at full capacity. Every animal that finds a home is a wonderful thing."

Just then the hostess came back with Prescott's to-go order, and to take Rosadel and Bethany to their table.

As Bethany and Rosadel sat down their table and ordered their drinks, Rosadel continued the conversation that had started with Prescott.

"It's so sad to hear that the animal shelter is full again. I hope that after the Holy Redeemer Parish Fair we get more people involved in fostering and adopting animals. It breaks my heart to think of poor innocent animals being euthanized."

Bethany shook her head in agreement. "Me, too, Rosadel. How do you think Cassidy does it? How does she not get overwhelmed by the sadness?"

"From talking to Cassidy, Pete and Prescott, Cassidy has done an amazing job since she has been here as director of St. Elizabeth Animal Shelter. So far, the only animals that have had to be euthanized have been too sick or too dangerous for adoption. Those are still sad, but so much less so than healthy animals in their prime. And as for the sadness, we're all vulnerable to getting overwhelmed, aren't we? Sadness comes in many different forms."

Bethany nodded as she spoke. "Truer words were never spoken, Rosadel. I'm so glad I have Michelle, or the sadness may have overwhelmed me when my husband died."

Rosadel reached across the table and clasped Bethany's hands. "Can you tell me about him? I know that after my Mom died the hardest thing was being afraid to talk about her for fear of upsetting people. My Dad took both of us to counseling, and we learned that talking about Mama was one of the healthiest things we could do. We learned to live with missing her, instead of tiptoeing around the emptiness."

Bethany sighed heavily before speaking. "I talk to Michelle about Derek all the time. I want her to know him. But talking about a Daddy and talking about a man are two totally different things if you know what I mean."

Rosadel nodded. "I sure do. There are things that I talk to my friend Bee about Clancy that I would never talk to the girls about. No matter how much you love them, husbands can be a trial. And then there is the whole remembering the courtship thing. The sanitized version for the eight-year old's is not what I want to remember all the time. Can you tell me about Derek the man?"

Bethany smiled and said. "He was smoking hot, and funny and my best friend. I miss him every single minute of every single day, and I'm so mad at him for leaving me I can't stand it." Bethany's smile had turned to trembling lips and tear-filled eyes as she spoke.

"We had so many plans. There was going to be at least one more baby, maybe two. Derek would have gotten out of the Army when Michelle was three, the perfect time to start trying for another baby. For the first year, I walked around in a fog. I would wake up and think Derek was alive and just still deployed. Then I would remember he was dead, and the grief would hit just as hard and fresh as the day they came to the door."

"How did you guys meet? How long were you together before Derek died?" Rosadel hoped to steer Bethany to more pleasant memories.

"We met freshman year in high school, when we both tried out for the cross-country team. Even though the boys and girls had separate teams, we trained together preparing for tryouts, and for meets. At the first tryout, Derek looked over at me and said, 'Hey stretch, shouldn't you be basketball or volleyball?' I was already almost five-ten. I said, 'Don't call me stretch, and I'm faster than I am tall'. I was faster than most of the boys, but not Derek. We got fussed every practice because we couldn't help racing each other. We also couldn't help the sparks that flew between us. Derek and I were never comfortable. We were always striking sparks off each other. But he was like my other half. Even when we were butting heads or competing like crazy, he was my rock, my anchor, the very beat of my heart."

"Me and Clancy met in high school too, and we both ran cross country and track. I only started running to be with Clancy though. Clancy is easy. He rarely gets angry. Being with Clancy is like being wrapped in the warmest softest blanket in the world. At the same time, he is so strong, and sure. We hardly ever argue. When we disagree, he listens, and then comes back calmly with compromise. But, for all that we are all smooth and calm, he lights me up, if you know what I mean. I'm so sorry, Bethany, that you lost Derek. I can't imagine the hole that would exist in my life if I lost Clancy."

"Thank you, Rosadel. One of the hardest things with my friends in Texas is that they could never be normal with me. You talk about Clancy when I talk about Derek without looking guilty. I don't want anyone to feel guilty because their husband is alive and mine is dead. I just want them to let me talk about Derek without all the sadness."

"Well, since we just met, you must have a thousand stories to tell, and I'd love to hear them."

Bethany smiled as the waitress brought their food. "I have a feeling you may be sorry you said that once I get going."

Rosadel smiled back. "Give it your best shot, I can tell a mean story too. And speaking of storytelling, there is no time like a good run for sharing stories. Do you still run?"

"Mostly on the treadmill now. When Michelle was smaller, I could put her in a jogging stroller, but now that she is too big for that, it is hard."

"Me and Clancy went through the same thing. We go to the track at the high school as often as we can. The girls play in the infield, and we do laps. You can join us anytime you like."

"Thanks, Rosadel. I think I'll do that. Are you sure I won't be taking away from your time with Clancy?"

"Clancy and I always find a way to make time just for each other, so this will be fine. It will be good for you and Michelle to get out more in the community. There are other people on the track in the evenings too, and other children playing in the infield. You'll see, it will be fine."

◆ ◆ ◆

Cassidy had just finished her Saturday chores when she heard the front door open. Maggie and Sophie woke up just enough to run to the door, but not enough to bark.

"I sure hope that it's you, Daddy," Cassidy called out. "My two old ladies aren't an early warning system at all."

"It is me, and I had to use my key to open the door, so you are doing the right stuff to stay safe without an early warning system." Prescott sat the bag of take-out on the counter and gave Cassidy a quick hug while Thor and the girls said their hellos. "How is my best girl doing?"

"To be honest, Dad, it has been a heck of a week. Let's get the food on the table and eat while it is hot and then I will tell you all about it."

As Prescott and Cassidy ate their lunches, Cassidy filled Prescott in on the conflict with Pete, making sure to include the revelation she had had the night before while talking to Bessie Chauvin. After Cassidy had told her story, Prescott sat back for a minute, obviously carefully choosing his words before responding.

"Whew! That is a whole bunch of stuff to process, Baby Girl. Jealousy is a dangerous emotion. I've seen it destroy people and relationships more times than I can count. But it is also a very human emotion, that most people struggle with at one time or another in their lives. I understand you not wanting to take a risk getting more deeply involved with Pete if he turns out to have an unreasonable problem with internally managing his jealous feelings. But knowing Harriet and George the way I do, it is hard for me to imagine Pete as an unreasonably jealous person."

"You're right there, Daddy. Pete told me that his Mom told him if he couldn't behave more maturely than to be jealous that he wasn't mature enough to have a romantic relationship. I got the impression that his Dad told him something too, but he didn't share that with me. And to be honest, when I called Pete last night and found out that he would be seeing Bethany and Michelle at Rosadel's today, I had to fight my own instantaneous jealous reaction."

"I think that taking your time is good, and I like that you told Pete about Gil, and Gil about Pete. This weekend will tell you a lot about Pete's commitment to not overreacting to your relationships with other men. But I need to tell you he will be sorely tested. Your old man doesn't pay much attention to what people look like. I like to see what a person is made of, not what kind of package they come in. Too many good people have had their appearance damaged in one way or another to put much stock in it. Gil Chauvin is one of those people who is so darned good looking that he turns heads everywhere he goes. We laugh about it at work. One time someone suggested that Gil should have a warning sign since so many people got bumped into when others turned their heads to follow Gil's movements. He isn't stuck on himself, and laughs about it, but go easy on Pete next weekend. I imagine he will have a hard time when he sees what Gil looks like."

"I'll see Pete tomorrow, and hopefully, we will have a good day. What do you think about what I told you about me reacting more to Mom and my history with her than really to what Pete did?"

"That is a hard one too, Cassidy. You are who you are because of the life experiences you've had. You are completely right in demanding that the people you allow into your life be emotionally available to you, and choose to be open and honest, instead of shutting you out when their emotions confuse them. The line between protecting yourself from a bad situation and being so protective you miss out on the richness of messy human relationships is crooked and blurry. A lot of where the line is and how thick it should be is determined by the other person in the relationship. You have had to protect yourself from Sandra's emotional roller coaster. I don't know that there will ever be another person in your life that needs that much from you. I think more of your relationships will be like ours. We might disagree, we might even get angry, but we always work through it. I always know you love me, and I hope you always know that I love you."

"Daddy, you know that our relationship has been the steadiest relationship in my life. I'm lucky that Mark, Candy and Chip are all easier than Mom, but no one is like you. I have never had a moment in my life when I wasn't sure that you loved me, or when I wouldn't pick up the phone and call you just because hearing your voice steadies me. I've met lots of people whose parents divorced when they were kids, and lots who grew up in intact families, and I can honestly say I don't know anyone who has a better relationship with their Dad than I do. Rosadel and Angus are like us, and it looks like the Marshall's all have that relationship with Mr. Marshall, so I know we are not the only ones, but that doesn't make me appreciate what we have any less."

"So, in light of the balance of your life, Mom being a challenge, and me being a constant, where does that bring you to how to manage your emotions related to Pete?"

"I think I may have overreacted to Pete's jealousy as badly as he overreacted to my excitement over talking to Gil. I guess both Pete and I need to mature in this relationship thing if we're going to stand a chance. I want us to work, Daddy. Before the mess this week, I can honestly say I have never felt more comfortable with anyone my age. I've always been comfortable with you, and my relationship with Grandma Bessie is amazing, but you know I've never really had close friends. Pete has been so easy to get close to and to trust. I guess that's why his distance hurt so much. I hope we can learn from this and grow together instead of apart."

"Me too, Baby Girl. Pete comes from good people, and from what I have seen of him as a Veterinarian, is good people himself. You two have so much in common, I think you have the right foundation to build on. The key is to remember that both of you will make mistakes, and that both of you will grow and change. In good relationships, the partners grow together, and stay connected through the trials. That all starts with good, open communications. Sounds like you and Pete had your first communication crisis, if you learn from it and get past it, you two have all the potential in the world to be a great couple."

"Thanks, Daddy. Now I want to hear about what is going on in your world. It feels like we hardly talked this week."

"Well, Cassidy, I've made some decisions. I'm going to announce my retirement on February 1, to be effective June 30."

"That is great Daddy, but what will you do when you are retired?" Cassidy knew Prescott did a lot of volunteer work with the VA but didn't think that was quite enough for her always on the go Dad.

"Well, Baby Girl, I've done really well with my investments since I've been working. I try to keep things low key, but I've accumulated close to $20 million dollars."

Cassidy couldn't believe her ears. "Daddy, I knew you weren't poor, but I'm speechless."

"I took some big risks over the years that paid off, and now I am about to realize a dream. I'm going to put all but a million dollars in a charitable foundation, and I'm going to buy a hundred acres in Terrebonne parish and build a sanctuary for military veterans and abandoned animals. I've been working on my business plan for the last year, and I meet with my attorneys on Monday to finalize everything. I'll be working with the VA on returning vets in transition. They will have a place to stay if they are having difficulty reentering civilian life. The plan is to develop some of the abandoned animals into emotional support and service animals, but to also have some just in sanctuary. Caring for the animals will be part of the therapy for the humans in residence. My plan is to have a psychologist on staff, and a vet tech, with a veterinarian on call. I will have a capacity of 10 vets, and up to 20 animals, with the animal population dependent on the human population. The property I'm looking at purchasing has a five-bedroom main house, where the staff will live, and we will serve communal meals for those who want to eat communally. I have a barn and a stable, so rescuing cows, horses, pigs and chickens is not off the table. There are four one-bedroom cottages, and three two-bedroom cottages. The animals will stay at the main house or in the cottages, with any large animals staying in the barn and stables."

"Oh my God, Daddy, this is an amazing idea. Are you sure that you want to take on something so ambitious as a retirement project?"

"I've been thinking about this for years, Cassidy, and my last financial windfall convinced me I could do it. I'll need to do fundraising to keep things going, but for as long as I'm alive, I can be making a positive difference in the world. And I won't be alone. I'll hire good staff and set up a board of directors for the trust and the facility. I want this to live on after I'm gone. It doesn't look like we will stop breaking people with war any time soon, and I want there to be a sanctuary for at least some of them. And after the way first Ulysses and then Thor have made my life better, I want to try to give that gift to as many as I can. And if I can also save some innocent animals who can't be service dogs and give them a good life, so much the better."

"I'm somewhere between so proud I could burst and so humbled I could cry. I love you, Daddy. And I'm so proud to be your daughter. This is a great thing you are trying to do."

"I need a name for the place, Cassidy. I just haven't been able to come up with anything, and I was hoping you could help. Do you have any ideas?"

"I don't Daddy, but I'll think on it. We have some time, don't we?"

"Yes, we do. I'm meeting with my attorneys on Monday. I'm not sure how the transfer of assets to the charity will work, or how long it will take or what the tax implications will be. I think the first step will be setting up the charitable foundation. I have a vision and mission statement, and a statement of intent. I just need a name. I think the attorneys will be busy just researching how best to move my money without losing too much to taxes. I'm sure we have a couple of weeks to come up with something."

"I'm sure we'll come up with the perfect name. I'm still a little in shock Daddy. Can I tell Pete and Grandma Bessie?"

"Yes, but only them until after I give my notice at work and hear back from my attorneys on how to proceed. I want to have more answers than questions when people start to hear about my plan."

"No problem, Daddy, we can keep the circle small for a while."

◆ ◆ ◆

The girls were playing with the kittens again, and Clancy and Pete were sharing a cup of coffee at the kitchen table while Roscoe, Laverne and Shirley napped.

Pete kept folding and unfolding a napkin, staring into space, when suddenly Clancy reached over and snapped his fingers right in front of Pete's face.

"What's on your mind, little brother? Something has been bothering you all day? You want to talk about it?"

Pete put down the napkin and took a sip of his coffee.

"Yes and no, Bro. I want advice, but I hate have to admit to you that I've been an ass."

"Whoa! What did you do? You're usually a pretty level, nice kind of guy, even though I hate to puff you up."

"It's Cassidy, Bro. She was all excited because Bessie's nephew Gil was able to get better rehabilitation tools for her. It was 'Gil this' and 'Gil that' every time I talked to her. I started feeling insecure and jealous and gave Cass the cold shoulder for a few days. I went to talk to Mom and Dad on Wednesday, and Mom raked me over the coals for being immature, and Dad told me Uncle Vinnie just about ruined his marriage with jealousy. So, I apologized to Cassidy and explained what had happened, and she told me that maybe we should cool things off, as she didn't want to be jerked around because I can't handle my emotions maturely."

"Man, that sucks, Pete. I know you really like Cassidy."

"So, she didn't totally throw me under the bus, she said we could be friends and we'll see if I can manage to not be a jerk. I don't want to be a jerk. But this jealousy thing is crazy. I never felt like this. Did you and Rosadel ever have a problem with jealousy? How did you handle it?"

"Pete, me and Rosadel have been together since we were kids, and I was half in love with her before we ever dated. I'm not even sure how to answer your question. Did it suck when I had to go away to college and leave her here? Yes. Did I give her Roscoe so that any new 'friends' would ask about her dog and she would have to say he was a gift from her boyfriend? Yes. Did it drive me nuts that her Advanced Biology lab partner senior year was Trent Guidry, who happened to be the quarterback of the football team and headed to LSU as a pre-med major? Yes. Was it worse when every other phone call was 'Trent this' and 'Trent that'? Oh My God, Yes. But while all that left me feeling insecure, I already really loved Rosadel. As much as I couldn't imagine my life without her, if she would have been happy with someone else I would have stepped aside. It might have killed me, but I love her that much."

"I think I could love Cassidy that much, Clancy, but I'm afraid of getting hurt."

"You know, Pete, Mom and Dad and Angus all were pretty freaked out when me and Rosadel got serious so fast. They all thought we were too young. Well, the good thing about being so young is being so sure that everything will be rainbows and puppies. We grew up together. So, I understand you are scared, but I can't really empathize, because me and Rosadel were too young to be cautious. Hence the triplets in the other room."

"Did Rosadel ever get jealous? Or is that something that just never happened in your relationship?"

"Wait a minute. I guess I didn't explain myself well enough. Of course, there were times I was jealous, I just never acted on that jealousy in a way that negatively impacted Rosadel. Every time I got jealous, I rededicated myself to being the very best man I could be for Rosadel. I turned the insecurity and anger into purpose. I would be the best thing that could ever happen in her life, no matter if she turned away from that or not. A kid's thinking, a kid's confidence, but it got us through.

"One time Bee Collins was dating a guy who was super jealous, he even resented the time that Bee spent with Rosadel. Rosie asked me why I never got jealous. It was almost like she felt that I couldn't really love her if I didn't get jealous. So, I told her the truth. I told her that I loved her so much that her happiness was the most important thing to me, and if her being happy didn't include me, I loved her enough to let her go. I told her what I just told you, that every time I felt jealous, I would use that emotion to be a better person, so I could be a better partner. She was real quiet for a few minutes, and then she threw her arms around me and kissed the daylights out of me. I asked her 'What was that for?' and she said, 'Because I love you that much too!'. And that is the only conversation I can recall in our fourteen years together on the subject."

"Thanks, Clancy. You've really given me a lot to think about. I'm going to be thirty this year, and I never even thought about falling in love before. I've been happy to go out and have fun. I've had girlfriends, but I think both of us always knew that the relationships weren't going anywhere, we just hung out and had fun till we both moved on. I had an 'Ah-Ha' moment while you were talking. If I want a long-term relationship with Cassidy, I have to focus on her, and on the relationship, not on me."

"Pete, if Cassidy is the right one for you, now that you've identified what you need to work on, it should be easy. I'm not saying it won't take work, because relationships, even the best ones, take work. But if you feel for Cassidy what I feel for Rosadel when I hold her in my arms, no amount of work is too much to enjoy that feeling for the rest of your life."

At that point the girls burst into the kitchen.

"We put the kittens away, cause we need a snack." Lou was always the first spokesperson.

"And then we want to play outside with Roscoe, Laverne and Shirley," said Grace, "Because Michelle doesn't have a dog to play with and she misses her Aunt Neetee's dog."

The dogs had all looked up sleepily when they heard their names. Clancy got up to start dishing up milk and cookies.

"Hopefully, the dogs will perk up while you have your snacks. They are all kind of old and maybe more interested in being pet than in playing."

Michelle smiled at Clancy. "That's OK, Mr. Clancy. I'm happy to just pet them if they are tired. Sometimes Neetee's dog just wants to be pet too. He is going to be the ring bearer in her wedding and walk down the aisle with me."

"You're going to be in a wedding?" asked Rosie. "We were in Pop-Pop and Gee-Jay's wedding. It was SO much fun!"

Pete and Clancy smiled at each other over the girls' heads, as the girls' conversation turned to dresses and hairstyles and flowers and whether or not eight was too old to be a flower girl and should Michelle really be a junior bridesmaid. As the girls chatter in turns amused and confused Pete, he had another moment of clarity. He wanted what Clancy and Rosadel had. A strong happy marriage, and a happy home with kids, and pets and a ready welcome when family stopped by. And he wanted it with Cassidy.

CHAPTER 25

What a difference a weekend could make. The shelter was still at capacity, but Dustin and Katelyn had taken a few applications on Saturday and had lined up a number of appointments for this week. As usual, the young dogs, puppies and young cats were generating the most interest. Knowing that Prescott would be starting a sanctuary gave Cassidy hope for all the future seniors she knew would be finding their way to the shelter.

Spending Saturday with Prescott had really helped Cassidy sort through her feelings for Pete, and she and Pete had a good day visiting Our Lady of Lourdes. Cassidy knew that there was still work to be done to restore her and Pete's relationship to what it once was, but now she was confident that they would succeed. Their time together Sunday had gone so well that they were planning for Pete to come over to Cassidy's after their visit to Bessie on Tuesday for Scrabble and supper.

It also helped Cassidy's mood that Bessie was progressing so well, and so quickly. Every day her speech was clearer, and her thoughts were being expressed more fully. Cassidy was pretty sure that Bessie would be moving from nursing care to assisted living before the end of February. Cassidy was still conflicted over losing Sophie. She would miss Sophie, but Maggie would miss her even more. The two dogs had really bonded since Sophie had come to stay with Cassidy in November, and Maggie depended on Sophie's company when Cassidy was at work. Cassidy decided to talk to Pete about it on Tuesday night, maybe Pete would have an idea that would help.

◆ ◆ ◆

Prescott was surprised at how relieved he felt after informing his boss of his plan to retire in June. The next step was to find a replacement so that he could start transitioning. His boss had asked him to start preparing a transition plan and was going to talk to human resources about potential candidates. Although the company had an internal job posting system, positions like Maintenance Leader for a site often involved both an internal and an external search. Prescott hoped they identified his replacement sooner rather than later, as he wanted to move on to the next stage of his life with a clear close to this stage.

Angus knocked lightly before sticking his head in the door of Prescott's office. "So, is the rumor true? You are retiring at the end of June?"

"Damn, Angus, that was fast. Yes, but I thought it would be kept quiet for a few days." Prescott was more amused than annoyed.

"I just left my boss's office. He asked me if I knew of anyone that might be interested. There are probably only about five people who know, and I think all of us will keep it quiet. You are such an important part of life at the plant, I'm pretty sure they want to have a replacement named before they announce you are leaving."

"I've been thinking about potential replacements myself, Angus. If you think of anyone, would you mind telling me before anyone else? I want to feel good about my replacement."

"Sure thing, Prescott. Do you have plans for what you are going to do when you retire?"

Prescott motioned for Angus to close the door and have a seat. "I'm going to open a sanctuary, Angus. A place for veterans transitioning to civilian life that are struggling, and a place for abandoned animals. I think there can be a symbiosis to exploit. I'm hoping to develop some of the rescue animals into companion dogs for the residents. I hope to move people in and out and back to society, but I'm comfortable if we end up with some permanent residents."

"Wow, Prescott, that sounds amazing. Have you told anyone? Where will it be?"

"I've told Cassidy and told her it was OK to tell Pete. JT Falgoust knows, as he will be moving into the sanctuary while he goes to school for his degree in psychology and social work. Eventually, he will live and work at the sanctuary full time. I also have a friend, Ed Adams, who worked for the Veterans Administration for years as a counselor. He retired two years ago, and then his wife was diagnosed with cancer. She died in November. He needs a purpose, and I need a counselor until JT graduates. Other than that, the attorneys that are drawing up all the papers, and now you. I'm looking at a property that used to be a plantation, then a small community of French, Houma Nation Peoples, and Free People of Color in Terrebonne Parish. If all goes well, I'll close on that property by the end of this month."

"I'm excited for you, Prescott, and if there is anything I can do to help with your transition, or to help with the sanctuary, please let me know."

"I'll be sure to do that, Angus, and thank you. I'm sure it goes without saying that I have no problem if you tell Jessie."

"As if I could keep a secret from her. That women can read me like a book."

◆ ◆ ◆

When Marie got home from work on Monday, she found Ricky Thibodaux and his crew putting the finishing touches on the fence enclosing her property.

"I never imagined you could finish this in a day!" exclaimed Marie.

"I brought on a few extra men," replied Ricky. "I wanted to finish so Max could have some off-leash time, Miss Marie. Speaking of Max, he barked quite a bit when we got here, so I went by the window closest to where the sound was coming from and told him it was me, and my guys would be building him a fence, and that he shouldn't worry. He quieted down then, just like he understood."

Marie felt bad that she hadn't thought about how Max might react to a work crew outside building a fence while he was contained in his crate. "Ricky, do you mind if I go get Max before I settle up with you? I want to make sure he is OK."

"No problem, Miss Marie. I'm going to walk the entire fence and inspect the job. When I'm finished my inspection, I'll knock at the back door, and then you and Max can come out and do a final inspection."

As Marie unlocked the door, she heard Max pawing the door of his crate. "I'm coming to get you big guy, just a minute." As soon as she stopped speaking Marie heard the steady thump of Max's tail against the side of his crate.

In just a little over a week, Marie's life had been transformed. The love that washed over her every day when she opened the door and heard Max, the love that she felt back from him as she opened his crate every day and they greeted each other was like nothing she had experienced since her Maw-Maw Aimee had died when she was seventeen.

Marie knelt on the ground as Max nuzzled her with his big head. "I'm sorry if you were worried by the people building the fence, Max. Ricky said you barked. I should have stayed home with you. But now we have a big fenced yard. I'm going to put you on a leash, and we'll walk around and check the fence with Ricky, and then you will have the run of the yard when I'm home with you."

Max tilted his head back and forth as Marie was speaking, and she was sure he understood every word. "Let's go see that fence!"

Marie leashed Max and took him outside. She knew Ricky would be coming to get her, but Max needed to get outside and do his business after being stuck in his crate all day. Marie sat down on her patio with Max and waited for Ricky, thinking about how nice it would be when she could just open the back door and let Max out when she got home from work. Then she could change her clothes and meet him in the backyard, so they could walk around while she told him about her day.

When Ricky found her and Max a few minutes later, he couldn't help the smile that covered his face. "Miss Marie, you and Max sure look like a poster for why everyone should have a dog. Both of you look so happy. Let's go see this fence of yours so that I can get home to my wife and baby. I think I need to talk my wife into going over to the animal shelter and getting us a dog."

✦ ✦ ✦

Sandra picked up the envelope and stared at the return address. Why? Why now? What did she want? Sandra put the envelope under a stack of bills and decided to leave it there until Mark got home. Mark would know what to do. Candace and Mark Jr. were due home from school any minute. Sandra knew she had to pull herself together so that the children wouldn't suspect anything. She went into her and Mark's bedroom and did some of the breathing exercises her therapist had taught her as a relaxation and calming technique. It didn't matter what Marie Theriot wanted from Sandra. Sandra had worked too hard to have this life with Mark and her children, and she wasn't going to let her past mess anything up.

The relaxation breathing worked. When Sandra heard the front door open and Mark Jr. run in calling "Mom!" she felt ready to face her children.

As she walked into the foyer, Mark Jr. couldn't contain his excitement. "Mom! In PE class today we played baseball, and I hit a homerun! Mr. Barbier said I should be playing Little League. I caught two fly balls too. And threw them to the right guy! Can I play Little League? Can I Mom?"

Sandra hesitated before she answered. Mark had been saying that Mark Jr. should be playing organized baseball and she had been against it. Now she was between a rock and a hard place. "I'm so proud of you that you did so well, Mark. Let's talk to your dad and see what he says."

"Yeah! I know Dad will say yes! This is the best day ever!" Even though Sandra had been against Mark Jr. playing baseball, his excitement and enthusiasm were impossible to not smile at.

"Let's go in the kitchen so that you can have a snack and get your homework done before Daddy gets home from work."

Mark Jr. continued to chatter away about his "best day ever" while Sandra prepared his snack. Just as she was setting his food out, the front door opened a second time. No excited yelling this time, as Candace walked into the kitchen looking like she had the weight of the world on her shoulders.

"Hi Mom, Hi Chip. Is there a snack for me too? I have a ton of homework to get through." Candace kissed Sandra on the cheek and leaned her head on Sandra's shoulder.

Even though Sandra was uncomfortable with Candace's casual affection, she cherished it. "Of course, there is a snack for you. You seem down. Are you OK?"

Candace kissed Sandra's cheek again. "Yes, Mom, I'm OK. Just a little overwhelmed by how much homework I have tonight. I wish the teachers would talk to each other and not all give big assignments on the same night. The only good thing is that with a bunch of tests and quizzes on Wednesday, the homework that night should be light. Is Cassidy still coming for dinner on Wednesday?"

Sandra nodded her head as she put a snack in front of Candace. "Yes, she is. Is there a special reason you want to see Cassidy?"

Candace stuck her tongue out at Sandra. "Just when we are having a normal family moment you have to go and ask a weird question like that. Shouldn't we all be excited whenever Cassidy comes over? Since she went away to college, it is like a piece of our family is always missing. I love it when she is here for dinner and our family is like it should be."

"Don't sass me like that Candace. I may have asked the question in a way you didn't like, but there is no reason to stick your tongue out at me or talk to me in that tone of voice." Sandra couldn't understand how Candace could be kissing her one minute and sassing her the next.

Mark Jr. hated when his mom and Candy got into it like this. It was like they tried to not get along sometimes. "Could you guys not fight for once? Candy, Mom is just trying to make conversation. Mom, Candy is a teenager, she sasses everyone without even trying. You make a guy too uncomfortable to eat his cookies, and they're chocolate chip."

Mark Jr. looked so put out that Candy started to laugh. "I'm sorry to ruin your cookie enjoyment Chip. And I'm sorry to be so prickly Mom. How about we start over?"

Sandra smiled at her middle child. "Let's do that. I'm glad you won't have too much homework and will get to enjoy Cassidy's visit Wednesday. Was that better?"

"Perfect, Mom. I feel just like a normal family."

As Sandra cleaned up after the children's snacks and started dinner preparations, she thought about what Candace had said about being a normal family. What in the world was a normal family? Sandra certainly didn't see one growing up. It all came so easily to Mark. He had grown up in an intact family, with a loving mother and father and brothers and sisters. Sandra watched the Guidry's when the family got together for holidays or parties and was always afraid to say too much. Sometimes the way the brothers teased each other seemed mean, but they always laughed. And there was so much hugging and kissing and leaning on each other. Sandra tried, but physical affection was hard for her. Except with Mark. Everything was easy with Mark. Thank goodness that Candace and Mark Jr. were like their dad. They were comfortable being affectionate with her even though she found it hard to initiate contact with them.

Cassidy was more like Sandra. She was guarded with affection, although Cassidy was much more affectionate with Candace and Mark, Jr. then she was with Sandra. It was better now than when Cassidy was younger. Before Sandra had married Mark, she and Cassidy had barely touched. Cassidy had been like a shadow at home, and it had hurt Sandra's feelings the way Cassidy would light up when Prescott called or came to pick Cassidy up.

Jealousy of Cassidy and Prescott's relationship followed, and Sandra knew she had been cold to Cassidy because she once again felt unloved and unlovable. Mark had helped Sandra see that Cassidy was just trying to keep Sandra happy, and since Cassidy could sense Sandra's discomfort with physical affection, had stopped offering any. Sandra could feel herself getting angrier and angrier as she thought about all the mistakes she had made so far in her life. She knew that blaming Marie and Burl for her difficulties in forming relationships wouldn't solve anything, but the resentment was there. Why had Marie written to her? Sandra felt like she was just making progress in her therapy. She didn't need any setbacks. Hadn't her mother messed up her life enough?

Sandra was still in the kitchen brooding and cleaning when Mark got home from work. As was his usual, he picked up the stack of mail and brought it with him into the kitchen. As soon as he saw Sandra ferociously cleaning the kitchen, he knew something was wrong. He walked up behind Sandra and placed his hand on hers. "Want to talk about it? Or would you like a hug? Or do you need space?" Mark had learned a lot over the years about how to comfort Sandra when she was distressed, and the first step was always to give her control over how to proceed.

"Can you just hold me for a minute? Then I need to you to look through that stack of mail. Then I want to talk."

Mark enfolded Sandra in a hug, not too tight, but tight enough, and rubbed her back. He just held her like that until he felt some of the tension leave her body, then he held her a little tighter. Finally, Sandra sighed deeply and stepped back. "Look through the mail," she said.

When Mark got to the envelope from Marie, he felt his heart still. Poor Sandra. Mark knew that resolving the issues of her childhood was necessary for Sandra to ever be really happy, and he knew she was working on it in therapy. What he didn't know was whether or not contact with Marie would help or harm the process.

"What do you want to do baby? You know you can just throw this away if you want. Or you can hang on to it and open it when you are ready. The return address is in Bayou Beni, out in Audela, so you could go years without running into her." Little did Mark know that Marie had already been in Bayou Beni for years.

"I don't know what to do Mark. I want to see her and tell her that in spite of her I'm fine. I want to ask her why she couldn't love me. I want to go back to yesterday and not have to deal with this." Sandra eyes filled with tears as she spoke.

"Don't you have an appointment with your therapist tomorrow? Why not take the envelope with you and talk to your therapist about it? You don't owe her anything, sweetheart. And me and the kids love you, so if she didn't, that is something that was wrong with her, not anything wrong with you."

"That's a good idea. I'll talk to my therapist tomorrow. I'm sorry I'm a mess. I worry that I'm too dependent on you and that you'll get tired of my drama, but I couldn't wait for you to get home. I was in a tailspin."

"Hey! How did the clothes I'm wearing get clean? And who shopped for and cooked that dinner I smell? And how did my kids get afternoon snacks and help with their homework if they needed it? And who makes this house feel like home? Honey, we depend on each other. That is what marriage is. Never worry that I'm the one you look for when you are upset or frightened. I look for you when I'm upset too. We take care of each other. The equation is perfectly balanced in my mind."

Sandra hugged Mark hard and kissed him. "Thank you. I don't know how I got so lucky to marry you, but I thank God every day that I did."

Mark kissed her back. "Me, too, Honey. Me, too."

CHAPTER 26

Prescott had just sat down at his desk with a cup of coffee when Angus poked his head in the door the next morning. "Mornin' Prescott. I have a name for you for your replacement if you're ready for it."

"Shoot. I'm happy to entertain any ideas." Prescott replied.

"Well, as soon as I mentioned your retirement and the search for a replacement to Jessie, she suggested Gil Chauvin."

Prescott chuckled as he shook his head. "Can't see what's right in front of my face sometimes, Angus. I spent Saturday with Cassidy. I told her about my retirement plans, and she told me that Gil is coming to town on Friday to see Bessie. You would think a lightbulb would have appeared above my head when Cassidy mentioned Gil, but I never even thought of him. I don't know if he has any interest in moving from Texas, but he would be a great fit. And I think he is ready for the job. I'll talk to the leadership team this morning and suggest his name. We could even interview him in person while he is here if he is interested."

"I'm the same way, Prescott. It is like I flip a switch in my head when I am with Rosadel. Work is just not on my mind when I'm paying attention to her and the girls. It is a little different with Jessie, because so much of what we talk about ends up being work related. So, I totally understand how you would fail to make the connection."

"It will be interesting if Gil decides to interview. I feel like a meddling old fool telling you this, but Cassidy and Pete had a little set to last week over Gil. Seems that Pete got jealous after Cassidy was excited after talking to Gil. And he's never met Gil yet. I hope that if Gil does take the job, it doesn't cause a problem for Cassidy and Pete. I know in my heart that Pete is the right man for my girl, and I hope they don't throw that away."

"You know, Prescott, I used to worry about Rosadel and Clancy because they are the only person either one ever dated. And they were just fourteen and sixteen when they got together. But as the years have gone by, I'm so grateful that they fell in love and stayed in love. The Marshalls are good people. I don't know your Cassidy that well, but I've watched Pete grow up, and he is a fine man. Seeing them together these past few months, they do look like they are made for each other. I sure hope everything works out."

"Me, too, Angus. Cassidy never really had a serious boyfriend before. She went on dates, but nothing that I would call a relationship. Cassidy has always been more comfortable with animals than people. She's lucky that she had Sandra and Mark's relationship to observe to see how marriage can work, but even that has a downside. Mark is so protective of Sandra, and to Cassidy, that relationship has always appeared lopsided. I've tried and tried to explain that no relationship is fifty-fifty. They all ebb and flow. And the only important thing is that both partners are getting what they need from each other to be happy. Pete has seemed very steady and careful to give Cassidy the time she needs, so this jealousy thing really caught her off guard and upset her. I'm hoping Pete just had a bad moment."

"Well, Prescott. I've known Pete since he was a sophomore in high school, and he never had a serious girlfriend. Dates, and sometimes enough dates that Harriet started to get excited, but nothing ever materialized. I trust that he realizes he made a mistake by acting out when he felt jealous. If Harriet got wind of it, I imagine she blistered his ear, and knowing how close Pete is to Harriet, I'm sure he talked to her. I'll put them on my prayer list."

"Thanks, Angus. Cassidy did tell me that Harriet had told Pete if he wasn't mature enough to handle Cassidy having male friends he wasn't mature enough to have a romantic relationship. Knowing Harriet, that was probably a gentler version than what Pete got."

Angus chuckled. "I have to admit, even after all these years of seeing Harriet and George regularly, I'm still scared to get on Harriet's bad side. She is something in full battle mode."

Prescott laughed as he responded. "The United States military missed out on one hell of a general when Harriet didn't enlist. I guarantee it."

◆ ◆ ◆

Sandra folded and refolded her hands and took deep calming breaths. She knew that the waiting time for her appointment with Dr. Mathieu was no longer than usual, but it seemed like forever. The letter from Marie was in her purse. She had almost opened it a hundred times last night and this morning.

Sandra was glad that the letter had arrived yesterday, the last nineteen hours had been torture. She was sure if the letter had arrived on Saturday she would have driven herself crazy by today.

The door opened, and Dr. Mathieu gestured to Sandra to come into her office. "Good morning, Sandra. How are you today?"

Dr. Mathieu had a soft, comforting voice, and Sandra always wondered if she was born that way or had practiced to have the perfect counselor voice. "I'm kind of a wreck, Dr. Mathieu, I have a letter from my mother in my purse."

"I can see that is very upsetting to you, why don't you sit down, and we can talk about it."

As Sandra sat down she opened her purse and took the letter out. "I don't know why she wrote to me. I don't know how she found me. I'm nervous and angry and frightened."

Dr. Mathieu nodded reassuringly. "Of course, you are feeling strong emotions. This is unexpected, and the unexpected always produces strong emotions. Even good surprises like winning the lottery. Talk to me more about all those feelings."

"I want to open the letter and see what it says, but at the same time I'm afraid of what it says. What if this letter just confirms that I'm not lovable? That my own mother could never love me?"

Dr. Mathieu leaned forward in her chair. "We have talked about this before Sandra. Your mother and her choices belong to your mother and not to you. You know better than to give her all that power."

"I know Dr. Mathieu. And I really was doing better. I can see that Mark loves me, and my children love me. I realize that I have to accept that every human is worthy of being loved simply because they exist. But the way I grew up has impacted me so deeply. It has taken me almost thirty years to get to the point where I don't feel like there is something wrong with me. And then a letter shows up in my mailbox and all my feelings of unworthiness come rushing back."

"Sandra, we both know how hard you have worked to break out of the thought patterns that make you feel unworthy. Why has this letter affected you so much?"

"I don't know. I think some of it is that I think there may be answers in this letter that I don't want. That there may be validation for why I wasn't loved by my parents."

"If parents don't love their children, that is not a fault of the child, Sandra. You know that. What are you going to do about the letter?"

"I want to read it, but I want to be here when I do. That way if I fall apart, I can process it with you before I try to process it with everyone else."

"You know that you don't have to read it, don't you? That you are free to ignore the letter entirely if that is what you choose to do?"

"I know. I thought about just throwing it away. But I want to know. I feel like so much of my life has been spent trying to figure out what was so wrong in my childhood. I keep thinking that if I could figure that out, everything else in my life would be so much easier."

"I need you to remember there is no gain in 'magic' thinking. No one thing will ever solve all life's problems. Whatever this letter says, it will just be information that you didn't have before you read the letter. You will still have to choose how to process that information. No magic. Just more data to work with."

Sandra smiled. "That is why I need to read it here. You nailed it. I have given this letter the power to make everything better, or to destroy all my hard work. It is just a letter with information from the person who is my biological mother."

"Exactly, Sandra. I'm proud of you for making that connection. Now, do you want to read the letter today, or save it for next week?"

"I want to read it today. I need to read it today." And so, Sandra opened the letter and began reading.

My dearest Sandra –

I don't blame you if you never read this letter. If you do choose to read it, I hope you read it with an open heart.

I am so sorry for being such a bad mother to you. I have been in counseling for several years now, and I know I did the best I could in a bad situation, but you were the one to suffer for my inadequacy.

I want you to know I love you. I have always loved you. Burl Theriot was a cruel and violent man, and the only way I knew to protect you from him was to push you into the shadows of our lives.

Burl hated for me to show anyone affection but him. When I realized that showing my love for you resulted in him abusing both of us, I stopped. I should have had the courage to leave, but Burl told me he would get custody of you, and you would be his target.

I should have had the courage to leave when you did, but I was so broken by then.

When Burl died, I hired a private investigator to find you, but then felt unworthy to ask your forgiveness.

I would love to be reconciled with you, and to meet your husband and my grandchildren. I realize that may not be something that you can do, and I respect whatever decision you make.

Please know that you were never the problem. You are a wonderful person, and were a wonderful little girl. I wish I could have given you a better childhood.

Whatever you decide, know that I love you with every breath in my body, and I am so proud of who you are.

Love Always,

Mom

As Sandra read, tears began streaming down her face. In her heart, she had known that Burl was abusive, even though she never remembered seeing physical abuse. She remembered his meanness, and his disparagement of Marie. So many memories came flooding back. And as the memories came back so did an astonishing amount of anger.

Dr. Mathieu sat silently while Sandra read the letter. She watched the tears, and the play of emotions on Sandra's face, and waited for her to speak.

Finally, Sandra looked up at Dr. Mathieu. "Aren't you going to ask me about the letter?"

Dr. Mathieu slowly shook her head. "You will tell me about the letter or not, depending on what you want to do, Sandra. I'm fine with whatever you decide."

Sandra's anger had to go somewhere, and right now, it felt good to direct it at Dr. Mathieu. "Do you know how angry you make me sometimes? You are so calm and distant. Do you ever feel anything?" Sandra was embarrassed and ashamed as soon as the words left her mouth.

"I can see you are angry, Sandra. Remember what we have talked about. Whatever the emotion, it is best to strive to stay in control. Once you are calm and in control, it is best to ask yourself is feeling this emotion making things better for you or worse. If being angry with me is making it better for you, that is fine with me. Your emotion belongs to you, and my response belongs to me."

Sandra's anger was extinguished as quickly as it had flamed up. "I'm sorry, Dr. Mathieu. I'm too full of emotion. I'm sad, I'm angry, I'm hurt, I'm relieved, I'm confused. I think I need time to process this before I talk to you about it. I want to talk to Mark, though. Do you think that is a good idea?"

"I think you need to trust yourself, Sandra. You just communicated with me very effectively about your current emotional state. We have talked about this before, and you have made tremendous progress. All emotion is legitimate. The proportion of emotion we feel is not right or wrong. An important part of being a highly functional human being is learning to control our emotions instead of letting our emotions control us. You have worked hard on your self-calming rituals. Practice your control, and you can talk successfully to anyone about anything."

"Thank you, Dr. Mathieu. I have no idea what I want to do about this letter, but I know I don't want to undo all the hard work I've done to learn more about myself. I'm going to talk to Mark, and collect myself, and talk to you next week about what I think my options are, and how I want to move forward."

"That sounds great, Sandra. Is there anything else you would like to talk about this week? We still have some time left in your hour."

"There is something else. The PE teacher told Mark Jr. he is a natural at baseball. Mark has been wanting Mark Jr. to play organized baseball since he was five. I have resisted because I'm afraid he'll get hurt. I know it will be good for Mark Jr., and for Mark but I'm frightened."

"It sounds like you have decided to let Mark Jr. participate."

"Well, I realized how illogical it is to forbid him. He will play baseball at school anyway. The more he knows, the less likely he is to get hurt from a failure to anticipate. Now I'm trying to figure out how to proceed so that I don't ruin Mark Jr.'s enjoyment of the sport."

"Do you think it will be easier for you if you don't attend his games? The "out of sight; out of mind" theory?"

"I think I would make myself crazy imagining, so I think I'll do better if I go."

"Do you think that as you go to games, and Mark Jr. doesn't get hurt, your fear and anxiety will go down?"

"I don't know. But I can always use my relaxation techniques. I realized that trying to control Mark Jr.'s life won't work, and that I have to start letting go. It was so much easier with the girls. Cassidy wasn't interested in anything other than animals, and it was exciting for me to have Candace show an interest in dance, as I had always wanted to have dance lessons but never did. Even though Candace didn't stick with dance lessons, it was fun while it lasted. I want Mark Jr. to have as normal a childhood as Mark and I can give him, so I feel like if he really wants to play organized baseball, I shouldn't stand in his way."

"It sounds like you have this figured out too, Sandra. You've had a productive session today."

"Cassidy is coming to dinner tomorrow night. Candace is very excited to see her. Candace told me yesterday that it has felt like a piece of the family is missing since Cassidy went away to college. It made me proud that my younger children don't look at Cassidy as a step-sister, but as a sister. Even in the midst of worrying about everything else, I focused on that good thing as my relaxation thought. It really helped. It feels good to know that my children love each other."

By the time Sandra had finished her appointment with Dr. Mathieu and was headed home, she was feeling much better than she had since she had seen Marie's letter. She had three great children who loved each other, a great husband, and a wonderful life. Mark would help her figure out what to do about Marie. Sandra was so glad that Mark had talked her into going for counseling and was glad that Marie had sought counseling too. Whatever the future held, Sandra was finally starting to feel confident that she would be able to handle it.

♦ ♦ ♦

Bessie Chauvin was waiting in the lobby of Our Lady of Lourdes when Cassidy and Pete arrived on Tuesday after work with the dogs. She was sitting in one of the armchairs with her cane across her lap.

"Grandma Bessie! Look at you, what a nice surprise!" Cassidy kissed and hugged Bessie while Sophie jumped into her lap.

"Assisted Living next week," Bessie said.

"Oh, my goodness! That is wonderful news! I'm so proud of you!" Cassidy hugged Bessie tightly, despite Sophie being in her lap. "I never thought we would see this day back in November when I took Sophie in to live with me and Maggie. You have worked so hard." Cassidy held tightly to Bessie's hand as she spoke.

Pete watched the two women he had come to care so deeply for over the last couple of months. He doubted Bessie would have made this progress without the steady comfort of Cassidy's love, and he realized he would indeed be a fool to ever jeopardize his relationship with Cassidy. Pete leaned over and kissed Bessie's cheek.

"Congratulations, Ms. Bessie. I'll bet you are looking forward to having some more space and privacy."

Bessie's speech was still slow but improving every day. "Looking forward to having Sophie all day."

"I'll bet you are, Grandma Bessie. And I'm sure Sophie is looking forward to it to." Pete saw the worry in Cassidy's eyes, and knew she was worried about how Maggie would cope with losing her partner. They had only been together for a few months, but Maggie had come to depend heavily on Sophie for company. Pete tucked that thought away for later, knowing that somehow, he could figure out a solution.

Bessie also noticed the worry in Cassidy's eyes, and thought about what the right answer might be. At ninety-three, Bessie knew better than to let things fester. She squeezed Cassidy's hand. "I know you are worried about Maggie missing Sophie. I promise no change until we know." Bessie hoped that in spite of her conversational shortcomings, Cassidy understood.

"We'll figure it out, Grandma. The most important thing is how well you are doing."

As Pete took Laverne and Shirley on their rounds visiting the patients in Assisted Living, Bessie and Cassidy took Sophie and Maggie visiting on the nursing home side. At each visit, Bessie shared that next week she would be moving over to assisted living. There was a definite air of celebration about the evening, as many of Bessie's fellow patients took encouragement from her progress, believing again in their own ability to recuperate.

As Pete and Cassidy were driving home after their visit, Cassidy confided her worries about Maggie to Pete. It felt good to feel close enough to share her worries again. Impulsively, Cassidy reached over and squeezed Pete's leg. "Can we try really hard to remember to talk things through instead of retreating from each other when we're upset? I missed you too much when we were at odds."

Pete took one hand off the wheel, picked up Cassidy's hand and brought it to his lips. "I learned something very important talking to

Clancy this weekend, Cass. He told me that whenever he felt jealous of Rosadel's relationship with someone else, he just committed more to be the best person he could be, because Rosadel deserves the best. I'm going to try my best to do the same thing. You deserve the best, and I'm going to focus my energy on being the best Pete I can be. So, I promise to talk things through, because I don't ever want to lose you."

CHAPTER 27

The phone rang just as Cassidy was about to get into her car to head to Sandra and Mark's house for dinner. Maggie and Sophie had been fed, cuddled and walked around the yard, and Cassidy was close to being late. She looked at the phone, saw it was her dad, and knew she had to answer.

"Hey Daddy, what's up? I'm almost late for dinner at Mom's. I've got about a five-minute cushion." Cassidy knew that Prescott knew how important punctuality was to Sandra.

"I'll make it quick, Baby Girl. Gil Chauvin is coming into town tomorrow to interview for my job. It is really a formality. If he wants the job, it will be his."

"That's great, Daddy! Grandma Bessie will be so excited to have him close. I know she misses him." Cassidy was being positive for Prescott's sake, but she was a little worried about how this would impact her and Pete.

"You don't have to pretend with your Daddy, Cassidy. I know this could be messy for you and Pete. That is why I called. I think it would be best if he hears this from you, rather than from anyone else, and Clancy could mention it without thinking it could be a big deal. Trust is the most important thing, and you don't want Pete to think that you were keeping this from him."

"Thanks for the advice Daddy. I think I better call Mom and tell her I'll be a couple of minutes late. I'll call Pete, and I'll text you later and let you know how everything goes."

"Sorry to be so up in your business, Cass. But as excited as I am for me, the company, Bessie and Gil, I would hate for this to hurt you and Pete. I can't help being an old meddler, but I think you and Pete are so good together."

"So, do I, Daddy. And me and Pete had a good talk yesterday. I think between what Mr. and Mrs. Marshall told him, and what Clancy told him, we are in a good place. But I don't want to take that for granted. I'll call him before I go to Mom's. I love you and I'll text when I am home tonight to let you know everything is okay."

"Love you too, Baby Girl. I'll look forward to your text."

As soon as Cassidy had hung up with her dad, she tried Pete's phone, but it went right to voicemail. "Hi Pete, there is something important I need to tell you. I'll call your office to try to reach you."

Crap. Cassidy needed to call Sandra before she did anything else. As she dialed Sandra's number, Cassidy thought about texting Pete the news about Gil. Nope. Too cold. She had to talk to him. Candy picked up the phone on the second ring.

"Hey Candy, is Mom there?"

"Sure Cass, you're not cancelling, are you?"

"No, Candy, but I'm running late, and you know how Mom is, can you let me talk to her real quick?"

"Sure, Cass. Mom! It's Cassidy."

Cassidy heard footsteps as Candy took the phone into the kitchen for Sandra. "Cassidy don't tell me you aren't coming for dinner." Cassidy could hear how upset Sandra was.

"No, Mom. I'm just going to be a few minutes late, and I didn't want you to worry. Something just came up that I have to take care of before I start driving. I'm in the car in front of my house, I just have to make another phone call, and then I'll be on my way."

There was a brief silence before Sandra replied. "I'm proud of you, Cassidy, for making your phone calls before you start driving. It is better to be late than to get in an accident because you are distracted."

Cassidy was stunned. She had expected a lecture about pre-planning and not getting into a last-minute crunch. "Thanks, Mom.

You don't know how much it means to me to have you tell me you are proud of me. I'll be there as soon as I can. Love you."

"Love you too, Cassidy. Drive carefully." As Sandra hung up the phone she could feel Candace staring at her. She raised her eyebrow at Candace.

"I'm proud of you, Mom, for not getting all up in Cassidy's business. You pulled off a perfect mom moment." And Candace hugged Sandra and gave her a smacking kiss on the cheek.

Sandra couldn't help but to laugh as she hugged Candace back. "You kids will teach me how to be a good mom if it is the last thing you do."

Mark Jr., who had been watching from a stool at the counter, chimed in. "You're already a great mom. Especially when you make chocolate chip cookies."

Sandra ruffled his hair as she went back to dinner preparations. She needed to keep reminding herself that she was a lucky woman with a great husband and great kids. And she was learning to be easier, on them and on herself. Whatever happened with Marie, Sandra was feeling emotionally strong enough to deal with it.

Uplifted by the positive interaction with Sandra, Cassidy tried to call Pete at the office. Hannah Falgoust answered the phone.

"Hey Hannah, it's Cassidy Bourgeois. Is Pete available?" Cassidy felt a little bad for being so abrupt. Usually she and Hannah chatted a bit.

"He's with a patient, Cassidy, and will be a little while. Can I help you?" Cassidy hesitated, not knowing exactly what to do. She decided to go all in.

"Hannah, I'm in a little bit of a bind. There is something happening that Pete should really hear from me, but I have to go to dinner at my Mom's house, and she is very sensitive about having my full attention while I'm there. I'm pretty sure Pete will hear about the thing he should hear about from me from someone else by the time dinner is over. I don't want him to think I was trying to keep something from him." Hannah was smiling broadly by the time Cassidy finished speaking. She had been hoping that Cassidy and Pete were getting serious.

"I'll tell Pete you called, and that he needs to understand you tried your best to reach him. Then I'll tell him that if he knows which side his bread is buttered on, he'll listen to you when you call him later and reserve judgement until then. How does that sound?"

"Hannah, you are one in a million. Please tell Pete I'll call him as soon as I get home from my Mom's house." As Cassidy hung up the phone, she was once again thankful to live in a place like Bayou Beni where people took care of each other. Surely this was the best place on earth.

In spite of doing everything she could to reach Pete and tell him about Gil, Cassidy was still nervous as she drove to Sandra's house for dinner. She took a deep breath as she walked towards the door. In just a couple of hours she would talk to Pete, she had to believe that everything was going to be fine.

Cassidy knocked on the door and then opened it and went in. "Hi, I'm finally here!" she called out. Candy and Chip raced into the foyer to greet her. "Cass! Cass! I'm going to play baseball." Chip threw his arms around Cassidy's waist as he talked. "Mom said 'yes'; isn't that awesome?"

"It sure is, buddy. I'll bet you will be really good. You have to tell me when you have a game, so I can come and cheer for you."

"Give me a turn to hug Cassidy, Chip, no fair hogging." Candy hugged Cassidy, and then looked at her closely. "Cass, we're the same height now."

"You must have grown this past month. Just cause you're taller don't forget I'm still the big sister."

Candy laughed as Sandra called from the kitchen, "Are you all going to let Cassidy come say hello to your mother?"

The three of them went into the kitchen, and Cassidy hugged Sandra and kissed her cheek. "Hi Mom, thanks for being so understanding about my being late."

Sandra gave Cassidy a squeeze. "Are you going to tell me what came up?"

Cassidy nodded. "I will Mom, but there is a lot of backstory I have to tell for everything to make sense. How about we eat dinner and then I'll fill you in?" Cassidy was already sorting through things in her mind to decide how much to tell Sandra.

As everyone cooperated to get the table set and the dinner on the table, Mark arrived home from work. He hugged and kissed Sandra, and then hugged each child, including Cassidy. "Looks like I timed my arrival perfectly," Mark joked as he looked at the table ready for supper. "Just let me wash my hands and then we'll eat."

Supper was a lively affair as Chip and Candy traded stories about their lives. Cassidy, Sandra and Mark only had to ask the occasional question or make an occasional remark to keep the conversation rolling. As supper was winding down, Sandra decided to find out more about what was going on with Cassidy.

"I'm too full to eat dessert right away, so how about we just sit and talk for a few minutes before we clear the table and start dessert?" Sandra was usually a stickler for getting the table cleared right away, and it was one of the things she was trying to be less rigid about. Her curiosity about what was going on with Cassidy helped tamp down her need to put everything in order right away.

Cassidy was kind of surprised that Sandra was willing to sit at the table and talk. She guessed that Sandra must really be curious. All the while Candy and Chip had been talking, Cassidy had been trying to figure out how to tell a story that wouldn't result in Sandra getting her feelings hurt because Prescott knew so much more about what was happening in her life than Sandra did. She hoped she had found the right balance.

"Cassidy, this is the perfect time to tell us that long story that is why you were late today."

"Well, I guess the only place to start is to tell you that I have been dating someone and I think we are getting serious." Cassidy waited a moment to see how that piece of information was received.

"Do we know him? How did you meet him? How long have you been dating him without telling us?" Sandra was both excited and nervous. Cassidy had never really had a serious boyfriend before.

"Well, I'm not sure if you know him or not, Mom. His name is Pete Marshall, and I've known him since we both volunteered at St. Elizabeth's Animal Shelter in high school. He is a veterinarian now, and he bought Dr. Russell's practice when Dr. Russell retired. We have been working together since I took the job as Shelter Director. Before

Christmas, his brother and sister in law volunteered to foster a momma cat and kittens, and so Pete and I started seeing more of each other. He asked me on a date, and we've been seeing each other ever since."

Sandra noticed that Candy was looking guilty. "Candy, you knew, didn't you?"

Candy blushed as she answered. "Yep, when me and Cass went shopping at Christmas time, it was for her and Pete's first date. Sisters share secrets sometimes, right, Cass?"

Cassidy knew she had to find a way to make sure Sandra didn't feel hurt or excluded. "I wasn't sure things would work out, and I didn't want to tell very many people, because I didn't want to have to answer a bunch of questions if things went bad. I wasn't keeping things from you, Mom. Candy is one of the only people I told."

Sandra was a little hurt, but she had learned enough in counseling to not make this about her. "I always wished I had a sister to confide in, I'm proud of both of my girls that you share so much with each other, even if my feelings are a little hurt. When will we get to meet this guy, and I still don't know what happened that made you late."

"Thanks, Mom. I can bring Pete over to meet you guys any time. So, what happened to make me late is another more complicated part of the story. So, you know that I took in Ms. Bessie Chauvin's dog while she is recovering from her stroke. Well, I was calling her nephew, Gil, to discuss her treatment plan and progress. Pete got jealous. I think we have worked through that, but I found out today from Dad that Gil is interviewing for a job in Bayou Beni."

Sandra knew there was still a puzzle piece missing. "What does your dad have to do with this?"

"Dad announced his retirement Monday. Gil works for the company in Texas, and Dad knew I know Gil from Ms. Bessie, so he let me know that Gil will be in town tomorrow for an interview. I was afraid that if Pete heard Gil might be moving here from someone other than me that the jealousy thing might pop up again. So, I wanted to call Pete and let him know from me before he heard it from someone else."

Sandra still felt like part of the puzzle was missing. "Why would Pete hear about something with your dad's job?"

"I told this was a complicated story. Pete's brother Clancy, and Clancy's father-in-law, Angus, both work at the company. I knew that if Pete talked to Clancy it was likely he would hear about Gil coming to interview."

"So, did you reach him? And are you sure you should get serious with someone who has a problem with jealousy?" Sandra was worried, remembering her own father and thinking about Marie's letter.

"I didn't get to talk to him, but I left him a message on his cell phone and with the receptionist at his clinic. We talked a lot about the jealousy issue. I think we put that behind us. He really is a great guy, Mom, from a good family. We're both new to this relationship thing. He told me I'm the first serious girlfriend he has ever had, and you know he is my first serious boyfriend. And we are old to be firsts. So, we are learning. He gets great advice from his brother, Clancy and his mom and dad. Now that you know, I can come to you for advice." Cassidy hoped that Sandra wouldn't ask about Prescott giving advice.

Sandra knew that Cassidy had probably been going to Prescott for advice, but since Cassidy wanted to play that down, Sandra was happy to let her. "Well, Cassidy, I think we need to meet this Pete Marshall sooner rather than later, so I know what kind of person I'm advising you on. Why don't you ask him to come over for dinner with us on Saturday night?"

"I'll check and see if he's free, Mom, and If so, we'll be here. How about I call you in the morning?"

"That will be fine. Now let's clear the table and get ready for dessert." As everyone helped, the clean-up was accomplished quickly, and they were soon eating bread pudding while the adults had coffee and Candy and Chip had milk.

"It is hard for me to imagine Prescott retiring, he always enjoyed his work so much," Sandra remarked as they were eating dessert.

"He already has plans to volunteer with veterans who are having a hard time adjusting to civilian life. His PTSD has been so much better since he has had service dogs, he will be working to train and match up dogs with vets who need them. I think it will be a perfect retirement job for him." Cassidy decided it was best to make it sound like Prescott would work for the charity, rather than found the charity.

"That does sound like a perfect fit for your dad," Mark replied, "And it should help you at the shelter too."

"It will, Mark. We will have another avenue for dogs we see potential in as service dogs. The charity that Dad will be working for is also going to have an animal sanctuary. It sounds like a great organization." Cassidy hoped she didn't talk herself into a corner.

"Do you know the name of it?" Mark asked.

"It is brand new, and I don't think it has been named yet. Dad will be one of the first employees. He is really excited about it. I think the charity will be based in Terrebonne Parish, so not too far away. I'll let you guys know as soon as I know the name. I'm hoping everything is lined up by the time of the Holy Redeemer fair at the end of the month. It would be great to have information at the booth the Animal Shelter will have there."

"I didn't know you were having a booth at Holy Redeemer Fair," Sandra wondered how that came about.

"Well, the momma cat and kittens that Rosadel Marshall is fostering were abandoned on the school playground. Rosadel ended up fostering them, but it turns out she didn't even know fostering animals was a thing until she was doing it. She thought more people would help if more people knew, so I went to a PTA meeting and pitched a booth at the fair. They use the booths to make money, and my booth won't so it was very generous of them, but I'll have a booth with adoptable animals and information. I've already had a dog and a few cats adopted by people who were at the meeting." As always, Cassidy became more animated when she talked about her work.

"Hey Mom," Chip asked, "Can we get a puppy or a dog?" Sandra knew that question was coming as soon as the conversation had turned to animals. "How about we worry about baseball for now and talk about pets later?"

"Ok! But I still want a dog someday. Can I be excused? I want to watch TV."

Mark smiled at his son, "Yes, you can be excused, Chip. Don't forget to take your dishes to the kitchen and put them in the dishwasher first."

"Sure thing, Dad. Hey Cass, make sure to come say 'Bye' before you leave." The adults and Candy all took their dishes to the kitchen, and soon it was time for Cassidy to leave.

"I'll call you tomorrow, Mom, and let you know about supper on Saturday." Cassidy gave each Sandra and Mark a kiss and hug goodbye.

"I'm gonna walk Cassidy to her car," Candy explained as she linked arms with Cassidy.

When they got outside, Candy immediately asked, "Did you notice the change in Mom? She is really trying hard to lighten up. I'm really proud of her."

"I did, Candy, and I'm proud of her too. Mark did a great job convincing her to go for counseling. I hope this lasts. I didn't feel like a disappointment once tonight."

"And you told her about Pete! I was so surprised! I guess that Lindy thing turned out to be nothing." Candy remembered how that has seemed like a big thing to her at the time.

"Yep, just friends. Lindy is going back to school to be a veterinarian, and she had told Pete that at lunch, so it was kind of emotional. It all worked out."

"Well, I'm excited to meet him and see how he does with Mom. This is a first for her, first boyfriend dinner. I hope she is like she was today."

"Me too, Candy. Now I have to get home to Maggie and Sophie. I hate to leave them in the evening after they have been alone all day. See you Saturday." As Cassidy hugged and kissed Candy goodbye, she thought again how lucky she was to have such a great relationship with her little sister. "You know I think you are the best, don't you?" she asked.

"Right back at you, Cass. Love you!"

As Cassidy drove home she thought about how different this visit with Sandra was from just about every visit in the past. No criticism, no drama. It was remarkable the difference in Sandra, and Cassidy hoped it would last. As she pulled up in front of her house, she saw Pete was sitting on the front steps. He stood up as she approached

"Hey you! I was going to call you as soon as I got inside." Cass walked up to Pete and put her arms around him. "What brings you here?"

"Well, your cryptic messages for one thing. What's going on? I took the girls home, fed them, and haven't answered the phone since Hannah gave me your message. I figured it something was that important to you I should wait to hear it from you."

Cassidy hugged Pete hard and kissed him. "You are a great guy, and a great boyfriend. Gil Chauvin is interviewing for Daddy's job, and he will probably get it and move to Bayou Beni. I wanted you to hear that from me, so you wouldn't think I was hiding anything from you."

Pete rested his chin on Cassidy's head. "And I have nothing to worry about because you are my girl. And I'm a great boyfriend."

Cassidy could hear Maggie and Sophie whining at the door. "Yes, you have nothing to worry about, and yes you are a great boyfriend, and we need to put my dogs out of their misery. Want to come in for a few minutes?"

Pete nodded his agreement with that plan as Cassidy opened the door. She took care of letting Maggie and Sophie out, and then sat down on the couch with Pete. "I need to text my dad and let him know everything is fine, because it is, right?" Pete nodded again as Cassidy quickly dispatched a text to Prescott.

"Want to go to dinner at my Mom's on Saturday night?" Cassidy figured it was best to ask right away.

"You're ready for me to meet your Mom?" Pete was a little surprised.

"How can I expect you to trust how important you and this relationship are to me if I'm afraid to introduce you to my family? Mom was amazing tonight. She was not critical at all. I imagine she will still backslide, but I want you to meet them and them to meet you. Can you come?"

Pete put his arm around Cassidy and hugged her tight to his side as he dropped a kiss on the top of her head. "You bet I can. And it makes me really happy that you want to introduce me to your family. I think you are starting to believe in us as much as I do."

"I do believe in us, Pete. And I'm excited for you to meet Candy and Chip. I'm a little nervous that tonight was the fluke and Sandra will be a tough case, but I know you will like Mark, because everybody does. We'll have a busy weekend with dinner on Saturday with my family and brunch on Sunday with the Chauvin's. You good with that much together time?"

"I haven't reached overload yet, so we'll see. I need to get home and get ready for tomorrow, but I needed to see you even more." Pete kissed Cassidy with all the relief and hope he was feeling and left both of them a little stunned.

"Wow!" Cassidy softly kissed Pete. "You sure know how to kiss a girl senseless."

"Just wait, "said Pete with a smile, "There is plenty more where that came from."

◆ ◆ ◆

Sandra and Mark had just climbed into bed when Sandra put her head on Mark's chest and hugged him tight.

"Thanks for everything, Mark. For loving me, for loving Cassidy and our kids, for pushing me to get counseling. I always think I can't love you any more than I already do, but then I love you more."

Mark hugged Sandra back. "You're welcome, Sandra. What brought this on though?"

"I've been thinking a lot since I got the letter and talked to Dr. Mathieu. I was afraid to open that letter. And if I hadn't already been going to counseling, I may have thrown it away. Something changed in me since I read the letter. I believe my mother loved me as best she could. I believe that none of what happened in my childhood is my fault. You have been trying for years to tell me that, Prescott tried to tell me that, but I couldn't accept it. Now I can.

"Tonight, when Cassidy called to tell me she was going to be late, I took a deep breath, and realized I was happier knowing she was okay than I was aggravated that she would be late. I thought about how I would want you to respond to me, and I thanked her for calling, and for making a good choice, and told her I was proud of her. When I hung up, Candace told me she was proud of me, and that I had done a 'perfect mom' moment. It made me feel wonderful.

"I realized that in spite of not always being a good mom to Cassidy, she has always loved me and given me another chance. Candace and Mark Jr. are more demanding. They call me to task when I am short-tempered or irritated. Cassidy just loves me, no matter how badly I behave. I realized tonight that ever since Cassidy was born I have been the recipient of unconditional love, and I have never appreciated that the way I should have.

"You and Prescott have done a great job in helping me to have the relationship with Cassidy that I have. You have both picked up my slack. And while Prescott is Cassidy's Dad, you're not. You never had to invest so much in Cassidy, but you did, and you did that initially because you love me that much.

"I'm sorry it took me so long to sort all this out. I'm going to wait until after Saturday dinner, but then I am going to go out with Cassidy and tell her the whole story. About me, her grandparents, and about why I wasn't always such a good mother. And I am going to write back to my mother. I'm not quite ready to meet yet, but I am ready to let her know that I am open to meeting her in the future. I feel like I need to invest in my relationship with Cassidy before I invest in forming a relationship with my mother."

Mark hugged Sandra tightly and kissed the top of her head. "You have always been worth the investment of time and love, Sandra. And while I may have started investing in Cassidy because I love you, I love her just for herself. She is an amazing compassionate person. I hope this Pete guy is good enough for her."

Sandra chuckled. "You sound just like a Dad. I'm pretty sure Prescott has been aware of this relationship from the beginning, and if he approves, I'm pretty sure Pete must be a good guy."

"You sound pretty certain that Cassidy has confided in Prescott, does that bother you?"

"It started to, and then I realized that the reason Cassidy doesn't confide in me is me. So, I let it go. I have to mend my relationship with Cassidy, because the brokenness has been all on my side."

"I'm proud of you Sandra. I know this hasn't been easy for you, and the progress you have made is remarkable. I see our lives just getting better and better from here."

CHAPTER 28

Gil Chauvin knocked lightly on Prescott's door as he stepped into the office. "Got a few minutes?"

"Sure thing, Gil. How did the interviews go?" Prescott gestured to the guest chair in his office as he spoke.

"They went well, Prescott. I think I have the job if I want it, and I want it. That is what I wanted to talk to you about. What is your transition plan and timeline?" Gil wasn't being arrogant, it had been made clear to him that the job was his if he wanted it.

"I had planned to officially retire at the end of June," Prescott replied, "But, frankly, I never thought the position would be filled this quickly. I'm fairly flexible with my timeline, but I'd like to transition slowly. I've got six weeks' vacation in the bank, with another prorated three this year, so altogether, nine weeks or a little more than two months. I had thought to slowly reduce my days per week until the vacation is all used up, with my replacement doing the job for the last six weeks to a month, and me just acting as a consultant."

"I've got to give the Texas plant time to replace me, and to train my replacement. I think we can have a job posting next week, and a replacement named by the end of February. If I could focus on training my replacement one week, and then shadowing you the next week throughout March, I'd like to be in this job full time the first week of April. I'll of course still consult with my replacement in Texas, but that will give us plenty of time as well."

"That sounds just about perfect to me, Gil. I have to tell you it is a great relief to me that you are taking this role. You are absolutely the best candidate for the job, and I believe you are excited to be moving back to Louisiana."

"I have been wanting to move to Louisiana for some time now. The family roots are here, although my father never left Texas after meeting my mother while stationed in Texas after he returned from Vietnam. We came back regularly when I was young to visit my grandparents and Tante Bessie. My sisters always teased me about feeling more at home in Louisiana than Texas. Even though I have plenty of family on my Mom's side in Texas, and Dad was an only child and Tante never married I had only distant cousins here, this place just suits me."

"It will do Ms. Bessie a world of good to have you close, Gil. She is one amazing woman, and according to Cassidy, thinks the world of you."

"And I her, Prescott. I want to share as much time with her as I can with the time she has left. She has always been so vibrant and youthful, until the stroke I kind of believed she would live forever, and that I had all the time in the world to hear her stories of long ago. Now I realize how lucky I am to have had her for so long, and how important it is to spend time with her now and write down all those family stories, so they don't get lost.

"Enough about me, Prescott. What are you planning to do in your retirement?"

Prescott proceeded to tell Gil about his plans to open a sanctuary. He shared his plans, including the fact that the only detail he was having difficulty with was a name for the facility. As he was describing the land he was negotiating to purchase, Gil's face showed extreme surprise.

"The land and houses you are working on buying, they wouldn't be the property that Zeke Thomas is selling, would they?" Gil asked.

"Yes, they are," Prescott's face now reflected his own surprise. "How could you possibly know that?"

"Zeke is a distant cousin. It is a long story, but my fourth great-grandmother was Ruth Thomas. Belle Terre was founded by a man named Jean Luc deBouchet. It was a plantation that he purchased prior to the Civil War. He freed all the slaves and deeded them land. The community was quite self-contained for many years leading up to and after the Civil War. Eventually, many people moved on, and the Thomas family bought up much of the land. As I understand it, no one in the current generation is interested in trying to keep the land, so Zeke is representing the impacted family and selling. I can't believe you are buying that land. What a perfect use for it. In its history, Belle Terre was sanctuary for free people of color, for a community of widows and orphans after the Civil War, a mixed-race community that closed ranks and protected each other through Jim Crow laws and the Civil Rights movement. The last fifty years or so of commercial use were a good effort to try to keep the buildings preserved, but to see it returned to a sanctuary is wonderful."

"I had no idea, Gil. I'm excited to tell Cassidy. I'll bet Ms. Bessie has even more stories than you do about that land."

"Absolutely, Prescott. Many of the stories I want to make sure get written down are the stories of Belle Terre. My fifth great grandmother was Mathilde Chauvin, her son, Robert, married Ruth. Tante has journals that Mathilde kept. The originals were transcribed by Tante in the 1940's into typewritten format, and Mathilde's handwritten copies were put in climate-controlled storage to preserve them. I don't think I've ever seen the originals, but Tante's transcripts were my favorite stories when I was a child. For all the events in the journals, Tante had stories. Ruth Thomas Chauvin lived to be ninety-eight, and Tante remembers her, as Tante was eight or nine when she died. Marguerite Chauvin, Robert's sister, lived until Tante was eleven. So many of the stories are first hand. I want to make sure those stories aren't lost."

"For a guy who didn't know his father, and whose mother died when I was young, I can't imagine having the kind of family history you have, Gil. What an amazing thing."

"My sisters aren't that excited about it, Prescott, but I always have been. The stories of Belle Terre should be told. It was an amazing community of tolerance and support, and they kept it that way by staying mostly separate from the surrounding communities in Terrebonne Parish. Many of the people there still spoke French as their main language until the 1960's. My father spoke a French patois until he went to school, and he was born in 1948. He taught all of us kids to speak French, but we all found out in high school that what they spoke in Belle

Terre had very little relationship with modern French. My sisters let it go, but I still use that language to talk to Tante. For one thing, Mathilde's journals are in that language, so until someone transcribes them into English, we could lose all that history if we lose our ability to read and understand that ancient French patois."

"I'm not a religious man, Gil, but I see the power of a great force in the universe. I feel like you relocating here is part of a bigger plan."

"Me, too, Prescott, me too. I feel like all the pieces of my life are about to fall into place, and it feels good."

◆ ◆ ◆

Marie loved coming home to Max every evening. His huge doggie grin warmed her heart, and his solid loving presence just made everything easier. The new fence was a great addition. Now when Marie got home from work, she let Max out first thing to run in the yard. After she changed her clothes, Marie would go outside and walk the perimeter of the property a few times with Max. Even with the fence, Max didn't like to get too close to the back of the property. Marie wondered why she had never noticed the dogs barking so much but realized that the noise was hardly heard inside the house with the TV or radio on. Since Max didn't like getting too close to the fence, they just kept their distance.

Still, with walking Max for twenty minutes to a half hour every evening, Marie felt better than she had in years. If only she could get her emotional health in a good place so easily. Marie knew that she may never hear from Sandra, or that it could be months, but it was difficult to not obsess over what could be, over what would be. Marie thanked God for Max, because she really didn't know how well she would cope without his steady company.

As Marie was preparing dinner for her and Max, she was startled by the ringing of the phone. Cautiously, she checked the caller ID. She picked up immediately when she saw it was Bee Collins.

"Hey, Marie. I was wondering if you would like to go out for breakfast after Mass this Sunday. We could go to nine o'clock and miss the brunch crowd that goes after the eleven o'clock. What do you think?"

"I think that sounds great, Dee. Where would you like to go?" Marie wasn't familiar with many places to go eat, as until recently she had mostly kept to herself.

"There is a new place called Breaking Dawn that I have heard good things about. It is right here in Bayou Beni, how does that sound?"

"It sounds great, Bee. I'm looking forward to it. While I have you on the phone, how is that online dating site working for you?" Marie really couldn't understand how a girl as sweet and outgoing as Bee had such a hard time finding someone. With her long, silky brown hair, dark blue eyes, and tall slender build, Marie couldn't imagine that Bee's looks were the problem.

"Oh my God, Marie, I went on a date last Friday. He was on CatholicMatch.com. He looked cute enough and nice enough on his profile. And he was cute and nice. And planning to go into the seminary in September. He wanted to date to make sure that he was really being 'called' to the priesthood. We had a great time, and I told him that there was no doubt about the fact he should be a priest. It was like going to lunch with Father LeBlanc, only younger."

Marie was laughing as Bee finished. "Well, honey, if you couldn't entice him away from the priesthood, I'm sure he is really being 'called'."

"Thanks, Marie. I don't know what I'm doing wrong. I really want to fall in love and get married and have a bunch of kids. Rosadel made it look so easy, and here I am twenty-eight and no prospects."

"Bee, twenty-eight isn't old, and if the Lord wants you to be married and have a bunch of kids, he'll put the right man in your path. Just have faith. You are such a good person, I'm sure the Lord has a great plan for you."

"I just wish He'd hurry up," replied Bee. "Oh, that sounded terrible. Sr. Dorothy would be lecturing me for sure if she heard that. She must have told me 'God's time, not yours, child' a thousand times when I was in school."

"The hardest lesson to learn, even at my age, Bee. I sent Sandra a letter, and now I'm driving myself crazy wondering when I'll hear from her or if I'll hear from her. I need to embrace that 'God's time, not yours, Marie' before I lose my mind."

"Marie, I had no idea you were ready to send a letter to Sandra. That took a lot of courage. I'm so proud of you and impressed with how far you've come and how hard you have worked to put the past behind you."

"Bee, honestly, I could never have done it without your friendship, and without you encouraging me to get counseling. That is why I'm sure that the Lord has a special plan for you. You give so much love to everyone in your world, there has to be something special in store for you."

"Awe, Marie, you are easy to be a friend to. Listen, if you start getting anxious about Sandra and need distraction, let me know. There are plenty of nights when all I am doing is watching TV or reading. I'm happy to go out, or to get together to play a board game or cards, or just get together to talk. Don't ever worry that you could be a bother to me. If I'm busy, I'll say so."

"Thank you, Bee. I may take you up on that. I don't like to leave Max alone in the evening after leaving him all day, but I'd love to have you over for dinner and conversation. When the days get longer, maybe we can go to the park with Max or something."

"Sounds great. I need to get going, my Mom is expecting me for dinner. I wanted to make sure we got Sunday booked before it got away from me. See you tomorrow at school."

As Marie hung up the phone, she said a quick prayer of thanks for Bee, and Jessie, and all the other friends she had made through Holy Redeemer. Whatever happened with Sandra, Marie knew she had to focus on all the good in her life, and just keep trying to be the person she had always been meant to be, before life and Burl had derailed her.

♦ ♦ ♦

Cassidy and Pete were surprised that Bessie wasn't waiting in the lobby for them when they arrived at Our Lady of Lourdes on Thursday night, but realized why not when they heard laughter coming from her room as they approached.

They both recognized Bessie's laugh, but the deeper pitched laughter was a mystery until they entered Bessie's room. "Soapy!" Bessie exclaimed as Cassidy dropped her leash and Sophie ran and jumped into Bessie's lap. Gil Chauvin stood as the couple with four dogs entered Tante's room. This must be Cassidy and Pete. Gil felt a quick stab of regret as he saw Cassidy's hazel eyed blond beauty and acknowledged to himself that Pete's tall slim build and dark hair made them a very attractive couple.

He held out his hand to Pete. "Gil Chauvin, and you must be Pete Marshall. I can see the resemblance to Clancy. Really pleased to meet you. Thanks so much for all you have done for Tante. I know she would never have made this amazing progress without all the love and care you have given her."

Pete shook Gil's hand and tried not to feel jealous. Gil Chauvin was the kind of handsome that everyone noticed. He had wavy dark brown hair, startling blue eyes, and cafe au lait skin tone. His features were strong and even, and he was easily 6 plus feet tall, and built like an athlete. Pete was determined to not behave in a way that would make Cassidy uncomfortable.

"Good to meet you, Gil. Ms. Bessie is a treasure, and it has been a wonderful experience for me to get to know her and spend time with her. I have been her veterinarian since I took over from Doc Russell, but only really got to know her well since coming to visit regularly with Cassidy. You are a lucky man to call her family."

Bessie was blushing prettily as Pete and Gil shook hands. "Pete's a charmer," she said with a smile. Pete walked over and kissed her cheek. "So are you, Ms. Bessie."

Gil took the opportunity to turn to Cassidy. "And you must be Cassidy. Would you think it incredibly forward of me if I hugged you? If Tante is your Grandma Bessie, we must be cousins."

Cassidy blushed and smiled as she hugged Gil. "Ms. Bessie was so excited that you were coming to visit. I think you must be her favorite nephew."

Gil smiled as he answered. "Besides my Dad, I'm her only nephew, so it is fair to say I'm in the top two. And I would never ask her to choose, would I, Tante?"

"No, indeed not. I love your Daddy like a son. It is so good to have you all together here. My heart is so full."

Cassidy hugged and kissed Bessie. "You are speaking so beautifully tonight, Grandma Bessie. It is almost like you never had a stroke."

Bessie smiled as she stroked Sophie. "Every day is better. Sometimes I can't find a word, but that happens less and less. I'm excited today, and that seems to help."

"Do you want to stay and visit with Gil, or do you want to make the rounds with Maggie and Sophie?" Cassidy wanted to make sure the other residents didn't miss out on their doggie time.

"I want Gil to come visit with us too. Gil, will you do that?"

"Sure, Tante. I'll come too. This sounds like fun." Pete kept repeating in his head, "Be the best man for Cassidy" as he took Laverne and Shirley over to the Assisted Living side of the home. He was doing the best he could to put on a happy face, but when he got to Sr. Dorothy Murphy's room, she saw right away something was off.

"Peter Marshall, there is a cloud in those blue eyes of yours today. Did something bad happen?" Pete kissed Sr. Dorothy's cheek, and picked up Shirley and placed her carefully in Sr. Dorothy's lap, while picking up Laverne and holding her in his arms.

"No, Sister. Just trying to be the man I should be, and sometimes it's hard." Pete really didn't want to go into the details with Sr. Dorothy.

"Aye, Peter. If it was easy to be a good man, there wouldn't be any bad ones. You're a good man, or you wouldn't feel the trying so much. The biggest challenge for you, boyo, has been the same since you were a wee lad. You are more than you think you are. More loving, more caring, and more worth fighting for. Have a little faith that others see what I see, and you'll be fine."

Pete felt his heart warm, and his insecurities about Gil fade. "Thank you, Sister Dorothy. I think next to my Mom, you have always been my biggest cheerleader."

"Ah, go on with yourself. I don't cheerlead. I simply see the good boy and good man God made. And I think you now have an even bigger fan than your dear sainted Mother and me. I think bonny Cassidy thinks you hung the moon."

Pete smiled at Sister's way of putting things. "I know I think Cassidy hung the moon, so I surely hope it is mutual. I'm glad I got to stop by and see you, Sister. Ever since I was afraid to start kindergarten at Holy Redeemer, you've helped me feel better about what I have to do, and how I should behave."

Sister Dorothy smiled at Pete, remembering all the stages of Pete's life so far. "The Marshall boys are special to my heart, as are Rosadel and her wee bairns. All my Holy Redeemer children are family, but you stole my heart when you were only five years old. Everything I believed about you then has come true, right down to your warm, charitable heart bringing these dogs to visit with us a couple of times a week. I've wished for you to find someone to share your mission, as it was always obvious to me that the married vocation was in store for you. I see you have found that someone in Cassidy. I'm looking forward to my wedding invitation."

"I promise you'll be the first after the parents to see the ring, Sister Dorothy. Now I just need to work on the right timing to make sure Cassidy says 'yes'. I need to get onto the other residents. I love you, Sister Dorothy. Thanks for helping me turn my mood around."

Dorothy Murphy smiled as she kissed Pete's cheek. "And I love you too, Peter. You make this old woman's heart smile every time I see you."

As Pete made the rest of his rounds, he thought about Sister Dorothy, and her ability to make everyone around her try harder to be the best person they could be. An angel in a habit, Pete felt blessed to have had her in his life for so long.

By the time Pete returned to Bessie's room with Laverne and Shirley, Bessie was looking worn out. Cassidy and Gil were talking about his interview, and it sounded like Gil would be moving to Bayou Beni.

"I had asked Tante before you arrived if it would be alright for me to stay in her house while we transition. She said I could just live there. I think that maybe she will progress to coming home, and maybe if I live there and we have someone checking in during the day, it can happen sooner. We'll have to see. But I'm very excited to be moving to Bayou Beni."

"I know Grandma Bessie will be thrilled to have you, won't you, Grandma?" Cassidy noticed Pete had entered the room and walked over and kissed his cheek. "You must have had some good visits, tonight."

Pete realized Cassidy was trying to reassure him, and it warmed his heart. "I did, Cassidy. How were things on this side?"

She smiled as she winked at Bessie. "Grandma Bessie was so busy showing off her nephew that the dogs weren't the stars of the show tonight. They still got plenty of lap time though."

Pete smiled as he thought of Sister Dorothy's pep talk. "Hey, it isn't every day that you get to show off your relatives, and we both know how much Bessie has missed Gil. It is good that the dogs gave her the opportunity to show Gil off to her friends here."

Cassidy knew when Pete said that that everything really was going to be fine. As they said their goodbyes and left Gil with Bessie, Cassidy felt as if she were walking on air. Life just kept getting better and better.

CHAPTER 29

Cassidy finished her Saturday chores just in time to shower and get dressed for Pete to pick her up for dinner at Sandra and Mark's house. She had spent the whole day distracted and worried about how Sandra was going to behave tonight, and how Pete was going to react to Sandra's behavior. She knew it was pointless to worry, as it was totally out of her control, but she couldn't help herself.

It was a relief when the doorbell rang, and it was Pete. Cassidy opened the door and gestured for Pete to come in. She stood on tiptoes to kiss his cheek. "You look very handsome tonight."

Pete was wearing a light blue shirt, jeans, and a grey sports coat. "I wasn't sure what to wear. I didn't want to look too dressy or too casual, and I figured I could lose the jacket if it was too much."

Cassidy gestured to the cotton jersey dress she was wearing. "I think we match, I was nervous too. I usually go to Mom and Mark's in whatever I have on, but today is kind of a big deal, so I wanted to dress up a little."

"Well, you look great, but then, you always look great to me. Do you want some help settling Maggie and Sophie?" Pete had squatted down to pet both dogs as they too had come to the foyer to greet him.

"I'm just going to fix them each a treat in their crates, and then we can go. I'm trying to calm down, but I'm worried that tonight might be a bad idea."

Pete stood up and hugged Cassidy. "I know you have had some rough times with your mom. I won't judge, I promise. I want to meet your family, and I want them to meet me. I plan to be part of your life,

Cassidy, and if that means I will have legit mother-in-law jokes to tell someday, then so be it."

Cassidy leaned into Pete and took a deep breath. "She was so great the other night, Pete. I just hope that we get that Sandra and not the one who finds fault with everything I do."

Pete kissed Cassidy's forehead. "Whatever happens, we'll find a way to laugh about it on the way home. My mom always said we can't control other people, but we can control how we respond to them. I'm not suggesting that I want to laugh at your mom, but you are such a terrific person, we can laugh at anything anyone does that suggests otherwise."

"Do you know how much I appreciate you, Pete Marshall?" Cassidy looked up at Pete.

"I'd ask you to show me, but then we might be late for dinner." Pete brushed a quick kiss over Cassidy's lips. "Let's get this show on the road. We don't want to get off on the wrong foot by being late."

When Cassidy got to the van, she noticed a bouquet of flowers on the back seat. Pete gestured to them. "For your Mom. My mom always taught us to bring something for the host and hostess when we were invited for dinner. Since the invitation came through you, I didn't get a chance to ask if I should bring something. I thought about getting a bottle of wine, but didn't know if Mark and Sandra drink, and that could be awkward if they don't. Flowers seemed like the best choice."

"They're beautiful, Pete, and I'll bet Mom will love them." As Pete drove to Sandra and Mark's house, Cassidy filled Pete in on what had been happening to prepare for the booth at Holy Redeemer's festival at the end of the month.

"We plan to have the booth open for four hours on Friday night, and for eight hours on Saturday. Dustin and Katelyn are each going to take an hour on Friday night, and swap out the dogs so that none of them are there for more than an hour or so. On Saturday, I've got myself booked for four hours, and Bee Collins and Rosadel are each booked for an hour. I only need two more volunteers and we'll be fully staffed."

"I'll bet either Hannah Falgoust or Lindy Russell will be happy to take an hour. And what about Angus and Jessie McPherson, have you asked either one of them? And I'll bet Bethany Williams would take a shift, it would help her meet people." Pete was full of ideas.

"Will you ask Lindy for me? I forgot until just now that Hannah volunteered already." Cassidy replied. "I'll ask Bethany. If we get two out of three of those we will be good."

"Sure, I'll ask Lindy. And I know you can count on Hannah. They love adoption events, and this one encouraging fostering will be a big hit with both of them. I'll let you know Monday afternoon what they say."

Pete pulled up in front of Sandra and Mark's house. He reached over and squeezed Cassidy's hand. "Let's see if I can charm your mother into inviting me into the family."

Sandra had been as nervous as Cassidy all day. She had made meatloaf, Cassidy's favorite meal, and had baked a red velvet cake for dessert. Candace and Mark Jr. had helped with straightening the house, and Mark had made sure the lawn and yard were in good shape. Sandra wanted to make a good impression on Pete for Cassidy's sake.

Mark Jr. went running for the door as soon as the doorbell rang. "Hey Cass! We're having meatloaf." Mark Jr. stuck his hand out to Pete. "I'm Chip, who're you?"

Sandra came into the foyer wiping her hands on a dish towel. "Mark Jr., that is not how to introduce yourself to someone. The correct way is 'Nice to meet you, I'm Mark Jr.'."

"But I want him to call me Chip like everyone else." Sandra took a deep breath and turned to Pete, just as he presented the bouquet of flowers.

"These are for you, Mrs. Guidry. Thanks so much for inviting me to dinner. How in the world did you know that meatloaf is my favorite?" Sandra blushed as she took the flowers.

"Thank you for the flowers, Pete. And you are very welcome for dinner. Meatloaf is Cassidy's favorite, that is why we are having it for dinner."

Pete looked at Cassidy, "How did I never know that?" he asked.

"Never came up?" Cassidy replied. "Hi Mom! Thanks for making meatloaf. The house smells great." Cassidy hugged and kissed Sandra as Candy came into the foyer.

"Hey Cass! Pete, I recognize you from when me and Cass saw you out with the girl that works for you. I'm Candy." Pete smiled as he responded. "Good to meet you, Candy. Cassidy talks about you all the time, and I'm glad to finally meet you in person."

"Does she talk about me?" Chip asked.

"She must, or I wouldn't know that you are finally allowed to play baseball." Pete responded.

"Yeah! Do you play baseball?" Chip was always looking for someone to toss a ball with.

"I played a little when I was in grade school and high school, but I wasn't good enough to make the high school team. I was more interested in spending time with animals than in playing sports."

"Pete is a veterinarian, Chip, and he used to volunteer at the shelter with me when we were both in high school."

Sandra chose that moment to interrupt. "We don't have to stand here in the foyer. Come on into the family room, while I put these flowers in a vase and put them on the dining room table. We have a few minutes to visit before dinner is ready."

Cassidy led Pete into the family room where Mark was watching television. Mark stood up and hugged Cassidy. "Hey girl, you sure look pretty tonight."

"Thanks, Mark. This is Pete Marshall." Mark stuck out his hand to greet Pete. "Happy to meet you Pete. What do you think about LSU basketball this year?" He asked as he gestured toward the television. And with that, Pete and Mark were off and running on LSU basketball and why they couldn't seem to put together a championship team.

Cassidy listened to their back and forth for a few minutes, and then went into the kitchen to talk to Sandra. "Hey Mom, can I do anything to help?"

"I think I've got it all under control, Cassidy. Where's Pete?" Sandra was bustling in the kitchen as she talked.

"He and Mark are talking basketball, I know Mark can do that for hours, and I think Pete can too, so I decided to spend my time with you. How are you doing with the decision for Chip to play baseball?"

"To be honest, I'm struggling, but I know I have to let him do the things he enjoys. It was easier for me with you and Candace. But Mark Sr. is thrilled, and I imagine the entire Guidry family will be out in full force at Mark Jr.'s games, so it will be good for the family." Sandra had stopped her bustling and had turned to face Cassidy sitting at the bar in the kitchen. "Cassidy, while we have a minute, I want to apologize for always being so hard on you. I'm learning a lot through counseling, and I don't want to get into everything tonight, but my need to apologize to you has been weighing on me."

"Mom, you have nothing to apologize for. You did your best. I know you love me. I turned out okay, don't worry." Cassidy was uncomfortable with the direction this conversation was going.

"I do owe you an apology, and an explanation. Can we have lunch one day so that I can tell you all about what I'm learning about myself in counseling?"

"That would be great, Mom, but it will have to be on a weekend day, I hardly get time to eat lunch at my desk at the shelter most days."

"Saturday it is then. Now tell me all about how your plans for the Holy Redeemer fair are progressing." As Cassidy filled Sandra in on the plans for the fair, she marveled once again at the change in Sandra. She was looking forward to next Saturday, and the next phase of her relationship with her mother.

Dinner was different than any Cassidy had experienced at her Mom and Mark's house. Pete and Mark acted like they had known each other forever, and Candy and Chip took turns asking Pete questions and getting questioned in return. There was so much laughing, Cassidy felt like they were at Mark's parent's house. Pete brought a fun and lightheartedness to everything he did, and it brought out the fun in everyone. Cassidy knew there was no turning back now, her family had fallen as much in love with Pete as she had.

Pete insisted that the "kids" do the dishes, since Sandra had cooked. Cassidy loved seeing how easily he charmed Sandra into going into the family room for "private time" with Mark. When he promised that they would call out before coming out of the kitchen so as to not interrupt anything important, Cassidy couldn't help blushing as Candy laughed and Chip looked confused. Mark high-fived Pete, and Sandra played along by beckoning to Mark over her shoulder like a vamp. Cassidy could hardly believe this was her family.

As they cleaned up the kitchen, Candy was the first to mention how great a night it was. "Daddy is always playful and fun, but to see Mom clowning around and joining in sure is great, isn't it Cass?"

"I know! I don't think I ever saw Mom like this before, and it's great." Pete looked from one to the other. "You mean you all don't mess around like this all the time?"

Chip shook his head no. "We see Daddy like this with his brothers and stuff, but I never saw Mom play like this before. I think you did it Pete."

Pete shook his head. "I just acted like I would at home. I hope I didn't make a mess."

Candy threw her arms around Pete and hugged him. "You didn't make a mess, you acted like we are normal, and Mom went along. I hope you always make it like this."

Pete gave Candy a hug back as he caught Cassidy's eye above Candy's head. Cassidy smiled at him like he was a hero, and Pete felt her love from across the room. "Maybe this is more about Mom than about Pete. She has been amazing lately."

"She always was amazing, Cass. She was just kind of scared. She's not as scared anymore." This came from Chip, who was an incredibly sensitive child.

"I think you're right, Chip." The door to the kitchen swung open as Sandra and Mark came back in the room.

"What is Chip right about?" asked Sandra.

"That you are amazing, Mom," answered Cassidy, and she meant it.

♦ ♦ ♦

Angus and Jessie were enjoying a quiet evening at home. "I'm looking forward to telling everyone I'm pregnant," said Jessie as they sat watching the fire in the fireplace, "I'm tired of people thinking I'm getting fat."

"Now why would you think anyone thinks that?" asked Angus. "You don't look any different to me."

"I need to go into maternity clothes soon, because all my clothes are getting tight. I can feel the baby move now, and I feel like he or she will grow better when my clothes aren't so tight." And Jessie wanted to start celebrating, because she was finally feeling confident that this pregnancy was going to end happily.

"Well, we told your brother and sister and their families on New Year's, Rosadel and Clancy know. As soon as we tell the triplets, we can tell everyone. Do you want to do that tomorrow?"

Jessie sipped her tea as she thought about it. "Yes, Angus. I know I had initially said I wanted to wait until I was twenty weeks, but I want to tell the girls and everyone else now. Are you okay with that?"

"Of course, I am, Sweetheart. I want what you want. You've given me a new lease on life. I'm so excited for this baby to be born and for us to be parents together. I think we're going to be great." Angus reached over and smoothed Jessie's hair back from her face. "I go back and forth picturing a little girl that looks like you, or a boy that looks like both of us. I'm glad we decided to wait to find out if our baby is a boy or a girl until you deliver. I think it makes the anticipation even better."

"Me, too, Angus. And I'm excited to tell the triplets. Do you want to call Rosadel and let her know there will be a special announcement at brunch tomorrow?" Angus nodded. "I think I should. Always better to be prepared with those three. I hope we don't end up with a biology lesson as well as brunch."

Jessie laughed. "I think at eight we're still in 'when a husband and wife love each other very much' stage of things."

"I hope so, Jessie, but with the Momma cat and kittens who knows what those three can come up with."

"There is never a shortage of entertainment with the triplets, is there? Go ahead and call Rosadel, and I'll get up and get supper started. Tomorrow is going to be an exciting day."

◆ ◆ ◆

Marie was talking to Max as they walked around the yard. "I'm going to breakfast after church in the morning, Max, so I'll be gone longer than usual. I'll get up early just like a work day and feed you before I go, and when I get home we'll walk and maybe watch a movie." As Marie and Max got closer to the back of the yard, Marie heard the dogs barking again. Max stopped and sat. "Do you want to turn around and go back, boy? We can. I don't really like the sound of those dogs barking either." As Marie headed back to the house with Max, she wondered why those dogs barking bothered Max. She wished he could talk. Well, she could keep him away since it made him uncomfortable. Marie knelt down and hugged Max. "I love you, boy. You're the best."

CHAPTER 30

Marie woke up before her alarm to the sound of rain. She reached out and felt Max sleeping and took a deep breath. Rain and storms were still stressful. After more than fifty years, you would think the fear of storms would have passed, but it never did. Marie listened to the rain for a few more minutes. No thunder, no howling wind, just rain. She breathed deeply, said a prayer and felt the fear recede.

Since she was awake early, Marie decided to go to church early and spend some time in prayer and meditation before Mass. Since sending the letter to Sandra, Marie felt unsettled, and knew that the best chance she had for finding peace was to seek peace through prayer. As she got herself coffee and Max breakfast, Marie was thinking about how lucky she was to have a friend like Bee. Marie wished she knew a nice young man to fix Bee up with.

Marie was surprised to see Bee already at Holy Redeemer when she got to church at a little after eight. Needing private time with her prayers, Marie sat in her regular seat and didn't make herself known to Bee. For the next forty minutes, Marie gave herself over to prayer and meditation, asking the Lord for patience and forbearance as she waited for His will to be done. By the time the church started to fill for Mass, Marie was glad to feel the peace of Christ in her heart.

Bee had arrived at church early for the same reason as Marie. Bee realized that she needed to take a step back from her quest to find a man. She was tired of herself. It was time to accept the life she had and enjoy it. If there was a man in her future, it would happen, if not, she would be happily single. Bee realized she was wasting the present by pining for an imaginary future. So, she came to church early, and prayed for peace and patience. For Bee, inner peace was still elusive, but she did feel better than she had since Christmas.

As the final prayers were said and the final hymn was sung, Bee made her way out of church. She had seen Marie at communion time and didn't worry that they would easily meet up in front of church.

Marie was waiting in the vestibule, as it was still raining on and off. Bee hurried over and gave her a hug. "Good Morning! Do you want to drive together or take both cars to breakfast?" Bee kept her arm around Marie as she asked.

"Well, since you know the way, how about we go together in your car? To be honest, I'm not that comfortable driving in the rain."

"My car it is. If we hurry, we can get to the car before another shower starts."

As Bee and Marie headed out for the restaurant, Marie began to reminisce. "My mother loved rain and storms. I remember when I was a little girl, she would take me outside to jump in the puddles. My little dog, Bijou, hated the rain. I can still see her sitting on the porch, with the saddest face you can imagine while me and Mom danced in the rain. When it would storm, my mother would stand by the window and watch. She was never the least little bit afraid."

"Do you have a lot of memories of your mother?" Bee knew that Marie had lost both her parents when she was young.

"Oh, yes. For most of my life I've pulled the memories of my life with my mother and father out and treasured them. Other than the first few years of Sandra's life, all my happy memories are from my life in Galliano with Mom and Dad. We had a very simple life. Dad was a commercial fisherman, and Mom ran the house. She had a huge vegetable garden, and canned vegetables and made fruit preserves and jellies. She made most of my clothes and made the curtains for the house. She also loved music and could play the guitar and the mandolin. On many an evening, Mom would play, and Dad and I would sing. We were so very happy, just being together."

"I can't imagine losing everything like you did, Marie." Bee reached over and squeezed Marie's hand. "It must have been so hard."

"It was worse than you can imagine. Not only did I lose my mom and dad and Bijou to the tornado, but I lost the life I knew. Life in White Castle was so different from Galliano. And I felt like I had to take care of my grandmother. She was so heartbroken. I went from a home full of music and laughter to one full of silence and tears. I understand how all of that worked together to set me up for Burl Theriot to take advantage of me. I wish that things were different back then, that sending a child to counseling would have been part of the normal response, but it wasn't. Thank God you talked me into going to counseling now. For the first time since I woke up in the hospital after the tornado, I am starting to feel like I deserve to be happy."

"Oh, Marie, I'm so sorry that so many years passed without anyone trying to help you. Honestly, I don't understand how that happened."

Marie patted Bee on the arm. "I was an expert at shutting people out. After all the losses I had suffered, I didn't want to care about anyone else. I wanted to be left alone, and I made sure that I didn't give anyone the opportunity to get close to me. I don't know why you were able to break through my barriers. I think it must have been God's will. But I'm grateful, and happy for the friendships that I now have."

"I got to church early this morning to ask God's help managing my emotions since contacting Sandra. I can honestly say that I am at peace with things for now. It is in God's Hands. I will hear or not hear from Sandra, and I'll go on with my ministry for other abused women and fill my life with friends."

"I went to church early too," replied Bee. "I have got to move on from this quest to find a man and just start enjoying my life. I don't think I'm at peace yet, but I'm moving in that direction. I realized I'm missing out on enjoying today by worrying about a tomorrow that may never come."

"Isn't it funny how easy it is to focus on what is missing rather than focus on what we have? For all the years here in Audela, I focused on what I lost. I didn't try to make friends or participate in the community. I worked, and went to church, and mourned. Even if I never speak to Sandra, or have a relationship with her and her children, I still have a lot to give to this world, and I finally realized that. Don't waste a minute,

Bee. Before you know it, you will be staring old age in the face and you don't want to be like me and regret most of your life."

Bee turned to face Marie as she parked the car in the restaurant parking lot. "I know I've got a good life, Marie. It just isn't the life I pictured. I'm going to appreciate what I have more and start making every day count for something. One of the things I'm thinking about doing is starting to work at the after-school care at Holy Redeemer as well as working in the office. I love kids, and that is a great way to have more access to them if I don't have my own."

"I think that is a great idea, Bee. Did you ever think about being a teacher?" Marie realized she didn't know much about how Bee had ended up the Holy Redeemer school secretary.

"That sounds like a great story to tell you over breakfast, let's go inside and get a table before there is a wait."

As Marie and Bee were getting settled and placing their orders, Bee thought about how to tell her story to Marie. Very few people knew the heartache that Bee had suffered, since it all happened while she was attending Nicholls State University in Thibodaux, LA.

"You came to Holy Redeemer to work the year Rosadel and I started high school, so you wouldn't have known us from school. If you would have been there, you would have known that Rosadel and I were like two peas in a pod. We did everything together. It stayed that way until Rosadel met Clancy, and then it was a threesome, or a foursome, as I dated quite a few different guys in high school. Anyway, Rosadel and I were sure we would go to college together and be roommates somewhere. Then after two years of being away from Clancy, Rosadel decided to go for a two-year RN at Delgado, and commute to school. I wanted the whole campus life thing, so I went to Nicholls State by myself.

"I had no idea what I wanted to do with my life, and I liked the feel of the campus there, so off I went. My roommate was a girl from Independence, and she introduced me to all of her friends on campus. That is how I met Gus. August Damiano. He was a three-sport athlete, not good enough for an LSU scholarship, but plenty good for Nicholls. We hit it off right away and were dating steadily by the end of our first semester.

"He was majoring In Human Performance Education. His plan was to teach high school and coach. I decided to major in Elementary Education. I would teach in a grammar school, and Gus in high school. We'd get married and have a bunch of kids and a perfect life."

Marie knew that hadn't happened and reached across the table to hold Bee's hand. "What happened Bee? What happened to Gus?"

"Right before Thanksgiving our sophomore year, Gus started feeling poorly. He thought maybe he had a cold or the flu. I was busy finishing up with assignments to go home for Thanksgiving, but on Friday afternoon, I went to his dorm room to check on him. He was burning up with fever, and disoriented. I tried to get him up to take him to health services, but he was too weak, and I called an ambulance. He had meningitis. By Monday, he was dead.

"My parents took me to Independence for the funeral, and then I went back to school. But I couldn't do it. I stayed in my bed. I didn't go to class. Rosadel was pregnant, about to have the triplets. She called every day. I know she called, because I would drag myself awake to talk to her, but I don't really remember anything. She got more and more worried and called my mother and told her that someone had to go to Nicholls to check on me.

"When my Mom got there, she couldn't believe what had happened. I hadn't eaten or bathed since I went back to school after Thanksgiving. She packed me up and took me home and took me to a psychiatrist. I was admitted to the hospital for a week. I had a psychotic break from grief. As long as I stayed in my bed, I could pretend that Gus was still alive. I really believed that his illness, death and funeral were a dream.

"After I got out of the hospital, I was very fragile. I was lost. Then Rosadel had the girls, and they were small, and had respiratory issues. Rosadel needed me. I spent hours and hours at the neonatal intensive care unit with her. After the babies got released, I stayed at her house whenever Clancy wasn't home. Later, when one or more baby would be in the hospital and the other or others at home, I was wherever Rosadel wasn't. Those babies pulled me out of my grief and made me want to live again.

"Rosadel insisted that I be godmother to all three girls. She said that she would feel like she was picking a favorite if I was only godmother to one girl. The girls' godfathers are Pete, Mike and Donnie, in order of age; so, Pete is Lou's godfather, Mike is Gracie's and Donnie is Rosie's. I spent the best part of the first year of the girls lives totally dedicated to Rosadel and Clancy and the girls. I still had no idea what I was going to do with my life without Gus."

"Oh, Bee. I'm so sorry you went through that. What about Gus's family? Why weren't they sharing your grief?"

"I was his college girlfriend, Marie, and I hadn't spent a lot of time with his family. He was an only child. His high school girlfriend was the daughter of friends of his parents. I think they thought I was temporary, and that he and his high school sweetheart would get back together someday. She sat with the family at the funeral, and I sat in the back with my mother and father. I think feeling invisible added to the sense of unreality for me. It was so hard.

"In a way, the girl that loved Gus and was going to be a teacher died when he died. As time has gone on, those years at Nicholls have faded in intensity. Most of my life is here in Bayou Beni. That year and a half in Thibodaux has a dream like quality, even in my memories. Gus was so busy with his sports and studies that Rosadel and Clancy were the only ones who got to know him at all besides me. When I dropped out after he died, I lost contact with his friends from school. There was no way for me to go back to Nicholls, and I was stuck, not knowing what to do next.

"At the end of the school year, Mrs. Abadie retired as school secretary. Sr. Dorothy came over to Rosadel's to check on the girls, and I was there with Rosadel. Sr. Dorothy told me I should apply for the school secretary position. I told her I never imagined being the school secretary. She told me that I needed to be in a loving environment, and that I only needed to stay until I figured out what I wanted to do next. I think you know from your years at Holy Redeemer that when Sr. Dorothy decides what someone will do, it is like fighting God Himself to say no. So, I started as secretary.

"I really liked it. I liked seeing the children. And interacting with the parents. Sr. Dorothy knew I wasn't challenged though and started pushing me to go to school at night so that I could become the network administrator and webmaster for the school and church. The parish was paying a service provider a boatload of money and weren't really satisfied with the service they were getting. I went to University of New Orleans, taking night classes and Saturday classes, and flexing my work schedule at Holy Redeemer to take daytime classes until I graduated.

"It has ended up being perfect for me. And now I think I'm ready to do some after school care. I want to spend more time with the children."

Marie was stunned. From the outside looking in, she had always thought that Bee had a charmed life, with nothing but wonderful moments.

"I had no idea, Bee. You always seem so happy and content. I would never have guessed that you had so much heartache in your life."

"It's okay, Marie. Just like you, I have become a master of hiding in plain sight. Everyone suffers heartache. Mostly, I don't want people to know. I like being Bee Collins, school secretary with the charmed life. Nothing changes the past, and I think I really have come to terms with the hand I was dealt."

◆ ◆ ◆

Pete and Cassidy had arranged to meet Gil at Our Lady of Lourdes so that they could go out to brunch with Bessie and only take one car. Once again, Pete and Cassidy could hear laughter coming from Bessie's room as they approached.

"As much as Grandma Bessie loves us, Gil just delights her, doesn't he?" Pete whispered to Cassidy.

"I know she really missed him," replied Cassidy. "And knowing someone their whole lives is really special. Can you imagine what it would be like to not see one of the triplets for a few months?"

Pete shook his head. "I hate when a week goes by. I don't even want to think about them growing up and moving away."

"Who's growing up and moving away?" asked Gil as they walked into Bessie's room.

"No one, yet," replied Pete. "Cassidy and I were just observing how happy it makes Ms. Bessie to have you here and comparing how she feels to how I'll feel if the triplets move away when they grow up."

Gil smiled, "That's right. You are the uncle of Clancy's triplets. I have to tell you, there has been many a break at a business meeting that has been reduced to hilarity at stories of those girls exploits. I hope I get the chance to meet them soon."

"You will probably get the chance after Mass. Rosadel, Clancy, the girls, Angus and Jessie all usually attend the eleven o'clock mass, and they go out for brunch afterwards. I'll admit I'm prejudiced, but they are beautiful and charming little girls." As much as he teased them, Pete was incredibly proud of his nieces.

"If they don't scare you with their questions," said Cassidy with a laugh. She playfully bumped Pete with her shoulder. "Now that they have successfully made a match for their Uncle Pete, you may get caught in their crosshairs."

"Sounds like I may get to play a starring role in one of Clancy's stories in the future. Did they really offer to find a wife for Father LeBlanc?" Gil still remembered that story.

Cassidy looked at Pete. "Really?" she asked.

"Really," replied Pete. "Loudly, after Sunday Mass, with a large audience. I thought Rosadel was going to die on the spot, and Angus, Jessie and Clancy all just laughed. So did Father LeBlanc after a minute. Angus composed himself enough to tell the girls that he would explain why Father LeBlanc would never get married, while Rosadel kept sputtering apologies. I felt too bad for Rosadel to laugh when it happened, but boy, did we all get a good laugh later. Even Rosadel can laugh at it now."

Bessie made a point of looking at her watch, and Cassidy picked up on the clue right away. "We better get going so that we can get into church and get Grandma Bessie settled in a seat. You know we will have to stop and greet everyone since we are bringing a celebrity with us."

Bessie blushed and smiled as she answered Cassidy. "Stop your teasing and get me to church. I have a nephew to show off." Cassidy brushed a quick kiss on Bessie's cheek, and they all headed to Holy Redeemer.

♦ ♦ ♦

Things were not going smoothly at the Marshall household. The kittens that had been claimed would start going to their new homes on Monday, and the reality of that was setting in with the triplets. Lou was pouting, Rosie was angry, and Gracie was struggling to not cry. Rosadel was on the verge of tears too. She had given up on any of the girls eating breakfast, reasoning that they would have brunch soon enough after Mass. The girls had stormed upstairs to get dressed for church, and Rosadel knew she had to go up in a minute and make sure they were making progress, but for the moment she just put her head in her hands.

Clancy walked into the kitchen after showering and getting dressed to find Rosadel head in hands totally dejected. He knelt down on the floor by her chair and put his arms around her. "Bad morning?"

"Oh, Clancy. I think I messed up big time bringing these kittens home. The girls are heartbroken that the kittens are leaving, and they are all acting out in their own way and I'm just as sad as they are and I'm at my wit's end. What in the world was I thinking with my big noble teaching compassion stupid idea?" Rosadel was angrily wiping tears from her eyes as she talked.

"Oh, Sugar, you didn't mess up. The girls will be sad, and they will grow from it. You are teaching them compassion, and strength, and how much it hurts to love sometimes. They were going to have to learn all those lessons someday. I know this is hard on all of us. But I've learned my lesson too. I have to take more responsibility for the hard parts of parenting. Why don't you get yourself a cup of coffee and go sit somewhere and pet Roscoe for a while? I'll go upstairs and talk to the girls and finish getting them ready for church." Clancy grabbed four tubes of yogurt and headed upstairs.

Clancy found the three girls deep in whispered conversation when he walked into their room. "What's this I hear about no one eating breakfast? You all at least have to eat a yogurt with Daddy."

"But my stomach hurts because I'm sad," said Lou.

"I know that, Lou. And Rosie is mad, and Gracie is sad. And your Mommy is crying in the kitchen." All three girls looked startled at that.

"I don't want Mommy to cry," said Gracie.

"And Mommy doesn't want you to cry either. But saying goodbye to the kittens is sad and hard. And it doesn't make it less sad or less hard to act like this. It is always okay to feel however you feel, but it is important to learn how to talk about feelings without hurting other people." Clancy looked at each of the girls in turn.

"That is what Pop-Pop said too." Lou sighed. "It's hard Daddy."

Clancy opened his arms for a group hug. "Let's eat our go-gurt and figure out what we can do to help Mommy feel better. The best way to take your mind off of yourself and your troubles is to help someone else."

"But Daddy," said Rosie, "None of us would have to feel bad if Mommy would let us keep the kittens. So, she can fix this."

Clancy hugged the girls again. "No, Rosie, Mommy can't fix this. The kittens have to go to their new homes. I know Gee-Jay explained that to you already. This is just one of those hard times when what has to happen is sad. We are lucky that we still have each other and Roscoe. And most of the kittens are going to homes where you will still get to play with them. So, this is nowhere near as sad as it could be.

"I know you girls think that me and Mommy can fix everything, and I wish that was true. But we can't. We can love you through everything though. Now what do you think we can do to cheer Mommy up?"

The girls had been eating their yogurt while Clancy talked. "We could get dressed for church and you could help us fix our hair and we could tell her we love her." Gracie was always the first with a solution.

"I think that is a great idea, Gracie. I'll go downstairs and check on Mommy, and when I come back I want you all dressed and ready to have your hair done."

Clancy found Rosadel on the sofa with both Roscoe and Holly. "Can we keep Holly?" Rosadel asked as soon as Clancy entered the room

"Sure thing, Sugar. I'm going to go back upstairs in a few minutes to help the girls with their hair, and then they will be down to go to church. You sure you want to keep Holly?"

"Yes, she and Roscoe really love each other. And I found out I like having a cat." Holly was purring in Rosadel's lap, while Roscoe was pressed up against Rosadel's leg.

"And you're not just doing this to make it easier on the girls?" Clancy knew the bulk of work always landed on Rosadel and wanted to make sure she was sure.

Rosadel flushed. "To be honest, that is where the idea started, the day after Cassidy brought people over to meet the kittens. But as I've kept Holly with me and Roscoe and away from the kittens, I've come to appreciate how happy it makes Roscoe to always have company. And so, it seems like a win for the family."

"Then Holly stays. I'll let you tell the girls whenever you decide is a good time."

"Not today. When they find out that Daddy and Jessie are having a baby, that will be a big distraction. I'll save this news for later." Clancy leaned over and kissed Rosadel tenderly. "I love you, Rosadel. And I'm proud of you. And I think you are a great Mom, and me and the girls are lucky to have you."

Rosadel put her hand on Clancy's cheek. "Stop or you'll make me cry again. I love you too."

As Father LeBlanc said the closing prayers at Mass, Rosadel said a quick prayer that the girls would be happy about Angus and Jessie's baby. They were so emotional right now, it was hard to predict what would happen from one moment to the next.

Angus and Jessie saw Pete, Cassidy, Bessie and Gil before Rosadel and Clancy and the girls came out of church. The early morning rain had given way to a cold and blustery day, and it took a while to wrangle three little girls into their coats.

"Ms. Bessie! It is so good to see you at church!" Jessie leaned over to kiss Bessie's cheek.

"It is good to be here." Bessie spoke slowly but clearly.

"Your speech is greatly improved, Ms. Bessie. I can tell you have worked hard in rehab." Jessie had put her arm around Bessie and gave her a squeeze.

Just then, the triplets ran over. "Pop-Pop! Gee-Jay! Uncle Pete! Ms. Cassidy! Ms. Bessie!"

Lou looked at Gil and said, "My name is Lou Marshall. Pleased to meet you." And stuck out her hand.

Gil took her hand in his. "Beau petite fille, my name is Gil Chauvin. Pleased to meet you too."

"Chauvin? Are you related to Ms. Bessie? And what were those words? I never heard them before." Grace and Rosie looked up at Gil expectantly, as if all three of them had asked the question.

"I said 'beau petite fille' which means 'beautiful little girl' in French. And yes, I am related to Ms. Bessie, she is my Aunt." Gil smiled as he spoke. "Can you introduce me to your sisters?"

Lou nodded. "This is Grace, and this is Rosie. I guess you know Pop-Pop, and Gee-Jay and Ms. Cassidy and Uncle Pete because you are with them. Do you know my Mommy and Daddy?"

"I know your Daddy, because I work with him, and I have met your Mommy at Our Lady when visiting Tante."

"Who's that?" asked Grace.

"Tante means "Aunt" in French, so that is what I call Ms. Bessie."

"We don't have Aunts," volunteered Rosie. "Well, we have Nanny Bee, but she is not really our aunt, just Mommy's best friend. And we call Gee-Jay's sisters our Aunts since she married Pop-Pop. And if Uncle Pete marries Ms. Cassidy, she will be our Aunt too."

Rosadel had been talking to the adults and heard her queue to enter the girls' conversation with Gil. Before she could speak, Lou did.

"We fixed up Pop-Pop and Gee-Jay, and Uncle Pete and Ms. Cassidy; do you need a girlfriend?"

"Lou, remember we talked about this. It isn't polite to offer someone you just met to find them a girlfriend or boyfriend. And Rosie, it might embarrass Uncle Pete or Ms. Cassidy to speculate about them getting married."

Before either girl could answer, Gil spoke up.

"Thank you for the kind offer, Lou. Cassidy told me to expect it. I am just visiting in Louisiana right now, so to find me a girlfriend here might be awkward. But when I move here, I'll be sure to ask if I need your help." Gil smiled at Rosadel as he spoke. He was charmed by the triplets and didn't want to be responsible for a dark spot on their day.

"The Chauvin men often know at first sight when they have found the woman of their dreams," said Bessie.

"Ms. Bessie! You can talk!" the triplets ran over to Bessie in their excitement. "We've been praying and praying for you to talk and sing again and to get all better!" That was Grace.

"We even prayed on our Rosary beads for you." That came from Rosie.

Bessie ran her hand over each little girls' face. "I knew there were powerful prayers helping me."

Angus noticed that Bessie and Jessie both looked chilled. "We need to get out of this cold. Girls, do you want to ride with me and Gee-Jay? We brought the car with the booster seats."

"Can we Mommy? Can we?" all three girls clamored to go with their Pop-Pop.

"Sure, just say your good-byes to everyone. We'll see you at the restaurant."

Rosadel was still shaking her head as she got into the car with Clancy. "I probably should give up on the matchmaking thing. They just won't stop."

"You know, Sugar, Gil handled it pretty well. Maybe we should only try to rescue the people that need rescuing. And, they may grow out of it."

"Gil certainly did handle them well. I'll bet Ms. Bessie is thrilled that he is moving to Louisiana. It is strange to think about Prescott retiring. I've been hearing his name since I was a girl, what with Daddy working with him and then you. He is so active, I have a hard time picturing him retired."

"He's not going to be idle. I hear that there is a new place opening in Terrebonne Parish, and combination animal sanctuary and transition facility for military veterans having trouble reentering society. The new place doesn't have a name yet, and the rumor is that Prescott isn't going to work there, he is founding the sanctuary."

"Wow! That sounds perfect for him. And what a relief for Cassidy. She will have more options for the shelter pets. Where in the world would Prescott come up with that kind of money?"

"My guess is that he has a benefactor. Maybe someone from a distinguished military family. Whatever, it sounds like Prescott will have a very happy and fulfilling retirement."

♦ ♦ ♦

Oddly enough, the conversation at brunch with Bessie, Gil, Cassidy and Pete was also about Prescott.

"Cassidy, did you know that the property that your dad is trying to buy in Terrebonne Parish belongs to my cousin?" Gil loved seeing the look on Cassidy's face as he asked.

"Are you kidding? What a coincidence. Can you put in a good word to help the sale go through faster? I know Daddy is dying to get started on the remodeling and finalizing the plans."

"I called Zeke yesterday, and told him about Prescott's plans. Zeke is excited to close on the sale, as a sanctuary is the perfect use for the property."

Bessie nodded, and joined in the conversation. "That land was once a plantation. It was won in a poker game by a Frenchman living in New Orleans named Jean-Luc DeBouchet. He moved his family, and the Chauvin family to the plantation, emancipated all the slaves there, and deeded them all land. Zeke is descendant from Paul Thomas and Marie Gerard DeBouchet. Paul was my ancestor Ruth's youngest brother. There ended up being four principal families, the DeBouchet's, the Chauvin's, the Thomas's and the Allard's. With intermarriage, the four families blended into many descendants. Gil and I both have the blood of all four families in our heritage."

"Wow, Grandma Bessie, that is so cool. I don't really know anything about my family beyond my dad and mom. Both of Dad's parents died before I was born, and he doesn't talk about them at all, and my mom has been estranged from her parents since before I was born, and it is something that is never discussed. I can't imagine having family stories going back so many years."

"Tante transcribed Mathilde Chauvin's journals from handwriting into type back in the 1940's, and I plan to translate them into English." Gil said. "The stories fascinated me as a child. Growing up seeing the buildings and land that had survived since Mathilde wrote of them in the 1850's made me feel part of history. Tante and I are the only ones still fluent in the ancient French of the journals, so we will work together on translating them to English. Isn't that right, Tante?"

"The only thing that Daddy doesn't have any idea about is what to name the sanctuary. I'm supposed to be helping him think of something, but I'm drawing a blank." Cassidy hoped that inspiration would have come to her by now, but so far, no such luck.

"I think I know the perfect name." said Bessie. "But to tell you, I must tell the story first. Gilbert, you will help me, as sometimes words are still hard to find."

"Of course, Tante." Gil placed his hand over Bessie's.

"As I said, Jean Luc DeBouchet won a plantation, called Teach Abhainn, from its owner, a man called Seamus O'Malley. When he moved his family to the plantation, he changed the name to Belle Terre."

Gil took up the story. "There was the main plantation house, which everyone called the plantation, and then the overseer's house and the slave cabins. Roby Thomas did not like that his house was called the overseer's house, as that carried the stain and the pain of slavery."

Bessie continued. "Marguerite, who was the child of Pascal and Mathilde Chauvin, and who I called Tante as a child, was a girl, and then a woman of great faith. She maintained throughout her life that angels spoke to her."

Gil once again spoke. "The family story, as recorded by Mathilde in her journals, is that upon the entire family being reunited at Belle Terre, Jean Luc was handing out assignments for work to improve the buildings on the property. Mathilde's son Gilbert, and Jean Luc's son Louis wanted to help, but were quite young. Roby, wanting to spare the boy's pride from being told they were too young to help, asked for their help with his house."

"Roby admitted that he didn't like calling the house the overseer's house, and Jean Luc joked that the house's all needed names. Marguerite then told Roby that his house should be called Angel's Watch, because her angel had told her that angels had been constantly watching over him and his family. So, I think the sanctuary should be called Angel's Watch." Bessie looked expectantly in Cassidy's direction.

"Grandma Bessie, I think you are absolutely right. Angel's Watch is a perfect name. I can't wait to tell Daddy. In fact, if you all don't mind, I'm going to text him right now."

♦ ♦ ♦

The Marshall's and McPherson's were also checking out the new Breaking Dawn restaurant and arrived just as Marie and Bee were leaving.

"Nanny Bee! Nanny Bee! We didn't know we would see you!" Bee dropped to her knee and was surrounded by laughing little girls with plenty of hugs and kisses to give.

"Hi girls! Mrs. Marie and I just had a real good breakfast, and I bet you will too." The girls then noticed Marie Theriot.

"Hi Mrs. Theriot." The girls were much more subdued with Marie.

"Hello, Lou, and Grace and Rosie. You all look very pretty today." Marie was trying harder to be more approachable to the children she encountered at school every day. She had always had a few to sneak past her defenses, but she had recently realized how much joy she had missed out on by keeping all the children at a distance.

"Thank you, Mrs. Theriot. Daddy helped us with our hair today." Grace thought it was important that her Dad get credit for helping.

"Well, he is certainly a man of many talents," said Marie.

"Yes, he is," said Rosadel. "Hi Mrs. Marie. It is good to see you." Rosadel had come a long way in her feelings about Marie. Where she had viewed Marie as a busybody at one time, she had come to know her and appreciate that Marie was a good person, and never meant any harm. "Maybe one Sunday we can arrange for you and Bee to join us for brunch."

Angus smiled warmly as he heard Rosadel's offer. He had counseled her to find a way to get past her animosity towards Marie, and apparently, it had worked. Jessie was quick to chime in. "We'd love that Marie. It would be nice for you to get to know the girls better."

Marie felt herself tearing up. The warmth that she had denied herself for so long could be overwhelming.

Bee saw Marie's emotion and answered for her. "We'd love that. This is the first time Marie and I got together for breakfast, but I'm sure it won't be the last. We'd love to join you for brunch some week. Now, we need to get going. Max is waiting at home for Marie, and my Mom expects me to help her clean out the attic this afternoon, while we have a cool rainy day."

Bee gave more hugs and kisses to the girls and gave a special hug to Rosadel.

"Bee, you know you owe me the story on your date last week," said Rosadel as they embraced. "Why don't you plan to come to dinner one night this week?"

"How about Tuesday?" Bee suggested.

"Perfect, Michelle and Bethany Williams will be there. It will give you a chance to get to know Bethany."

"It's a date," promised Bee, and she and Marie headed for home.

After everyone was seated at the table and orders were placed, Jessie reached over and clasped Angus' hand as she looked at the girls.

"Lou, Grace and Rosie, Pop-Pop and I have some very important news to share with you." The girls looked puzzled as they turned to Angus.

"Girls, Gee-Jay and I are having a baby." Angus knew his face would hurt tomorrow he was smiling so hard.

Lou was the first to speak. "But you're old." Rosadel gasped. "Wait, that sounded bad." Lou knew she was in trouble. "I mean, I thought only young people had babies."

Angus smiled. "Well, Lou, mostly, that is true. But Jessie never got married when she was young, so this is the first chance she had to have a baby. We are older than most parents, but I think we'll be good at it."

"So, you can have a baby whenever you want?" Grace was intrigued by this.

"Not quite," Jessie replied. "It can be harder to have a baby when you are older, and sooner or later, women get too old to have a baby. Pop-Pop and I are really excited, and we hope you girls will be excited too."

Rosie spoke up. "Babies are cute. I think I can be excited. Mommy, what do you think?"

Rosadel blew Rosie a kiss. "I'm very excited, Rosie. I never had a brother or sister, and now I will have one. And you girls will have an aunt or an uncle. And Jessie will get to be a Mommy, which is the very best thing that has ever happened to me. So, I think this is wonderful."

Lou still looked skeptical. "How can the baby be our aunt or uncle if the baby is younger than us?"

"Sometimes it works that way," said Jessie. "As a matter of fact, my Daddy has a nephew that is older than he is. His oldest brother's oldest son was three years old when my Daddy was born."

"But we're eight," said Grace. "But I think I am getting excited. Will you and Pop-Pop still come see us and have brunch and stuff? Or will the baby take our place?"

Angus reached over the table to squeeze Grace's hand. "You will see us just as much, and maybe more. And no, the baby won't take your place. Nothing can ever take your place. The baby will be just another person to love who will love you back."

The triplets looked at each other, and Rosadel and Clancy knew that the weird, silent communication they had with each other was taking place. Finally, Lou spoke. "We're excited. When will the baby get here, and where is it now?"

"The baby is growing in Gee-Jay's tummy. And pretty soon, Gee-Jay will look pregnant. You remember other kid's mommies being pregnant, don't you?" Rosadel was trying to remember which one of their classmates had recently gotten a brother or sister.

"Sean Tastet's mom had a baby. She looked really fat, and then she was skinny again. Is that going to happen to Gee-Jay?" Grace remembered Mrs. Tastet kind of waddling into church.

"I hope I don't look really fat, but yes, that will happen to me When the baby gets bigger, you will be able to feel him or her move around when you touch my stomach." Jessie hoped that wasn't too much information.

The girls exchanged looks again. "So, when will the baby get here?" Lou asked again.

"Sometime in June," replied Jessie. "We think after your Mom and Dad's birthdays but maybe before."

"So, after our First Holy Communion in May," said Rosie.

"Yes," answered Rosadel, wondering why that was important.

"Because Sean's Mom had to leave the Christmas pageant because her baby was crying, and Sean was upset. We don't want Gee-Jay or Pop-Pop to miss our communion." Grace answered Rosadel's question without it ever being asked.

"Everything will be fine at your First Holy Communion," Angus assured the girls as breakfast arrived.

As Angus and Jessie headed home, Jessie reached over and put her hand on Angus' hand. "I think that went pretty well, what do you think?"

"I think it was amazing. And I don't think you will ever look fat. Just big and beautiful with my baby. I love you, Jessie girl, more every day."

"I love you too, Angus. I'm excited to be sharing my life with you."

CHAPTER 31

Cassidy wasn't surprised to hear Sandra's voice when she answered the phone in her office on Monday morning.

"Hi, Mom, what's up?"

"Hi, Cassidy. Thanks for bringing Pete over to dinner on Saturday. He sure is nice. The flowers still look beautiful."

"He is a nice guy, Mom. I really like him. He liked all of you too."

"I'm glad to hear that, Cassidy. I know sometimes I can make a bad impression."

Cassidy wasn't sure how to answer that and was relieved when Sandra continued talking.

"I know you are at work, honey, so I don't want to take up a bunch of your time, but would you be able to have dinner with me one night this week? Just the two of us? I need to talk to you, and I know lunch is too busy for you, and I don't want to wait until Saturday lunch."

"I can be available any night, Mom. Are you okay? Is there something going on?" Cassidy couldn't ever remember just her and Sandra going out to dinner.

"I'm fine, Cassidy. I just want to talk to you about my family. I received a letter from my mother, and want to talk to you about it, and about me and you, and why I do some of the things I do. I thought I could wait until Saturday, but I want to talk to you as soon as you can be free."

"Wow, Mom, I didn't even know your mother was still alive. Would tonight be too soon? I'm anxious to hear this story."

"Tonight will be fine, Cassidy. How about I meet you at the Hungry Pelican at six? Does that give you enough time after work?"

"That will be fine Mom, I'll see you then. Love you."

"I love you, too, Cassidy. See you tonight."

Cassidy was still staring at the phone a few minutes later when Dustin stuck his head into her office.

"We're almost empty again, Cassidy. This has been the best winter I ever remember for finding homes for our animals."

"That is great news, Dustin. I'll never understand why we go through peaks and valleys with adoptions, but I love when we have an almost empty shelter. I love my job, but I would be happy if no animal ever needed to go to a shelter again."

"Me too, Cassidy. Maybe someday. In the meantime, I'm taking pictures of the few cats and dogs we have and posting them on Facebook and Petfinder."

"Thanks, Dustin." As Dustin left the office, Cassidy realized she needed to call Pete and let him know that she now had plans with Sandra for tonight.

Hannah Falgoust answered the phone at Pete's clinic. "Hey Hannah! Is Pete available by any chance?"

"Hey Cassidy. He just went into his office, let me put you through."

As Cassidy waited for Pete to pick up, she tried to imagine what she would learn this evening. Cassidy wasn't sure if she was more excited or nervous.

"Hey Cassidy! This is a nice surprise, what's up?"

"Pete, my mom just called, and she wants me to have dinner with her tonight. She wants to tell me about her family, my family, I guess. I'm kind of freaked out. She said she got a letter from her mother. I didn't even know if her mother and father were alive or dead."

"Whoa! Take a deep breath, Cass. It will be okay. This could help you figure out your relationship with your mom. Tell me what I can do to help you calm down."

"That is really why I called. I'm supposed to meet Mom at six at the Hungry Pelican. I'll just have time to run home and feed the girls and I'll have to run right back out. I hate for them to have so little time with human company."

"I can help with that. How about I meet you at your house and take Maggie and Sophie back to my place? I'll feed them, and they can hang out with me. You can call when you get home and I'll bring them to you, or you can come to my house and tell me all about your evening and then take them home."

"I'll come to your house. Thanks, Pete. I didn't just want your help with the dogs. I needed to talk to you. I knew talking to you would help me calm down and feel better."

"You know I'm always here for you, Cassidy. I want us to be like Clancy and Rosadel, and like my Mom and Dad. Best friends who always have each other's backs. I think you want the same thing."

"That is exactly what I want Pete. I'll see you at my house at around 5:30 then?"

"I'll be there Cassidy. And I'll be looking forward to you telling me all about your dinner with your Mom afterwards."

♦ ♦ ♦

Prescott shook his head in amazement as he hung up from the call with his lawyer. One call to Zeke Thomas from Gil and agreement was reached on the terms of the sale. Prescott's lawyer was executing the paperwork to finalize the sale and was confident that Prescott would be able to close the deal and sign all the necessary paperwork on Friday. The text from Cassidy yesterday had answered Prescott's last question of what to name the sanctuary. Angel's Watch was the perfect name.

Prescott planned to have the utilities turned on as soon as he took title to the property, and have JT moved in the next week. The buildings were all livable, but needed updating, and Prescott planned for JT to oversee the renovations. Prescott needed to call JT to let him know it was time to give his notice at Home Depot. Prescott would pay JT a salary while he acted as a property manager, and then a reduced salary and any school expenses that VA benefits didn't cover while JT got his undergraduate and graduate degrees in Counseling.

JT would have work responsibilities at Angel's Watch while he finished school, but Prescott was far more invested in JT achieving his educational goals to support the long-term mission of Angel's Watch than in the short-term arrangement.

Prescott also needed to call Ed Adams and let him know that any time after next week, he was welcome to move to Angel's Watch. Prescott didn't plan to have any residents until after he retired in June but hoped that Ed would be moving in soon. Prescott hoped Ed would volunteer at the VA and start building relationships with some of the local veterans who may need some help. He had also talked to Ed about visiting missions and shelters in New Orleans, Houma and Baton Rouge to identify any veterans out there who may have fallen through the cracks.

JT was surprised when his cell phone rang just as he pulled into the Home Depot parking lot. He was even more surprised to see the caller was Prescott.

"Hey JT! Looks like I'll be closing on the property on Friday. If all goes well, the utilities will all be on by the end of next week, and you can move in any time after that. I'll put you on salary as of two weeks from today, so you may want to give your notice."

"Wow Prescott! That happened quick. I'll give my notice today. And tell my Mom that I'll finally be moving out."

"I don't know how long you'll be there alone, JT. I'm about to call Ed and tell him the news. Are you comfortable with being out there by yourself until Ed gets here?"

"The first job I'm overseeing is perimeter fencing and a security system, right? And the house has locks? I'll be fine, Prescott. It isn't as if the property has been vandalized while it has been sitting vacant. Seems like a safe and quiet location."

"It does to me too, JT, but sometimes too much quiet can be just as much of a problem as too much noise."

"Stop worrying. I'm good. And Prescott, thanks. I don't know if you can appreciate just how amazing this opportunity is for me. I was drifting and lost since I got back from Afghanistan. Now I have dreams, and a purpose, thanks to you."

"No thanks needed, JT. You are going to help me do the most important work of my life. And by the way. We have a name for our sanctuary. It will be called Angel's Watch, and there is a heck of a story behind that name. I'll tell you all about it next time I see you."

Prescott hung up feeling good about how things were going with JT and checked his schedule to see if he had enough time to call Ed Adams. Prescott sighed as he thought about what Ed was coping with. Prescott had met Ed at a conference on veterans' mental health issues over thirty years ago. Ed had spent his career as a psychologist at the Veterans Administration, treating countless patients over the years. Ed and his wife Shirley had a wonderful marriage and a wonderful life together. They had raised three great kids and were planning to travel around the world when they both retired two years ago. Shirley had been diagnosed with pancreatic cancer within six months of her and Ed's retirement. They had at least gotten to go on an African safari as their retirement gift to themselves before Shirley's diagnosis.

The remaining months of Shirley's life had been fighting through chemo, a short remission with a trip to Australia and New Zealand, and then an aggressive return of cancer that had ended Shirley's life in November. Prescott had held Ed as he cried after Shirley's funeral, not knowing what to say. But when Ed asked, "What will I do without her? My whole life after retirement was about Shirley and finally having all the time in the world to spend together", Prescott had an answer.

Ed grabbed onto the idea of working at the sanctuary like a lifeline. As he and Prescott had talked over the last few months, Ed had been working on cleaning out the house he shared with Shirley and getting ready to move to the sanctuary. Prescott knew Ed was anxious to get started, anxious to start on something to fill his mind and his time.

"Hey Prescott! I was hoping to hear from you soon. How are the plans progressing?"

"Things have really started to come together, Ed. I should take title to the property on Friday, and the utilities should all be on by the end of next week. You are welcome to head over and get settled in as soon as you want to."

"That's great, Prescott. My youngest, Jancy, freaked out when I said I was selling the house. She talked her husband, Todd, into buying the place. I told her that I would sell it to her just as if she were a stranger, and then divide the proceeds among the three of them. Well, to make a long story short, her purchase was contingent on the sale of the house she and Todd already owned. Their house sold immediately, and they have to be out by March 1, so they are ready to start moving in here. I've been looking for a short-term rental, but now I won't have to. I'll be over there in two weeks, ready to start learning the lay of the land."

"I love it when a plan comes together, Ed. Why don't you plan to stay at my place the first night you get here, so that you can have a full day to move your stuff into the cottage you pick for your own."

"Sounds, great, Prescott. You can expect me two weeks from today."

As Prescott hung up from his call with Ed, he once again felt like the universe was conspiring to make sure his vision of a sanctuary came to fruition. And boy did it feel good.

♦ ♦ ♦

Bessie Chauvin looked with satisfaction around her small assisted living apartment at Our Lady of Lourdes. It wasn't as good as being at home, but it was definitely better than a room on the nursing home side. Today Bessie planned to contract the local pet walking business to arrange for someone to come and take Sophie for a couple of walks a day. Once that was done, Bessie would be ready to have Sophie living with her again.

Bessie knew Cassidy was worried about how Sophie moving out would impact Maggie. It was a dilemma for Bessie as well. Bessie would happily take both dogs, but that would leave Cassidy without her companions. Bessie knew in the logical part of her brain that Cassidy had always hoped that Sophie would be a temporary pet, but Cassidy had made a long-term commitment to Maggie. Bessie knew that tomorrow night she and Cassidy would have to have a difficult conversation. She planned to pray for guidance on what the right answer was between now and then.

As Bessie walked to her speech therapy session, she marveled at how quickly she was progressing with her speech and occupational therapy. Her occupational therapists were ready to do a set of benchmark tests, and Bessie was confident that she had returned physically to her pre-stroke baseline. Bessie really believed that within a month she would be ready to graduate from speech therapy too.

And in many ways, it was all thanks to Cassidy. After the stroke, while Bessie was missing Sophie and feeling alone, she had thought about just praying for a happy death. And then Cassidy came along, and helped Bessie realize that she still had a lot to live for. And now Gil would be moving to Bayou Beni, and Bessie was hoping they could share her house. And they would finally translate Mathilde Chauvin's journals into English, so that the stories would be preserved for future generations. God was indeed good.

◆ ◆ ◆

Cassidy was surprised that the day had passed as quickly as it had. She had expected the minutes to drag as she thought about what she would learn from her mother tonight but working on the details for the Holy Redeemer Church fair and finalizing her report to the St. Elizabeth Parish President on the financial performance of the animal shelter for last year and projecting this year's needs had made the day fly by.

Pete was waiting for her when she got to her house. The dogs were excited to see Pete, and happily got into his van. Pete gave Cassidy a hug and held on for a moment. "I know you're nervous, and anxious, about what you will learn tonight. Just remember, none of it will change who you are. This might be the worst time to tell you this, but there is a guy in Bayou Beni who loves you very much and will be waiting for you to come home."

Cassidy hugged Pete tightly. "Hold that thought. I'll see you in a couple of hours." Cassidy kissed Pete and got in her car and left. "Well girls," Pete turned to the four dogs in his van, "I was hoping for an 'I love you, too'. Guess I'll just have to keep waiting on that."

Cassidy couldn't believe that Pete picked tonight to tell her he loved her. She felt bad about not responding better, but he had surprised her. And she was nervous. Cassidy took a deep breath and reminded herself that Pete understood her better than she realized, and that everything would be fine when she saw him later tonight.

Sandra was waiting in the vestibule of the Hungry Pelican when Cassidy arrived a few minutes before six. "Hey Mom! I hope you haven't been waiting long."

"Hi Honey. I just got here myself." Sandra reached out and squeezed Cassidy's hand. "Thanks for making time for me tonight."

"I'll be honest, Mom. I really want to hear about your life and your family. The more involved I've gotten with Pete, and the more I have seen his extended family, the more I have wondered about my family. Dad's really got nothing besides the names of his mom and dad. And with you I didn't even have that."

"Let's get a table and order, and then we'll talk."

As Cassidy and Sandra were shown to a table by their hostess, Cassidy thought about the last time she was here with Candy, and how much had happened in her and Pete's relationship since then. In a way, life had entered warp speed at Christmas time, and there was no indication it was going to slow down anytime soon.

After their orders were placed and their drinks delivered, Sandra reached across the table and held Cassidy's hands.

"Cassidy, I know I have been very hard on you at times, and that I am very fortunate that we have the relationship that we have given some of my behavior. You know I have been going to counseling, and I've been working very hard to change my destructive patterns. I want you to know I'm sorry that I haven't been a better mother to you, and I appreciate very much the way you always loved me in spite of myself."

"Momma, you don't have to apologize. I am who I am because of everything that happened to me up to this point, and I am happy with who I am and where I am. You have been a good mother, I never wanted for anything."

"Cassidy, thank you for that, but we both know that I could have done better." When Cassidy opened her mouth to speak, Sandra held up her hand. "I love you for forgiving me, and I love you for telling me that I did a good job as your mother, but I know how hard I made it for you to keep on loving me. I know that your Dad and Mark were incredible and helped you to see my fear and insecurity for what it was and never hold it against me. You have a beautiful heart, Cassidy, and I am so grateful for that.

"And that is why I need to talk to you. I need to tell you about my childhood, and my family. I came from a very dysfunctional home. My father was an abusive bully, and my mother his favorite target. I have a hard time thinking about my childhood, and I think I've only talked about it to my counselor, Dr. Mathieu, and to Mark.

"Through my counseling sessions, I've come to appreciate that I personally experienced very little physical abuse as a child. I think now that my mother shielded me as best she could, but I didn't see it that way until recently.

"My mother did everything she could to appease my father, and I stayed out of the way as much as I could. Many nights I would eat dinner by myself, so that I would be in my room when my mother and father ate. I had hardly any time alone with my mother. She would pick me up from after school care when I was young, and that five-minute car ride was about it. Once we were in the house, my father insisted that she focus all of her attention on him.

"When I aged out of after school care, she would leave me dinner to heat up and notes, so that I saw my father as little as possible. I would make up stories about my family to tell my friends, I knew I lived in a strange world, and so I painted a false picture of my home life.

"I would hear my father hitting my mother, and my mother crying, and I would put headphones on and listen to music to drown out the sounds. As I child, I thought my mother loved my father and not me. As I've gone to counseling, I've come to accept that my mother was struggling to survive."

"How terrible, Mom. What about her family? Didn't they help?" Cassidy hated the thought of her mother growing up in such a difficult environment.

"My mother had been orphaned, and her grandmother died when she was in high school. As far as I know, she had no relatives. I left home as soon as I graduated high school, and never looked back. I held my mother responsible for everything that went wrong, and every bad decision I made. I carried a lot of anger.

"After you were born, I got even angrier. And then I started to wonder about me. If even my mother couldn't love me, maybe I was unlovable. And that tainted my relationship with you. I wanted to be loving and gentle, but instead I was always demanding and cold. Your dad tried to get me to go to counseling when you were little, but I resisted. It took years for Mark to convince me I needed to get out of my bad patterns."

Cassidy was at a loss as to what to say. "Mom, honestly, you've been a good mother. When you talk about your childhood, I can't even imagine. Lots of kids have demanding parents. I never felt like my life was that much different than the kids I went to school with, except that my divorced parents got along, and there was never any holiday drama about who I was going to spend time with. Please don't beat yourself up about your relationship with me. There were times when I did get my feelings hurt, but that happens with every mother and daughter. I'm just glad you are getting the help you need for you, so that you don't have to feel bad anymore."

"Thank you, Cassidy. I know I don't say it often, but I love you dearly, and am so very proud of the woman you have become. I'm beyond grateful to your dad and Mark for helping me raise you. Especially your dad. He might not have been a good husband for me, but he is a great dad to you and a great partner as a parent.

"The reason I needed to talk to you about all this is because I got a letter from my mother. After all this time, she wants to reconnect. I think I want that too, but I wanted to talk to you, and then Candace and Mark, Jr., before contacting her."

Sandra took the letter out of her purse and handed it to Cassidy. "Please read this, and then we will talk some more."

My dearest Sandra –

I don't blame you if you never read this letter. If you do choose to read it, I hope you read it with an open heart.

I am so sorry for being such a bad mother to you. I have been in counseling for several years now, and I know I did the best I could in a bad situation, but you were the one to suffer for my inadequacy.

I want you to know I love you. I have always loved you. Burl Theriot was a cruel and violent man, and the only way I knew to protect you from him was to push you into the shadows of our lives.

Burl hated for me to show anyone affection but him. When I realized that showing my love for you resulted in him abusing both of us, I stopped. I should have had the courage to leave, but Burl told me he would get custody of you, and you would be his target.

I should have had the courage to leave when you did, but I was so broken by then.

When Burl died, I hired a private investigator to find you, but then felt unworthy to ask your forgiveness.

I would love to be reconciled with you, and to meet your husband and my grandchildren. I realize that may not be something that you can do, and I respect whatever decision you make.

Please know that you were never the problem. You are a wonderful person, and were a wonderful little girl. I wish I could have given you a better childhood.

Whatever you decide, know that I love you with every breath in my body, and I am so proud of who you are.

Love Always,

Mom

As Cassidy set the letter down, she noticed the return address on the envelope. Something about that address was familiar. Theriot – Burl Theriot. Could it be?

"Mom is your mother's name Marie Theriot?" Sandra looked surprised at Cassidy's question.

"Yes, Cassidy, but why?"

"Because I know her. Well, not really know her, but she adopted a dog earlier this month from the shelter. His name is Max, and I was really worried about him finding a home. He is a big dog, around sixty pounds, and black, and a pit bull mix. His family lost their jobs and their home, and he was so miserable in the shelter, and I couldn't find a foster for him. Mrs. Theriot came in to see about adoption, and she and Max bonded immediately.

"I felt like she was the saddest, loneliest person I ever met, and when she took Max to see Pete for his initial veterinary appointment, Pete felt the same way. She's nice Mom. Sad and reserved, but really nice." Cassidy didn't know if she was making things better or worse.

Sandra just looked stunned. "Well, I can honestly say that I never expected this. I guess this makes it even more important that I get in touch with her. It never occurred to me that you might have met her."

"I'll follow your lead, Mom. She will just be Mrs. Theriot who adopted a dog from the shelter until you tell me to handle it another way. I know how hard this is for you and I don't want to make it any harder."

Just then, the server brought their meals to the table. Cassidy gave the letter back to Sandra, who put it back in her purse.

"I know you probably have more questions for me, Cassidy, but can we talk about something else now? I'm in emotional overload."

"Sure, Mom. I know I updated you on the booth at the Holy Redeemer fair on Saturday, but have I told you that Bessie Chauvin is moving over to assisted living at Our Lady of Lourdes today?" As she brought it up, Cassidy realized she had stumbled into another emotional minefield, but maybe the distraction would be good for Sandra.

"Wow, Cassidy. That is amazing. She has made an incredible recovery."

"She has, Mom. And she has worked really hard. Now that her nephew is moving to Bayou Beni, I know she is planning to move back to her home after he is here permanently. They have old family journals in a French patois that they are planning to translate to English. I can't imagine being in my 90's and still having ambitious goals like Bessie does."

"I'd love to meet her someday, Cassidy. Candace still talks about her and would also love to see her again."

"I tell you what, Mom. After the Holy Redeemer fair, I'll have you all and Bessie and her nephew and Pete over to dinner at my house. That way everyone can meet."

"I'd love that Cassidy. Now that Ms. Chauvin is in assisted living, will her dog be going back to live with her?"

"I'm sure Bessie wants Sophie to come live with her, and for myself, I've been ready for that day since I took Sophie in as a foster. But I'm worried about Maggie. She has gotten very dependent on Sophie, and I'm afraid she will grieve losing her companion. I honestly don't know what to do."

"I never would have thought of that, Cassidy. What options do you think you have?"

"I've thought about bringing Maggie to work with me, but the shelter is a stressful environment, and may do more harm than good. I thought about asking Rosadel if Maggie could come over to her house for a transition. I also thought about asking Dad if Maggie could come hang out with Thor. I don't know if any of those will work though. I'm kind of at a loss."

"I'm way out of my element to try and give advice, Cassidy, but is Maggie going with Sophie to live with Bessie an option?"

"I don't know. Two dogs are a lot more than one, and I don't know if that would be too much for Bessie. I would miss Maggie terribly, but I'd be a terrible example to all the people I encourage to foster animals if I didn't want what is best for Maggie. I'm sure that Bessie and I will talk about this when I visit with Sophie tomorrow night. Maybe between now and then something will come to me."

"I know whatever you decide it will be the right thing, Cassidy. And I hope you know I'm here if you need to talk."

As Cassidy drove to Pete's house after her dinner with Sandra, she thought about what she had learned. It seemed so silly to make a big deal over Sandra's parental shortcomings after hearing about Sandra's childhood. Cassidy felt like she had unfairly judged Sandra all these years, even though she knew that she had never acted on those internal feelings. As much as Cassidy wanted to talk to Pete, she wanted to talk to her Dad, and to thank Prescott for making sure she always treated Sandra gently. No wonder why Prescott and Mark were so protective of Sandra. And that led to Cassidy wondering if anyone had ever protected Marie.

Pete and the girls had had a nice evening. Four dogs might be a lot to some people, but these four old ladies were pretty easy and amazingly good company. When Cassidy pulled into his driveway, Laverne and Shirley went to the door, and Sophie and Maggie struggled to wake up.

Pete opened the door before Cassidy had a chance to knock. Cassidy stepped inside the door, and then put her arms around Pete's neck. "I love you too, you know. I'm sorry I didn't tell you that before dinner. I was too deep in my own head. And then I worried about it, but only for a minute, because I know you know me better than I know myself sometimes." And then she kissed him.

Pete held Cassidy until the dogs started whining for attention. "Your girls and my girls want some love, too."

Cassidy moved to the couch and sat down so that all four dogs could surround her. As she loved up on the dogs, Pete watched quietly, waiting for Cassidy to collect herself and tell him about her evening.

"Well, Pete, I don't know where to start. But I'll tell you this. I love and admire my mother more than I can say. She has done a great job overcoming her past."

As Cassidy shared what she had learned with Pete, he thought again about how lucky he was to have been born into the Marshall family. He made a note to himself to thank his Mom and Dad the next time he saw them. He couldn't imagine the life that Sandra had lived, much less the life Sandra's mother had lived. As Cassidy finished sharing what she had learned, she divulged the final piece.

"And Pete, you'll never guess who my grandmother is. Marie Theriot, the lady that adopted Max."

"Holy Cow, Cassidy. What are you going to do about that?"

"For now, nothing, Pete. You know, I'll talk to my Dad, but until Mom restores contact, I'm just going to treat Marie Theriot like someone

I met when they adopted a dog. I don't see how I can do anything else without potentially hurting my Mom."

"Poor Marie, no wonder she wears that air of sadness all the time. I hope for all of your sake that this reconciliation has a happy ending for everyone."

CHAPTER 32

By the time Rosadel got the triplets off to school on Tuesday morning, she was exhausted. Michelle Williams was coming over this afternoon after school, and she and Bethany were taking Pokey and Boo home with them. This morning, Miriam Devereaux was picking up Cuddles, soon to be known as Marshall, and tomorrow after school, Grace White would be picking up Snuggles, soon to be Elyse.

The girls' tearful goodbyes to Cuddles before they went to school had torn at Rosadel's heart. She was glad that she had been able to tell the girls that Holly would be staying with them, as that had eased their sorrow. Rosadel was also glad that she had invited Bee for supper, as she would need reinforcements tonight when Bethany and Michelle left with Pokey and Boo. She didn't know whether to hope the last two kittens got homes sooner or later. The longer the process lasted, the longer the tension and sadness would hang over the house.

As if she had conjured a call from the universe, Rosadel's phone rang and she saw the call was from Cassidy. "Hey Rosadel, I have a couple of people interested in the last of your kittens. Will you be home today?"

"Hi Cassidy, I can be. How many people and when?" Rosadel hoped the visits would be while the girls were at school.

"I've got a couple that were hoping for early afternoon, and a family that was hoping for an after-school visit. Would that work?"

Rosadel sighed and sent up a quick prayer for help. "That will be fine, Cassidy. Miriam Devereaux is picking up her kitten this morning. I have to pick the girls up from school at three o'clock, we should be home and settled in by three forty-five. So, the first visit will have to be before say two? And the second after three forty-five."

"I'll set the visits up for two and four. Thanks for being so accommodating Rosadel. I'll see you later." Rosadel hung up the phone and looked down to see Roscoe sitting by her feet looking up.

Rosadel dropped to her knees and hugged Roscoe, putting her face against his. "I know we'll get through this too, Roscoe. I just hope the girls will learn something from all this misery."

Rosadel got up and looked at the clock. She had enough time to straighten the house, get some laundry going and meet Miriam Devereaux before two, but only if she got going right away.

Miriam arrived right on time at ten and left with Cuddles/Elyse and a promise to text pictures for Rosadel to show the girls once she got Elyse settled in her new home.

Two o'clock arrived faster than Rosadel would have believed. When the doorbell rang, Rosadel was surprised to see Cassidy with two women, one who was wearing a scarf covering an obviously bald head. The women looked to be in their forties and looked like a couple.

"Hi, I'm Rosadel, come on in and meet the kittens," said Rosadel as she opened the door.

The woman in the scarf held out her hand. "I'm Arlene, and this is my wife, Julie. Pleased to meet you. Thank you for opening your home to us on such short notice."

"No problem at all," said Rosadel as she shook Arlene's hand. Rosadel then shook hands with Julie. "Nice to meet you too."

Cassidy had been standing quietly in the background while the women introduced themselves. Rosadel turned and gave Cassidy a quick hug. "Now on to those kittens. I'm sure Cassidy told you that three of them already have homes, so only the orange kitten, who my girls call Pooh, and the orange and white kitten, who my girls call Peanut are available. Pooh is a female, and Peanut is a male. They both will come with a spay/neuter already paid for."

Rosadel noticed as she led them into the dining room that Arlene appeared frail, and that Julie was very careful to support her without hovering. "Why don't you have a seat, and I'll get Pooh and Peanut out for you to play with."

The other kittens meowed their displeasure when Rosadel got Pooh and Peanut out and left them behind. Rosadel set Pooh and Peanut down on the floor. Arlene and Julie immediately sat on the floor to watch them. Pooh ran over to Arlene and climbed immediately into her lap.

Julie reached over to pet Pooh. "Look like she picked you, Arlene." Arlene picked Pooh up and snuggled her against her face. "What do you say, little one? Do you want to be my baby?"

Pooh responded by rubbing her little face against Arlene's. "I think she answered you, sweetheart," said Julie. "I think we found our baby."

Julie looked at Cassidy and Rosadel. "We definitely want this one. What is the next step?"

Cassidy answered. "Your application has been approved, so all we have to do is complete the paperwork. We could actually take Pooh with us and fill out the papers back at the shelter."

"Um, Cassidy, can we move a little slower please? The girls will be heartbroken if they don't have the chance to say goodbye to Pooh."

Arlene looked up at Rosadel. "Girls?"

"Yes, Arlene. I have eight-year-old triplets who have been taking care of the kittens since they were abandoned with their mother before Christmas. They are having a hard time letting the kittens go as it is, and if they didn't get to say goodbye, I'll have three heartbroken little girls on my hands."

Julie and Arlene exchanged a look. "We can come back for Pooh, don't worry about it. But we would like to pick her up soon."

Rosadel thought about the visit at four this afternoon that could result in Peanut leaving. "The girls will get home from school at about three forty-five. Cassidy is bringing someone over to meet Peanut at four. Do you want to come back later today?"

Again, Julie and Arlene exchanged what appeared to be a silent communication. "We would hate to mess up your dinner time or interfere with the other family who wants a kitten."

Rosadel nodded. "We eat dinner between six and six-thirty most nights, so if you could come at five, I think it will work just fine."

Rosadel was on pins and needles knowing the emotional storm that was coming, and she hoped that having Michelle at the house helped to temper the girls' reactions. She was still relieved to see Bee supervising the pickup line at Holy Redeemer.

"Hey Bee! Can you come over as soon as you can? We have kitten pickups and I could use reinforcements."

"Sure thing, Rosie. I'll be there by four, and I'll just let myself in." Rosadel hugged Bee tightly. "You really are the best friend ever."

As Rosadel got the triplets and Michelle buckled into the van for the ride home, she told them that Pooh had found a home, and that a family was coming to meet Peanut.

The ride home was quiet, with an occasional sniffle from the back, battering Rosadel's already hurting heart.

As the girls unloaded at the house, Grace hugged Rosadel hard. "I know you are as sad as us, Mommy. I'm going to try really hard to not make it harder for you."

Rosadel hugged Grace back. 'Thank you, baby. You are a very special girl with a wonderful heart, and I love you very much."

Michelle was looking upset as Rosadel settled the girls in the kitchen for a snack, and Rosadel wanted to make sure she was okay. She walked up and knelt down next to Michelle's chair. "Are you okay, honey? You look sad."

Michelle nodded, and her eyes filled. "I don't want Pokey and Boo coming to live with me to make Lou, Rosie and Grace sad."

The triplets all jumped up and surrounded Michelle's chair. "Those are the only ones we aren't even a little sad about." said Lou.

"That is like if Pop-Pop and Gee-Jay or Grandma Harriet and Grandpa George took kittens." said Rosie.

"Don't be sad, Michelle," said Gracie. "You are our best friend. We never want you to be sad at our house."

"Okay, girls, let's have our snacks. Ms. Cassidy and the family who wants Peanut will be here soon, and we want to be finished our snacks."

Rosadel hoped Bee would arrive before Cassidy and wondered how soon was too soon to have a glass of wine. This day was a killer. Just then the door opened, and Bee called out, "No worries! It's me!"

"Nanny Bee! Nanny Dee! You're early! Do you know our friend Michelle? Her mommy is coming for dinner too! Pooh has a home, and a family is coming to meet Peanut. Mommy said Holly can live with us forever! Did you find a boyfriend yet?"

Bee laughed at the barrage of questions and information bubbling out of the triplets and didn't even try to determine which one said what.

"Give me some sugar, girls, and let me take my coat off. Hi Michelle. I've seen you at school, but it will be nice to get to know you better. Rosadel, can we have some coffee?" Bee handed Rosadel a bag. "This is wine for dinner, but coffee would taste good right now."

As the girls were kissing and hugging Bee, the doorbell rang, signaling the arrival of Cassidy and the next prospective family.

"Bee would you get that while I have a quick conversation with the girls?"

"Sure thing, Rosadel, just don't forget my coffee."

Rosadel sat down at the table. "Girls, you are welcome to come into the dining room and meet this family, but I expect you to be polite and helpful if you do. You can also go upstairs and do homework if that would be better. If they decide to take Peanut, you can come down and say goodbye."

The girls looked at each other. "We'll be good, Mommy. We promise."

The Gregory family were adorable. Mother, father and two teenage girls. The girls had been very bored in the foyer, but as soon as they saw the kittens they forgot to have attitude.

"Hi, I'm Rosadel Marshall, these girls are Lou, Rosie, Grace and Michelle. I'm sure Cassidy told you the only kitten without a home is Peanut, the orange and white male. Lou, why don't you let all the kittens out and you girls can play with them while the Gregory's meet Peanut."

The dad spoke, "I'm Carl, my wife is Katy, and the girls are Olivia and Sophia. Thanks for opening your home to us."

As the kittens tumbled out to play, Peanut made a beeline for Olivia, and tried to climb her leg. "Look, Daddy, he wants me," she said as she picked Peanut up and cuddled him. "I think we should take him home."

"Let me hold him, Livie," Sophia said. "He's going to be a family cat, not your cat." Olivia turned her back and continued to cuddle Peanut.

Katy Gregory interjected. "Livie, let your sister hold the kitten. I would have thought the two of you would have grown out of this sort of behavior by now."

Olivia gave her mother a dirty look but handed the kitten to Sophia. Katy turned to Rosadel, Cassidy and Bee. "I'm sorry. I keep thinking they are old enough to behave in public but we're just not there yet."

Rosadel answered, "No problem. I never had a sister, so I had no idea how normal arguing was until I got to be friends with Bee, and we would eavesdrop on her older sisters. They fought all the time."

Katy looked at Bee. "Didn't you fight with them?" Bee shook her head no. "They were ten and eleven years older than me. My name should be 'Ooops', not Belinda. Mom and Dad thought they were through when I surprised them. My brothers are even older. So Rosadel is more like a sister, and my siblings' kind of like aunts and uncles."

Cassidy listened to the exchange in wonder. She still marveled at how easily Rosadel and Bee engaged people like they were lifelong friends. Maybe if she spent enough time around Rosadel she would learn how to be more like her.

The girls had been quiet since coming into the room, but even as they played with the kittens, they were watching intently.

Carl Gregory looked at Katy and when she nodded he said to Cassidy, "I think we are taking that little fellow home."

"Your paperwork is all in order, and I have the adoption kit in my bag. We'll fill out the papers, and your family will be bigger by one."

As Cassidy took out the paperwork, Lou approached Sophia. "Would it be okay if I held Peanut for a minute to say goodbye?"

Sophia immediately handed over the kitten. Rosie and Grace crowded around Lou. "Please don't forget us Peanut. And be good for your new family. We will always love you." All three little girls had tears in their eyes as they said goodbye. Bee felt an intervention was in order.

"C'mon Chickens, let's go upstairs. I promise it will be easier if you leave Peanut than if he leaves you. Now say goodbye to the Gregory's too and let's go."

As Bee shepherded the girls upstairs, Rosadel blinked back her own tears. Cassidy put her arm around Rosadel's shoulder. "You did a great thing by fostering these kittens Rosadel. I know it is hard, but I'm so grateful to you."

"Are you on Facebook, Rosadel? I promise I'll post pictures of Peanut regularly, so you and the girls can see him grow up. Thanks for giving him such a good start in life." And then Katy hugged Rosadel.

As Rosadel closed the door behind the Gregory's and Cassidy, she realized Bee had never gotten her coffee. She went upstairs to check on everyone and found Bee and all four girls snuggled up in Lou's bed.

"Hey Rosie, want to jump in? I needed some snuggle time, and the girls were happy to help."

"Mommy, did you know Nanny Bee had a date with a man who wants to be a priest? We could have told her priests don't have girlfriends, cause Pop-Pop told us when we tried to find a girlfriend for Father LeBlanc." Lou was excited to share Bee's dating stories.

"No, I didn't know that. Bee, I never got your coffee, do you still want a cup? And girls, we have to do homework, so let's go down to the kitchen and get going."

As the girls went downstairs, Bee put her arm through Rosadel's. "Well, my tragic dating life at least works as a great distraction."

"So, the future priest story is true?" Rosadel couldn't help the chuckle that escaped.

"Sadly, totally true. I think I am about to embrace my single vocation and stop trying."

"You know I am useless for advice, Bee. But I really believe your dream man is out there somewhere."

"I hope you are right Rosie, and I hope the girls finish their homework before the next couple get here to pick up their kitten, so that you and I can start drinking wine when they leave. I might drink too much and sleep in the girl's room tonight."

"You know you're welcome to the guest room if you want to stay. We haven't had a sleepover in too long."

The girls had finished their homework and were playing with the kittens when the doorbell rang. Rosadel had told Cassidy there was no need for her to come back with Arlene and Julie, so this time it was just the two women.

Pooh ran right to Arlene when they walked into the dining room. Lou walked over to Arlene and Julie. "Hi, I'm Lou Marshall. I'm glad to meet you. And that is Grace, and that is Rosie, and that is Michelle."

Arlene and Julie were immediately charmed. "Hi, Lou. I'm Arlene and this is Julie. Thank you for taking such good care of these kittens."

"You're welcome. What are you going to name Pooh?"

Arlene had picked up the kitten and was cuddling her. "My last cat was orange too, and her name was Ginger Rogers. I think this one will be Lucille Ball and we will call her Lucy."

"What happened to Ginger Rogers?" asked Rosie.

Arlene sighed. "Ginger died right after I was diagnosed with cancer. We decided to wait until I was finished with chemotherapy before getting another kitten."

"What's chemo that word mean?" asked Grace.

Rosadel intervened. "Chemotherapy is one of the ways that cancer is treated. Sometimes, when people have chemotherapy, they are very sick and tired until it is over."

"Did Mom-Mom Allie have chemotherapy?" asked Lou.

"Many times," replied Rosadel.

"I'm sorry you are sick with cancer," Grace told Arlene. "I hope you get better and that Pooh, I mean Lucy, helps you feel better faster."

Arlene knelt down so that she could look Grace right in the eyes. "Thank you, Grace. I actually started feeling better as soon as I met Lucy."

"We have been kind of getting mad at everyone because they are taking our kittens away, but I'm starting to understand what Gee-Jay told us. I hope that Lucy makes you feel better too." said Lou.

Arlene looked somewhat helplessly at Rosadel, not sure how to answer.

"They're mine, and I can't always follow the conversation, Arlene, so you are not alone. My mom, that would be Mom-Mom Allie died from cancer when I was twelve, and Gee-Jay is my dad's wife. I think what Lou just told you is she finally understands that these kittens are meant to live with other people who need them more than we do."

"That's right, Mommy," said Grace, "See you do know what we mean."

Arlene's eyes filled. "Thank you, girls. I really do need Lucy right now, she will help me not miss Ginger so much. I can't go back to work for a while, so I get lonely while Julie is at work. Lucy will keep me company until I feel well enough to go to work."

The girls said goodbye to Pooh/Lucy with no tears, and with hugs for Arlene and Julie. "We'll pray for you to get better on our rosary beads," promised Grace. "Sister Dorothy gave them to us because we're grown up enough now."

"I'll make sure to send pictures and progress reports so that you can watch Lucy grow up." Julie gave Rosadel a card. "My email address is on this, if you send me a message, I'll send back pictures."

When Rosadel returned to the kitchen, Bee had opened a bottle and poured two glasses of wine. "Too late for coffee now, and I think we both could use these."

Rosadel took a sip and settled the girls back at the table to finish their homework. "Thanks, Bee. I'm glad supper is cooked. I just need to put the pot of minestrone on the stove and take the macaroni out of the fridge. I'll get things heating up so that when Clancy gets home, and Bethany gets here we can eat."

The girls were just finishing up their homework when the doorbell rang. "That's my Mommy!" Michelle jumped up and headed for the door, with the triplets hot on her heels. They didn't even get there before the door opened and Clancy yelled, "I'm home!" Resulting in four little girls excitedly greeting their mommy and daddy in the foyer.

Clancy and Bethany came into the kitchen with the four girls to find Rosadel and Bee sipping wine and setting the table. Clancy kissed Rosadel, "Tough day, Sugar?"

"Yes, and Bee and I are drinking wine and having a sleepover, so you are in charge. Hi Bethany! Next time I'll plan better, and you can have a sleepover too."

Clancy smiled at Bethany. "And this is why Rosadel hardly ever drinks. She gets silly within the first glass."

"What's silly about Bethany and Michelle having a sleepover with us?" Rosadel was confused.

"Well, Sugar, for one thing it is a school night, and for another thing, you and Bee are the only grown women I know who still have sleepovers, so you kind of have to warm people up to the idea."

Bethany was smiling as she replied. "See how much you know, Clancy. My sister Neetee and sister-in-law Deedee and I used to have sleepovers all the time before I moved here. But the school night thing is legit."

"Well, put me in the slow group," said Clancy. "I had no idea."

With everyone helping, in no time at all dinner was on the table and it was time for the blessing. Michelle had decided to join the girls in offering what she was thankful for, and as a guest, she went first. "I'm thankful for my good friends, Lou, and Gracie and Rosie, and for Pokey and Boo." Lou went next, "I'm thankful that Holly gets to stay with us and be our cat." Rosie was next, "I'm thankful that Lucy is going to help Ms. Arlene feel better." Clancy raised an eyebrow and Rosadel gave him the "I'll explain later" look. Grace finished, "I'm thankful that we had the kittens to love for a while, and that they are with their forever families now."

Rosadel blinked away tears. Maybe fostering the kittens hadn't been such a bad thing after all.

◆ ◆ ◆

Cassidy was glad that she didn't have to go back to Rosadel's with Julie and Arlene, as that gave her a chance to call Prescott.

Prescott answered the phone on the first ring. "Hey, Baby Girl, how are you?"

"I'm good, Daddy. Before I say anything else, I just wanted to thank you for always helping me be understanding and gentle with mom. I'd be a wreck today if I had ever acted out on some of my feelings."

"It was my job as a good father to help you understand your mother better, Cass, so no thanks needed. Now how about you tell me what is going on?"

Prescott was silent as Cassidy told him about her dinner with Sandra, the letter from Marie, and everything that Cassidy had learned about Sandra and her life. After she finished, Prescott knew he had to fill in the last piece.

"Cassidy, when you told me that Marie Theriot had adopted Max, I had to do some detective work. I couldn't take a chance that it was the same Marie Theriot, and that somehow, she would disrupt Sandra's life in a negative way. I called her and talked to her. I apologized to her for not recognizing the abusive situation she was in and not trying to help. She told me that she wanted a relationship with Sandra and you and your siblings, but that it would be on Sandra's terms. I have been waiting for something to happen and have been hoping it would be a positive thing when it did."

"Wow, Daddy. You are still so protective of Mom. Knowing what I know now, I really appreciate that. I couldn't help wondering last night if anyone had ever protected Marie."

"I don't think so, Cassidy. And I feel really bad about that. I hope you all can get to know her and offer her some of the love that has been missing from her life since she was orphaned as a child."

"Mom is planning to make contact with Marie. I hope for all of our sakes that it goes well. I think Mom will only be truly happy after she reconciles with her mother and her past. And it is past time for Mom to be truly happy."

Pete noticed Cassidy was kind of quiet on the way to Our Lady of Lourdes. "You okay, Cass?"

"Sorry, Pete. I'm feeling sad. The girls were all having a hard time not crying as the kittens left today, and Rosadel looked exhausted. I'm not usually so emotionally involved with my foster families, so I've been kind of immune to how much it can hurt to let an animal you have cared for go to a new home. Then I talked to my dad this afternoon about my mom and our conversation and Marie Theriot and found out that he investigated after I mentioned a Marie Theriot adopted Max and has kind of been waiting for all of this to come out. And I still don't know what to do about Maggie. I know Grandma Bessie wants Sophie to come live with her, and I'm not sure how my old girl will manage without her companion."

"First things first," said Pete. "Are you upset with your dad?"

"No, I understand that he was kind of between a rock and a hard place, and just had to be ready to pick up the pieces if Sandra ever learned Marie was in Bayou Beni. He has always maintained that Sandra's story was hers to tell, not his, so I'm not upset. It is just weird because once you find out something really big that impacts your life that you don't know, it makes you wonder what else is going on that you don't know that is going to stop you in your tracks."

"I totally understand why you feel that way. Life will always find a way to surprise you. And my mom always told us that the more times life slaps you upside the head, the better you handle it the next time. You are going to be unflappable soon."

Cassidy laughed, just as Pete intended her to. "I guess there is always an upside. I just hope that Rosadel and the girls are finding one."

Pete reached over and squeezed Cassidy's hand. "Tell you what, Cassidy. I'll call Clancy as soon as we finish visiting and see how things are going over there. I know my nieces, and they never stay down for long, and Rosadel is the most resilient person I know. I can give you an update on how all of them are doing. As for Maggie, we'll figure something out, I promise."

Cassidy squeezed Pete's hand back. "Thanks, Pete. I'm sure something will work out."

Bessie was once again waiting in the foyer for Pete and Cassidy when they arrived with the dogs. Since this was the first visit since Bessie had moved to the assisted living side, Cassidy wasn't sure how things were going to proceed.

"Hi Grandma Bessie. Do you want to go visit on the nursing home side with Sophie and Maggie, or visit over here?"

Bessie smiled as Sophie jumped into her lap to be pet. "I think the girls do a world of good in the nursing home, so let's take them there. But first, I want to show you my apartment."

As Bessie took Sophie's leash and led Pete and Cassidy to her new apartment, Cassidy once again marveled at the amazing progress Bessie had made. It was hard to believe that at Christmas they had used a wheelchair to bring Bessie to Christmas dinner.

After the visits were finished, Pete met Cassidy and Bessie back at Bessie's apartment. He found Bessie and Cassidy seated on Bessie's small sofa, each with a dog on their lap. Cassidy was in the middle of telling Bessie about her dinner with Sandra the night before. He wondered if Cassidy was going to tell Bessie the final piece about Marie Theriot being her grandmother.

"Grandma Bessie, the next piece is the hardest part, and before I tell you, I have to ask you if you want to know something that you will have to keep a secret for a while. If you would rather not know, I'll wait and tell you when everything is out in the open."

Bessie reached over and held Cassidy's hand. "I think it might be better if you wait, Cassidy. This sounds like it is your mother's story to tell, and so you should wait until she is ready to tell it."

"Thanks Grandma Bessie. And even though I know now that I have a grandmother alive, it doesn't change anything between us."

"I know, sweetheart. And because we are family, and family talks about the hard things, we need to talk about Sophie coming back to live with me. I can have her now. I have talked to the local dog walking service, and they can add me as soon as I say the word. I'll never be able to put into words how much it means to me that you have taken care of her for me all these months, but it is time now for her to come home."

"I know, Grandma, and I'm ready to bring all of Sophie's things over here and give her back to you. My dilemma is Maggie. Since Sophie came to live with us, Maggie has become quite dependent on her. I'm afraid that Maggie will go into a rapid decline if she loses Sophie. I've been talking to Pete about options to help Maggie with the transition, and I'm sorry to say we haven't come up with any good ones yet."

Bessie squeezed Cassidy's hand. "Would you think about Maggie coming to live with me and Sophie? I hate to take away your companion, but I think you are right about Maggie's dependence on Sophie, and you know she loves it here. You would be able to see her every time you visit, and you could come every day. I feel selfish even making the suggestion, but it is the best idea I could come up with."

Cassidy squeezed Bessie's hand back. "After all the times I've given pep talks to long-term foster parents about letting go, I can give myself my own pep talk. As much as I'll miss having Maggie, she belongs with Sophie more than with me. And I can borrow them once in a while, right?"

Bessie nodded as Pete said, "And you can borrow Laverne and Shirley too." Hearing their names, both dogs stood up and started wagging and barking, breaking the tension, and the conversation moved on to other topics.

As Cassidy and Pete walked out to the van, Pete bumped shoulders with Cassidy. "It is a wonderful and generous thing you are doing Cassidy. I'm so proud to be part of your life."

Cassidy leaned into Pete's shoulder as they approached the van. "Can you come in for a while when we get to my house. I think I need to be held for a while."

"That is an invitation I'll never turn down. We'll just sit and chill. And you can decide if you want me to call Clancy tonight or tomorrow to check on Rosadel and the girls."

"I think I'll sleep better if I know, will it get too late to call if we wait?'

Pete checked his watch as they got the dogs buckled into the van. "Nope, we have plenty of time. I'll text Clancy, that way even if it is after the girl's bedtime we won't cause a problem."

Pete reached over and squeezed Cassidy's hand after they got into the van. "You know I think you are amazing, don't you? You did such a great thing for Ms. Bessie keeping Sophie, and now you are giving up Maggie because it is what is best for her. You always do what is best for everyone else. I hope you know that just makes me want to do everything I can to make you happy, because you truly deserve it."

Cassidy leaned over and kissed Pete's cheek. "Thank you, Pete. I'm feeling a little like crying, so don't be too nice to me. Let's go to the house."

When Pete and Cassidy arrived at her house, they got the dogs settled and then sat down on the couch. Pete put his arms around Cassidy, and she rested her head on his chest. "Every day when I get home, I'm afraid it is the day that I will find Maggie has died, and I hate the thought that she could die alone. I know now she will always be surrounded by love. "

"You know, Cass, Maggie is really quite healthy for a sixteen-year-old dog. She could have a couple more years in her."

"I know that Pete. But I also know that a sixteen-year-old dog is not something to take for granted. I don't know quite how to explain what I'm feeling. I don't know how I'll sleep without the dogs in the bed, but I'll figure it out. And if I get too lonely, there is always another dog needing a foster home."

"I meant what I said about borrowing Laverne and Shirley. They can spend the night with you anytime you like."

"And then what will you do?" Cassidy leaned up to look Pete in the face.

"Probably cry myself to sleep," he answered, and Cassidy laughed just as he had intended her to.

"Why don't you text Clancy now and check on everyone?" Cassidy knew she would worry until she knew how everything had turned out.

Hey Clancy - How are Rosadel and the girls? Cassidy is worried about kitten withdrawal.

All good, Pete. Bee brought wine. Tipsy karaoke. Bethany and Michelle left with kittens. I put girls to bed. Rosadel and Bee looking at Bee's suitors on CatholicMatch.com, and giggling like seventh graders. The storm has passed for now.

Pete chuckled as he read Clancy's text and showed the phone to Cassidy before responding.

All good now. Talk to you tomorrow.

Cassidy sighed with relief and put her head back on Pete's chest. "Well, I guess that is one less thing to worry about."

"Honestly, Cass, that is the thing about Rosadel. I'll bet that all the kittens families have become part of Rosadel's circle. I wouldn't be surprised if she hosted an annual reunion or something. She just has this amazing ability to bring people in, and to care about them from the time she meets them. It really is astounding. And she has no idea that everyone isn't just like her. The world would be a much better place if there were more Rosadel's in it."

Cassidy couldn't agree more.

CHAPTER 33

Marie's days had fallen into a predictable routine. Get up, walk and feed Max, settle him in his crate with some toys, go to work, come home, check the mail for a response from Sandra, walk Max, eat dinner, walk Max again, watch some TV or read, go to bed, do over.

Although Marie was anxious to hear from Sandra, it had only been a little over two weeks since Marie's letter had been mailed. Sandra could have thrown the letter away. Marie was at peace that she had done all that she could do, and that it was in God and Sandra's hands now, but she couldn't help the sense of anticipation as she retrieved the mail each day.

Max was softening Marie in ways she couldn't explain. She had taken a picture of him and it was now the background on her phone. She had asked Bee for help to print out the picture and kept in in her badge holder behind her employee ID so that she could flip the ID over and see his sweet face during her workday.

Multiple students had seen Marie looking at the picture of Max and had asked about him. She was slowly becoming Mrs. Marie instead of Mrs. Theriot, as she warmed up to the students and they warmed up to her. Marie was rediscovering the tenderness in her heart that she had buried after the death of her parents and marriage to Burl. It was as if having Max to love had opened a door in her heart that she had believed closed forever.

Marie realized that even if she never had relationships with her own grandchildren, there were many children at Holy Redeemer to love, who would love her back simply because she was kind to them and cared about them. Marie prayed daily thanking God for opening her eyes to the opportunity to heal from the past and learn to really enjoy the present.

Max had settled in beautifully to life with Marie. They simply enjoyed each other's company. Marie had started to consider leaving Max loose in the house while she was at work. He was so calm and easy going, she didn't think he would be a problem, and wondered who she could talk to about the idea. As much as Marie wanted to call Cassidy, she was nervous about how much contact to initiate. Marie didn't want her relationship with Cassidy to impair her ability to reconcile with Sandra.

Marie had noticed that Max continued to be skittish near the back fence on their daily walks. There was always barking from the dogs on the adjacent property, and the barking bothered Max. He never barked back but put his ears back and his tail between his legs and got as far away from the fence as possible. Marie thought it sounded like an awful lot of dogs on the property but thought it might just be the echoes of their barking.

After worrying about the barking on the adjacent property, and whether or not to continue crating Max, Marie decided to call the St. Elizabeth Animal Shelter and ask for advice. She decided to not ask to speak to Cassidy, but just ask whoever answered the phone.

"St. Elizabeth Animal Shelter, this is Katelyn," Marie heard on the other end of the phone.

"Hello, Katelyn, this is Marie Theriot, I adopted Max from the shelter a couple of weeks ago."

Katelyn felt her heart sink, she had so hoped that Max had found his forever home. "Is there a problem with Max?" Katelyn asked.

"Oh, no, no problem with Max at all," said Marie as Katelyn breathed a sigh of relief. "I was just calling for some advice as I haven't owned a dog since I was a child, and I wasn't sure who to ask."

"I'm happy to help, Mrs. Theriot, what would you like to know?" These were Katelyn's favorite kind of calls. People who cared so much about their pets that they wanted to make sure they were doing the right things.

"I've been crating Max whenever I leave the house since I brought him home. He doesn't seem to mind, but I feel bad leaving him in the crate while I'm at work all day. He has never shown any tendencies to mischief, and I've been thinking about letting him have the run of the house when I'm not home."

"Well, Mrs. Theriot, dogs are a lot like children, and it is best not to expand their boundaries too quickly. It might be stressful for Max to go from his crate to the run of the house in one step. Do you mind me asking which room Max's crate is in?"

"Not at all," replied Marie. "His crate is in my bedroom."

"Well, I would recommend that you start there. When you go out for a short time, like to the grocery store, put Max in his crate but don't shut the door, and then close the door to your bedroom. If he does well with that, then you can try him loose in your bedroom while you go to work. Make sure there is nothing in the bedroom he can hurt himself with. If he continues to do well loose in the bedroom, slowly expand his access to the rest of the house. You can use baby gates to restrict him or close the doors to certain rooms. Most dogs will work really hard to not soil their crates but may feel like a spot in the house is permissible. That is something you will have to watch for while you are allowing Max freedom in your bedroom, to see if he will need to either have access to outdoors to potty, or a designated space with pee-pee pads in the house."

"I'm glad I called you, Katelyn," said Marie. "I never would have thought this was so complicated."

"It's not really complicated, just cautious. Dogs love routine and security. Whenever a dog has a change to his routine, it is stressful. Just like humans, stress can cause dogs to act out. By making one small change at a time, and letting Max get used to it before another change, we can reduce his stress and not upset his sense of security."

"Maybe I should just keep crating him," said Marie. "I don't want to stress him."

"That is up to you, Mrs. Theriot. Most dogs view their crate as their personal space, and like the security of it. What made you worry about Max staying in the crate all day?"

"Well. Katelyn, this may be silly, but I get stiff if I can't change positions and walk around frequently, and I was afraid the same thing could happen to Max. He takes his time some days stretching when he gets out of the crate, and I worry that he may be stiff."

"Dogs are smarter than us, Mrs. Theriot, and they like to stretch everything out before they move to make sure their muscles are ready, so his stretching is just a sign that Max is taking good care of himself. But, as dogs age, they can get stiff if they don't have the opportunity to move around. It is not a bad idea to see how he does without being crated. But it is also not a problem to continue to crate him."

"Thanks so much, Katelyn. You have given me a lot to think about. I appreciate you being so patient with me and answering my questions so thoroughly.

"No problem, Mrs. Theriot. We love to help people keep their pets safe and happy at home. You feel free to call any time now."

It was after Marie hung up the phone that she realized she had never asked Katelyn about the dogs on the adjacent property and Max's response to them.

◆ ◆ ◆

Sandra was surprised at how well everything went when she told Cassidy about her parents and childhood. She hoped things would go as well with Candace and Mark Jr., but understood that because of their ages, she would have to handle those conversations differently. She decided to talk to Candace first, and then to Mark Jr. Sandra debated asking Cassidy to join her when she told Candace, knowing that with Candace's personality, there may be a heated argument.

Cassidy was surprised to see Sandra's name on the caller ID when the phone rang at the shelter on Wednesday morning. "Hi Mom! What's up?"

"Hi Cassidy, I called to ask for advice."

Cassidy pulled the phone away from her ear and looked at it in disbelief. This was truly a change. "Are you there, Cassidy?"

"Yes, Mom. You surprised me, that's all. What can I help you with?"

"Well, I know that telling Candace about your grandmother will not go as smoothly as telling you did, and I wondered if it would help if you were there when I tell her?"

Cassidy took a deep breath before answering. "Mom, I would love to be there for you, but it might make Candace feel bad. I think if you sit with her one-on-one, she can call me afterwards to talk about it. I think it is important that she has time with just you to ask the questions that are important to her."

"You reinforced what I was thinking, Cassidy, but I have to tell you I would love backup when I talk to her."

"Mom, I'd be happy to watch Chip, or take him out somewhere so that you and Mark can talk to Cassidy together. That would give you support and would feel more natural. Mark owns part of this story too. He knew about your childhood and agreed with you to keep your children away from your family, and to keep your family a secret from your children. I think it is fair for him to share telling Candy and Chip."

"How'd you get to be so smart, Cassidy? Do you think I should tell Mark Jr. and Candace at the same time?"

"To be honest, Mom, I don't know. My guess is Candy will want a lot more information than Chip, and that he will get bored with the conversation. I don't think it hurts anything to tell Chip much less formally than you tell Candy. He might surprise me, but I think Chip will just accept that he has a grandmother he didn't know about, and his questions will come later as he gets older."

"What is your schedule like this week? When can you take Mark Jr.?"

"How about Pete and I pick him up on Saturday? We can take him to New Orleans to City Park. We can play miniature golf and rent bikes and paddle boats. If that doesn't take enough time, Pete can always bring a baseball, a bat and a few mitts and he and Chip can play ball. We'll plan to pick Chip up around eleven and have him home by five. Will that work?"

"That sounds perfect Cassidy. Can you and Pete stay for dinner after?"

"Since I just planned Pete's whole Saturday without asking him about it, how about I give you a tentative 'yes' and confirm after I talk to Pete?"

Sandra laughed as she replied. "You are more like me than I realized. I commit Mark all the time before asking, and then realize I might have gone too far."

Cassidy laughed too. "I feel better now that I realize I came by this honestly. Mom, Pete is so easy going I'm going to have to be careful not to steamroll him."

"Oh, Cassidy! I'm sure Pete wouldn't be as successful as he is without the ability to stand up for himself when it is important. You are usually very easy going, but when you have a problem to solve you have always been full speed ahead. I think you two will be fine. A perfect yin and yang for each other."

"Thanks Mom. I sure hope you are right. Now I need to get back to work, and let Pete know we have plans for Saturday."

As Cassidy hung up, she realized that she had not told Sandra about Maggie going to live with Bessie and Sophie at Our Lady of Lourdes. When Cassidy and Pete visited Bessie on Thursday, they would be leaving Maggie and Sophie with Bessie. They would go back on Friday to check on how things were going, and Cassidy knew she would visit daily for the next couple of weeks. The nights without the girls would be the hardest. And that made Cassidy pick up the phone to check on Rosadel. She'd talk to Pete tonight.

Rosadel was slightly hung over, but the second cup of coffee was really helping. She couldn't believe how Bee had woken up just fine. Bee swore the trick was to drink twice as much water as you did wine, and from this morning's result, Rosadel was starting to believe her. The girls were so excited to have Bee at breakfast that they didn't pine for the kittens too much.

After Bee left to go home and get dressed, the girls played with Roscoe and Holly, and then got ready for school. As Rosadel loaded them up in the van for the drive to school, she gave each girl a hug and thanked her for being so grown up and responsible about the kittens going to new homes. Rosadel knew there would be more tears in the future but was still really proud of how well the girls were handling things.

Rosadel was surprised and not surprised when the phone rang, and she saw the St. Elizabeth Animal Shelter on the caller ID. She had expected a call from Cassidy this morning, but not quite so early.

"Hi, Cassidy. We're fine, honest we are. The girls didn't even cry this morning."

"Wow, Rosadel, that's great. I didn't expect to hear that after how things were going when I was there yesterday."

"It really was strange, Cassidy. It was a combination of things. Michelle almost crying because she felt so bad taking her kittens was one thing. Then when the girls met Arlene and Julie, things really changed. It was like they realized that some people really NEEDED their kittens. And even though they love the kittens, they know they don't need them. This morning, they played with Roscoe more than they have in years, and he just loved it. I know we have some rough days ahead, and I'll weather them, but I think the girls have really grown through the experience. I think they learned that love can be hard, but it is always worth it."

"I'm struggling with that myself this week, Rosadel."

"What's the matter, Cassidy? Did something happen with Pete?"

"No, thank goodness. Me and Pete are fine. It is the foster thing. You know I have been fostering Sophie for Grandma Bessie. Well, she is ready to have her back. The hard thing is that Maggie has gotten so dependent on Sophie, that I'm afraid she will grieve herself to death without her. When you take a senior rescue, you don't know what will happen. Maggie loves me, but she needs Sophie. So tomorrow, both of them are moving in with Grandma Bessie. If I let myself, I'll start crying now and I don't know when I'll stop."

"Oh, Cassidy. I'm so sorry. I know how much you have loved having Maggie and Sophie with you. Tell you what, why don't you plan to stay here on Thursday and Friday night? We have a guest room, you will have Roscoe and Holly to distract you, and it will be a thrill for the girls. It will also help them see that you don't grow out of hurting when you do the right thing, but you just keep on doing it."

"I don't know, Rosadel, that seems like an awful imposition. I'm going to have to get used to my empty house sooner or later."

"I know, but if you have a couple of nights with the sounds of my family around you as you get used to sleeping without them, I'm sure it will help. And it will be a help for me too, as the girls adjust to life without kittens. Please say you'll do it."

Cassidy thought for a long minute. She had actually thought about asking either Sandra or Prescott if she could stay at one of their houses, so this was a great solution. Rosadel couldn't know that Cassidy had never slept at anyone's house other than her own or her parents, so couldn't know what a big deal this was.

"Thank you, Rosadel, I'll take you up on your offer. I won't be there until kind of late either night, as I'll be going to Our Lady of Lourdes after work. And I have to leave early Saturday to pick up my younger brother Chip for the day."

"No problem at all, Cassidy. I'll see you tomorrow then. The girls are going to be thrilled."

As Cassidy hung up the phone, she thought about how much her life had changed since the triplets got involved with rescuing the kittens. Rosadel may think they were holy terrors, but Cassidy felt like they had been just the divine intervention she needed to move her life in the right direction. Life had been fine before, but with the Marshall family in it, especially Pete, life was really, really good.

CHAPTER 34

Pete finished loading the dog beds, the dog crates, the dog food and the dog toys into the back of his van. Maggie, Sophie, Laverne and Shirley had watched the entire process with great interest, but none of them seemed overly concerned.

Pete was thrilled that Cassidy would be staying with Rosadel and Clancy for a couple of days. He had thought about inviting her to stay at his place but was afraid that it would sound like a cheesy come on. Cassidy staying with Rosadel was a perfect answer. Pete was also excited that Cassidy had planned a day for them to spend with her little brother. It made him very happy that Cassidy felt comfortable enough about their relationship to plan an outing for her brother without asking him first.

As Cassidy brought the dogs out to the van to fasten them into their car seats, Pete asked, "Are you sure we have everything?"

"I think so," Cassidy answered, "But since I'll be going back every day for a while, I can always bring anything I forgot later. Are you sure we shouldn't just take two cars? I don't need you to follow me to Rosadel's right now to drop the car off."

"Cass, we talked about this already. I want to stop in and see everyone anyway. It just makes sense to run your car over there now so we can go back there together after we visit. Think of it as reducing your carbon footprint."

Cassidy dropped a quick kiss on Pete's lips before getting into her car. "You win. I'll see you at Rosadel's."

As Pete put the car in gear to follow Cassidy, he offered up a quick prayer that everything would go smoothly with the transition for Maggie and Sophie. Especially Cassidy's part in that transition.

Bessie Chauvin was again waiting in the foyer of Our Lady of Lourdes when Pete and Cassidy arrived. Pete had pulled the van up in front, so that they could unload the dogs' supplies before he parked. Sister Dorothy Murphy was waiting in her wheelchair with Bessie.

"I thought you would have lots to unload, so brought myself down here to hold the leashes for darling Laverne and Shirley. I know as I'm their favorite, it would be a big help." Pete leaned down and kissed Sister Dorothy's cheek.

"You are indeed their favorite, and I thank you very much," answered Pete as he handed over the leashes. "Behave, Laverne and Shirley, I know she seems like a cupcake, but Sister Dorothy is ferocious if you cross her."

"Oh, go on with yourself!" Sister Dorothy laughed as she lightly punched Pete's arm. "You know I'm as gentle as a lamb."

It was Pete's turn to laugh. "Begging your pardon, Sister Dorothy. But you weren't able to keep over five hundred school children in line with the raise of one eyebrow because you are a lamb."

Bessie turned to Sister Dorothy in admiration. "I thought I had good control of my classrooms, but that sounds truly impressive, Dorothy."

Sister Dorothy chuckled. "Don't be fooled by Pete's blarney. It took more than a raised eyebrow, but I did have a knack for keeping the children in line back in the day."

As Sister Dorothy and Bessie started to exchange stories about their experiences in the classroom over their many years of teaching, Pete and Cassidy made short work of moving Maggie and Sophie's possessions into Bessie's apartment.

Cassidy looked at Maggie and Sophie's things and felt the tears welling in her eyes. Pete wrapped her in his arms. "You can cry if you need to," Pete said as he hugged her tightly.

Cassidy rested her head on Pete's chest. "I know, but it won't do anyone any good. Give me a minute to compose myself, and then we'll act like this is any other night. I can't do anything to make this hard on Grandma Bessie. I'll cry later if I have to."

Pete kissed the top of Cassidy's head. "You know I love you, and you are wonderful," he said.

"I love you too, Pete. I'm glad you're here. It really does make everything easier."

Cassidy's emotions were still perilously close to the surface when she and Pete arrived at Rosadel and Clancy's house later that evening. Maggie and Sophie had looked a little surprised that they were staying at Our Lady of Lourdes but didn't cry or try to follow Pete and Cassidy out the door. Cassidy promised Bessie that she would call as soon as they got to Rosadel's to check on how things were going.

As soon as Pete rang the doorbell, he and Cassidy could hear the pounding of three sets of feet headed for the door. "It's Uncle Pete and Ms. Cassidy!" they heard Lou shout as Grace opened the door.

"Ms. Cassidy! Ms. Cassidy! We're so excited that you are sleeping over. We're sorry about your dog going away. We know how sad you feel." As usual, it was hard to separate which triplet was saying what, but Cassidy was glad for their chatter.

All three girls grabbed Cassidy and Pete in a group hug. "Uncle Pete, we didn't know you were coming over. Are you sleeping over too?"

"No, Kukla, Fran and Ollie. I'm just dropping Ms. Cassidy off and visiting for a few minutes. I missed you guys."

Lou put her hands on her hips. "If you missed us you should try to get our names right."

Cassidy, who had been close to tears, started laughing. "You know he has to tease all the time, don't you Lou?"

Rosie answered. "Yes, we do, but we wish he would grow out of it."

Clancy chose that moment to come into the foyer. "I've been hoping Uncle Pete would grow out of a bunch of things for a long time, girls. Join the club."

"Hey! Is it pick on Pete night?" Pete asked.

Grace took his hand. "Uncle Pete, if you start teasing, you have to be able to take teasing. If you can't take it, don't start."

Clancy clapped Pete on his shoulder. "It's that easy, bro. Even an eight-year-old knows it."

Rosadel called out from the kitchen, "Girls, last call for a snack before bedtime!" and the triplets went running for the kitchen.

Clancy reached out to take Cassidy's bag. "I'll put this upstairs in the guest room, Rosadel can show you where everything is after the girls are in bed."

Pete took Cassidy's hand as they went into the kitchen with Rosadel and the girls.

Rosadel set a plate of cookies on the table and turned to give Cassidy a hug.

"How're you doing?" she asked.

Cassidy blinked back tears for what felt like the thousandth time since she left Our Lady of Lourdes. "I'm hanging in there, Rosadel, but it's hard."

Roscoe bumped Cassidy with his nose, and she knelt down to hug him. "Hey, big guy. You know just what to do to make me feel better, don't you?"

Lou, Rosie and Grace all left the table and crowded around Roscoe and Cassidy. "You can cry if you need to, Ms. Cassidy. We all cried over the kittens. Roscoe is good at licking tears."

Cassidy wasn't sure which triplet said what, but she was grateful for their support.

"C'mon and eat your cookies and drink your milk," said Rosadel. "Maybe Ms. Cassidy and Uncle Pete will tuck you in and hear your prayers if you are good."

"Would you, Ms. Cassidy? Please?" asked Gracie.

Cassidy wiped her eyes yet again and nodded.

"Would you like a cup of coffee or tea or a glass of wine or a beer or anything?" Rosadel asked.

Cassidy thought for a minute. "I'm not much of a drinker, but I think tonight a glass of wine would be great. I need to call Grandma Bessie, I promised her I would call and check on how the girls were doing."

Rosadel gestured to the dining room, and Cassidy went in and shut the door to make her call. Bessie answered on the first ring.

"Hello, darling girl. I'm sitting here on my sofa with Maggie on one side and Sophie on the other, enjoying a little TV before bed. They are as calm and happy as can be."

"That's great Grandma Bessie. I thought that would be the case. Why don't you give me a call tomorrow morning and let me know how things are going? And then I'll see you tomorrow evening."

"I'll do that Cassidy. How are you? Are you OK?"

"I'm good Grandma. I'm at Rosadel's with Pete. I'm going to go upstairs and hear their bedtime prayers and read them a story in a few minutes. They are very good for me right now."

"Those girls are good for everyone. They bring so much joy."

Cassidy smiled as she answered. "I'll be sure to tell Rosadel you said that. I love you, Grandma Bessie. Talk to you tomorrow."

"Love you too, Cassidy. Sleep well, sweetheart."

Cassidy went back into the kitchen to find the girls finishing up their cookies and milk, with a large glass of wine at the empty seat at the table. Rosadel had a similar glass in front of her.

"I figured if we were only having one, it should be a good one," Rosadel joked.

"I'll sleep well tonight for sure," replied Cassidy.

The girls put their plates and cups in the dishwasher, and kissed Rosadel and Clancy goodnight.

"We're going to brush our teeth and wash our faces and put our pajamas on, so you can come up and hear our prayers and read us a story," said Lou.

"It will take us only a little while," said Grace.

"Ten minutes," said Rosie.

"We'll be there, Snap, Crackle and Pop," Pete answered.

As the girls rolled their eyes at Pete and headed upstairs, Clancy raised an eyebrow and asked, "Do you think you will ever run out of trios?"

"I've been re-using for years," replied Pete. "No one really pays attention to which names I use. And as much as I aggravate them, they'll miss my teasing if I ever stop."

Cassidy took a sip of her wine and felt some of her sadness start to melt away as she listened to Pete and Clancy's banter. She would miss Maggie and Sophie, but she did the right thing. And she was so lucky to have become friends with Rosadel. Cassidy hoped that she and Pete would be forever, but she knew that even if that didn't happen, her relationship with Rosadel was forever.

Lou, Grace and Rosie were all clustered on one bed when Pete and Cassidy entered their bedroom.

"We read here, and then we get in our own beds and you tuck us in and hear our prayers," said Lou.

"Tonight, the prayer order is Rosie, Lou and then Grace." said Rosie.

"We take turns going first, middle and last," said Grace.

"Hey, those are three nicknames I haven't used yet," said Pete, earning him a dirty look from all four girls in the room.

"What are we reading tonight?" asked Cassidy as she settled into the bed with the girls. Pete climbed in so too, so that they all resembled a pile of puppies.

"We're reading 'Because of Winn-Dixie'" replied Grace, "And we're on Chapter 3. We get a chapter a night."

"I love this book! Even though I was a teenager when it came out, I read it as soon as I heard about it." Cassidy was excited to get reacquainted with Opal and Winn-Dixie and the other characters in the book.

As Cassidy read to the girls, they snuggled closer to her, their simple affection lifting Cassidy's spirits and healing her heart. As the chapter came to an end and the three sleepy little girls climbed into their beds, Cassidy knew that coming to Rosadel's tonight had been a better idea than she had understood at the time.

While she and Pete listened to their prayers, Cassidy noticed that each girl prayed for the kittens, and the families that had taken them home. As Cassidy kissed each girl goodnight, they hugged her and whispered, "I love you, Ms. Cassidy." And she answered, "I love you, too."

As they turned out the light and pulled the door shut, Pete took Cassidy's hand. "I don't want to scare you, but that made me look forward to reading stories to our children someday."

Cassidy leaned her head on Pete's shoulder. "That doesn't sound scary at all, Pete."

CHAPTER 35

The week leading up to the Holy Redeemer Church fair passed in the blink of an eye. Cassidy was still adjusting to a home without dogs, but she had been to visit Maggie and Sophie every day. They were so obviously happy it made it much easier to accept that she had truly done the right thing.

Friday was a beautiful late February day. The sun was shining, and the temperature was predicted to be in the low seventies. Cassidy was manning the booth from five to seven, and Dustin was relieving her at seven to stay until the fair closed at nine. Pete was planning to come with Laverne and Shirley at around five-thirty, to talk about the joy of rescuing senior dogs.

Prescott was scheduled to spend an hour on Saturday at the booth with Thor, talking about emotional support animals, and the amazing difference they can make in a person's life. He and Thor had a repertoire of tricks that they would perform as people stopped by the booth. Mostly though, the booth would be manned by Bee, Rosadel, Hannah, and Lindy, and of course, Cassidy.

The shelter had very few animals currently in residence, which was great. Rosadel and the girls were going to bring Holly and talk about fostering the kittens until they were old enough for forever homes. Bessie was determined to bring Maggie and Sophie for at least a few minutes, even if they just visited the booth. The idea born at Rosadel's kitchen table had finally come to reality, and the staffs of both St. Elizabeth's Animal Shelter and Bayou Beni Animal Hospital were very excited for the opportunity to advocate on behalf of shelter animals with the people of Holy Redeemer.

◆ ◆ ◆

Sandra had been surprised at how little Candace and Mark Jr. had reacted to the news that she had been contacted by her mother. She had a feeling that there was more going on with Candace than she was communicating, but Mark had cautioned her to be patient. Sandra was pretty sure that Candace would talk to Cassidy about it more than she would talk to Sandra and was proud that she felt more gratitude than jealousy about that.

The thing Sandra hadn't figured out yet was what to do to get in touch with Marie. She had thought about sending a letter but couldn't really figure out what she wanted to say. She knew that Cassidy had Marie's phone number in the files at the animal shelter, but she knew Cassidy was not supposed to disclose that information. She had checked with information, and Marie's phone number was not listed.

Sandra had talked to Dr. Mathieu about it in her session on Wednesday, and Dr. Mathieu has listened to Sandra talk through options but had left it up to Sandra to decide. Sandra knew she was thinking herself in circles about it and decided that Monday was soon enough to make a decision.

◆ ◆ ◆

Ed Adams hugged his daughter Janey as he handed over the keys to their family home. He was ready to leave for Bayou Beni as soon as they left the lawyer's office.

"I've got everything I want out of the house Janey, and I've left the few pieces of furniture that you said you wanted. Everything else went with your brother and sister, and I had Habitat for Humanity pick up all the other furniture. I even had a cleaning service come in and give the place a good scrub, so it should be all ready for you to move in."

"Thanks, Daddy. You know you can stay with us for a few days, you don't have to leave so fast."

Ed put his arm around Janey. She looked so much like Shirley, and like Shirley, she was a nurturer. "I know I can stay, Janey, but I am excited to go start the next stage of my life. The work that Prescott will be doing with veterans is just what I need right now. I'll never not miss your mother but doing work that is rewarding and important will help me get through the days. I'm not going to be that far away. I'll be back for a visit in a few weeks."

Ed decided to make a quick call to Prescott before he got on the road, as he knew he was not expected until Monday. If necessary, Ed decided to spend the weekend in New Orleans, but he really hoped to stay in Bayou Beni and start to get a feel for the place. Prescott answered on the first ring.

"Hey Ed! Good to hear from you. How is everything coming along?"

"Just great, Prescott, just left the lawyer's office, the house is now Janey's. I'd like to head over to Bayou Beni right away, if you don't mind company this weekend."

"Don't mind company at all, Ed. The Holy Redeemer Parish fair is this weekend, and I've got a commitment to bring Thor over to talk about service dogs, but other than that, I'll be spending most of my time at Angel's Watch getting things done. I'd love to have another pair of hands, and it will be good to visit."

"Great, Prescott. I should be there sometime early this evening. I put your address in my GPS, and it estimates my arrival time at around six."

"I'll see you then, Ed. Looking forward to getting our work here started."

♦ ♦ ♦

Gil put his bag in the overhead bin and settled into his seat on the plane. In a little more than an hour he would be touching down in New Orleans, and then on to Bayou Beni for the weekend. It was hard to believe it had only been a couple of weeks since he had interviewed for the Maintenance Leader job at the Bayou Beni plant. His replacement had already been named, and the transition plan would start in another two weeks.

Gil was planning on spending his weekends in Bayou Beni until he started spending his weeks at the plant. Gil was anxious to get settled into Bessie's house, and to start the process to bring Bessie from Our Lady of Lourdes and back into her own home. He hoped that the strange restlessness that had possessed him for the best part of the last year would be satisfied by the move to Bayou Beni, but he knew any relief would be temporary.

Gil knew that the real problem was that he never imagined that he would be in his thirties and not married. Gil knew he was born to be a husband and father. He thought he would be married and have a couple of children by now. He had dated many women, but none of them felt like forever. Gil knew he was somewhat cursed by the Chauvin family legend that the Chauvin men knew the second they laid eyes on their future wife that she was the one. He often wondered if he didn't give his dates a fighting chance because he had never experienced that "struck by lightning" feeling.

This weekend would be a surprise visit for Bessie, and Gil hoped to bring her to her house in Bayou Beni and start looking over the transcriptions of Mathilde's journals. As important as it was to Gil to get married and start a family, he also felt a tremendous responsibility to get those journals translated with Bessie's help. Gil hoped that the journal translation process would help calm his restlessness and give him a focus beyond work. Gil was also looking forward to renewing his spiritual life. Holy Redeemer had felt more like home than any church he had attended since he was a child. High on his list of activities once he moved to Bayou Beni was figuring out how to really belong to the Holy Redeemer family.

As the plane touched down in New Orleans, Gil collected his bag and made his way to the rental car facility. He decided to go the store on the way to Bessie's house, so that once he was in he could stay in. He had gone over to Bessie's house the last time he was in Bayou Beni to check on the state of the house. The utilities had never been turned off, and Gil had arranged for a cleaning service to come in and dust and make up the beds with fresh linens. He would use the guest room he had always used when coming to visit Bessie in the past. He would talk to Bessie this weekend to find out how she felt about changes to the house. Gil thought that some modifications to the layout would make it an easier house for Bessie to live in. He also wanted to adapt the house so that if Bessie did become confined to a wheelchair at a later date, she would still be able to stay at home with him.

The positive by product of Gil staying single so long was that he had saved most of his income, and now had money put away so that he could provide in home nursing care should Bessie need it. He knew that Bessie had some money of her own put away, so was confident that as long as it wasn't medically necessary, he would be able to keep Bessie at home until she went to her final home with the Lord.

◆ ◆ ◆

The Holy Redeemer fair was in full swing when Pete arrived with Laverne and Shirley. The fish fry had a line of customers waiting for seating and to-go orders. The children's amusements were doing good business, and the sounds of music and laughter filled the air. Laverne and Shirley were looking all around but were both amazingly calm for the chaos they were walking through.

Pete saw Cassidy before she saw him. She was kneeling down, talking to a little boy who looked to be around eight years old. She looked so beautiful, it took Pete's breath away. If all went well, Pete planned to propose to Cassidy tomorrow. He had already talked to Prescott and Sandra, asking both for their permission to ask for Cassidy's hand in marriage. Pete knew that he was old fashioned, but he also knew that he wanted to do everything exactly right when it came to him and Cassidy.

Just then Cassidy looked up and saw Pete. "Here are a couple of puppies, Sean. I told you Dr. Marshall would be here soon."

Sean turned and looked at Pete, Laverne and Shirley and then looked back at Cassidy. "Are you sure they don't bite, Ms. Cassidy?"

"I'm sure, Sean. Pete, Sean has a friend that was bitten by a dog, and he wanted some advice from me on how to not get bitten. I told him that if the dog is loose, to be a tree, and stand as still as he can without looking at the dog. If the dog still comes near him, I told Sean to feed the dog a jacket, a backpack, something to keep between him and the dog, and I told him if he falls down to curl into a ball with his fingers locked together to protect his neck and ears. But Sean wants to know what to do when he meets a friend's dog, and I told him we would show him when Laverne and Shirley got here."

"Thanks for the background, Cassidy. Sean, you can call me Dr. Pete. The first thing to do is to ask the dog's owner if it is okay to pet them. If they say 'yes', then you should offer the dog the back of your hand to sniff. Ms. Cassidy will show you how with Laverne."

Pete told Laverne to sit and stay, and Cassidy placed the back of her closed fist under Laverne's nose. Laverne sniffed Cassidy's hand, and when she determined Cassidy wasn't holding a treat, looked up at Pete.

"Now that Cassidy has let Laverne check her out, she can pet Laverne on the shoulders or chest. Petting a dog on the face can feel threatening to them, so we never do that with a dog we don't know well."

Cassidy scratched Laverne's chest and Laverne's tail started sweeping the ground behind her. "Would you like to try, Sean? You can pet both Laverne and Shirley."

Sean carefully offered both Laverne and Shirley his closed hand, and then gave each of them a quick pet.

"They're so warm and soft!" Sean exclaimed. "I didn't think they would feel like that."

"Dogs are great company," said Pete. "Do you think you will be less afraid now?"

"I think so, Dr. Pete. Thanks for letting me pet Laverne and Shirley."

As Sean scampered away, Cassidy looked around for a pencil and paper. "I think I just had a great idea, Pete. I think Grandma Bessie and Sister Dorothy could bring Maggie and Sophie to Holy Redeemer once a week and read to kids in the library. That way all the kids at Holy

Redeemer could learn about how to approach dogs safely and learn to not be afraid of dogs. What do you think? Who should I talk to?"

Pete released Laverne and Shirley from their sit/stay and gave Cassidy a quick kiss. "Bee or Rosadel would be where I would start. One of them will know what you will need in a proposal. You can shop your idea to Grandma Bessie and Sister Dorothy tonight when we leave here to go visit them."

There wasn't any additional time for conversation, and the booth was very busy now that Laverne and Shirley had arrived. The girls were well behaved and charming, and a number of people showed real interest in senior rescue. By the time Dustin arrived for his seven o'clock shift, both dogs were sleeping comfortably in one of the crates Cassidy had brought to the booth.

"Do you think we'll have to carry them to your van?" Cassidy asked.

"Nope. They'll be fine after their nap. I think it might be too much for them to go to Our Lady tonight though. I'll take them home and get them settled, would you mind picking me up on your way over there?" Pete was gently waking the dogs up as he spoke.

"That will be fine, Pete. I'll be over in about a half hour."

The visit that night with Bessie was a cheerful affair. Sister Dorothy and Bessie had become fast friends since Bessie moved over to the assisted living center. They had found that visits with the dogs were best in the afternoons, so, on Mondays, Wednesdays and Fridays, the dogs visited with the assisted living patients, and on Tuesdays, Thursdays and Saturdays, they visited with the nursing home patients.

Sister Dorothy loved the idea of going to Holy Redeemer one day a week to read to the children. She had tried as hard as she could to be stoic about her disability, but she missed children, and feeling like she was making a positive difference. Helping Bessie visit with the dogs had really brightened her world, but to have a chance to work with children again? Truly a gift from God.

By the time Cassidy and Pete left Our Lady of Lourdes, the idea of bringing the girls to read to the children was entirely out of Cassidy's hands. "Sister Dorothy will have all the details worked out, up to and including transportation to and from school for her and Bessie and the dogs," said Pete as they walked out to Cassidy's car. "When Sister Dorothy sets her mind to something, it is as if the Lord Himself is driving progress. She is an amazing woman. You did good with this idea Cassidy. It will make both of them very happy to feel like they are making a valuable contribution."

"I'm in awe of both of them, Pete. I can't imagine being in my nineties like Grandma Bessie, or in my eighties and crippled with arthritis like Sister Dorothy, and still have such a strong drive to make a contribution and to be the difference in people's lives. So inspiring."

"Let's try to be just like them when we're that age." Pete put his arms around Cassidy and kissed her as they reached her car.

As Cassidy got ready to head over to Holy Redeemer on Saturday for another day at the fair, she ran through a mental checklist to make sure she had everything she needed for another successful day. Cassidy would man the booth from ten until noon, then Bee, Rosadel, Hannah Falgoust and Lindy Russell would each take an hour, with Cassidy coming back from four until six. Prescott would show up sometime during the afternoon. That would complete the weekend.

Dustin and Katelyn would take turns bringing shelter pets over to the booth, and Bessie was planning to bring Maggie and Sophie. The triplets had been leash training Holly for the past week and were excited to show her off. Cassidy was confident that the work that had gone into planning for the booth at the Holy Redeemer Fair was going to pay huge dividends.

CHAPTER 36

Marie planned to take Max for a couple of loops around her property before heading over to the Holy Redeemer Fair. She had thought about volunteering to bring Max to the St. Elizabeth's Parish Animal Shelter booth but didn't want to spend too much time with Cassidy until she heard from Sandra.

As Marie and Max neared the back of her property, Max started to whine. Marie noticed that the barking seemed to be louder and more insistent, and the barks were accompanied by howls and crying. Marie knew she could no longer do nothing and took Max inside and called the animal shelter.

Katelyn answered the phone on the first ring. Dustin was on his way to Holy Redeemer to drop off a couple of adoptable dogs at the fair.

"St. Elizabeth Animal Shelter, this is Katelyn, how can I help you?"

"Katelyn, this is Marie Theriot. The property behind mine apparently has a number of dogs, and I always can hear them barking when I walk Max around the property. Today, they are howling as well as barking, and it sounds like the dogs are in trouble. I don't know what to do, so I called you."

"You did the right thing calling us, Mrs. Theriot. If you give me the address, I'll text Dustin and have him go out to the property and check on the dogs."

"I'm not sure of the address, Katelyn. The roads out here in Audela are winding and not very predictable. Do you want me to drive around and get the address and call you back?"

"Would you mind if I sent Dustin to your house? Then you could direct him to the right address."

"That would be fine, Katelyn. How long do you think it will be? Those dogs sounded pretty desperate."

"I've already texted Dustin, but he hasn't answered yet. I'm thinking he will be there within the half hour. I'll call you back when he answers my text and give you an estimated arrival time."

"That will be fine, Katelyn, thanks for the help."

Dustin had heard his phone beep when Katelyn's text came in and waited until he was parked in Holy Redeemer parking lot before looking at his phone.

> *Need you to investigate a complaint. Call me ASAP.*

"What's up, Katelyn?"

"We had a complaint that needs immediate investigation. Have you dropped off the dogs with Cassidy yet?"

"No, I just got here. Give me the address, and I'll text you when I'm leaving here."

"Kind of complicated. The complaint is out in Audela, and the complainant doesn't know the address, as the property backs up to hers. I'm sending you to her house, and she'll lead you to the property."

"Good enough. It is easy to get lost out in Audela, and the GPS doesn't have great accuracy out there. Text me the address, and I'll text you when I'm leaving here."

Dustin had brought two dogs with him to leave with Cassidy. Trent was a lab mix, and Tabitha was a beagle mix. They were both cute, friendly dogs, and Dustin hoped they would find forever homes today. There would need to be good news to offset investigating a complaint. Those usually did not have a happy ending.

Cassidy was happy to see Dustin arrive with the dogs, as she had turned away many disappointed children who were just there to see the dogs. As Dustin got Trent and Tabitha settled, he told Cassidy about the complaint.

"Keep me posted, Dustin. I have to stay here for another hour, but I can come out after that if you need me."

"I'm hoping it's nothing," said Dustin. "But Katelyn sounded worried, so I'm afraid of what I'm going to find."

Marie jumped when the phone rang, glad to see it was Katelyn calling her back.

"Dustin will be there in about twenty-five minutes," Katelyn said. "He'll be driving the parish animal control truck."

"Thank you, Katelyn. I appreciate your help."

When Dustin arrived at Marie's house, they decided the easiest way to get Dustin to the right house was to have him follow Marie. Marie put Max in his crate and got in her car.

"Please let those dogs be alright," Marie prayed as she drove. If only she had mentioned the barking the last time she had called the shelter.

As Marie pulled up in front of the house, she immediately noticed that it looked abandoned. The yard was overgrown, there were no cars, and no shades or curtains on the house and the rooms looked empty. Dustin pulled in behind her.

"Do you mind if I wait here to find out what is going on? I'm worried sick about those dogs," said Marie.

"You can wait right here, and I'll let you know." Dustin tried the gate, and finding it unlocked, went up and banged on the front door. Marie noticed you could hear the dogs from here, but it was much fainter as it was all the way on the back of the property, but it was still obviously the sound of animals in distress.

When no one answered the door, Dustin took off at a jog for the barn at the back of the property. What he found there had him running back to Marie. "Marie, I need you to call the sheriff, and get someone out here right away. I need to call Cassidy."

When Cassidy saw Dustin's name on her cell phone, she felt a chill go through her. "What is it Dustin?"

"We've got an abandoned puppy mill, Cassidy. I've got the sheriff on the way. You need to get here as fast as you can." He gave Cassidy the name of the road and told her to look for the truck.

379

Cassidy hung up the phone and looked frantically around the grounds. She spotted Bee and waved as hard as she could. Bee came running over.

"Is there a problem Cassidy?"

"Yes, Bee. I have to go to investigate a cruelty case. Can you start your shift at the booth early? And I'm supposed to pick up Grandma Bessie to bring her over, and I may still be tied up."

"I can start now, and I'm planning to go pick up Sister Dorothy after my shift, so I can get Bessie too. What time was she expecting you? Do you need me to call her?"

"No, that will get you there right after they finish lunch, which was when I was planning to go. Thanks, Bee."

"No problem, Cassidy. I'll be praying for you."

As Cassidy gathered up her things and walked to her car, she realized she needed to call Katelyn.

"Katelyn, I just heard from Dustin. We've got an abandoned puppy mill. I don't know how bad it is yet. Could you please call the shelters in the nearby parishes and check for space? And can you call Pete and give him the address and ask him to come out there? I'll try to call when I get out there and let you know what we are facing."

"I'm on it Cassidy. I'll run out to Holy Redeemer when the shelter closes and pick up Trent and Tabitha. We'll have to forgo sending the other dogs out this afternoon."

"Thanks for thinking of that, Katelyn. I'm so rattled, I forgot about that."

Cassidy knew she had to get to Dustin, but she also knew she had one more call that needed to be made.

Prescott was surprised to see Cassidy's number on his caller ID, as he thought she would be too busy with the Holy Redeemer fair to call him today. And he planned to head over there with Thor in a couple of hours. He excused himself to Ed and answered the phone.

"Hi Daddy. We may have a crisis at the animal shelter. Dustin found an abandoned puppy mill. I don't know how many animals we are dealing with. I just needed to tell you before I head out there, in case it is bad enough that it makes the news."

"Oh no, Cassidy. Call me if you need me. I'll be sending all the positive energy I can to you."

"Thanks, Daddy. I'm on my way now. Love you."

As Cassidy drove to Audela, she wondered if she should call Sandra, and decided she would wait and see what she found. As she turned onto the street in Audela, Cassidy saw multiple sets of flashing lights as the sheriff's department had sent a couple of cars. Cassidy saw an officer talking to Marie Theriot and wondered what in the world Marie had to do with this case. That answer would come later, as Cassidy had to find Dustin.

The first thing that shocked Cassidy was the smell. These animals had obviously been unattended for a while. Cassidy found Dustin filling water bowls with small amounts of water as a sheriff's deputy took photographs of the barn. The barn was literally filled with cages, stacked two and three deep, with six rows of fifteen to twenty cages, depending on size. Most of the cages were open and appeared to be empty, but there were probably twenty cages with animals inside. All of the animals were barking or crying.

"I don't know where to start, Cassidy." Dustin looked like he wanted to cry. "This is horrible."

Cassidy called to the deputy. "Can we start ministering to the animals?"

"I've got enough pictures, and they surely need help. What can I do?" The deputy looked as upset as Dustin.

"We'll go cage by cage and offer water first. Be careful. These animals are frightened and probably not socialized. I have tranquilizers on the truck but given that we don't know how fragile these dogs are, I want to wait until the vet gets here if we can.

"We'll give them water and get a count and start to triage based on condition. While Dustin and I are examining the animals, if you could go out to our truck and bring in some food, that would be great. We don't have enough on the truck to fill them up, but we can give the dogs who appear well enough something."

By the time Pete arrived with Dr. Russell and Lindy, all the animals had been identified. There were two litters of puppies, a dachshund litter of six, and a boxer litter of five. Both mothers were very exhausted and depleted but appeared to be relatively healthy. They had both been separated from their puppies and fed.

The rest were mostly female and appeared to be dogs that had been bred multiple times and were at the end of their usefulness. There was a French bulldog, two Yorkshire terriers, and two golden retrievers. They were emaciated, and frightened, but not aggressive.

The final dog was the one in the worst shape. It was a lab puppy, about twelve weeks, with a deformed paw that looked like it would need to be amputated. He was the friendliest, but also the most fragile.

From the general condition of the dogs and the barn, Cassidy estimated that the dogs had not been fed or had their cages cleaned for less than three days. Thank God they had gotten a complaint so quickly. These dogs would have been dead in a few more days.

Pete asked the question Cassidy had forgotten to ask in her rush to aid the dogs. "How did we find out about this?"

Dustin answered. "The neighbor called in a complaint when she heard the sound of dogs in distress. Thank God she did. She lives on the property that backs up to this one. She didn't know the address, but knew how to get here, so she led me in. She called the sheriff for me and was giving them her report when I came back here to see to the dogs."

"That was what Marie Theriot was doing here," thought Cassidy. Just then the deputy who had been searching the house came out to the barn.

"This is a rental property, and we contacted the owner. He had no idea the tenants had vacated the property. We have their names, and it appears that they represent themselves as legitimate breeders in Mississippi. There was a complaint against them in Mississippi, and when officials went to the property there, they found a situation similar to what we have here. Looks like they pulled up and are laying low for now. The Humane Society has been advised. We will be issuing warrants for their arrest, and the State Police cybercrimes unit will be following up to see if the web sites they use start to point to other locations."

"Thank you, Officer. Is there anything you need from me?"

"I'll be taking statements from all of you on the condition of the animals and this dwelling. We want to make sure we charge these people to the fullest extent of Louisiana law. If Mrs. Theriot was a less observant and concerned neighbor, this could have been a barn full of dead dogs. How bad are they Ms. Bourgeois? Hard to tell from the smell."

Pete and Dr. Russell had each started with one of the litters of puppies. Pete let Dr. Russell take the lead. "The conditions in here are deplorable, but from a preliminary check, these dogs were all fed within the last twenty-four hours and have only been without water for about eight hours. Given the mild February temperatures, they are not too bad. I don't think the others were getting adequate nutrition, just from the looks of them, but they weren't being starved either. It looks like these moms and puppies were getting fed to be a cash crop. My guess is the mill owners took as much as they could, and these were the least valuable puppies.

"We'll finish examining the rest of the dogs, but I think the only one we will have to take to the clinic is the lab pup. Looks like they were just letting him die."

"Can we come in and make our statements early next week? I'd like to get these dogs out of here and cleaned and fed if that would be okay."

"Absolutely, Ms. Bourgeois. We can send an officer to the shelter on Monday to take statements from you and Mr. Tassin."

Cassidy turned to Pete. "Pete, do you all have everything under control here? I want to call Katelyn and tell her what to expect, and to thank Mrs. Theriot."

"We're good, Cassidy. I know you have enough room for the dogs on the truck, but I'd like to get a couple of good whelping boxes to move the litters in my van. Lindy and Dr. Russell will transport the lab puppy first, as we want to get an IV started for him right away."

"I can call my dad to pick up two whelping boxes from Katelyn at the shelter and ask him to bring them to you. I'm going to go talk to Mrs. Theriot, and help Dustin load up the dogs. Dad should be here almost as fast as we can load the dogs. I'll see you at the shelter in a bit then."

Cassidy looked at Pete, Dr. Russell, Lindy and Dustin. "Thank you all so much for the quick compassionate response. I've always known how special a place Bayou Beni is, but the way you all responded to this just brings it home. I'll never forget this. Dustin, I'll be back in a few minutes to help you load the dogs in the truck to take to the shelter."

As Cassidy walked back towards the front of the property, the first call she made was Prescott. "Daddy, there are two litters of puppies, and I need two whelping boxes to transport them to the shelter. Can you go by the shelter and pick them up and bring them out here?"

"Course I can, Baby Girl. Just give me the address. I'll bring Ed Adams with me, as he is staying with me for the weekend. We'll be out there in less than forty-five minutes."

"Thanks Daddy. I'll call Katelyn and let her know."

Cassidy hung up and called Katelyn. "Katelyn, I've got eighteen to bring to the shelter. Five adults, and then a mom and litter of six, and a mom and litter of five. Any luck finding openings in local shelters?"

"The closest with an opening is Louisiana SPCA in New Orleans, and they would need us to transport. We have five in residence. Eighteen will take us over our limit."

"I'll have to report a deviation, Katelyn. There isn't much we can do, and there is no way we can transport to New Orleans today. We'll work it out. Dustin and I will be there with the dogs within the hour. My dad is coming to pick up two whelping boxes for the puppies, and then Pete will bring the puppies to the shelter."

"I'll make sure the dog washing station is well stocked and be waiting for you. If I'm not here, it is because I am at Holy Redeemer getting Trent and Tabitha."

"Thanks, Katelyn. I know you'll be putting in extra hours today, and I appreciate it."

Cassidy had reached the front of the house, where she found Marie Theriot leaning against her car and working a set of rosary beads in her hands.

"How bad is it?" was the question that burst from Marie's lips when she saw Cassidy.

"It is so much better than it would have been if you hadn't been paying attention and called right away. Only one puppy is in crisis, and I think Dr. Russell and Dr. Marshall will be able to save him. If this had gone on for days, the outcome would have been much worse."

"It was Max who did it Cassidy. He is the one who made me see that something was wrong. I never even noticed that there were dogs over here until I got Max and started walking him around my property every evening. He didn't want to get close to the fence. He knew something wrong was happening back here. I meant to tell Katelyn when I called about Max and his crate, but I forgot. I feel like I failed these poor dogs."

Cassidy reached out and took Marie's hands in hers. "Mrs. Theriot. Even the deputy said it is a remarkable thing you did. You and Max saved nineteen lives today by paying attention and following through. You'll never know how many people would have decided it wasn't their business. You should be very proud. Now I know this has been upsetting for you. Is there someone you can call to spend time with?"

"I'll be fine, Cassidy. I was planning to go over to the Holy Redeemer fair after Max and I had our walk. I'll go home now and check on Max, and head over to the fair. Do you need my help at your booth? I figure you won't get back to it."

"Oh, Mrs. Theriot. I am supposed to do a two-hour shift from four to six, and I know I won't be able to do that. I need to make some phone calls."

"Don't you worry, Cassidy. I'll take Max and take your shift. I'm sure some of the ladies will help me break down the booth, and I'll give your things to Rosadel. Max and I are the best advertisement for rescuing a dog the good people of Holy Redeemer will ever see."

As Cassidy headed back to the barn, she thought about how in a crisis, her grandmother had come through to help. She was starting to believe what Pete's mom was fond of saying. The Lord surely did work in mysterious ways.

♦ ♦ ♦

Bee Collins hurried through the door of Our Lady of Lourdes and headed for Bessie Chauvin's room. Rosadel had told Bee that Bessie was usually waiting in the lobby for Cassidy, but if Bessie wasn't in the lobby Bee should just go to her apartment, knock on the door and let herself in.

So Bee knocked, and opened the door calling, "Hey Ms. Bessie, Cassidy had some shelter work she had to take care of, and I was picking up Sister Dorothy anyway, so here I am."

As Bee entered the sitting area she stopped in her tracks. Sitting next to Bessie on the couch was simply the most beautiful man Bee had ever seen in her life. Bee felt the heat climbing her cheeks. "I'm sorry to barge in like that Ms. Bessie, I didn't know you had company."

Gil rose to his feet and held out his hand. "I am a surprise visitor for Tante this weekend. Gil Chauvin, very pleased to meet you."

"I'm Belinda Collins, pleased to meet you, too." Bee felt like she had touched a live electrical wire when she touched Gil's hand.

Ms. Bessie smiled at Bee and Gil, hoping she was seeing what she thought she was seeing. "Oh, Bee! I was so surprised to see Gil, I forgot to call Cassidy. We could have brought Sr. Dorothy with us."

"It's no problem Ms. Bessie. I'll bring Sr. Dorothy with me, but it would be a huge help if you could bring her back with you. I'm not sure how long Rosadel will be, and I may be needed at the fair."

Gil smiled as he answered. "I'll be delighted to give Sr. Dorothy a ride. We'll see you at the fair?"

"I'm the chairperson this year, so I'll be everywhere. Ms. Bessie are you still going to bring Maggie and Sophie to the Animal Shelter booth now that your nephew is visiting?"

"Of course," replied Bessie. "They are a great advertisement for rescue seniors and for therapy dogs. We'll see you when you stop by the booth."

As Bee hurried down the hall to collect Sr. Dorothy, she shook her head in bemusement. Gil Chauvin unsettled her. It wasn't just his remarkable looks. There was something about him that made Bee want to stop everything and spend as much time with him as possible.

Sr. Dorothy was waiting in her travel wheelchair when Bee got to her room. "I'll have to depend on the kindness of others to push me around the fair," Sr. Dorothy said as Bee came into the room. "My motorized wheelchair needs a van."

"I'm sure there will be volunteers lining up," replied Bee. "You know you are always a star at Holy Redeemer."

Sr. Dorothy looked closely at Bee. "You look flustered, child. Is something wrong?"

Bee knew better than to even try to fib to Sr. Dorothy. "I just met Ms. Bessie's nephew, and he is so handsome, I am flustered. And Cassidy had to leave the fair because of an emergency animal cruelty case, so one thing on top of the other has me out of sorts."

"That Gil Chauvin is so handsome, I get flustered. It's a wonder he's not yet married." Sister Dorothy smiled as she spoke. "I know Bessie would love for him to marry a Louisiana girl and settle here forever."

Bee was not the only one feeling flustered. As she left Bessie's room, Gil reached out and clasped Bessie's hand. "Tante, I've been told my whole life that the Chauvin men know immediately when they meet the woman who is to be their wife. I never believed it. But now I do. Belinda Collins is my destiny. I know it in my heart."

Bessie squeezed Gil's hand. "I felt the energy change, Gilbert. She is the one."

CHAPTER 37

Prescott arrived at the house in Audela just as Cassidy and Dustin were finishing loading the dogs into the truck. When Cassidy saw her dad, all the feelings she had been successfully managing bubbled to the surface.

Prescott took one look at her and opened his arms. "Oh Daddy!" said Cassidy as she hugged her dad. "This is unbelievable. I have no place to put all the dogs. I'm going to have to go over my allowable number of dogs."

"Just a second, Cassidy. Angel's Watch isn't ready to open yet, but with JT and Ed, we can manage the dogs you currently have in the shelter. I'll just need to go get some crates and food and pick them up. I'll call JT before I leave here. I can fill out the foster paperwork when I pick up the dogs. You know they'll be fine with us."

"You're an answer to a prayer, Daddy. I'll see you at the shelter then." Cassidy breathed a deep sigh of relief and told Dustin the good news. "I need to call my mom, Dustin, so I'll be a few minutes behind you. Can you handle things with Katelyn until I get there?"

"No problem Cassidy, take your time. We'll have it under control."

Cassidy dialed Sandra before thinking through everything she wanted to say and hoped the new improved Sandra could handle it. Cassidy started talking as soon as she heard Sandra's voice.

"Mom, it's Cassidy. We had an animal cruelty report and found a puppy mill. I had to leave the Holy Redeemer Fair and I'm not going to get back there, so if you were coming to see me, I won't be there. And you'll never guess who called in the report of animal cruelty. It was

Marie Theriot. And she is going to cover my booth at the fair for my four to six shift."

"Whoa, Cassidy! Take a breath. How bad is it? Are the animals okay?"

"Pete and Dr. Russell said the animals had only been abandoned within the last twenty-four hours, so they are mostly okay. One puppy with a deformed paw is in pretty bad shape. Dr. Russell took him to the clinic to start an IV. Dustin is on his way to the shelter with the dogs. Pete is loading up the puppies. Dad is going to take the five dogs we currently have at the shelter as fosters so that I don't go over capacity."

Sandra knew that there were many details missing from Cassidy's summary, but decided not to press her. "Do you need my help with anything? What can I do?"

"I think I'm okay for now, Mom. I'll call you later this evening after things have calmed down. I'll be sleeping at the shelter for the next few nights until we have had time to evaluate the new dogs and puppies."

"I know the shelter is typically closed on Sundays, but can I come see you there tomorrow? I want to make sure that you are alright."

"Sure you can, Mom. I'll be fine. It was just so scary and overwhelming when we got here before we were able to check everything out. I've got to go now and help Dustin and Katelyn at the shelter, I promise I'll call later this evening."

Sandra went looking for Mark as soon as she hung up the phone. "You know how I've been worrying and worrying about how to contact my mother?"

"Yes, I know it has been on your mind." Mark patted the couch next to him and Sandra sat down.

"I need you to tell me if this is a crazy idea. The whole situation is crazy, so maybe that has influenced me. Cassidy just called. She was working at the fair at Holy Redeemer and got a call about an emergency animal cruelty case. She had to leave to go investigate, and it turns out that there was a puppy mill in Audela. I don't know how many animals, but according to Cassidy it looks like they will all live. Here comes the crazy part. My mother called in the complaint. I don't know how she knew. But she is going to cover Cassidy's booth at the fair from four until six. I think we should go, and I should meet her there. Is that crazy?"

Mark reached over and held Sandra's hand. "What will you say to her? Have you thought that out?"

"Not a lot, Mark. But I thought I would thank her for helping Cassidy. And introduce you and the kids to her. And tell her that I want to establish a relationship, but I don't really know how, and I decided that meeting like this in public was the easiest way to start."

"Well, sweetheart, if that is what you want to do, I say we do it. I hope it is not too much of a shock for your mother, but she has to know in the back of her mind that you might have planned to come to the fair to see Cassidy."

◆ ◆ ◆

Katelyn and Dustin had unloaded most of the dogs by the time Cassidy arrived at the shelter and were settling them into the kennels. The dogs were subdued and obviously frightened, so the first course of action was to provide comfort. The Golden Retrievers seemed to be the least frightened, so Dustin and Katelyn each took one to bathe. Cassidy distributed blankets to the other dogs and provided some toys.

It seemed like only minutes before Pete arrived with the mothers and puppies in the whelping boxes. The puppies were the least fazed of all, as long as their litter mates and their mother were available, they were too young to react to all the changes. Both mother dogs were showing high anxiety and so wouldn't be bathed until they settled down.

"Your dad will be here in less than an hour to pick up the dogs," Pete told Cassidy as he unloaded the puppies. "I'm going to go check on the pup, and then I'll be back. Lindy will be spending the night with him at the clinic."

"I'll be staying here for the next couple of nights or until we find foster homes for the puppies. I don't want to leave them alone until we're sure they can thrive." Cassidy hated the idea that any of the rescued puppies would die.

"They seem pretty healthy, Cass. I'll bring worming supplies and worm all of them today. I think they are about three weeks old, and no telling if they have been treated yet, so we'll get them started. I'll also bring puppy food for the moms, and we can start trying the puppies on some solid food tomorrow. I'm optimistic about all the outcomes, Cassidy, I really am."

"From your lips to God's ears, Pete. I need to call Bee and let her know I won't be back to the fair, and that Marie Theriot will be manning the booth there."

"I can't wait to get some time with you to hear that story. This has been one crazy day."

Bee was thrilled to hear that Marie had volunteered to cover the booth, and that the emergency, though grave, was nowhere near as bad as it could have been. Rosadel and the girls had extended their shift from an hour to an hour and a half, and Hannah Falgoust was covering the other half hour so that Lindy could stay at Bayou Beni Animal hospital with the lab pup.

Cassidy hung up the phone feeling better than she had since she got the call from Dustin. From Bee's account, word had spread that St. Elizabeth Animal Shelter had found an abandoned puppy mill, and the parishioners were ready to help in any way they could. The triplets had charmed multiple people with stories of fostering the litter of kittens, and how much fun it was, and Rosadel had told Bee she thought that Cassidy would have multiple offers to foster future litters.

By the time that Prescott got back with the supplies to take the five dogs in residence to Angel's Watch, the rescued dogs had all been bathed, and the mothers and pups were resting comfortably. Cassidy was trying to get all the paperwork in order. Dustin and Katelyn had gone home for the day.

"I'll be heading over to the fair with Thor once I get these pups settled in with Ed and JT," Prescott told Cassidy. "I should be there by five, so that will give me an hour until the booth shuts down."

"Marie Theriot is covering the booth for me with Max. We really haven't vetted Max with other dogs, but I think he will be fine."

"If there are any problems, I'll move on out. It will be good to see Marie and thank her in person for saving all these dogs."

"Daddy, it is kind of a miracle, you know? I wish I could have told her that I know she is my grandmother, but I have to wait on Mom. But it just felt amazing, the way she jumped in to help and take care of me."

"Your Mom is going to do the right thing, Cassidy. I'm sure it won't be too long before you can interact with Marie as your grandmother."

◆ ◆ ◆

Marie was having a wonderful time at the Holy Redeemer Fair. Max loved the attention and was a docile and friendly as could be. Bee kept coming over to check on Marie, and finally just pulled up a chair and sat down to visit.

"I know they will need me when the bands start playing at six and we close up some of the booths, so I'm going to rest a bit and visit with you. Are you okay? That must have been so upsetting for you this morning."

"It was, Bee, but I'm okay now that I know all the dogs will be fine. So many people have stopped by to ask about the rescued dogs and when they will be available for adoption. Max has been a real star, and I'm so proud of him. I can't believe a day that started so badly is working out so well."

As Bee was about to respond, she saw Marie turn white as a ghost. "Marie, what happened?" Bee asked, as she looked in the direction that Marie was looking.

While Bee had never seen the resemblance between Cassidy and Marie, seeing Sandra provided the missing link. "Holy Moly, Marie, do you want me to stay with you?"

"Please, Bee, I'm shaking like a leaf."

As Sandra, Mark, Candace and Mark, Jr. walked toward the booth, Bee could see Marie visibly trembling. She had no idea what to do, or what would happen next. Sandra walked up to the booth, looking as nervous as Marie.

"Hi, Mom," said Sandra. "Thanks for helping Cassidy out like this. I don't know what I'm supposed to do, but I want to try to have a relationship with you."

Marie teared up. "I'd love that Sandra."

"This is my husband, Mark, and my daughter, Candace, and my son, Mark Jr." Mark reached out and shook Marie's hand.

"Pleased to meet you," he said. "That's a mighty fine-looking dog you have there." Marie smiled a real smile.

"His name is Max, and he is a rescue. He was already eight years old when I got him earlier this year. Puppies aren't the only ones who need homes, and an older dog can be a perfect fit for a busy person or family."

"Mom won't let me have a dog," complained Mark Jr.

Marie was at a loss to answer that, and Bee jumped in.

"Dogs are a lot of responsibility," she said. "Most of the time one of the children wants a dog and the mom ends up taking care of it. I think if you really want a dog, you should take on a chore and show your mom that you can be responsible and follow through."

Sandra smiled at Bee. "Sounds like you know what you're talking about. Do you have children?"

Bee laughed. "No children of my own, but I'm the school secretary at Holy Redeemer, so I always joke that I have four hundred children. You learn a lot being in a school all day."

Marie continued to watch Sandra and her children while Bee talked. "I don't want to take up a lot of your time today, Mom. But I have been trying to figure out how to contact you and couldn't think of a good way. When Cassidy told me that you had volunteered to take over her time at the booth, it seemed too good of an opportunity to miss out on. I know we have a long road ahead. How about I call you in the next few days, and set up some time for us to have dinner or something?"

"Oh Sandra, that would be wonderful. Thank you so much for giving me a second chance."

"I think it is a second chance for both of us." As Sandra and her family started to walk away, Mark turned around and gave Marie a thumbs' up sign.

Marie sat down, and Max put his big head in her lap. She lowered her head to rest it on his.

"Well, Marie, that was about as close to a Hallmark movie moment as I've ever seen," remarked Bee. "I think you are going to get your happy ending."

♦ ♦ ♦

Pete arrived back at the shelter a little after six. "Laverne and Shirley are spending the night with my mom and dad so that I can stay here with you. I know you only have one cot, so I have a cot and a sleeping bag in the van. I also have a picnic basket with food from the fair, and my scrabble board, so we should have a good night after I see to the puppies."

"You don't have to stay with me, Pete. I've stayed here by myself many times, it will be okay."

"Now don't go hurting my feelings, Cassidy. I want to stay with you. Let me get the rest of my stuff, and then I'll give you all my good news."

Cassidy smiled as Pete went outside to the van to unload. Life with Pete would never be dull, and it was amazing how he could turn any day into a good one.

As Pete wormed the puppies, he filled Cassidy in on the big news of the day. "So, your mother talked to your grandmother at the fair."

"What? How do you know?" Cassidy was stunned.

"Bee told Rosadel, who told Clancy, who called me at the clinic. And, my mom wants to foster the dachshund puppies once we clear them. And she wants to keep the mama dog. Dad has been after her for a while to get another dog, and this decided her.

"From what Clancy said, you can expect a bunch of families next week to adopt dogs. Even though we had less opportunity to bring the shelter dogs out, with Laverne and Shirley, Maggie and Sophie, Max and Thor and Trent and Tabitha, quite a few families were inspired to get a pet. I know we have to keep a close watch on the rescued dogs, and find experienced foster families to help them socialize, but we should have rehomed all of them before summer."

"Wow, Pete, this is unbelievable. How is the little lab?"

"His name is Trey, and JT wants to adopt him. He is stable and will be fine. Doc Russell and I think the best thing to do is to amputate that undeveloped paw, but we'll let him get a little stronger first. Hannah took a picture of him on her phone and sent it to JT and he begged us to let him have the pup. Seems like a great fit."

A few hours later, after a feast on fair food and a couple of rousing games of scrabble, Pete turned his chair to face Cassidy.

"Today didn't turn out anything like I pictured. It was supposed to be an easy day at the clinic, and then we were going to have a wonderful, successful day at the Holy Redeemer Fair, and all your residents would have potential adoptions.

"Instead, together, we faced one of the most frightening situations that a local animal shelter can face, the discovery of a puppy mill. We were so lucky that we were able to save all the dogs. And we were also lucky to have each other.

"I am so proud of you, Cassidy. You kept your composure, you listened to advice, you made decisions and you kept moving us forward so that we are in the best place we could be this quickly.

"You inspired the people who care about you to step up and step in and make the booth at the fair a success in spite of the crisis you had to manage."

Pete slipped out of his chair and down on one knee, taking a ring box out of his pocket as he did so.

"I planned to ask you to marry me today, but I planned to be in a restaurant with both of us wearing nice clothes. I thought about waiting until another day, but then I thought about what marriage is. Marriage is the whole thing. The good days, the bad days, the heartbreak, the joy. Today was one of the toughest days I could ever imagine, even though it turned out better than I could have dreamed. And through it all, I was so glad we were together. Because with you the hard times are easier, and the good times are better. I love you, Cassidy. I want to spend the rest of my life with you. Will you marry me?"

Cassidy slipped out of her chair and knelt in front of Pete, as she took his face in her hands and kissed him. "I love you, Pete, and I want to spend the rest of my life with you. So, yes, yes, yes."

EPILOGUE

Cassidy looked around the table at the Hungry Pelican and marveled at the changes in her life in the past six months. It was a big group, with Harriet Marshall, Bessie Chauvin, Marie Theriot, Rosadel and the triplets, and Sandra and Candace. They had all been out shopping for wedding clothes that morning.

Pete and Cassidy had opted for an informal wedding, they would be married at Holy Redeemer, with a reception at Mark and Sandra's house in August. Cassidy was attending mass regularly at Holy Redeemer and was signed up to participate in the Rite of Christian Initiation of Adults in September, with plans to receive the sacraments at Easter the following year.

Lou, Grace and Rosie were thrilled to be participating in their second wedding. They had picked out matching dresses in different colors for their roles as flower girls. Candace was excited to be a bridesmaid, and Mark, Jr. an usher. Rosadel would stand as Matron of Honor for Cassidy, and Clancy was Best Man. Marie and Bessie would have places of honor as grandmothers of the bride.

Rosadel thought about the past year, and how frustrated she was with her girls when they put those kittens in the manger scene at school. And then she looked at Cassidy and thought about how she thought that Cassidy and Pete were perfect for each other but may have never moved forward without the push from the girls.

And they were doing better with impulse control using the system proposed by Mrs. White. They still had their mishaps, but far less often. And having Michelle for a best friend had helped too. Clancy had gotten a big enough bonus that they had gone to Disney World with Angus and Jessie for spring break.

Rosadel placed her hand on her abdomen as she thought about the decision she and Clancy had made to try for more children. By Cassidy and Pete's wedding, Rosadel might need a bigger dress. Thank heaven Cassidy had picked a forgiving empire waisted style.

Bessie reached over and squeezed Marie's hand. Marie returned the gesture and smiled at Bessie. "Who would have thought at this time last year that we would be shopping for grandmother of the bride dresses together. This world is full of unexpected blessings."

UNEXPECTED BLESSINGS

Dear Readers,

Thanks for visiting Bayou Beni! I hope you have enjoyed meeting all the wonderful characters who live here. My next book will be a historical novel, where you will learn more about Bessie Chauvin's ancestors. I hope you enjoy that book too!

I'd love to hear from you.

Best -
Anne Marie
authorannemariestclair@gmail.com

Made in the USA
Middletown, DE
19 September 2018